The Duke's Men

They are an investigative agency born out of family pride and irresistible passion . . . and they risk their lives and hearts to unravel any shocking deception or scandalous transgression!

Acclaim for this "steamy" (*RT Book Reviews*) series from *New York Times* and *USA Today* bestselling author

SABRINA JEFFRIES

WHAT THE DUKE DESIRES

"A totally engaging, adventurous love story with an oh-so-wonderful ending."

—*RT Book Reviews*

"Full of all the intriguing characters, brisk plotting, and witty dialogue that Jeffries's readers have come to expect."

—*Publishers Weekly* (starred review)

WHEN THE ROGUE RETURNS

"Blends the pace of a thriller with the romance of the Regency era."

—*Woman's Day*

"Enthralling . . . rich in passion and danger."

—*Booklist* (starred review)

More praise for the Duke's Men novels

HOW THE SCOUNDREL SEDUCES

"Scorching. . . . From cover to cover, it sizzles."

—*Reader to Reader*

"Marvelous storytelling. . . . Memorable."

—*RT Book Reviews* (4½ stars, Top Pick, K.I.S.S. Award)

IF THE VISCOUNT FALLS

"Jeffries's addictive series satisfies."

—*Library Journal*

The *New York Times* bestselling "must-read series"
(*Romance Reviews Today*)

THE HELLIONS OF HALSTEAD HALL

THE TRUTH ABOUT LORD STONEVILLE

"Launches a sparkling series. . . . Lively repartee, fast action, luscious sensuality, and an abundance of humor."

—*Library Journal*

"Delectably witty dialogue, subtly nuanced characters, and scorching sexual chemistry. . . . A captivating series."

—*Booklist*

A HELLION IN HER BED

"A tempting new series. . . . A spirited battle of wits and wiles, and a lively plot blending equal measures of steamy passion and sharp wit come together."

—*Booklist* (starred review)

"Overflowing with scintillating wit and heart-stopping sensuality."

—*Library Journal*

HOW TO WOO A RELUCTANT LADY

"Delightful. . . . Charmingly original."

—*Publishers Weekly* (starred review)

TO WED A WILD LORD

"Wonderfully witty, deliciously seductive, graced with humor and charm."

—*Library Journal* (starred review)

"A beguiling blend of captivating characters, clever plotting, and sizzling sensuality."

—*Booklist*

A LADY NEVER SURRENDERS

"Jeffries pulls out all the stops. . . . Not to be missed."

—*RT Book Reviews* (4½ stars, Top Pick)

"Superbly shaded characters, simmering sensuality, and a splendidly wicked wit . . . *A Lady Never Surrenders* wraps up the series nothing short of brilliantly."

—*Booklist*

Sabrina Jeffries

What the Duke Desires

POCKET BOOKS

New York London Toronto Sydney New Delhi

Pocket Books
An Imprint of Simon & Schuster, Inc.
1230 Avenue of the Americas
New York, NY 10020

This book is a work of fiction. Names, characters, places, and incidents either are products of the author's imagination or are used fictitiously. Any resemblance to actual events or locales or persons, living or dead, is entirely coincidental.

This Pocket Books paperback edition July 2015

POCKET and colophon are registered trademarks of Simon & Schuster, Inc.

For information about special discounts for bulk purchases, please contact Simon & Schuster Special Sales at 1-866-506-1949 or business@simonandschuster.com.

The Simon & Schuster Speakers Bureau can bring authors to your live event. For more information or to book an event, contact the Simon & Schuster Speakers Bureau at 1-866-248-3049 or visit our website at www.simonspeakers.com.

Designed by Leydiana Rodríguez-Ovalles

Manufactured in the United States of America

10 9 8 7 6 5 4 3 2 1

ISBN 978-1-5011-0722-1
ISBN 978-1-4516-9351-5 (ebook)

To all the wonderful people who adopted me in my college years since I couldn't go home to visit my parents in Thailand—Aunt Shirley and Uncle Harvey Peshoff, Aunt Judy and my late uncle Jimmy Martin, my late aunt Gloria, and the entire Owens family: John, Donna (now deceased), Diane, Joyce, Johnny, and Pam. You'll never know what your love and care meant to me.

The Manton and Bonnaud Family Tree

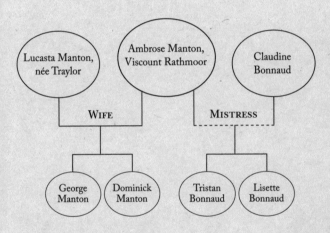

| Lucasta Manton, née Traylor | Ambrose Manton, Viscount Rathmoor | Claudine Bonnaud |

WIFE　　　　**MISTRESS**

| George Manton | Dominick Manton | | Tristan Bonnaud | Lisette Bonnaud |

PROLOGUE

Yorkshire
1816

"*Sacre bleu*, girl, stop that pacing and come eat breakfast before you make me dizzy."

Fourteen-year-old Lisette Bonnaud halted, only to stare out the front window of the cottage. "But Maman, how can you not be worried about Tristan? He's never gone all night! What if something happened to him while he and Papa were hunting yesterday?"

Claudine Bonnaud waved her hand with the sort of elegant flourish that had made her a celebrated actress on the Continent before Papa had brought her back from one of his travels and ensconced her in this cottage. "Then we would have heard of it by now. Your papa would have sent a servant to fetch us, at the very least. More likely Ambrose took Tristan drinking after the hunt, and they ended up staying until dawn at the Green Inn."

Maman was probably right. It figured that Papa would take her brother somewhere interesting. Tristan always got to do *everything*. She never did. And Tristan wasn't even that much older than her—just three years. It wasn't fair.

"Perhaps I should walk to Ashcroft to make sure that they're there." She cast a wistful glance out at the green woolly hills of the Yorkshire wolds that stretched for miles and miles.

Maman lifted one perfectly plucked blond eyebrow. "You cannot go off to town alone, *ma fille*. It's not seemly."

Blowing out a frustrated breath, Lisette returned to pacing. "As if anyone cares about propriety for a bastard."

"Lisette Bonnaud!" Maman said sharply. "Do not use that awful word to describe yourself! You're the daughter of the Viscount Rathmoor. Never forget it."

"The *illegitimate* daughter of the Viscount Rathmoor," she grumbled. "What happened to all of Papa's promises to marry you?"

Maman's lips tightened into a line. "It's . . . a complicated matter. He had to wait for the war with France to end. Marrying a Frenchwoman will create a very great scandal for your papa as it is. And for his legitimate sons."

Lisette eyed her mother askance. "The war ended a year ago, Maman. And the only one who cares about scandal is George. Waiting won't change that."

Twenty-six-year-old George Manton was Papa's *legitimate* son and heir, half brother to her and Tristan. He'd hated them ever since Papa made Maman his mistress. Even after George's mother had died years ago, he'd still loathed the woman whom his father continued to dote on. And the children born of his father—*their* father.

"George will come around," Maman said dismissively, obviously uncomfortable with this line of conversation. "He will have no choice once your papa marries me." She began to spread jam on a piece of toast with delicate strokes of the knife.

Everything Maman did was delicate. Meanwhile, Lisette didn't have a delicate bone in her body. She was unnaturally tall for a girl her age, with bony hips and large breasts that made her look off-balance. And her hair wasn't Maman's buttery blond, which gentlemen always seemed to admire. It was Papa's ink black.

She did try to make it attractive with the ribbons Papa brought her from his travels, but it was so wild and curly that such an endeavor was fruitless. Most of the time she ended up using the ribbons to embroider her gowns instead.

"Maman, am I pretty?"

Her mother blinked. "Of course you're pretty, *ma chérie*. You're my daughter, aren't you? Don't fret, one day men will vie for your attention."

She wasn't sure she wanted that. Maman's looks had only gained *her* a lifetime of waiting around for the man she loved to marry her. As a little girl, Lisette had believed in Papa's promises to make them a real family one day. But lately she'd begun to lose faith in him.

A heavy knock came at the entrance door. "I'll answer it," Lisette called out as she dashed into the hall to open it. She smiled when she saw her other half brother, nineteen-year-old Dominick Manton, standing on the doorstep.

"You're back at last!" she cried.

Dom was as different from George as peas from pears. He'd been a childhood playmate to Tristan while George was off at school. As Lisette had grown older and begun trailing about after them, he'd been kind to her even though the villagers weren't—and she adored him for that.

But today he didn't look happy to be here. "May I come in?"

Her heart faltered as she noticed his bloodshot eyes, his colorless lips . . . the way he held himself as if he were made of porcelain. Something bad had happened. Oh, Lord.

"Tristan!" she whispered. "Is he hurt?"

"Where is he?" Dom countered.

The question confused her. "I don't know. He's been gone since yesterday. You should talk to Papa; they went out hunting together."

He muttered a curse, then squared his shoulders. "Father is dead, Lisette."

The bald words were a slap to her face. As she gaped at Dom, wondering if she'd misheard, a choked gasp came from behind them.

Maman stood frozen, the blood draining from her features. "Dead? *C'est impossible!* How can that be?"

Dom ran a gloved hand through his thick black

locks. "I can't tell you much, Mrs. Bonnaud. I'm still piecing together what happened while I was in York. As best I can make out, while Tristan and Father were hunting, Father's gun misfired and exploded in his chest. Tristan and the groom got Father back home and into his bedchamber, where George joined them. The groom fetched a doctor; George and Tristan stayed by Father's side. They were both there when Father died shortly after sundown last evening."

As the truth of Dom's words started to sink in, tears stung Lisette's eyes, then slipped down her cheeks. Behind her Mama was quietly weeping, too, and Lisette went to her side. They stood there crying, wrapped in each other's arms.

Papa couldn't be dead. She'd seen him just yesterday, when he'd come to fetch Tristan.

Oh, Lord, Tristan!

She shot Dom an accusing glance. "If Tristan was there when Papa died, why hasn't he come home to tell us?"

"I don't know. I didn't arrive at the manor myself until a couple of hours ago. But . . ."

At his hesitation, Maman stiffened. "B-but what?"

"We have to find him. George will be here any minute looking for him."

A horrible chill struck Lisette. "Why would George come here? He doesn't think Tristan *killed* Papa, does he?"

"No," Dom said tersely, "though he probably would have tried to claim that if the groom hadn't witnessed what happened." Dom rubbed a hand over his weary features. "But George does think that Tristan stole Blue Blazes last night."

Shock made her gasp. Blue Blazes was Papa's—and Tristan's—favorite Thoroughbred. Papa had promised to give the horse to her brother one day. "You don't think Tristan would do such a thing, do you?"

"I don't know. None of the servants is very clear on what happened after Father died. They said that Tristan eventually left, but George claims he returned in the dead of night to steal Blue Blazes. He's gathering up men as we speak to capture Tristan so he can be charged with the crime."

Her blood ran to ice. "Oh, Dom, no! How can he?"

"You know how George resents Tristan. He'll do anything to ruin his life."

"Is that why you're here?" Tristan strode forward from the end of the hall nearest the cottage's back entrance, his blue eyes fierce upon Dom. His coat was torn as if he'd been running through the woods, and his trousers had mud caked up to the knees. "Have you come to witness my ruin?"

"Tristan!" Lisette cried. "Don't speak to him like that!"

"I'm here to warn you," Dom put in, his voice even. "If you did take Blue Blazes, you have to give him back."

A flush darkened Tristan's cheeks as he marched inexorably forward. "Why? He's mine. Father willed him to me, a fact that your arse of a brother could confirm if he weren't determined to deny me my birthright."

"What are you talking about?" Maman whispered.

Tristan laid his arm about Maman's shoulder, then shot Dom a belligerent glance. "On his deathbed, Father wrote a codicil to his will. He left the horse to me, the cottage to Maman, and his collection of gewgaws to Lisette. He also provided an annuity for the three of us. George and I both witnessed him signing the document."

"Oh, Papa," Lisette whispered as tears slid down the back of her raw throat. He *had* cared about them, enough to think of them in the end. And he knew how much she loved the small artifacts he'd bought in the various countries he'd visited, his tales intoxicating her with heady glimpses into what it might be like to travel the world.

Tristan's gaze blazed with unusual fervor. "But as soon as Father drew his last breath, George burned the codicil in front of me. He said he'd die before he let us have one penny."

Lisette reeled from the same shock that lit Dom's face. Why did George hate them so much?

Dom scowled. "George said naught of it to me."

"And that surprises you?" Tristan snapped.

A pained breath escaped Dom. "No."

Tristan left Mother's side to face down Dom. "So yes, I took the horse that belonged to me."

"You have to give it back," Dom said. "Horse thieving is punishable by death. Somehow we have to sneak it back into the stables or have it be found wandering the fields or—"

"Too late for that," Tristan said calmly. "I sold it to a gypsy horse trader to give my family something to live on until I can find a way to provide for us."

"You *sold* it?" Dom snapped. "Are you mad? George will have you hanged for certain!"

"Just let him try," Tristan snarled. "I'll tell the world what he did, what a lying, duplicitous scoundrel he is, and—"

"No one will believe you, *mon cher*," Maman said in a choked whisper. "They'll say you have everything to gain by lying. George is the heir. He will win, and you'll be hanged." She began to cry again.

Tristan crumbled in the face of her misery. "Aw, Mother, I won't be hanged!" He went to gather her up in his arms. "Shh, shh, don't go on so."

Lisette turned to Dom. "You have to do something. You can't let George arrest Tristan!"

"Damn it to hell." Dom squared his shoulders. "All right, this is what we'll do. Tristan, you've got to leave. Now. You can probably make it to the cave before George arrives. I'll meet you there as soon as I can get away tonight."

"What cave?" Maman asked.

The three siblings exchanged a glance. It was their private playground, the place where they'd always escaped parents and guardians—and George—kept secret by mutual agreement all these years.

"Don't worry, Mother, I know which cave he means." Tristan glowered at Dom. "But I don't see why *I* should be the one to run when it is George—"

"Listen to your brother!" their mother cried. "I'm sure Dom will do what he can to make this right, but if you stay here and George has you prosecuted, it will mean ruin for all of us."

Lisette held her breath. Maman had been wise to use guilt on Tristan. Otherwise, the reckless fool would defy George up until the moment they put the noose around his neck.

With a sullen glare, Tristan crossed his arms over his chest. "All right, Dom, suppose I *do* flee to the cave. Then what?"

"I'll try to convince George to do the right thing," Dom said. "He's more likely to do it without you around provoking him."

Hope sprang in Lisette's heart. If anyone could convince George, it was Dom. "Listen to Dom, Tristan."

Tristan let out a long breath. "Fine. But if George persists in his lies—"

"You'll go to France," Maman said stoutly. "I have family in Toulon." She turned a pleading glance on Dom. "If it comes to that, can you get him there?"

"I can get him onto a fishing boat at Flamborough Head. He'll have to make his way to the port at Hull on his own. Then he can use some of the money he got for the horse to buy passage to France."

"Fine," Maman said. "He will do it."

"Now, see here, Mother—" Tristan began.

"No!" she cried. "I will not lose you *and* your papa! Do not ask it of me!"

Tristan gritted his teeth, then gave a terse nod.

"Come," she said, taking his arm, "we'll pack your things for the journey."

"No time for that," Dom bit out. "I can get his things to him tonight. But he's got to go *now*! George will be here any moment."

"Yes, go, Tristan!" Lisette urged, pushing him toward the back door. "Before George finds you."

Tristan paused at the end of the hall. "One thing you should know, Dom. Father also left money to *you* in that codicil that George burned. So if his actions go unpunished—"

"I understand," Dom said. "Now leave, damn you!"

With a scowl, Tristan was gone.

"I'd best gather up what he'll need for the journey." Maman disappeared down the hall, leaving Lisette alone with Dom.

Dom took her hands. "I'm sorry, dear girl. About George, about Father . . . about all of it."

"It's not *your* fault," she mumbled. "We both know George does as he pleases, and as for Papa—"

When tears fell again, he drew her into his arms to comfort her. She couldn't believe Papa was dead. Just yesterday he'd given her a kiss and promised to take her riding sometime soon. So many promises, and now he could never fulfill them.

Tears spilled down her cheeks, soaking into Dom's fine blue coat as he murmured soft words of comfort. She wasn't sure how long they stood that way, but it seemed like mere moments later when the noise of horses outside broke them apart. As she exchanged glances with Dom, a hard rap at the door made her jump.

"We should fetch your mother to answer it," Dom said in a low voice. "His seeing me here might tip our hand too soon."

"But the sight of Maman will infuriate George. Let me answer."

"Lisette—"

"I can play dumb, and he might believe me. We have to stall him long enough to give Tristan time to get away."

Dom stared intently at her, then sighed and stepped back. "I'll be right here if you need me."

Casting him a grateful smile, she opened the door.

Then she froze, taken off guard by the mob George had brought with him. There was his nasty man of affairs, John Hucker, and two of the more brutish grooms, along with several villagers who disliked that "French bastard," as Tristan was often called in town, all because he had the viscount's favor.

She fought not to react to this show of strength, reminding herself that George was still unaware that she knew about Papa. Or the Thoroughbred. "Good morning, my lord. What brings you here so early?"

Though George possessed the sturdy build of a country laborer, his features and clothing and manner were pure aristocracy. He had the fine pale brow of a lord who rarely ventured into the sun, the perfectly tailored suit of a gentleman who never worried that work might muss his clothes, and the sheer arrogance of a viscount's heir.

Plenty of women would call him handsome, too, with his broad chest and wavy brown hair and the toothsome smile he bestowed on those females who met his exacting standards. But Lisette was immune. She knew the darkness lurking within that chest.

Typical of him, he didn't even bother to climb down from his favorite gelding. "Where is he?" he barked without preamble.

"Who?" she barked back. If he wouldn't attempt civility, why should she?

"You know who. Your sly arse of a brother."

Only with difficulty did she contain her temper. "He's your brother, too."

"Or so your mother claims," Hucker drawled.

The cruel remark made her gasp, even as it set the other men laughing. How dare he? And how dare George not only allow it but laugh at the remark?

She fought to hold her tongue, for Tristan's life might depend upon it. Unfortunately, her silence only fired up the men. They edged nearer on their horses to make crude comments about her bosom, and to propose things she only dimly understood but which sounded vile.

Within seconds, Dom appeared in the doorway. "Call off your dogs," he snapped at his brother. "She's in mourning every bit as much as us. How can you let them insult her? She's your sister, for God's sake!"

George raised an eyebrow but wisely said nothing to that. "What are you doing here, Dom?"

"I'm here to commiserate with my family—*our* family."

A sneer crossed George's face. "Are you sure you're not just hoping to take up with Mrs. Bonnaud where Father left off?"

Lisette blinked, then lunged forward. "Why, you beastly, awful man!" Only Dom's iron grip restrained her from jerking George off his gelding so she could slap his face.

"Enough, *monsieur*!" Maman cried from behind her. She came out to stare coolly at George. "Your quarrel is with me. Leave them out of it."

George's expression chilled to ice. "My quarrel is with Tristan."

Not for nothing had Maman been the toast of Toulon society when she was an actress. Though she couldn't hide her red eyes or her pale cheeks, she could play nonchalance very well. "Oh? What has my son done now to annoy you?"

"Stolen my property. And we're here to make sure he pays for it."

She waved her hand. "I know nothing of that." A disbelieving smile crossed her lips. "Can you *prove* he stole your property?"

Hucker was the one to answer. "Witnesses saw him take Blue Blazes from the stables last night."

As Maman paled, Lisette went limp. Witnesses. That wasn't good.

Yet Maman persevered. "Be that as it may, it has naught to do with me. I cannot control my son. I'm sure he will return the horse soon. It may very well be back in the stables now, if your lordship would just go—"

"I'm not going anywhere, Mrs. Bonnaud. The first place Tristan would come is here, if only to tell you of Father's passing." George stared at her with the lazy arrogance that made them all hate him. "So I'll make this simple enough for even a French whore to understand. Either tell me where Tristan is, or vacate this cottage by first light tomorrow."

As Dom cursed under his breath, Lisette spat, "You can't do that!"

"I most certainly can." George glanced at Maman. "Do you have this month's rent?"

"Of course not," she said, her face now ashen. "Ambrose owns it."

"*Owned* it. My father is dead, remember?" George said coldly. "So now the cottage belongs to me, and I require rent. Can you pay it? Because if you can't, I have the right to evict you." He smiled his bullying smile. "Hell, I have the right to evict you anyway. Especially since you've been harboring a thief."

Dom stepped forward. "Show some mercy, George. They're still reeling from the news of Father's death. We all are. Allow them time to grieve, to get through the funeral and the reading of the will."

"I hope you're not siding with them, brother mine," George said acidly as his horse danced back and forth. "Because there's nothing in Father's will for you. He wrote it shortly after I was born, and he hasn't changed it since."

Judging from Dom's sharp intake of breath, he hadn't known that. "That can't be true," he ground out.

"Consult with Father's solicitor if you don't believe me. He's been trying to get Father to update his will for years." George cast his brother a smug smile. "So I suggest you figure out whose side you're on. Because I'm more than willing to be generous to my *legitimate* brother and give him what Father neglected to leave to him legally. Or . . ."

His malevolent pause made Lisette's blood run cold.

"Or?" Dom prodded.

"I can end your future career as a barrister just like that." He snapped his fingers. "If you help them hide Tristan from me, you won't get a penny of Father's fortune—no allowance, no property, nothing. And you'll find it very difficult to continue studying law without money."

Despair gripped Lisette. Dom's life would be over before it even started. He hadn't agreed to that when he'd agreed to help Tristan.

"How can I hide him from you when I have no idea where he is?" Dom said with a calm mien, though she could feel the tension in him.

George frowned. "Be very careful what choice you make, little brother. I mean it when I say I will cut you off."

A heartbreaking look of pure betrayal crossed Dom's face. "You really did burn that codicil, didn't you?"

The color drained from George's face. "I don't know what you're talking about."

"I heard that Father wrote a codicil to his will on his deathbed that provided for all of us, including me. And you burned it."

"Aha!" George leaned forward in the saddle. "You *do* know where Tristan is. Otherwise, you wouldn't—" He broke off with a chagrined expression.

"Have heard about the codicil?" Triumph lit Dom's gaze. "I thought you didn't know what I was talking about."

George wasn't about to let anything so inconvenient as the truth stop him from his course. "Don't try your legal tricks on me, little brother. You're not a barrister yet, and I'm not admitting anything. Where is he, damn you?"

"I told you. I have no idea."

"You're lying."

"So are you," Dom bit out.

"You can't prove that. You have only the word of a worthless thieving bastard who has nothing to lose by slandering me."

"And you can't prove that I know where he is."

"I don't need proof. I'm the heir. My law is absolute." He tightened his fist on the reins. "So are you with me, little brother? Or with *them*? Because if you choose them, I swear I'll leave you with nothing."

Lisette held her breath. Even the horses seemed to halt their fidgeting, waiting for Dom's answer.

He stared at George for a long, hard moment. Then he turned to offer Lisette his arm. "Come, sister. It appears we will have to pack your and your mother's belongings before tomorrow."

Shock lined George's face. Then he narrowed his gaze. "Fine. You've made your choice. Tell Tristan that your ruin is on *his* head." Whirling his gelding toward the other men, he barked, "Search the house! Search the fields and moors and every inch of land between here and the sea! He must be here somewhere!"

As his men rushed into the house, Lisette said, "Dom, you shouldn't—"

"Keep quiet until they're gone, dear girl," he whispered. "Then we'll talk."

He was right to be cautious, but it took all her restraint not to protest as Hucker pawed through her closet, and the others turned furniture upside down, ignoring Maman's French curses. Hucker was smoking his vile Spanish cigarillos, and the thought of the sickening scent permeating her clothes was almost more than she could bear.

Battered by the day's events, Lisette wanted to scream at them, but there was no point. Nothing would ever be the same anyway. Papa was gone. There'd be no more lazy breakfasts with him reading funny parts of the paper aloud or regaling them with stories about his latest trip. No more walks along the cliffs at Flamborough Head with him and Maman. No more nights staring up at the stars with Dom and Tristan.

Tears burned her eyes again. How would she bear it? And what was to become of them without Papa?

It didn't take long for George's men to figure out that Tristan wasn't inside. As soon as they'd left to check the surrounding property, Maman approached Dom with a look of worry. "My boy, you mustn't do this. George will leave you penniless for certain. Your father wouldn't want that."

"You'd rather I give Tristan over to him?"

"Of course not, but perhaps if you reason with George—"

"You saw how well that worked."

Maman frowned. "What if Tristan gave him the money he got for the horse? Surely George couldn't . . . wouldn't have his own brother hanged. Would he?"

"He could and would, I'm afraid. If he's willing to trample over the wishes of our dead father, he'll do anything." Dom gazed out the window to where George was spurring his men on in the search. "Besides, I suspect that even if I were cruel enough to hand Tristan over, it would gain me little except a lifetime of slavery to George. He'd use the bludgeon of his fortune time and again to require my compliance with whatever scheme he concocts, and I refuse to live like that."

"But how *will* you live?" Lisette asked. Dom was her brother, too. She didn't want him to suffer.

Dom chucked her under the chin. "I'm a grown man, dear girl. I can take care of myself. My legal education may not have progressed far enough to gain me a position as a clerk or solicitor, but I have a friend in the Bow Street Runners who might hire me on the strength of it." He broadened his gaze to include Maman. "I'm more concerned with how you three will live."

Maman squared her shoulders. "We shall slip away with Tristan to my family in Toulon."

Dom frowned. "That means leaving everything behind."

"Not everything," Maman corrected him. "I have my

children. Besides, my possessions were bought for me by your papa, so George will claim that they belong to the estate anyway." She tipped up her chin. "I won't have any accusation of thievery laid upon *my* head. Or Lisette's. We will take our clothes, that is all."

"But how will you live in France?" Dom asked.

"I can find a position as an actress again." She tilted her head coyly. "I am still young and pretty enough for that, no?"

Dom smiled at her show of vanity. "Yes. And you have whatever money Tristan got for the horse."

"He shouldn't keep it," Maman whispered.

"Ah, but he should. Father wanted him to have it." Dom turned pensive. "At least we know that Father *meant* to do right by us all, even if George thwarted him in the end."

The shadow of grief that darkened his face made Lisette feel sorry for him. "Papa should have put you in his will. It was very wrong of him not to."

"You know how he was, always off somewhere exploring a new city or island or lake." An edge entered Dom's voice. "He had no time for things like family responsibilities."

"Do not blame him too much," Maman said. "He might not have been good at such things, but he did love you." Her gaze stretched to include Lisette. "He loved you both very much."

That started Maman crying again, and she left to find a handkerchief. After she was gone, Lisette whispered, "Yes, he loved us. Just not enough."

That was the trouble with relying on a man to save you. Men were unreliable. Papa . . . George . . . Even Tristan had made matters worse with his anger. Of the important men in her life, only one had always done the right thing—and much as Dom wanted to help, even he could do little more than pack them off to France.

Maman had been wrong to place her faith in Papa. All it had gained her was grief for her and her children.

Lisette dashed away fresh tears. Well, she would never be so foolish. First chance she got, she would make her own way in this world, no matter what it took. She wasn't going through this kind of betrayal ever again.

1

Covent Garden, London
April 1828

THERE WASN'T A single letter from Tristan in the
whole lot.

As the misty morning brightened to a less gloomy
gray, Lisette tossed the mail onto the desk in Dom's
study. Typical. When she'd left Paris, Tristan had promised to write her once a week. But though he'd started
out well, two months had now passed without so much
as a line from him.

She was torn between worry over what had stopped
the flow of letters, and a desire to string her feckless
brother up by his toes and let *him* see what it was like
to be left hanging.

"Are you sure you don't want to accompany me to
Edinburgh on this case?" Dom asked. "You could take
notes for me."

Lisette looked over to see her half brother loung-
ing in the doorway. At thirty-one he was leaner and
harder than when they were young, and he now had a
scar across his cheek that he wouldn't talk about, which

came from God knew where. But he was still in her camp.

Most of the time. She scowled. Sometimes he could be as bad as Tristan.

Ever since Dom had fetched her here from France six months ago, she'd worked hard to turn his rented town house into a home. Just because it also served as the office for Manton's Investigations didn't mean it had to feel cold and impersonal. But what had her efforts got her? Nothing but another *man* to govern her behavior.

Sitting back in the chair, she lifted an eyebrow. "You don't need me to take notes—you remember everything word for word."

"But you're better at descriptions than I am. You notice things about people that I don't."

She rolled her eyes. "I will only go if you let me do more than describe things and make you tea."

He eyed her warily. "Like what?"

"Interview witnesses. Follow suspects. Carry a pistol."

To his credit, he didn't laugh. Tristan would have laughed. And then tried, *again*, to find her a suitable husband from among his swaggering soldier friends in Paris, who acted as if a half-English bastard like her should be grateful for every crumb of their attention.

Instead, Dom eyed her consideringly as he came into the room. "Do you even know how to use a pistol?"

"Yes. Vidocq showed me." Only once, before Tristan put a stop to the lessons, but Dom needn't know that.

He was already cursing Eugène Vidocq, the former head of the French secret police. "I can't believe our brother allowed you anywhere near that scoundrel."

She shrugged. "We needed the money. And Vidocq needed someone at the Sûreté Nationale whom he could trust to organize all his index cards containing descriptions of criminals. It was a good position."

And to her surprise, she'd enjoyed it. After Maman's death three years ago, when Lisette had moved to Paris to live with Tristan, she'd craved useful work to take her mind off her grief. Vidocq had offered it to her. She'd learned about investigating crimes from him. Vidocq had even proposed hiring her as an agent for the Sûreté, as he'd done with other women, but Tristan had refused to allow it.

She snorted. Tristan thought it perfectly fine for *him* to be an agent for the Sûreté all these years, but his sister was to be kept wrapped in cotton until she found a husband. Which got more unlikely by the year. She was already twenty-six, for pity's sake!

"What is your answer, Dom?" she prodded her half brother. "If I go with you, will you let me do more than take notes?"

"Not this time, but perhaps one day—"

"That's what Tristan always said." She sniffed. "Meanwhile, he was plotting behind my back to get me married, and when that didn't work, he packed me off to London with you."

"For which I'm profoundly grateful," Dom said with a faint smile.

"Don't try to distract me with compliments. I'm not going to marry any of *your* choices for husband, either."

"Good," he said cheerily. "Because I don't have any. I'm too selfish to want to lose you to a husband. I need you here."

She eyed him uncertainly. "You're just saying that."

"No, dear girl, I'm not. You've got a wealth of information about Vidocq's methods stored up in that clever head. I'd be mad to marry you off and lose all that."

Lisette softened. Dom *had* been much more accommodating about her learning his business than she'd expected. Perhaps it was because he'd struggled so hard to gain it, after George had cut him off entirely. Or perhaps it was because he remembered their childhood together fondly.

Whatever the case, she would allow him some time. Perhaps eventually he would consider giving her broader duties. More exciting duties. She might finally get to travel, to satisfy the wanderlust she'd inherited from Papa. It was a measure of how much Dom trusted her that he was leaving her here for a week with only the servants for company. This was the first time he'd done so.

"So you think I'm clever, do you?" she said.

"And managing and opinionated and a pain in the arse—" At her frown, he softened his tone. "But yes, also very clever. You have many good qualities, dear girl, and I do appreciate them. I'm not Tristan, you know."

"I know." She thumbed through the letters spread out on the desk. "Speaking of our rapscallion brother, I haven't heard from him in months. It's not like him to be so silent. Generally he writes once a week."

Dom strode up to the desk to collect some papers for his trip. "He's probably on a case for Vidocq."

"But Vidocq was forced to resign as head of the Sûreté last year."

After Vidocq had left, Tristan had retained his position as an agent by the skin of his teeth. Because she hadn't been an agent, she'd lost her position entirely. So her brother had decided it was time that she find a husband, even an English one. And since he dared not return to England because of the theft warrant against him, it had been left to Dom to take her to London.

"Then he's probably on a case for the new fellow," Dom said as he shoved documents into his satchel.

"I doubt that." She rose to wander toward the window. "The new head of the Sûreté doesn't exactly like Tristan."

"That's because Tristan is damned good at what he does. That new fellow couldn't investigate a fruit seller for bruising an apple, so he resents anyone who shows him up." He shot her a side glance. "Although, to be fair, our brother can try any employer's patience. He makes his own rules, keeps odd hours, and has a tendency not to tell anyone what he's up to."

"You've just described yourself," she said dryly.

A laugh sputtered out of him. "All right, I'll concede that. But I work for myself, so I can act that way—he has superiors who expect regular reports."

"True," she said absently as she gazed out the window, her attention caught by a man in a gray surtout across the street, who was staring at the town house most intently. He looked familiar. He looked like . . .

She moved closer to the glass, and the man disappeared into the fog. A chill skittered down her spine that she forced herself to ignore. It couldn't be Hucker. He wouldn't be in London; he'd be in Yorkshire with the rest of George's minions. If he even still worked for George.

Dom walked toward her. "There's also the fact that he has an annoying tendency to land himself in trouble without even trying."

"Who?" she asked, startled into turning from the window.

"Tristan." He steadied a curious gaze on her. "That *is* who we're discussing, isn't it?"

"Yes, of course." She forced herself to forget about Hucker. "His penchant for getting into scrapes is precisely why I'm worried. Even Vidocq used to say that Tristan purposely courts danger."

"True, but he always manages to extricate himself from it, too. He doesn't need you for that." Dom's gaze on her softened. "I, on the other hand, need you for lots of things." Holding his gloved hand out to her, he pointed to a rip in the palm. "You see? I did that just this morning. Can you fix it?"

He was trying to distract her from her worries, which was sweet of him, though completely transparent. Wordlessly, she drew off his glove, took out her mending box, and began sewing the rip closed.

As she worked, her mind wandered to the man she'd seen outside. Should she mention him to Dom? No, that would be foolish. He might decide to stay in London, which they could ill afford. His business was growing by the day, but he still couldn't pass up a case as lucrative as the one in Scotland.

Besides, she wasn't even sure it was anything to be concerned about. It had been years since she'd left the estate—the man might not be Hucker at all. No point in alarming Dom for no reason.

She'd nearly finished repairing his glove when Dom's lone manservant—butler, valet, and footman all in one—entered the room. "It is nearly nine, sir. You have only half an hour to make it to the docks."

"Thank you, Skrimshaw," Dom drawled. "I know how to read a clock."

The florid-faced fellow stiffened. "Begging your pardon, sir, but 'Like as the waves make towards the pebbled shore, So do our minutes hasten to their end.'"

When Dom began to scowl, Lisette smothered a laugh and said hastily, "I'll make sure he gets off in time, Shaw. He'll be along soon."

Skrimshaw looked unconvinced but turned and left.

"I swear, if that man quotes any more Shakespeare to me, I'll turn him off," Dom complained.

"No, you won't. You'll never find another who'll do what he does for so little salary." She tied off the thread and handed the glove to Dom. "Besides, you provoked him by using his real name."

"Oh, for God's sake," he said as he jerked his glove

on, "I'm not going to call my servant by a stage name, no matter how he spends most of his evenings."

"You should be kinder to him, you know," she chided. "Because of your insistence that he stay here to look after me at night while you're gone, he gave up his minor role that begins rehearsals this week. And in any case, he's right. It's time for you to leave." She fought a smile. "All those minutes are hastening away."

With a muttered oath, Dom turned for the door, then paused to glance back at her. "About Tristan. If you haven't heard from him by the time I return from Scotland, I'll see what I can find out."

"Thank you, Dom," she said softly, knowing what a concession that was.

"But don't think I'll be running off to France after the rascal," he grumbled. "Not unless someone pays me for it."

"Perhaps while you're in Edinburgh I'll solve a case or two," she said lightly. "Then *I* can pay you."

He scowled. "That's not remotely amusing. Promise me you won't try any such fool thing."

Casting him an enigmatic smile, she glanced at the clock. "You'll miss your ship if you don't leave."

"So help me, Lisette, if you—"

"Go, go," she cried as she pushed him toward the door. "You know perfectly well I'm teasing you. Don't worry about me. I'll be fine."

At last he left, muttering about insolent servants and troublesome sisters. With a laugh, she returned to dealing with the mail, sorting each letter by the case it involved, then putting the inquiries for new cases into a pile to go through last.

She spent the day responding to the correspondence, making notes on the cases she thought Dom might take, and dealing with household matters. It was nearly midnight before she got to bed. There was no point in retiring before then—crowds of theatergoers thronged the streets most evenings. She enjoyed the noise and the bustle, which reminded her of the theaters where Maman had acted in Toulon.

The streets were a bit quieter once she did go to bed and they generally stayed that way until midday, at least at their little end of Bow Street.

So when a pounding on the door downstairs awakened her just past dawn, she nearly had heart failure. Who could be coming here so early? Oh dear, had something happened to delay Dom's ship to Edinburgh?

Hastily donning her dressing gown over her night rail, she hurried into the hall just in time to hear Skrimshaw grumbling to himself as he headed for the door downstairs. He'd scarcely gotten it open when a male voice snapped, "I demand to see Mr. Manton."

"I beg your pardon, sir," Skrimshaw said, donning his butler role with great aplomb. "Mr. Manton does not see clients at this early hour."

"I'm not a client. I'm the Duke of Lyons," the man countered, his tone iced with the sort of anger only the aristocracy could manage. "And he'll see me if he knows what's good for him."

The bold statement sent Lisette rushing forward in a panic.

"Otherwise," the duke went on, "I will be back with officers of the law to search every inch of this house for him and his—"

"He's not here," she said as she flew down the stairs, heedless of how she was dressed. The last thing Manton Investigations needed was an officious duke barging in with a crowd of officers merely because he was up in the boughs over some foolish matter. The gossip alone would ruin them.

But as she reached the bottom of the stairs and caught sight of the man, she skidded to a halt. Because the fellow looming in the doorway beyond Skrimshaw did not *look* like a duke.

Oh, he wore the clothing of a duke—a top hat of expensive silk, a coat of exquisitely tailored cashmere, and a perfectly tied cravat. But every duke she'd seen depicted in the papers or in satirical prints was gray-haired and stooped.

This duke was neither. Tall and broad-shouldered, he was the most striking man she'd ever seen. Not handsome, no. His features were too bold for that—his jaw too sharply chiseled, his eyes too deeply set—and his golden-brown hair was a touch too straight to be fashionable. But attractive, oh yes. It annoyed her that she noticed just how attractive.

"Dom's not here," she said again.

"Then tell me where he is."

The expectation that she would just march to his

tune raised her hackles. She was used to dealing with his sort—the worst thing she could do was let him bully her into revealing too much. After all, she still didn't know what this was about. "He's on a case out of town, Your Grace. That's all I'm at liberty to say."

Eyes the color of finest jade sliced down, ripping away whatever flimsy pretensions she might have. In one savage glance he unveiled her age, family connections, and station in life, making her feel all that she was . . . and was not.

Those all-seeing eyes snapped back to her. "And who are you? Manton's mistress?"

His words, spoken in a tone of studied contempt, had Skrimshaw turning positively scarlet, but before the servant could speak, she touched his arm. "I'll handle this, Shaw."

Though the older man tensed, he knew her well enough to recognize the tone that presaged an epic setdown. Reluctantly, he stepped back.

She met the duke's gaze coldly. "How do you know I'm not Manton's wife?"

"Manton doesn't have a wife."

Supercilious oaf. Or, as Maman would have called him . . . *English*. He might not look like a duke, but he certainly acted like one. "No, but he does have a sister."

That seemed to give the duke pause. Then he caught himself and cast her a haughty stare. "None that I know of."

That *really* sparked her temper. She forgot about his threat, forgot about the early hour or what she was wearing. All she could see was another George, full of himself and his consequence.

"I see." She marched forward to thrust her face right up to his. "Well, since you know so much about Mr. Manton already, you obviously don't need us to tell you when he's returning or how you can reach him. So, good day, Your Grace."

She started to close the door, but he pushed forward to block the motion. When she lifted her livid gaze, she found him staring at her with the merest hint of respect. "Forgive me, madam, it appears that you and I got off on the wrong foot."

"*You* got off on the wrong foot. I merely watched you shove it into your mouth."

He raised an eyebrow, clearly unused to having people of her inconsequence speak to him in such a fashion. Then he nodded. "A colorful way to put it. And perhaps apt. But I have good reason for my rudeness. If you will allow me in to explain, I promise to behave like a gentleman."

When she eyed him skeptically, Skrimshaw stepped forward to murmur, "At the very least, miss, come away from the open door before someone sees you dressed as . . ."

It suddenly hit her that she was standing here practically in view of the street wearing only her night rail and dressing gown. No wonder the duke thought her a mistress. "Yes, of course," she mumbled and backed away, allowing him to enter.

The duke closed the door behind him. "Thank you, Miss . . . Miss . . ."

"Bonnaud," she finished.

Before she could even explain why her name was different from Dom's, the duke said in a strained voice, "Ah. You're *that* sister."

The wealth of meaning in his words made heat rise in her cheeks. "The bastard one?" she said tightly.

"The one who's also a sister to Tristan Bonnaud." His hard gaze flicked down her again.

Alarm rose in her chest. "You know my other brother?"

"You might say that. He's the reason I'm here." His eyes narrowed on her. "I was hoping Manton would reveal where the scoundrel is hiding in London. But I don't suppose there's much chance that *you* will do so."

A chill coursed down her spine. This wasn't good at all. If Tristan had been fool enough to come to England . . .

No, it was impossible. "You must be mistaken, sir. Tristan hasn't visited London in years. And if he did, we would be the first to know. But Dom and I have had no word from him."

He searched her face. "Which only proves me right about his character. I did think it odd that a man of Manton's sterling reputation would countenance Bonnaud's actions, but if he was unaware of them—"

"What actions, sir?" she asked, her pulse jumping

up a notch with the duke's every word. "What has my brother done?"

"Forgive me, madam, but I prefer to discuss this with a more disinterested party. Tell me where Manton is, and I will leave you in peace."

After hinting that Tristan had done some awful thing? Not a chance. "As I said before, I'm not at liberty to do so. But if you'll reveal what it is you think Tristan has done, I promise to be as impartial a judge of his actions as you have been."

Skrimshaw let out what sounded like a laugh, which turned into a cough beneath the duke's withering glance.

"It seems that we have come to an impasse," the duke told her icily.

She crossed her arms over her chest. "It does appear that way, doesn't it?"

"I'm not leaving without the information I seek."

"And I'm not telling you anything without knowing what's going on. So you have two choices, Your Grace. You may speak to me clearly and honestly of your grievance, and I will help you resolve the matter. Or you can bed down in our parlor for the next week or so until Dom's return."

"A week!" the duke exclaimed.

"As I told you, he is on a case. Sometimes they go on for a while."

Lyons muttered an oath under his breath. "You realize I could bring half a dozen officers in here to search the place for the information I seek."

It was her turn to cast *him* a withering stare. "You

could. But you'll find that such behavior will only make me more recalcitrant. By the time you can return with officers, I will have spirited away any information of use to you. And then you'll have to toss me in gaol to get anything out of me."

He blinked, then surprised her by letting out a harsh laugh. "You make a formidable adversary, Miss Bonnaud."

"I take that as a compliment," she said archly.

"Of course you do. Very well, I'll tell you what I know if you'll tell me what *you* know." He nodded at Skrimshaw. "But only if we can continue this conversation in private."

Now that she'd won the skirmish, she began to be worried about the battle. If he wanted privacy, Tristan must have done something very bad indeed.

"Certainly, Your Grace," she said shakily, then turned to Skrimshaw. "If you'd be so good as to ask Mrs. Biddle to bring us tea, we shall take it upstairs in the study. I believe this discussion is going to require it."

"It will require something more than tea, I expect," Skrimshaw muttered as he took the duke's hat and coat, then headed for the back of the house.

Lisette began climbing the stairs. "If you'll follow me, sir, I'm sure we can sort out this muddle."

The duke fell into step behind her. "I damned well hope so."

So did she. Because if she couldn't handle this to the duke's satisfaction, she had a feeling the result would be disaster for both of her brothers. And she would do just about anything to prevent that.

2

MAXIMILIAN CALE, THE Duke of Lyons, followed the young woman, marveling that she'd called
his bluff. And his threat to bring in the authorities *had*
been a bluff—he didn't want them involved if he could
avoid it. Given the enormity of the situation and the
gossip it would spawn if it were known, he was better
off dealing with it privately.

Still, he'd hoped to bully her into giving him Manton's whereabouts. He stared at the rigid back of
the woman who climbed the creaking stairs before
him, then shook his head. Apparently he had underestimated Miss Bonnaud's tenacity.

He dredged his mind for the little information
he'd gleaned about the Manton and Bonnaud families
through the years, but could only remember that Tristan
Bonnaud and his sister were the illegitimate children of
the Viscount Rathmoor by a French actress.

It showed. Her accent was tempered with a softness
in the consonants that reminded him of the French,

even though her word choice was thoroughly English. And though her forthright manner and surprising height differentiated her from the delicately flirtatious Frenchwomen who nightly populated the theaters, like them, she had a flair for the dramatic.

No doubt she would have a flair for something else, too. Her thinly veiled derriere, displayed at his eye level, gave him an excellent view of certain feminine charms. She moved with an economy of motion so fluid that he wondered if she would move the same way in bed.

Holy God, what was he thinking? He wasn't here for that, and she was the last person he ought to be noticing in such a fashion. Though it was hard *not* to notice when she was dressed so . . . informally, her raven hair tumbling down her back in a welter of black curls that shimmered and swirled with every step.

And the scent of some elusive French perfume that wafted down to him in her wake—

"Do you live here, Miss Bonnaud?" he asked in an attempt to keep his mind off the seductive form ahead of him. "Or are you just visiting?"

"This is my home." She reached the top and moved down the hall to stand before an open door. "I manage the administrative portion of Manton's Investigations for my brother."

"Ah."

As he came abreast of her, she gestured into the room. "If you'll wait in here, sir, I'll go make myself more presentable."

He would prefer that. Even in the dim light, he

could see the ripe curves of her breasts outlined in semitransparent linen.

He suppressed a groan. "Of course."

After she left, he shook off his absurd preoccupation with the woman's appearance and glanced about, noting the cheap but clean draperies, the battered oak furniture, and the surprising touches of feminine color—a vase filled with lilacs and an elaborately embroidered cushion. The place didn't *look* sinister, but then, what did?

He strode to the desk to see what he could find, but Bonnaud's sister must be a very capable office manager indeed—nothing worthy of perusal lay on top. The drawers were locked, probably to keep their contents from the prying eyes of servants, and the bookshelves revealed only tomes with such titles as *Elements of Medical Jurisprudence* and *The Newgate Calendar* and *The Proceedings of the Old Bailey*. Clearly Manton took his duties as an investigator very seriously.

"Find anything of interest?" Miss Bonnaud clipped out from the doorway.

Returning the book he was holding to its shelf, he said unapologetically, "You know I did not. You have everything in this office locked up tight. It makes a man wonder what you are striving so hard to hide."

"No more than you are, I imagine," she said in that same throaty voice that had first made him mistake her for Manton's mistress.

Her gown did little to correct that misapprehension. Oh, it was respectable enough, but its excellent cut showed her figure to good effect, and the blue and green stripes set off skin as creamy as Sevres porcelain and a red mouth as lush as it was unsmiling.

She was a French rose growing wild amid the hothouse flowers of London. And when she sat down behind the desk and shimmied to adjust her billowing skirt, his eyes again went inexorably to the impressive bosom that filled out her bodice.

"Now, what exactly has Tristan done to have you show up here at the crack of dawn?" she asked bluntly.

He jerked his gaze up to meet the cool blue eyes glittering at him from beneath a fringe of riotous black curls barely contained by hairpins.

"For one thing, your brother asked me to meet with him at a tavern last night, then disappeared before I could arrive."

The color drained from her cheeks. "Tristan really is in London? No, it's impossible. He wouldn't come here."

"Why not?" he asked as he approached the desk.

Her gaze grew shuttered. "Because . . . because he doesn't like England." She forced a smile. "And he has a very good position working for the . . . authorities in France."

That was so vague as to make him suspicious. "What authorities?" He leaned forward to plant his hands on the desk. "Where? Doing what?"

Her gaze shot up to his, obstinate once more. "I'm not telling you anything until you explain what he's done wrong. I hardly think missing a meeting with you is a crime."

Pushing away from the desk, Maximilian bit back a curse. How much should he say? At the very least, he had to explain what the rest of England had known since he was a boy. It was the only way to impress upon her the seriousness of the situation. "Tell me, Miss Bonnaud, what have you heard about my family?"

"Nothing, I'm afraid," she admitted almost apologetically, which made him inclined to believe her. "I lived in France until recently, and I didn't keep up with the English papers. Since I've been here, I've had little time to do more than help Dom organize his office."

"So you're unaware that I had an elder brother."

"If that's true, then why isn't *he* the du—" She halted with a flush. "Oh, you *had* an elder brother."

"Precisely. Peter was kidnapped very young, and we had no word of him until the year of his seventeenth birthday, when he was found dead in Belgium."

He could still hear Mother's voice in the hours before her own death. *Where is my son? I want my son!* And she hadn't been calling for Maximilian.

Shoving that painful memory back into the fortress he kept it in, he went on. "Last night a boy came to my London town house while I was at dinner with friends. He bore a note for me from a gentleman at a tavern near the docks, who turned out to be your brother, saying he had information regarding Peter." He fixed her with a hard gaze. "He claimed that Peter is alive."

She paled, clearly recognizing the ramifications of that.

"He knew that would draw me out," Maximilian

went on. "He said he would wait for me at the Swan and Bull until three a.m. But when I arrived before midnight, your scoundrel of a brother was nowhere to be found."

"What did the messenger boy have to say about that?" she asked shakily.

"Nothing. He disappeared the minute he saw that the 'gentleman' was gone." Anger roiled in him again. "I waited until three, but neither the boy nor your brother ever returned. Thinking I might have somehow missed Bonnaud, I went home to see if another note had been left there. Nothing. So I remembered his connection to Manton, woke my friend Jackson Pinter to learn of Manton's whereabouts, and came here, hoping to find Bonnaud here as well."

He could tell from her agitation that he'd shaken her. Good. She needed to understand how important this was.

"I swear to you that neither of my brothers is here."

"I believe you." If she were hiding Bonnaud, she would have tried to hurry him out the door instead of inviting him upstairs for this chat. "But he must be somewhere in London, or he wouldn't have requested that meeting."

"Are you absolutely certain it was my brother?" she asked, clear worry in her voice. "There must be any number of Frenchmen with his name."

"Ah, but none that I *know*. You see, I met Bonnaud once at a race when your father brought him and introduced him around. Rathmoor said he was planning to buy your brother a commission in the cavalry when he came of age, so he spoke to my father about the regiment Father supported. While they talked, Bonnaud and I chatted about horses. The note alludes to that."

She swallowed. "You have the note with you?"

He hesitated but saw no reason to keep it from her. Drawing it out, he tossed it onto the desk.

She snatched it up and read hastily. He knew exactly what she was seeing. He'd already memorized every word.

> *Dear Duke of Lyons,*
>
> *You may not remember, but we met on a hot summer day when I was fourteen. At the time, I remarked on the handsome handkerchief you refused to use to wipe your brow, and you explained that it had sentimental value, being a special one made just for members of your family.*
>
> *I recently saw another of its kind and realized that the man carrying it, whom I consider a friend, bore a remarkable resemblance to Your Grace. Judging from things he has told me, I believe he may very well be a certain missing relation of yours whom you and I discussed briefly on that day years ago.*
>
> *I can say no more at present, in case this falls into the wrong hands, but for proof of my suspicions, I enclose a rubbing of the embroidery on the handkerchief. If you will be so good as to accompany this messenger to meet*

me, I will show the item to you in person, and
you may judge its veracity then.
              Your servant,
              Tristan Bonnaud

"Well?" he snapped. "It's his signature, is it not?"

She raised a stunned gaze to him. "Yes. But I don't understand. How could Tristan possibly have come across your brother's handkerchief?"

"That's what *I* want to know. More importantly, I want to know what he's trying to get from me. I doubt seriously that he has noble intentions. He wants money, I daresay, for introducing this impostor to me."

"Now, see here," she protested. "If he had such nefarious motives, then why didn't he show up for your assignation?"

The question was a valid one. "Perhaps after he considered the matter, he feared I would bring the authorities. Or perhaps he got cold feet. Or . . ." He scowled at her. "I don't know. But I could ask you the same thing—if this is *not* a nefarious endeavor, why didn't he show up?"

"Obviously he was prevented by something or . . . or someone."

The way she said "someone" gave him pause. "Like who?"

"I-I don't know. An enemy of some kind. He did mention being afraid that the note would fall into the wrong hands." She frowned. "Though it is odd. I mean, if Tristan really had found your brother and wanted to reunite the two of you, he should have just brought Peter to see you. That would be simplest."

The fact that she would point out something that cast even more suspicion on her brother's actions made him feel better about trusting her with the story. She truly didn't seem to know why Bonnaud had approached him.

He fixed her with a dark glance. "He didn't bring the impostor to me because he wanted me to come to him. That's how sharpers work. The swindler lures the target of his fraud away from his friends, to get him alone and confused. It makes the target easier prey."

"My brother is *not* a sharper!" she protested. When he lifted an eyebrow at her, she said stoutly, "He isn't."

"Are you sure?"

Two spots of color appeared in her pretty cheeks. "Yes," she said, though she dropped her gaze to the desk, where she was worrying the note with her hands. "I'll admit he can be wild sometimes and he gets into trouble occasionally, but he's a good man. He'd never prey on someone's grief."

She'd gone right to the heart of Maximilian's anger. "Then he'd be the first to have such scruples," he said bitterly. He paced the room, fighting his churning emotions. "Do you know how many men have approached me and my family in the years since my brother was kidnapped? How many have claimed to know Peter? To *be* Peter?"

And how many his parents had momentarily been swayed by, desperate to have their son back. The son

and all his earthly belongings went up in flames in Belgium fourteen years ago!"

As the angry words echoed in the room, a knock sounded at the door. He jerked his gaze to the aging woman who stood waiting in the doorway, a tray in her hands.

Miss Bonnaud rose slowly, as if afraid he would pounce on her if she didn't use small, careful movements. "Ah, Mrs. Biddle is here with our tea, Your Grace." Instead of calling the servant in, Miss Bonnaud swept toward the door, keeping a wary eye on him.

It unnerved him. He'd seen that look before, leveled on his mad father. That look was why Maximilian generally took great care with his every remark, his every action. People were always watching and waiting for him to exhibit the same symptoms. And Maximilian would never give them the satisfaction of thinking they had seen something . . . off in him.

It annoyed him more than he liked that Miss Bonnaud had just seen him lose his temper. This situation had him all out of sorts.

Taking the tray from the servant, she brought it back to set it on the desk. "Will you have some tea, sir?"

Tea. It was so normal, so everyday. Right now, he wanted nothing more than to feel normal and everyday. "Yes," he clipped out. "Thank you."

The calm he'd forced into his voice seemed to translate to her as well, for she relaxed her shoulders. "And how do you take it?" she asked as she prepared the brew.

"Strong. Black. No sugar."

"How odd," she said as she set the cup and saucer on the desk in front of a chair, unsubtly inviting him to sit down. "So do I. So did my father. Maman thought us both quite mad."

Had she mentioned madness on purpose to provoke him? He slanted her a wary glance. "Then she would have to consider me so, as well."

"Ah, but she would not. You're a duke." Her voice turned acid. "Dukes are above reproach."

She couldn't possibly know about his family's dance with madness, or she wouldn't speak so glibly of it. And she hadn't even known about Peter, so she wouldn't know the rest. "I take it you do not share your mother's opinion of dukes."

"She's dead now," she said with a small hitch in her voice, "but no, I did not share her opinion." She met his gaze boldly. "In my estimation, no man is above reproach."

"Except your brothers?" he drawled.

She released a sigh. "Not even them. They often try my patience sorely."

In spite of everything, he smiled. She was making small talk to put him at ease, and it was working. She must be good at managing Manton's clients.

Watching as she poured her own cup of tea, he took a seat and sipped the brew. It was exactly as he liked it. And it was of surprisingly good quality, given the obviously strained finances of her and her half brother.

"Now then," she asked when she took her own seat,

"how can you be sure that this handkerchief belonged to your brother? You said you were young when he . . . um . . . left."

"Was kidnapped. Let us not mince words. And the handkerchief has certain distinguishing marks. The embroidery is distinctive, for one."

"But any embroidery design could be copied. I copy designs in my own embroidery all the time, whenever I see something pretty on a gown."

"You'll have to trust me when I say it can't be copied. It's more than what was in the design. Each handkerchief's embroidery is unique to its owner. No one but the family knows how. Unfortunately, it requires that I see it to be sure it's the right one."

"How would you even recognize it? I mean, if your brother was taken when you were barely old enough to remember anything . . ."

"Before we received word of Peter's death, my father gave me a written account of everything Peter was wearing or carrying when he was abducted, including the handkerchief. That's why it's imperative that I meet with your brother. So I can get to the bottom of this."

Furrowing her brow, she sipped her tea. "It makes no sense, you know. If Tristan had uncovered an heir to the dukedom and then had traveled to England to reveal that, he would have told Dom and me."

"Perhaps he *did* tell Manton. And Manton left you out of it."

"Dom would never do that."

"Then where is he? It can't be a coincidence that

Manton ran off right before I was supposed to meet
with Bonnaud. He has probably gone to join the scoundrel somewhere."

She glared at him. "Dom began planning this trip to
Edinburgh weeks before you received that note from
Tristan. I have the letters he received from the client,
notes about the information he's been—"

"Edinburgh?" Maximilian cut in, as hope of speaking to Manton died. "He's in *Scotland*?"

A sigh escaped her. "I suppose you might as well
know. He left by ship yesterday morning."

"Confound it all. He has a day's start, then."

"Following him won't do you any good. He doesn't
know where Tristan is any more than I do. In fact, before he left we were discussing our concern that Tristan
hasn't written for months, which isn't like him."

"Obviously Bonnaud was already planning his trip
to England."

"I don't think so. He would have written us about it.
Dom and I and Tristan are very close. We have no secrets from each other. Dom would have told me if he'd
heard from Tristan."

"Unless *Dom* is part of your brother's scheme."

Anger flared in her face. "He would never be part of
any 'scheme.'"

Maximilian considered that a moment. He had to
admit that Manton had an excellent reputation as a
man of good character and principles. It was hard to
believe he would countenance a fraud, especially one
involving a duke.

Manton's half brother, however, was another matter entirely. "So your Tristan didn't tell either of you. That just points to his guilt. He was probably ashamed to admit that he sought to defraud me."

She shook her head. "I still say something bad must have happened to him. That is the only logical explanation."

Not as far as Maximilian was concerned, but clearly she had blinders on when it came to her brother. "In any case, none of this helps me find him. He didn't even leave a note with the tavern keeper or inform the messenger boy what to do if he was gone when we arrived. You have to admit that looks suspicious."

"Yes. And it's not like him at all."

"Have you no idea of where he would go in London?" he pressed her.

"I'm telling you—he can't possibly be in London. Not willingly, anyway."

He sifted through his memory. "Then perhaps he went to the family seat. It's in Yorkshire, is it not?"

A hard laugh escaped her. "It is indeed, but clearly you know as little about my family as I know about yours. My eldest half brother, George, hates us all, even Dom. Dom stood up to him on our behalf, so George cut *him* off, too."

"Too?"

Pain slashed over her features. "Because of my father's negligence in providing for us and because of . . . other things, George was able to cut off all three of us. Why do you think Dom works in such an ungentlemanly profession? Because he has no choice." A contemptuous edge laced her voice. "I assure you, Yorkshire is the last place Tristan would ever go."

Frustrated by her answers, Maximilian drained his cup, then rose to pace again. "The tavern was near the docks. Perhaps he stayed on board a ship. I can go through the manifests of every one that has recently been at port in France."

She lifted an eyebrow. "Good luck. Thousands of ships come through the Port of London every year, and that isn't counting the smaller vessels. You forget that steam packets make the journey daily. If he took one of those, he might already have returned to France, having missed you."

Damn it all. "Steam packets don't travel on Sunday, so perhaps he's still nearby."

"And perhaps he took the coach to Dover or Brighton or Southampton to pick up a packet in those towns tomorrow morning."

"So you do think he might have returned to France."

She shrugged. "It's possible he never left France. He could have sent that note from anywhere."

"He mentioned the messenger and set up an assignation."

"True." She worried her plump lower lip with her teeth. "Perhaps the note is forged."

He narrowed his gaze on her. "You're grasping at straws, madam."

She rose. "I know my brother's character. He would

never coax a duke to meet him unless he had every intention of being there."

A curse escaped him. It did bother him that Bonnaud hadn't come to the town house. A sensible swindler would have come in person, asked for money to bring the impostor to him, and taken what he could get. And if Bonnaud's purpose had been to get Maximilian off where he could demand money easier, why hadn't he stayed around?

He hated to admit it; she was right—this made no sense. But that didn't mean he would stop looking for the man. He couldn't, not if there was any chance in blazes that Peter was alive.

"Then I have no choice. I have to find your brother. I cannot sit here doing nothing in hopes that he seeks me out again. I must have my answers." He stalked up to the desk. "You mentioned reaching him through his employer—I can use that, too. I'll travel to France myself to speak to his employer if you will but give me the man's name and address."

She stared him down. "Not on your life."

He stiffened. He couldn't believe it. The impertinent chit was actually *refusing* to help him! "I don't think you understand, Miss Bonnaud. I will—"

"Oh, I understand completely. You mean to go to Tristan's employer and ruin his reputation by making wild accusations about him, with only a possibly forged letter as proof. I will not allow it." She crossed her arms over her chest. "Tristan has a good position working for the

French government, and I'm not sending you off to destroy that over what is probably some misapprehension."

"Misapprehension!"

"But having already been worried about his silence of late, I want to know the truth as much as you. So I will help you find him. Under one condition."

He glowered at her. He should have known how this would end. "You want money, I suppose."

"Certainly not!" She drew herself up. "I want you to take me with you."

3

IF CIRCUMSTANCES HAD been different, Lisette would have laughed at the look of sheer outrage carving deep lines into the duke's brow. But much as she would normally enjoy shocking a haughty English lord, this was not about that.

It was about making sure that Tristan didn't find himself at the end of a hangman's noose. Because if he *were* in London or if the duke made a big to-do over finding him in Paris . . .

It didn't bear thinking on.

No, she had to avoid having the duke speak to the new head of the Sûreté, who would use any excuse to dismiss Tristan. She would talk to Vidocq, who was Tristan's friend. He might know what this was about.

But that meant she had to be there. The wily Vidocq would never reveal anything to the duke.

"You have lost your bloody mind," Lyons said in a low hiss.

She squared her shoulders. "I have not. I know how men like you work. You run roughshod over whomever you please, simply because you can. Well, you're not going to run roughshod over my brother."

He glowered at her. "And *you* won't stop me from prosecuting him to the fullest extent of the law if I find he has attempted to defraud me."

A chill froze her blood. She ignored it. "And I won't try, either. *If* he's guilty of such a horrible thing, I'll hand you the shackles to secure him, myself."

Clearly that caught him by surprise. "Is that a promise?"

"It is," she vowed. "But I'm not doing anything until I determine that you have the right culprit."

A muscle ticked in his jaw. "How do you propose to do that?"

"I don't know," she said truthfully. "I only know that if I hand you the means to find him and you muck up his life and future in France, I will never forgive myself. He and Dom are my only family. I owe them better, for all the years they've looked after me."

That seemed to give him pause, thank goodness. He scrubbed one hand over his face, and she realized that he looked quite weary. If he'd been up since yesterday morning . . .

A sudden pang of sympathy made her scowl. Why should she care if he was tired? He was threatening to hunt Tristan down like some common criminal, with nothing more to go on than that note.

And Tristan's inexplicable disappearance.

She suppressed that thought. Tristan couldn't be guilty of fraud. He could *not*!

"What if I swear to treat your brother fairly?" he said.

She eyed him with suspicion. "Men like you do not—"

"You know nothing about men like me," he snapped.

"I know more than you think." She thought of George's determination to destroy Tristan. "Besides, I have connections of my own to the authorities in France. If you attempt to malign Tristan unfairly, I'll have some recourse. But only if I am *there* when you do it."

The duke prowled before the desk like, well, a lion . . . all tawny hair and muscular brute of the forest. He was a rather frightening fellow in a temper. His words and manner might be cold, but a terrifying anger simmered just beneath the surface, showing only in the wild glint of his eye and the tautness of his jaw.

So she didn't wait for more of his protests. "I can be a help to you. I know not only where Tristan lives, but how he works, how to find him, where his haunts are." And Vidocq still had friends in high places. Not to mention a few in low places who might be useful.

The duke glared at her. "But you cannot travel alone with me, so I'll lose precious time finding a chaperone for you."

Was he joking, for pity's sake? "I don't need a chaperone. No one cares about my reputation. I'm a nobody."

"You're a respectable woman."

She snorted. "That's not what you said earlier."

That brought him up short. He stared at her, his gaze unreadable. "That was rude of me, and I apologize."

"No need," she said, though the apology gratified her. She doubted he offered one very often. "I've grown used to people making such assumptions through the years. What people think of my mother is bound to reflect upon me."

That was why she was so wary of men. Even Tristan's soldier friends were only interested in dallying with her. Her brothers couldn't see that; they seemed to believe she could find a husband anywhere if she just tried. She knew better.

"All the same," he said earnestly, "I won't ruin any chance you have for a decent marriage by carrying you off with me unchaperoned to France."

A bitter laugh burst from her. "I assure you I have few prospects for a 'decent marriage.' I'm nearly twenty-seven. I have no connections or fortune. Not to mention that I'm the daughter of a French actress."

"And a viscount."

"Who chose not to marry my mother." When he looked as if he would say more, she added, "If the thought of damaging my reputation truly bothers you, just tell people I'm your relation. Your sister, perhaps."

He shot her an incredulous glance. "I'm the Duke of Lyons. Everyone knows I don't have a sister."

"Then choose something else, something they would never know was a falsehood. Tell them I'm your mistress."

She regretted the flip statement the moment something hot and fierce and raw flared in his eyes, something distinctly ungentlemanly. It provoked the oddest fluttering in her belly.

"Because coaches leave frequently for Brighton on Sundays. In fact, there's one that leaves from the Golden Cross Inn at two. Since we can't take a steam packet, we can still move forward and be ready tomorrow morning for the packet to Dieppe."

"Ah yes, Dieppe shortens the route to Paris by ninety miles," he said smoothly.

But she caught the calculating glint in his eye. The sly devil was still trying to figure out where Tristan was. "It shortens the route to Rouen and Dijon, too. And any number of French towns." She wasn't about to reveal that they were headed for Paris, not yet. She couldn't take the chance that Lofty Lyons would abandon her once he knew their eventual destination.

With a scowl, he crossed his arms over his chest. "You're really not going to tell me where Bonnaud has been living or who he's been working for."

"No." She tilted up her chin. "Not unless you take me with you."

"I could travel to Edinburgh to find your half brother. No doubt *he* would tell me where Bonnaud lives and works."

"He might. But Edinburgh is only where Dom is disembarking from the ship—he's traveling on elsewhere in Scotland, and I'm not going to tell you where that is, either. So while you're rambling about Scotland, I'll be off to France to warn Tristan that you're hunting for him, and if you're right and he's guilty, he'll be long gone by the time you reach him."

What an idle threat—she couldn't afford a trip to

Dover, much less a trip to France. But *he* didn't know that.

Lyons studied her a long moment, the small crease between his eyes deepening until it mirrored the small crease in his chin. The intensity of his gaze sent tremors of apprehension down her spine.

Apprehension, yes. That's what it was. She knew better than to feel tremors of anything else for an English lord of his consequence. A very attractive, very virile English lord of the highest consequence in the land.

"So what's it to be, Your Grace?" she said, as much to remind her of the gulf in their stations as to stop that intrusive stare. "A masquerade? Or are you going alone to search for a needle in a haystack in France?"

He scowled at her, then propped one hip on the edge of the desk. "I would play your brother," he said, as if trying the idea on for size.

"Yes." She fought to hide her relief from him. At least he was considering her proposal. "We'll make it simple, which is always best. You can use your real surname, since that will make it easier for you to remember. No one will connect Mr. Cale with the Duke of Lyons, especially since Cale can be spelled so many ways. And I'll be Miss Cale. It's probably less conspicuous than my own French name anyway." She tapped her chin. "Oh, but I'll want to call you by your Christian name. What would that be?"

Though that impertinence made him raise an eyebrow, he said, "Maximilian," in that oh-so-cultured voice of his.

"That won't do at all. I'll call you Max." At his dark stare, she added wickedly, "To throw off suspicion. 'Maximilian' sounds far too lofty a name for plain Mr. Cale, the cotton merchant."

"Cotton merchant? You said to keep it simple. What the blazes do I know about cotton?"

"You don't need to know anything about it; I know plenty already. Dom had a case once involving that industry. I'll field any questions you're asked."

"Right. Because *that* won't look odd in the least," he said sarcastically. "Nor will anyone notice that we have different accents. And before you suggest it, no, I cannot change my accent. Unlike you, I'm unaccustomed to playing a role."

Was that supposed to be an insult—implying yet again that she and her family were devious? "What do you mean—'unlike you'? Do you think I play roles routinely?"

"You must," he said dryly. "You seem to think it the easiest thing in the world."

"Oh," she said, slightly mollified. "Well, it is. My mother *was* an actress, you know."

"Have you ever done any acting yourself?"

She colored. "No, but I know all the techniques. I spent years helping Maman prepare for her roles."

And she'd always wanted to be an agent for Vidocq, to pretend to be someone else while traveling to exotic places and infiltrating the highest and lowest levels of society. To be a spy. It sounded very exciting.

He was watching her now, his gaze hooded. "All the

same, no one will ever believe that you and I are brother and sister. We sound too different, look too different." His voice dropped to a rough thrum. "And I can assure you, I will never be able to treat you like a sister."

That got her dander up again. "Because I'm too far beneath you?"

"Because you're too beautiful." When she stiffened, he added ruefully, "I can't pretend I don't notice. And the last time I checked, brothers weren't supposed to notice such things about their sisters."

The bald statement threw her off guard and made a stealthy warmth creep under her defenses. She steeled herself against it. He was probably using flattery to try to get his own way, since blustering hadn't worked. Obviously he thought she would melt at the idea of being thought beautiful by a duke. Then she would relent in her plans.

Arrogant beast. "It doesn't matter if people believe it. As long as they don't know who we really are, they can speculate all they want. We are two relatively anonymous travelers. No one will ever connect the real me to the real you. Hardly anyone knows *me* anyway. I only returned to England six months ago."

He cocked his head to one side. "Yet you backed out of the doorway to keep your neighbors from seeing you speaking to me in your night rail and wrapper."

A blush heated her cheeks. "That's different. I can't have my neighbors gossiping about me, because it would reflect badly on Manton's Investigations."

"Exactly," he drawled.

"But my neighbors won't be taking the coach to Brighton or the packet boat to Dieppe. As long as I don't join you in your coach to travel to the Golden Cross Inn, no one will be the wiser. We'll arrive there separately and let Shaw deal with my neighbors. He's good at telling tales. He actually *is* a professional actor."

"Your *butler* is an actor?" he said incredulously.

"Well, he's not exactly a butler, more like a jack of all trades. But he's an excellent actor. So you see, there's nothing to worry about."

"Right." He lifted his gaze heavenward. "Just the possibility of disaster when either you or I let something slip that unmasks us."

"Come now, Your Grace, think of it as an adventure," she said firmly. He was *not* going to talk her out of this. "It sounds as if you could use one, quite frankly."

He shot her an arch glance.

"The coach from the Golden Cross will land us at the coast well before midnight," she continued, "and we can be up at dawn to take the packet for Dieppe."

"Can we indeed?" he said dryly.

She ignored him, determined to have her way in this. "I know that leaving at two allows us only a few hours to pack, but you won't want to take much with you anyway—just Dom's clothes and a few essentials. Nothing fancy that will call attention to yourself. And no big trunk, either—public coaches don't have room for such." She walked to the window. "You mustn't show up at the inn in your coach either, or—"

"You're forgetting one thing, Miss Bonnaud."

She turned from the window to find him standing with legs apart and hands clasped behind his back, looking every inch a duke as he fixed her with a steely glance.

"And what is that?" she asked, feigning nonchalance.

"I haven't yet agreed to your plan."

She girded herself for battle, ignoring the tremor of alarm that swept down her spine. "But neither have you suggested any other workable plan that I will agree to. So unless you can read my mind for the information you seek, you will have to work with me. Or let the matter of your brother's handkerchief remain an intriguing mystery."

He scowled at her. She stared right back at him.

At last he let out a low oath. "Given that time is of the essence, you leave me no choice."

"None," she agreed. She'd actually won!

She headed for the door, now that the worst was over. "I'll see what clothes Dom might have that would fit you—"

"I'll find my own clothes," he interrupted. "I'm sure one of my servants can provide attire different enough from my 'usual finery' to suit you."

"Oh." How could she have forgotten that he would have legions of servants to order about and borrow clothes from? "Of course."

They walked out into the hall and down the stairs in utter silence. When they reached the entrance, where Skrimshaw already had the duke's greatcoat and hat waiting, Lyons faced her with eyes glittering.

"Forgive me for being blunt, Miss Bonnaud," he said

irritably, "but I think you should know that the reason you've remained unmarried until now isn't your age or lack of connections or even your illegitimacy. It is the fact that you are a royal pain in the—" He caught himself as Skrimshaw cleared his throat. "In the derriere."

She burst into laughter. "Dom said exactly the same thing to me before he left yesterday, except that he used the more colorful version. It appears that you *can* play the role of my brother after all. Obviously it comes naturally to you."

The duke must have missed the humor in that, for he glowered at her. "Then it's a good thing I never had a sister. Because I would have throttled her before she was even grown."

The statement was so similar to something her brothers might have said that she couldn't resent it.

"You wouldn't have done any such thing," she said softly. "You would have fought to protect her with every ounce of your strength, the same way I'm fighting to protect my brother."

He studied her with eyes the color of a summer forest. "Then for your sake, I hope that Bonnaud proves worthy of your faith in him."

"He will." He'd better, in any case. Or she would throttle *him*.

"Very well, then. It seems we have a plan." Taking his coat and hat from Skrimshaw, he dipped his head. "I shall see you in a few hours at the Golden Cross."

"I'll be there."

Once Lyons walked out the front door, Skrimshaw

came to stand beside her as she watched the duke get into his coach. "Are you sure about that?" Skrimshaw murmured.

"About what? That I'll be there?"

"That Mr. Bonnaud is worthy of your faith in him. 'There is a method in man's wickedness, / It grows up by degrees.' And it sounds as if your brother is edging a trifle too close to criminal behavior this time."

"Tristan isn't wicked *or* a criminal, and besides—" She scowled. "Wait, were you eavesdropping on my conversation with the duke? That's very rude."

"Is it? Half of the plays in the world contain eavesdropping. I assumed it was a common practice."

She eyed him askance. "You assumed no such thing, you sly dog. You're well aware of the bounds of propriety when you want to be."

Skrimshaw stared earnestly at her. "Yes, which is why I know you are tempting fate with this wild scheme. His Grace is right about that."

Swallowing her apprehension, she turned for the stairs. "I have no choice. I have to make sure Tristan is all right, and I see no other way to do so."

He fell into step behind her. "You could write to Mr. Manton in Scotland and let him handle the matter."

"And how would that get rid of the duke?"

"You could tell *him* what he wants to know."

"So he can rage over to Paris to ruin Tristan's future with the Sûreté? Not on your life."

"You assume that disaster will ensue if His Grace goes off without you, but perhaps he will find Mr. Bonnaud and discover that your brother has indeed located *his* brother."

She paused on the landing to glance at him. "I doubt that. I'm sure Tristan has merely leapt to a conclusion that won't bear up under the facts. A duke's long-lost elder brother appears out of nowhere to claim the dukedom? It's like something out of a play."

"*As You Like It* comes to mind."

"Exactly. Which is why I have to be there when Lyons discovers the truth, whatever it is." She continued up the stairs. "Someone has to ensure he doesn't make Tristan bear the brunt of his anger."

"Mr. Bonnaud is a grown man, you know. He can take care of himself."

She snorted. "No man can take care of himself entirely. I should never have left him alone in France."

They climbed in silence a few moments before Skrimshaw ventured another remark. "Perhaps that is the real reason you wish to embark on this mad journey. Because you miss your home, and you're seizing your chance to return."

Halting at the top of the stairs, she considered that possibility. "Perhaps. I do miss Paris sometimes . . . the people, the food, the art." She headed down the hall. "But I like London, too. That's the trouble—in a perfect world, I would visit both regularly . . . and Venice and New York and even Timbuktu." A long sigh escaped her. "But it isn't a perfect world, is it?"

"No." He stayed her with one hand. "Which is why you shouldn't be going off with a stranger. You don't even know the man, yet you mean to travel with him?"

"We'll be crowded into coaches and packets with several other people, for pity's sake. What can he do? And as sister and brother, we'll have separate rooms at any lodging, so I needn't worry."

Skrimshaw narrowed a particularly stern gaze on her. "You told the man you'd play his mistress if that's what it took."

Lord, he really had heard everything, hadn't he? "All right, I'll admit that was foolish of me, but I was trying to make a point. And I didn't mean I would actually *be* his mistress. He knew that."

"Did he?" Skrimshaw sounded skeptical. "Take care, miss. You're letting the gentleman's high rank, fine attire, and subtle flatteries sway your good judgment. 'All that glisters is not gold.'"

"I realize that. Still, do you think I learned nothing from Maman? I know how easy it is to fall under such a man's spell—and how dangerous. I'm well shielded against such nonsense. You're worrying over nothing. It will be fine."

"I daresay Mr. Manton would think otherwise if he were here."

"Ah, but he's not here," she said with a wave of her hand. "And why do you care what he thinks? With me gone, you can begin rehearsing the part of Diggory in *She Stoops to Conquer*. It might lead to greater things."

He eyed her askance. "Yes, like being turned off for allowing you to travel with the Duke of Lyons on some wild expedition to France."

"What a bag of moonshine. Dom would never turn you off." When he still looked nervous, she added, "I won't let him—I swear it."

"And what am I to tell people if they ask where you have gone?"

"Tell them I went with Dom." She steadied her shoulders. "I know what I'm doing. Go enjoy being in your play, and don't fret over me." She headed for her room. "But first, fetch Mrs. Biddle to come help me pack."

Still, as she prepared for the journey, she wondered if Skrimshaw was right. *Was* she letting the duke's high station and wealth tempt her into trusting him? Or worse yet, his flatteries?

Because you're too beautiful. I can't pretend I don't notice.

That same dratted fluttering arose in her belly. The man certainly knew how to give a compliment. It had seemed devoid of pretense and winking insinuation.

But that didn't mean it was real. How could it be? She wasn't the fragile, wilting flower that every fine gentleman wanted. Even Papa had called her his wild filly, and if she knew one thing about the English, it was that they didn't like wild women. The duke had made that abundantly clear when he'd called her a pain in the "derriere."

That brought a smile to her lips. How ludicrous that Skrimshaw was worried about him—why, the duke couldn't even bring himself to say the word *arse* to her. Once he'd determined that she wasn't a loose woman, he'd been the soul of propriety.

Except for that moment when she'd proposed that she play his mistress.

Remembering how boldly his eyes had raked her, she caught her breath. Perhaps "soul of propriety" wasn't the best description of him, either. He was an enigma, one she wished to unwrap.

She frowned. No, certainly not. Men like Lofty Lyons were more trouble than they were worth. And she didn't need that kind of trouble. She was finally making inroads with Dom; one day soon he might actually let her investigate a case, or at least do some of the important parts.

That was what she'd dreamed of all these years— being in control of her own life, being able to pull her own weight instead of having to depend on feckless men. Taking up with a duke would not help her plans.

So she had to keep a distance between herself and Lyons. She had to ignore his compliments and the absurd attraction she felt for the man. This was a matter of saving Tristan's future. That was all.

✦ ✦ ✦

A FEW HOURS later, when she arrived at the Golden Cross Inn with her bag, she had to remind herself of that. Because the haughty duke had once more defied her expectations.

Dressing in lower-class attire ought to have made him look ordinary and workaday, dulling his virile appeal. Instead, it amplified it. With his greatcoat slung casually over one shoulder, he looked like a rakish adventurer out to conquer the world.

And she had a decided weakness for rakish adventurers.

Drat it all. She couldn't blame his clothes; the fustian suit was what any merchant might wear—a medium-brown coat, buff breeches, and a dark brown stock tied simply about his neck.

But the soft brown color brought out the warm green of his eyes. And his brown leather high boots, with their creases and weathering, made him look rough and daring, a man to be reckoned with. Worse yet, the bold features and unfashionably straight, gold-streaked hair that had seemed wrong for a rich lord were perfect for an adventurer in fustian.

Then he spoke, and the duke returned in full force, arrogant accent and all. "There you are. I thought that you had forgotten what time the coach left."

She forced a smile as she approached. "It took me forever to get packed." Mindful of the people milling about the coach office, she added, "Were there any more notes waiting for you at home from . . . our brother?"

His expression hardened. "No. No word of any kind."

She released a sigh. Part of her had hoped that Tristan had just been delayed somewhere and would have tried to reach the duke again. But it had been over twelve hours since Tristan had first sent that note. It wasn't looking good.

Feeling a sudden chill down her spine, she glanced about the coach office, but nobody seemed to be paying them much mind. She'd had the oddest sense that someone was watching them, but it must have been her imagination, spurred by her worry about Tristan. "I suppose you've purchased our tickets already."

"Of course. Did you bring your passport?"

"Certainly."

"Give it to me. I'll need it to book passage aboard the packet boat."

She handed it over and watched as he shoved it into his coat pocket. "Where's your bag?"

"Already loaded."

"Then I should—"

"Miss Bonnaud!" cried a voice behind her. "I can't believe you're here!"

Her heart sank into her stomach as she turned to see Mrs. Greasley, one of her neighbors, bustling toward her with her stoic husband in tow. Oh no. The biggest gossip in her street just happened to show up at an inn halfway across London? What were the odds?

"Going on the coach, are you?" Mrs. Greasley continued as she caught sight of Lisette's bag.

Steady now, Lisette told herself. *If she asks who's accompanying you, all you need do is claim that Dom is running late.* Lots of coaches left from the Golden Cross Inn, and the woman might not even be here to travel on one.

"Good day, Mrs. Greasley," she said smoothly. "Fancy seeing you here."

"We're off to Brighton to visit our daughter," Mrs. Greasley said cheerily. "I suppose you're off to Brighton, too, eh?"

Lisette froze. This couldn't be happening. How was

she to play Miss Cale if the Greasleys were in the coach with them all the way to Brighton? "I—I—"

But Mrs. Greasley didn't seem to require an answer, for she went on without pause: "I spoke to the coachman, and he said he had a gentleman and a lady booked for the inside seats with us, but I never dreamed it were you and your half brother." She glanced about the inn. "Where is Mr. Manton, anyhow? The coach will be leaving soon, our driver said."

Panic seized her. She couldn't be Miss Cale, and Mrs. Greasley knew that she had no other brothers, so she couldn't claim that the duke was another Mr. Manton or Mr. Bonnaud or—

"I'm afraid the cat has got her tongue," Lyons said smoothly beside her. "You'll have to forgive her—it's been a busy week." He bowed to Mrs. Greasley. "The lady is going with *me* to Brighton."

"You!" Astonishment mingled with outrage in Mrs. Greasley's voice.

"Yes. Allow me to introduce myself. Max Cale, at your service." As Lisette's panic grew to a fever pitch, he took her hand and placed it firmly in the crook of his arm. "I am Miss Bonnaud's new husband."

4

MAXIMILIAN COULD FEEL Miss Bonnaud's fingers digging into his arm, but he ignored them. It was her fault they were in this ridiculous situation. She was the one who'd dreamed up this idiotic plan and was now reduced to a blithering fool at the first obstacle.

But my neighbors won't be taking the coach to Brighton.

Naïve female. He'd known this wouldn't work from the beginning, but she'd jammed him between a rock and a hard place with her refusal to tell him where Bonnaud was, so he'd had no choice.

Now it was left to him to salvage things. As always.

"Oh my word," the plump Mrs. Greasley breathed, then turned on Miss Bonnaud with obvious incredulity. "Husband? You got *married*?"

He held his breath, praying that Miss Bonnaud wouldn't fall apart right there and confess all.

After their earlier encounter, while preparing for the trip, he'd sent a servant to the area around Bow Street to ask about her and Bonnaud. Everything she'd told him so far had proved true. Bonnaud had never been seen at Manton's Investigations, and her role at the place was strictly administrative.

Judging from all reports, she was as forthright as she seemed. Which probably explained why the appearance of her neighbor at the coach office was throwing her into a panic. He braced himself for any reaction.

But she rose to the challenge, leaning close to look up at his face with feigned adoration. "Yes. I'm Mrs. Cale now."

Mrs. Greasley was having none of that. "But . . . but . . . I saw your brother last week and he said naught about it! Why, I didn't even know you *had* any beaus!"

When Miss Bonnaud stiffened at the veiled insult, an inexplicable urge to throttle her busybody neighbor seized Maximilian. "Didn't you?" he said coldly. "She was the belle of the ball in France. That's where we met. I had great difficulty persuading her to choose me over the others."

"Others?" Mrs. Greasley squeaked.

Warming to the subject, he patted Miss Bonnaud's hand. "She came to England to avoid her French suitors. Fortunately, I'm English, so I just followed her to London after I returned from doing business on the Continent. Then I courted her relentlessly until she agreed to marry me."

The woman still looked skeptical. "The banns weren't called."

"We married by special license," he said smoothly. "Mr. Manton had to take an emergency trip to the north, so he prevailed upon the archbishop to grant us the license so he could accompany us to the church before he left. I'm sure you know that Mr. Manton has friends in high places."

That certainly knocked the good Mrs. Greasley off her game. "A special license," she breathed with clear reverence. "What did you say your name was?"

"It's Kale," Miss Bonnaud said quickly. "With a K. My husband is a—"

"Land agent," Maximilian broke in. He was having none of this cotton merchant nonsense. He didn't know a damned thing about cotton. Or being a merchant, for that matter. "I'm land agent to a gentleman in . . . Have you ever visited Devonshire, Mrs. Greasley?"

She was staring at him wide-eyed. "Afraid not."

"Ah, a pity. That's where I'm a land agent. Big estate. Lots of sheep." It wasn't entirely a lie. Among his several estates was a rather large one in Devonshire that brought in most of its income from wool.

"Oh my, a land agent," Mrs. Greasley said, obviously impressed. "That's why you speak so well."

"Doesn't he, though?" Miss Bonnaud said with false sweetness. "My husband has improved himself wherever he can. He's very ambitious."

"I can see that." Mrs. Greasley nudged her husband, who'd done nothing but stand there like a lump. "You could use a bit of Mr. Kale's ambition."

"Aye," the poor man answered. "But then you wouldn't have nobody at home of an evening to listen to your harping now, would you?"

"Mr. Greasley!" she protested.

Maximilian kept his face carefully blank, though he was laughing inside. Clearly Greasley had his own way of dealing with his busybody wife.

A horn sounded from the front of the inn.

"That's the ten-minute warning," Mrs. Greasley said. "We'd best hurry."

"We'll be right there," Miss Bonnaud said. "I just need a moment with my husband."

"All right, but they'll leave you if you're late," Mrs. Greasley cautioned as she tugged her husband toward the door.

As soon as the woman was out of earshot, Miss Bonnaud whirled on him. "My *husband*? Are you out of your mind?"

"You gave me no choice. You stood there gaping like a fish about to be filleted, and one of us had to do something. I realized you couldn't go by another name when she already knew yours, and you couldn't invent another brother, so I improvised. I gather she is familiar with both your brothers?"

"She knows Dom." She hit her forehead. "Oh, Lord, I should have told her you were Tristan! She's never met him."

"I somehow doubt she would believe that I am your half-French brother," he said. "Besides, a husband will be easier to pass off, since then we don't have to look or sound alike, or pretend we have the same background and family connections. And a husband is far easier to get rid of than a brother."

"What do you mean?"

He shrugged. "All you need do when you return from France is claim I had an accident while we were abroad. I drowned or dropped off a cliff." He fought a smile. "Or dueled with one of your many suitors and died tragically in your arms, wounded by love."

"That's not funny," she muttered. "And if I claim you died, then I become a widow. I'll have to put on widow's weeds for a year, not be able to marry for a year, not . . ." Her eyes lit up. "Wait a minute, what a fine idea! You're brilliant!"

"I always thought so," he drawled.

"If I'm a widow, I'm free!" She lifted a shining face to him. "My brothers can stop their fruitless search for a husband for me. Widows can do as they please . . . well, not *completely* as they please, but they can do far more than a spinster. I could travel . . . I could work for Dom! He wouldn't be so reluctant to train me, and I could actually *be* one of his men."

He eyed her askance. "I doubt that becoming a widow magically alters one's sex."

"You don't understand. Shaw and I are always telling new clients that Dom and 'his men' will handle their cases, even though we know that Dom can't afford to hire other investigators." She grinned up at him. "But he wouldn't have to hire anyone else if *I* worked for him. I could be one of Dom's 'men'!"

The idea of her striding about town asking questions of strangers all alone sent a chill down his spine. "Why would you want to do that?" he asked sharply.

A noise in the inn yard made her glance out the window. "We've got to go. The coach is about to leave." She grabbed her bag.

"I'll take that," he said as he extricated it from her hand. "You have a husband, remember?"

Her eyes gleamed at him. "Not for long." Then she hurried ahead to the coach.

With a frown, he quickened his steps. "You don't have to be so cheerful about it, Miss Bonnaud. Or so confounded eager to kill me off."

"Stop calling me 'Miss Bonnaud,'" she reminded him. "I'm your wife Lisette for the time being."

"Right. Lisette." He'd forgotten her Christian name. It suited her.

He handed her bag up to the footman, then helped her into the coach. Oh yes, the name suited her very well. Her French blood showed in the delicate flick of her wrist as she settled her traveling cloak and her skirts about her, in the way that she didn't hurry to cover her ankles or hide the bottom of her petticoat . . . even in the unconsciously provocative smile she shot Greasley when he drew back his booted foot to keep from soiling her hem.

Maximilian had seen women in Paris move and smile in such a fashion. It came naturally to them, was part of who they were. Lisette had that French feminine instinct, too, though it was mercifully joined to a healthy dose of English pragmatism and good sense.

He liked that about her. But given what she'd said, other men didn't appreciate that mixture at all. They must all be daft.

Obviously women recognized her sensual appeal enough to view her as a threat, or Mrs. Greasley wouldn't be so catty to her. The old biddy probably couldn't abide having a French rose like Lisette growing wild in her neighborhood.

He settled into his seat in the carriage. If that were the case, Mrs. Greasley was going to have heart failure by the time they reached Brighton. Because this was a damned small coach, and they were in very close quarters.

Between the ladies' petticoats, his height, and the small items protruding from every nook and cranny, he felt like a horse in a hatbox. There was scarcely any room for his legs, and his head butted up against the ceiling.

It was even worse once they set off, with the body of the coach swaying and lurching at every rut in the road. Holy God, did people actually travel like this? How did they stand it?

He couldn't imagine how *he* was going to stand it. He'd never been in a public coach. Even when he'd been in school, some servant had always come to fetch him in one of the many family equipages.

Lisette had said he should look on this as an adventure, but clearly her idea of adventure differed vastly from his. His would never have included having a packet that reeked of mutton lodged under his arm, or being jabbed in the ankle by an umbrella every time the coach made a stop.

And there were several stops before they even left the city—to pick up a young woman from her home, to intersect with an incoming coach in order to acquire a load of goods, to maneuver around another carriage blocking the road. He couldn't believe the number of delays.

By the fourth one, he was chomping at the bit. He glanced over at Lisette, wondering if she was, too, but she was gazing out the window with an expression of rapt attention. They were passing Kennington Common now, where some orator was boring the crowd with his opinions and the nearby Church of St. Mark's was disgorging its worshippers. Then came Brixton Road and a long line of moderately pretty terrace houses. Mundane sights, all.

Yet every one seemed to fascinate her, for she alternated between craning her neck to see things and pressing her face to the glass. Had she really traveled so little? She'd spent part of her life in France, after all.

Then again, if she'd been living with her brother all that time and then come straight to London with her half brother, she might not have had many other chances to travel.

Her enthusiasm made him envious. When he rode in his own coach, he never noticed the world outside. He was too busy sorting correspondence or reading the papers. But now, through her eyes, he noticed the beautiful carving on one impressive edifice and the glistening of sunlight on the River Effra.

An adventure? Perhaps.

They had just reached a more rural stretch of road when Greasley bent down to remove from his satchel what looked—and smelled—like a peeled raw onion. He bit into it and, catching Maximilian's hard stare on him, explained, "It's good for the constitution, you know. I eats one every day." He thumped his chest. "Keeps me strong and healthy."

"Put that thing away," his wife mercifully said. "You're going to stink up the whole coach!"

"It's your mutton pies that's stinking up the coach," Greasley retorted.

"Our angel likes my mutton pies, she does. I promised her I'd bring her some." Mrs. Greasley turned a flirtatious smile on Maximilian. "So do *you* like mutton pie, Mr. Kale?"

"I don't eat mutton," he said hastily. *Unless it's prepared by my French chef and not by a woman who thinks it improves with age.*

"Then you just haven't had it cooked right, that's all," the woman said. "I warrant once you taste *my* mutton, you'll have a right healthy appreciation for it."

As her husband fell into a coughing fit, Maximilian fought to maintain his composure. Obviously Greasley knew what his wife did not—that "mutton" was a vulgar term for something else. And though Maximilian doubted that anyone, even her husband, had ever tasted the harpy's mutton, he sure as blazes didn't want that confirmed or disproved. Indeed, he would do almost anything to get that image out of his head.

So it was fortunate that Lisette chose that moment to join the conversation. "How long do you mean to stay with your daughter in Brighton, Mrs. Greasley?"

Sparing a frown for her still coughing husband, Mrs. Greasley let Lisette change the subject. "A week at least, I expect. She just bore our first grandson—that's why we're going. Mr. Greasley put our son Danny in charge of the drapery shop until we return." She shot her husband a dark glance. "I daresay *he* will make it pay."

"The devil he will," her husband muttered, having finally stopped coughing. "The lad's got bacon for brains. We'll be lucky if the shop's still standing when we return."

"Don't you listen to Mr. Greasley," the woman replied with a sniff. "My Danny is a sharp one, he is. And my younger daughter Sally . . ." She cast Lisette a calculating glance. "Isn't it about time Mr. Manton started looking for a wife?"

Lisette snorted. "Dom can barely support *me*, much less a—"

"My wife keeps forgetting that she's married now." Grabbing her hand, Maximilian squeezed it in warning. "Her brother doesn't have to support her anymore."

Her hand stilled in his. "Of course. I-I'm not used to having a husband yet, I suppose."

"I'm sure Mrs. Greasley understands," he said, trying to smooth over her gaffe. He flashed the older woman a smile. "I suppose you had the same trouble when you were newly wed, eh, madam?"

"Not a bit," Mrs. Greasley said stiffly. "We'd been courting nearly a year by the time *we* married. I was so eager for it that I'd been calling him 'husband' in my head for months. But in my day, young people didn't leap into marriage willy-nilly."

When Lisette stiffened beside him, he squeezed her hand again. "No doubt you were wise to be cautious. Lisette and I should probably have been more so." That was an understatement. "But what could we do when our hearts ran away with us? We had to follow after."

He'd probably got that out of some book, but it was apparently one Mrs. Greasley hadn't read, for she beamed at him. "Oh my, that's a lovely sentiment, Mr. Kale. Isn't it lovely, my dear?"

The man grunted but didn't protest when his wife patted his arm affectionately.

Lisette relaxed beside Maximilian, but he kept hold of her hand. At first it was to be sure he could prevent her from blurting out anything else that might give them away. Then it was because he couldn't let go. Now that he had hold of her, he indulged his urge to explore—running his thumb along the curves of her fingers, stroking the knuckles, caressing her palm.

And to his surprise, she let him, though her breath seemed to quicken and the rest of her body go taut. He exulted in that. She had a lovely hand, with slender fingers and bones more delicate than he'd have expected for a woman of her height.

It suddenly occurred to him that if he moved her hand merely an inch over, it would be resting firmly on his thigh. The urge to do so was so powerful, he nearly acted on it. But the thought of her hand on his leg made his mouth go dry and his muscles go taut in places they should not, and that was definitely unwise.

Abruptly he released her hand. If he held it any longer, he feared he might want a wedding night in truth. And considering that they would probably have to share a room at the inn in Brighton to maintain their masquerade, that would push him over the edge.

She shuddered so lightly that no one but him would notice, yet it set his blood pumping higher. Confound it, now he was aware of her thigh pressed against his, her breast just inches away. This was proving to be worse torture than even Greasley's onion eating.

As if she'd read his lustful thoughts, Lisette said brightly, "Do you think we'll be stopping for dinner anywhere? Or does the coach go straight through to Brighton? I confess I'm famished—I had no time to eat this morning, what with preparing for the trip."

"I imagine not," Greasley said with a wink at Maximilian. "Being as you only just got married yesterday, I'll wager you didn't rise early enough to do more than run for the coach."

Confound the fellow—now Maximilian had new images to torment him. Lisette as a blushing bride on her wedding night. Lisette letting down her hair. Lisette in nothing but a flimsy night rail and a wrapper, climbing the stairs in front of him with her bottom just close enough to—

"Speaking of getting married," Mrs. Greasley put in, "isn't your half brother over thirty, Mrs. Kale?"

"Yes," Lisette said in a quiet voice, making Maximilian wonder if she could sense the rampant urges in him.

"Then that's more than old enough to be looking for a wife," Mrs. Greasley said. "I daresay Mr. Manton makes a good deal of money with his business. And if you're not keeping house for your half brother anymore, he'll need someone to look after him. You've only got the one other brother in France, right?"

"Right," Lisette said, then went on hastily, "But truly, is there no stop along the road for luncheon or dinner?"

"There's a short stop at Crawley if you want to have a bit to eat there," Greasley offered, but Maximilian's mind was now elsewhere. The Greasleys seemed to know a great deal about Lisette's family, which she obviously didn't want him to hear.

Perhaps there was another way to find out where Bonnaud was hiding. Somewhere along the route, he could take Greasley aside and find out what the older man knew.

If he had to guess from what she'd said about Bonnaud having a government position, the man's employer was probably in Paris. Then again, that was only if the man worked for the national government. Bonnaud might have a regional position in some obscure town. She'd never said where *she'd* been living in France, so anything was possible. A needle in a haystack, she'd called it.

Well, he meant to shorten that haystack a bit. He liked to know where he was headed. And if he *could* learn where Bonnaud had been living and it proved to be some small village, then he could leave the meddlesome Lisette in Brighton and put an end to this mad farce.

Not exactly the gentlemanly thing to do, old boy.

He scowled. This expedition hadn't been *his* idea. Besides, she could head back to London on the next coach and be home in her own bed by midnight. Maximilian would see to it that the coachman received compensation for making sure she was let off right at her door.

One way or the other, though, he was going to interrogate Mr. Greasley at the first opportunity. He deserved *some* reward for being crammed into a coach with the bloody arse and his bloody wife.

He got his chance the next time they stopped to change horses. Lisette and Mrs. Greasley disembarked in haste, obviously eager to find a necessary, and that left Maximilian alone with Greasley, who'd already begun lighting a cigar.

"So," Maximilian said in a casual tone as soon as the women were inside the inn, "have you ever met Lisette's brother in France?"

Greasley took a puff or two. "Can't say as I have. Manton's a good fellow, though. Treats his neighbors right, and don't make too much racket like some young gentlemen. That's probably on account of his having Miss Bonnaud around. Though I'll have to start calling her Mrs. Kale, eh?"

"Yes." Maximilian refused to let him change the subject. Taking a stab in the dark, he said, "I met Mr. Bonnaud in Paris, myself. Seemed like a good enough chap."

"In Paris?" Greasley tipped some ash from his cigar onto the floor. "I thought the two of them had lived in Rouen."

Maximilian bit back a self-satisfied smile. "Well, I'm not sure," he said, congratulating himself for obtaining what he needed to know so easily. "I only know where I was introduced to him."

Greasley glanced out the window. "Ah, there's the mistress. I'll ask her. She ought to know."

"That's all right." Maximilian suppressed a curse as he glanced over to see Mrs. Greasley bearing down on the coach. Lisette couldn't be far behind. "I'll just ask my wife."

But Greasley was already shouting out the window, "Where did Miss Bonnaud and Mr. Bonnaud used to live?" He leapt out to help his wife into the coach. "It was Rouen, weren't it?"

"No, you old fool. It was rue Something." Mrs. Greasley settled into her seat with a sniff. "*Rue* is the word for *street* in French, you know. Not Rouen at all. It was a *rue* somewhere."

As Mr. Greasley climbed in beside her, Maximilian leaned forward and lowered his voice. "It's as I told you, Greasley. I met him in Paris."

"But I don't think he *lives* in Paris," Mrs. Greasley said. "I could have sworn it was Toulon, where she lived before. No, wait. She might have mentioned Paris." Suddenly she eyed him suspiciously. "Don't you know where they'd been living? You being married and all?"

"I only met her brother once, in Paris. I assumed

that's where they lived. She doesn't like to talk about her life in France much." As he saw Lisette approaching, he began, "No need to bother her about it. I don't like to—"

"Where is it you and your brother lived in France, Mrs. Kale?" Mrs. Greasley asked as Lisette reached the coach. "I remember your telling me, but I forgot where it was exactly."

Gritting his teeth, Maximilian leaped out to help Lisette board. She shot him a veiled glance as she climbed in and settled onto the seat. "He lives in a villa, of course. A very nice one on a river."

Maximilian got in. "Yes, but in what city?" he persisted. In for a penny, in for a pound, and now that it was out in the open, he could use the Greasleys to learn what he wanted to know. They would think it odd if she refused to answer such a simple question. "Greasley said Rouen and Mrs. Greasley said Toulon, while I assumed it was Paris. That's where you and I met, after all."

He watched for a telltale reaction to any of those choices but got only a stony stare. Then her expression virtually crumbled right before his eyes.

As the coach swung into motion, she began to cry. "I can't believe that you don't remember the first place we met. It wasn't Paris at all, as you ought to know. Yes, we danced in Paris, but that's not where we met."

To his horror, tears—real tears, for God's sake— began sliding down her cheeks. She dug inside her cloak for her handkerchief, her shoulders heaving with distress. "How could you forget such a thing? I remember every minute of that day!"

Holy God. He could only gape at her, wondering where this pitiful creature had come from.

"You've b-broken my h-heart," she blubbered, very convincingly. "Y-you don't c-care about me at all, d-do you? M-my brother was right. I sh-should never have m-married you!"

What the blazes? She really seemed upset. How could that be? Was he supposed to do something about this?

"Now you've gone and done it, man," Greasley mumbled. "Even if you don't remember some things, you got to pretend to remember. The ladies put great store on a man's memory of the important things."

Mrs. Greasley glared at him. "We certainly do, and rightfully so. Are you saying that you *pretend* to remember things about me? What have you been pretending, Mr. Greasley? Have you forgotten where *we* met?"

"No, no, of course not, my angel!" he protested, shooting Maximilian a daggered glance. "I wasn't speaking of you and me, mind. I'm no young fool like Mr. Kale there. I remember everything. We met at the assembly at Middleton Hall, we did."

Pure outrage lit Mrs. Greasley's face. "We did no such thing! We met at your cousin's dinner!"

The look of a cornered fox swept Greasley's face. "I-I don't think so," he said uncertainly. "That came later. Didn't it?"

"It did not!" his wife said, then dissolved into tears herself. "L-leave it to a m-man to forget the most im-

portant things in a woman's life. Do I m-mean so little
to you? All the years that we've sh-shared, did they
mean s-so little?"

"No, my angel, no!" Greasley said, flashing Maximilian a panicky look.

Bloody hell. As if Maximilian could do anything
about it. Lisette was rivaling Mrs. Greasley for feminine distress beside him. How the blazes had it come
to this? Women were not supposed to cry over such
things. Were they?

Even though he *knew* it was just her pretense, it was
beginning to upset him. It smacked too much of the
strange fits of tears that had often followed the demented accusations Father had flung at poor Mother,
tears that had always kept Maximilian off balance.

He didn't like being off balance. And how could Lisette really be crying, anyway?

My mother was an actress, you know.

Confound the woman. He should have given that
statement more credence. Clearly she had mastered the
finer points of acting.

With her little ploy, the minx had effectively backed
him into a corner, and there wasn't a confounded thing
he could do about it without alerting the Greasleys to
their masquerade.

He was half tempted to do so. She wasn't playing
fair and deserved to suffer the consequences. He could
certainly make her do so. After all, she'd said she didn't
care if people thought the worst of her. She'd even offered to masquerade as his mistress.

Yet she'd backed away from the door to keep her neighbors from seeing her in her night rail. And blushed as she did so.

Despite all her bold assertions, she wasn't as immune to public opinion as she pretended. And the gentleman in him couldn't let her be shamed in front of the Greasleys.

As Greasley continued to profess his great affection for Mrs. Greasley, Maximilian bent to whisper in Lisette's ear, "Very well, you win. For now. You can stop the tears. I won't ask them any more questions about your brother."

With one last sniffle, she dabbed at her eyes, which really were red, and flashed him the smallest smile of triumph he'd ever seen.

Then it vanished, and she stared up at him with a teary-eyed glance that would do her actress mother proud. "Oh, my dearest Max, that is the sweetest apology. I forgive you."

As he fought to suppress a snort, she tucked her hand about his arm, then laid her head against his shoulder. "And now I confess I'm very tired. I believe I shall sleep a bit."

The woman then actually proceeded to sleep. Or feign sleep. He wasn't sure which. But as Greasley managed to assuage his wife's temper, and intimate whispers became the only sounds in the carriage, Maximilian realized he had vastly underestimated Miss Bonnaud's determination to protect her brother.

Not to mention her ability to pull the wool over people's eyes.

His eyes narrowed. She was indeed a more talented actress than he'd given her credit for. Had he been too hasty in assuming she wasn't in league with Bonnaud? Could she be part of the man's fraudulent scheme?

No, the servant he'd sent to Bow Street earlier would surely have uncovered some connection between her and her brother. Though she'd managed *this* contretemps well, she'd been flummoxed at the Golden Cross when confronted by Mrs. Greasley. And there was no way she or Bonnaud could have anticipated that he would show up at Manton's this morning.

Something she'd said earlier leapt into his mind. *I could be one of Dom's men.*

Ah, yes. She was feeling her oats, trying out her prowess at pretense. And doing it rather effectively.

Well, she'd got the best of him this time, but it wouldn't happen again, not if he could help it. He didn't like being made a fool of, and he damned well didn't like not being sure what she was up to.

From now on, there would need to be an understanding between them. She could pull her tricks on anyone else they needed to fool. But she wasn't going to pull them on him. There would be truth between *them* at least.

A smile crept over his face. And he had a way to ensure that, too. Miss Bonnaud was about to find out that two could play her game.

5

LISETTE HAD SERIOUS trouble feigning sleep once Mrs. Greasley started talking again.

"Forgive me, Mr. Kale," she asked, "but what does a land agent do, exactly?"

Holding her breath, Lisette waited to see how the duke would manage this. He'd been stubborn about taking up *her* choice of profession, and now she couldn't even help him with his choice without giving up her pretense of sleep.

"He collects the rents," Lyons answered handily, to her surprise. "He makes inventories. He surveys the farms, keeps a terrier of the common lands . . ."

As he continued to list an impressive number of duties, Lisette marveled at his knowledge. She could not have helped him with this, to be sure. Papa had always just said that his land agent "managed the estate," indifferent to what the man actually did. And Papa had only been a viscount. She'd assumed that a wealthy duke with vast properties would have even less need of such knowledge and would know little about the inner workings of his estates.

In Lyons's case, she'd been wrong. Mr. Greasley asked more questions, and the duke answered every one easily. Astonishing.

As the two men began to talk of leases and enclosures and things that were far beyond her ken, the rumble of Lyons's voice and the swaying of the carriage began to lull her into a doze. She *had* been up very late and had risen very early. And they wouldn't reach Brighton for some time . . .

She came slowly awake a while later to find the coach dark and the duke's arm about her shoulders. Her head had slid down to the center of his chest, and her hand was on his waist.

Horrified, she jerked herself upright, embarrassment filling her cheeks with heat as he pulled his arm from around her shoulders. "Where are we?" she asked, trying to get her bearings.

"On the outskirts of Brighton," he said in that low timbre that did something unseemly to her insides.

She couldn't look at him. She'd been practically on his lap! How mortifying. He must think her the most vulgar creature imaginable.

"You were sleeping very sound," Mrs. Greasley offered. "You must have been tired, dearie."

It was said so kindly that Lisette winced. She felt a little guilty about how her fake tiff with her "husband" had led to a very real tiff between Mr. and Mrs. Greasley. Still, they seemed to have patched it up. The woman was leaning companionably against him, and he didn't seem to mind.

Lisette turned her face to the window. Thank God this nightmare stretch of the trip was almost over. The incident with the Greasleys had proved only too well that she couldn't necessarily travel with impunity.

The duke had known it, too, and tried to take advantage. She couldn't fool herself that she'd gained the upper hand with her little performance. She'd just gained a reprieve, that's all. He could have chosen to drop the facade the moment he realized he might get the truth out of the Greasleys. He could have revealed that she was *not* married to him and asked them flat out what he wished to know. And in one fell swoop, he would have ruined her and possibly Dom's business.

Why hadn't he? Because he was a gentleman?

More likely it was because he could tell that the Greasleys didn't know enough to help him. Thank God she'd mentioned both Toulon and Paris to them in the past, and thank God the two cities were in very different parts of France. Otherwise, she was almost certain Lofty Lyons would have abandoned her in Brighton to hunt down Tristan in whichever one they'd named definitively.

She'd made a narrow escape. Too narrow.

Fortunately, she had little chance of encountering more neighbors. So once they parted from the Greasleys she ought to be safe from discovery, at least until they were on their way to Paris.

Surely Lyons would never abandon her in France.

That would be most ungentlemanly, and he was nothing if not a gentleman.

Most of the time.

A shiver skittered down her spine as she remembered the feel of his strong arm about her shoulders. And worse yet, the way his hand had toyed with hers earlier. She should have tugged hers free. Why hadn't she?

Because it had been so . . . intimate. No man had ever held her hand in such a fashion, boldly but tenderly, too. It had utterly unnerved her. Even now, with her hand still tucked in the crook of his arm and his thigh pressed against hers, she felt that same quivering in her belly that she'd felt when he'd caressed her hand.

She stiffened. Skrimshaw was right. She'd better take care. The duke had been the one to assert he was her husband, and that shifted everything. Now there was no reason for him to treat her like a sister, no reason for them to have separate rooms . . . anywhere.

Her pulse gave a flutter at the thought of spending several nights on the road alone in an inn room with him.

Lord save her. She'd better be careful.

She slanted a gaze up at him. He was looking entirely too unreadable. After her little display, she'd expected him to be a good deal angrier. But he'd conceded defeat and acted as if nothing had happened. It had put her on her guard again. He had something up his sleeve. What could it be?

They reached the coaching inn a short while later. As the Greasleys took their leave, Mrs. Greasley surprised her by murmuring, "Don't let the man bully you, dearie.

If you don't stand up for yourself at the beginning of the marriage, he'll be no good to you for anything but grief."

The sage advice, coming from a woman who clearly had her own husband tied neatly in knots, bemused her. Had Mrs. Greasley noticed more about their relationship than Lisette had given her credit for? Or was that just the woman's usual advice to newly married women?

It didn't matter—Lisette only had to survive the duke's presence long enough to extricate Tristan from this trouble. And standing up to Lyons when he tried to bully her wasn't the problem. She could manage that. It was when he was being sweet that he was most dangerous.

Was that his current course—to kill her with kindness?

Trying to figure out his game consumed her throughout the next hour, while he went off with the innkeeper to arrange for their room and their passage to Dieppe, have their bags sent up, and ask that a meal be provided. So much for traveling as a regular person. Clearly he had no idea how a regular person traveled.

Then again, he'd changed the rules by claiming to be a land agent. Such men did have some money—they would be able to afford a decent room in an inn, and they would be used to giving orders.

She had to admit it had been rather clever of him to hit on that role. It put him in that nebulous land between gentleman and tradesman. He worked for a living, but his position required a certain amount of polish and skill. It meant that his accent wasn't *too* odd, his knowledge of certain things too unbelievable. And clearly he had realized that he knew the part well enough to play it.

She only wished she knew the role of wife half as well. Would a real wife let him handle all the arrangements without voicing an opinion? Would she complain that the rooms they were led to were too small?

Thank God there were two of them—a bedchamber and a sitting room. That somewhat eased her fear of being alone with him. One of them could sleep on the settee while the other took the bed. They wouldn't be quite as much in each other's pockets as she'd feared.

He must have planned it that way, and for that she was grateful.

As soon as the innkeeper left, scurrying off to arrange for their dinner, His Grace shed his greatcoat, then walked over to the ewer, poured some water in the basin, and began to wash his hands.

The silence stretched maddeningly between them. "I imagine that you find the public coaches very dirty, Your Grace," she said as she took off her cloak and hung it on a hook, longing to wash her hands as well.

"I find traveling very dirty regardless of the coach." He dried his hands, then faced her, leaning back against the sturdy bureau that held the washbasin and crossing his arms over his chest.

His unreadable stare made her feel the first tendrils of alarm.

She ignored them. "It is, that's true." She walked over to her bag and opened it, determined to appear as nonchalant as he.

"That was a very enlightening performance you put on in the carriage," he said at last. "I was impressed."

She didn't suppose "Thank you" was the appropriate answer. "You pushed me into a corner," she said defensively. "I didn't have a choice. We agreed that I would help you find Tristan if you would let me go along. You couldn't expect me to jeopardize his safety by telling you too soon where he is."

Her voice had grown stronger the longer she talked, but it didn't seem to change his stance any. He just kept staring at her with a piercing gaze. An oddly compelling piercing gaze.

It was most unsettling. "Because you know very well," she went on, "that the minute I do, you'll abandon me and go off on your own."

"True."

She gaped at him. He hadn't even bothered to deny it. "Well, I can't have that. I have to protect my brother."

"Do you?" He pushed away from the bureau. "I begin to think you have a darker goal."

That took her completely by surprise. "Darker goal?" she asked, her blood freezing in her veins.

"When I first met you, I assumed you weren't part of his scheme. But your playacting today proved that you are masterful at pretense. How do I know that our entire conversation this morning wasn't a charade? That you aren't leading me away from London at this very moment for some devious purpose?"

Devious purpose? *Masterful at pretense*? He thought she was some sort of swindler! "That's a vile accusation! I would never do such a thing!"

"And why should I believe you?" He strode nearer, his face dark with threat. "You've proved yourself very good at dissembling. For all I know, you and your brother cooked up this plan together."

"B-but why? Why would I do that?"

"That's what I want to know." He loomed over her. "I ought to have you tossed in gaol until you tell me the truth."

"Because I *cry* well?" she squeaked.

"Because you are attempting to defraud me," he said in an ominous tone.

He was going to throw her in irons, all because she could do some acting in a pinch. Oh, Lord, Manton's Investigations would be ruined! Dom would never forgive her!

"I swear I'm not doing any such thing," she began, her heart in her throat. "You know why I insisted on your taking me with you. You do! I don't know where you've got this daft idea that I'm some . . . some swindler, but nothing could be further from—"

Inexplicably, he started laughing. She gaped at him, now all at sea.

That merely made him laugh harder. He paused just long enough to gasp, "You're not the only one . . . good at pretense."

And suddenly she understood. This was revenge for her playacting this afternoon.

Planting her hands on her hips, she glared at him. "You are a horrible, *horrible* man! How dare you terrify me like that? Why, I ought to—"

He dropped onto the settee, laughing so hard he could scarcely speak. "If you . . . could only have seen . . . your face . . . when I mentioned . . . gaol . . ."

She walked up to hit him on the arm. "That was not remotely amusing!"

He just laughed even more. "I . . . beg to . . . disagree . . ." he choked out, holding his stomach as he lost himself in mirth.

Glowering at him, she strode over to the ewer, brought it back, and poured its contents on his head.

He jumped up off the settee sputtering. "What the blazes was that for?"

"For making me think you were going to pack me off to gaol, you . . . you . . . oaf!"

"Oaf?" he said as he removed a handkerchief from his pocket and began to wipe his face. "That's the best insult you can offer?"

She narrowed her eyes to slits. "Cretin. Devil. *Arse.*"

He smirked at her. "Careful now. Aren't you supposed to be a respectable married lady?"

"You nearly gave me heart failure!"

"You deserved it after all that crying and nonsense." He mimicked her. *"M-my brother was right. I sh-should never have m-married you!"*

Tossing the empty ewer onto the settee, she crossed

her arms over her chest. "The words might have been feigned, but the sentiment is still valid."

"It wasn't my idea to do this," he reminded her.

"It wasn't *my* idea to pose as a married couple. Thank God *that's* pretend." She headed for the other room, hoping to find another ewer of water so she could wash her hands.

"Oh yes," he said irritably as he followed close behind her. "You would hate being married to a wealthy duke who could buy you whatever you wanted and show you the world you so obviously crave to see."

That he had noticed so much about her love of travel vexed her more than she liked to admit. She whirled on him in a temper. "I would hate being married to any man who would own me. Who would want to tell me what to do, when to do it, how to do it, and with whom. No thank you."

He slicked back his wet hair. "Is that really how you see marriage?"

"As a prison for women? Yes."

"And you see no advantage in it," he said as he came right up to her.

"None."

"What about children?"

"My mother had two. She wasn't married." Though Lisette would never follow that example, she wasn't about to admit it to His High-and-Mighty Grace.

He lifted one arrogant brow. "And you ended up in poverty as a result."

"So did my half brother, and *he* was legitimate. The

truth is, in this country, unless you're the eldest, you inherit at the whim of your father. Marriage is no protection against that."

"That's not true. Women's families can insist that any children be provided for in the marriage settlement before the couple even weds."

"Only if the women have something to barter with." She lifted her chin. "Dom's mother married above her when she married the viscount; she brought no wealth to the union. So she couldn't make any demands on her husband, even after he took my mother as a mistress. She had no recourse. Poor women never do."

"All right, I'll grant you that, I suppose," he muttered. "Forget about the financial aspects, then. What about companionship?"

"I have two brothers who will never abandon me. That's companionship enough for me."

"And love?" he asked softly. "What about love?"

She glanced away, not wanting him to see her ambivalence on *that* subject. "Love is the chain men use to hold a woman prisoner. They offer her love, and in exchange for her devotion, they give her none. In that regard, I learned well from my mother's example." Forcing a bright smile to her face, she met his gaze once more. "So you see, Your Grace, I find no advantages to be had in marriage."

"You're forgetting one more," he said, his eyes locked with hers.

"Oh, and what might that be?"

"Desire."

She fought a shiver at the sensual way he said the word. She hadn't forgotten that one. She'd ignored it. There was a big difference. "Desire is only an advantage for the man." She'd been telling herself that for years, but it somehow rang hollow when she said it to *him*.

"You can't be that naïve." His voice was now a low thrum. "Surely your mother enjoyed her nights in your father's arms."

"I wouldn't know. She didn't talk about such things." Maman had been determined to act respectably outside the bedchamber, probably thinking that it would convince Papa to marry her. Obviously it hadn't worked.

"And you? No man has ever tempted you with desire?"

"I've been kissed a time or two. But it never tempted me to do more. I was always too aware that desire brings nothing but trouble."

Something flickered in his face. The thrill of challenge, perhaps. Or something darker, more visceral. "Then clearly you haven't been properly kissed."

And before she could even react, before she could even think, he grasped her head in his hands and bent toward her.

She froze. "What do you think you're doing?"

"Tempting you," he murmured, then covered her mouth with his.

Oh, Lord help her. His lips were on hers, hot and hard and demanding, and that annoying fluttering in her belly began. The whole world seemed to tilt sideways, sending her spiraling down into a place where heat and longing and need seemed perfectly appropriate.

At some point she must have opened her mouth, for his tongue swept inside, surprising her. Then melting her. He delved deep in a motion far more intimate than the play of their hands earlier.

She shouldn't let him do this, shouldn't let him plunder her like the rakish adventurer she'd glimpsed this morning, but she couldn't seem to help herself. He did it so very well. Every stroke of his tongue deepened her awareness of him as a man, one who made her blood roar and her heart thunder. He smelled of the most expensive cologne water, the heady scent adding to the sensual fog swirling about her.

Though her mind protested his outrageous possession of her mouth, her body wanted to sink into it, to join the conflagration he was stirring deep inside her. The intensity of her sudden urge for more alarmed her.

Tearing her mouth from his, she murmured, "Please, Your Grace . . ." but he seemed not to hear her, for he merely shifted to scatter kisses over her cheek, then her ear, which he tugged at with his teeth. Did he mean to devour her in truth?

"Your Grace, please . . ." she said again, and when he did not answer, she added, "Max, you mustn't."

That got his attention at last. He paused in caressing her ear with his mouth. "Why not?" he breathed.

"Because I do not wish it."

He drew back to stare at her, his gaze heavy-lidded,

his breath coming quickly. "Are you sure about that?" he rasped.

She wasn't. And her hesitation to lie to him had him seizing her mouth once more. Only this time, his hands slid down to grip her waist, to pull her against his body so she could feel the hard heat of him through the damp fabric of his waistcoat and shirt, feel the hard thrust of him lower down. It was alarming.

It was heavenly. He offered kisses so all-consuming they made her breath burn in her throat. Soon she was gasping and clutching at his shoulders, slipping into some seductive oblivion where all she could feel and think was that he kissed more gloriously than she could possibly have imagined.

So this was how desire was *supposed* to feel— intoxicating, maddening, and yes, tempting. That made it dangerous. Oh so dangerous.

Now he was tangling his tongue with hers, inviting her to play, to tease, and that was more enticing than he could know. No other man's kisses had affected her so. She felt herself lifting her hands to clasp his neck, sliding her body flush against his. His mouth turned positively ravenous.

A knock came at the door.

She froze, then shoved him away. They stood there staring at each other, both breathing heavily, both tense.

"Mr. Kale, I've brought your dinner," said a voice from out in the hall.

Max grimaced, then glanced at the door. "Yes, of course," he called. "Come in."

A servant hurried in with a large tray. Seemingly oblivious to the tension in the room, he set out the dishes, bowed, and scurried out, probably rushing to take care of all the other guests who'd been disgorged by coaches.

As soon as the door closed behind him, Lisette whispered, "You must promise never to do that again."

Max's eyes blazed at her. "Why?"

She glanced away, unable to face that heated look. "Because I have no intention of ending up a duke's mistress. Bad enough that I watched Maman throw her life away on a man who could not love her. I will not follow in her footsteps."

"Ah. *That* reason I can understand. I was afraid you were going to claim you didn't feel desire between us." His gaze bore into her, clearly seeing far too much of what she fought so hard to hide. "We both know that would be a lie."

She wanted to deny it. She wanted to argue that his arrogant assumption was wrong.

But he hadn't said it arrogantly. And she wasn't in the habit of denying what was blatantly true. "So you agree to do as I ask? Never to . . . kiss me?"

"If you will agree to do something for me in return."

Her gaze shot to his. "What?"

"Never lie to me."

She stared at him, perplexed. "To my knowledge, I never have." She'd omitted bits of the truth but had spoken no out-and-out lies.

"This afternoon, when you burst into tears, for a moment I . . ." He muttered a curse. "I couldn't tell it was feigned. I knew it had to be, but it felt real. It felt horrible. With my father, I was never sure—"

He halted, then turned coolly nonchalant. "I understand that in playing this 'role,' you'll have to say things that aren't true. But when you and I are alone, I want to be sure you're speaking the truth to *me*, being forthright in your dealings with *me*. Can you promise that?"

"Yes, of course." How many lies had he endured in his life to make him even ask such a thing? To make him so bothered by her pretense of tears? What was it that he'd never been sure of with his father?

She would dearly like to know, but it was clear he didn't want to tell her.

"Thank you," he said tersely. "Then I believe we have a bargain."

"I believe we do."

Thank goodness. She did not need him bringing all his sensual powers to bear on her for his temporary amusement. Because what other reason could he have for it? He would never consider marriage to her.

But as they sat down to dinner, with the air between them still thick with desire, she realized that for some tiny, aberrant part of her it didn't matter whether he would consider marriage to her.

That part of her would still very much like to have him kiss her again.

6

DINNER WAS A tense affair. Not that Maximilian was surprised. He'd just been ravishing Lisette's mouth, after all. It would be damned near impossible for either of them to forget that.

And what a mouth she had, too—soft and far too sweet. He'd expected more resistance, more outrage. He certainly hadn't expected the fire that had flamed between them the second his mouth touched hers. At least now he knew he wasn't alone in his attraction. She had definitely responded to that kiss.

The thought of it aroused him all over again, made him ache to touch her, to caress her. Her skin was as delicate as wild rose petals, as silken as any man could want. And he had wanted, oh, how he'd wanted, to lay her down on that settee and show her what real desire was.

That hunger still coursed through him, the need that had made him take her mouth with overwhelming force and intensity and—

Passion. He'd never considered himself a passionate man. There had been too much passion in his parents' lives—too much emotion and chaos in general—which was why he kept an iron control on his mind and body, relegating his feelings to the dungeon in the fortress of his heart.

Oh, he satisfied his urges when necessary, and he and his friend Gabriel Sharpe had done some sowing of wild oats in their time, but not that often. He hadn't been that keen on going to demireps, all too aware that his father had once caught syphilis. He'd always thought it odd, since Father had never struck him as the kind to go to whores, but perhaps in his younger days he'd been indiscreet.

Father had been lucky—the disease hadn't had any lasting physical effects—but Maximilian had never wanted to take any chances. Especially since he hadn't found casual swiving satisfying. It had always been purely physical, like scratching an itch or quenching a thirst.

Kissing Lisette had been more than scratching an itch. The damned female got under his skin as no woman ever had.

So he wasn't altogether disappointed that she wanted to halt it before it blossomed into anything. Because he didn't like feeling that much out of control of his senses. It reminded him that one day he could expect to be like Father—completely out of control of his senses.

It wasn't a pleasant thought.

He started to pour himself a third glass of wine, then reconsidered. This was no night for drowning his fears in drink.

Lisette was toying with her own wineglass. "I take it that you've had some experience with people lying to you."

Bloody hell. He should have known she would be clever enough to ascertain why he'd made his demand. "Some, yes."

When he would have left it at that, she prodded, "Who would dare to lie to a duke?"

A cynical laugh escaped him. "Nearly everyone. The servants who will say anything to keep me happy, the tradesmen who will say anything to sell me something, the matchmaking mamas who will claim anything to gain their girls a duke for a husband, and my family, who—"

He caught himself. He hadn't meant to say *that*. But she had this way of drawing things out of him with her forthright nature.

"Your family?" she said, pouncing on his slip.

He scrambled for an explanation. "I have a few spinster cousins who plead poverty regularly, in hopes that I will pay their gaming debts. To save the honor of the Cale name, of course."

"And do you?"

"Sometimes. Depends on the cousin. And the debt."

"Of course." She steadied her shoulders. "I thought perhaps you meant your parents."

He had, but he wasn't about to reveal that. Because

then he'd have to explain what they'd lied about and why.

Her long, slender fingers turned her wineglass round and round. "My own parents lied to me a great deal."

The bald statement took him by surprise. "About . . ."

"Oh, Papa lied about how he was going to marry Maman one day, which he never did. And Maman lied about how Papa loved us madly."

"Perhaps that was true."

"Then he should have provided for us," she said stoutly. "He shouldn't have made it so we had to leave our home the day after his death."

Holy God. "How was that even possible? I know your eldest half brother cut you off, but surely your father signed some agreement with your mother that ensured you at least had a home."

"Sadly, no. Maman was young and naïve when they first met in France. She'd had one spectacular season in the theater, and this handsome viscount came along, wanting to whisk her away to England, away from the war and the poverty of her family. I think she would have done anything to escape France at that point, even take up with a married man. So she didn't sign any papers."

She glanced away, her voice turning hollow. "By the time his wife died, Maman was well-established as his mistress. I think she really did believe they would get married after that, especially once Tristan was born. She clung to that promise all through the war, even when he said he dared not risk a scandal by marrying a Frenchwoman. And after the war, he kept saying that they would have a fine wedding as soon as Dom was settled into a law practice, or George had married. There was always some reason it wasn't convenient."

Her tone grew bitter. "Then he very inconveniently died, and that was that." She sighed. "He was always worried about scandal or making things harder for his legitimate children. And I suspect he thought he had plenty of time. He was only fifty-three when he died."

Fifty-three wasn't exactly young, something she surely must realize. "For a man of that age to be so careless with his children, illegitimate or no—"

"Ah, but he was a careless sort, my father." She sighed. "I loved him dearly, but he was the kind of man who preferred to roam the world looking for adventure. We only saw him when he got bored with travel. He would whisk in with presents and stories, and in a few weeks, he'd be gone again."

Maximilian knew men like him, whose own needs and wants took precedence over their duty. He wasn't one of them, and he felt a strange need to impress that upon her. "Is that why you don't trust men of rank? Because they're unreliable?"

"And because they have a tendency to lie."

"I don't."

She eyed him askance. "Never?"

"Never. There's no need." He shot her a cocky smile. "I'm a duke. I say what I please, and everyone just has to put up with it."

That made her laugh, as he'd intended. "Yes, I could tell from how you bullied your way into my house."

"Ah, but you got the upper hand in that encounter."

The minx had the audacity to smile. "True." Her smile faltered. "But not for long. You would have left me today if either I or the Greasleys had told you where Tristan was. You already admitted it."

"Yes, but I wouldn't have left you destitute or without resources. I would have made sure you climbed back on a coach to London, and I would have paid the coachman to deposit you safely on the doorstep of Manton's Investigations."

She studied him a long moment from beneath incredibly thick black lashes. "Why didn't you tell the Greasleys the truth about us? Is it because you realized they didn't know anything anyway? Or . . ." She dropped her gaze. "Never mind, it doesn't matter."

"Do you really think I would have ruined you as easily as all that?" he said irritably. "Embarrassed you before your neighbors and made it impossible for you to live a respectable life in Bow Street again?"

She toyed with her fork, not looking up. "No, I suppose not. But you didn't want this, and you could have taken the chance to get out of it."

"Not like that. We're not all your father, you know. Or your elder half brother."

"I gathered as much." The fire illuminated her tenuous smile. "You knew more about your imaginary estate than Papa ever knew about his real one."

"That's because it wasn't imaginary. I actually do

have one in Devonshire. And it does have a lot of sheep. You see? It's as I told you—I never lie."

Finally, she met his gaze, but only to shoot him a skeptical look. "You're not really a land agent."

"All right," he grumbled, "but you can't blame me for that lie. You pushed me into it. I told you from the beginning I was uncomfortable with playacting."

"You did, that's true," she conceded. "And you were clever enough to see what I could not—that it made more sense for you to play a land agent than a cotton merchant. I was assuming that you would be as unaware of the inner workings of your estate as my father. And now George."

"Rathmoor doesn't take good care of his estate?"

She snorted. "After he inherited, he alienated all the competent people who'd worked for Papa, including the land agent, Mr. Fowler. Then George raised the rents, forcing several tenants to leave land they'd leased for years. Now the entire place is going to hell in a handbasket."

That roused his curiosity. "How do you know all this? I thought you and your siblings hadn't been there in a while."

"Dom keeps abreast of it." She thrust out her little chin pugnaciously. "If there is any justice in the world and George dies prematurely, Dom will have to pick up the pieces. So he has a spy keeping him informed of what goes on in Yorkshire."

"Ah. Very wise of him." He settled back against his

chair. "You really are close to Manton and Bonnaud, aren't you?"

A faint smile played across her lips. "Dom and Tristan are only two years apart, so they grew up together. Since Dom's mother died in childbirth, my mother became a sort of second mother to him. The boys played together, and I . . . adored them both, so they let me come along sometimes. Papa didn't hide us, you see. He actually encouraged us to be one big happy family. Perhaps that was wrong of him, but—"

"The Duke of Clarence, present heir to the throne, doesn't hide any of his ten illegitimate children by an English actress, so I see no reason your father should have hidden his two by a French one." He did some quick figuring in his head. "If I remember right, Bonnaud is two years older than you."

"Three, actually."

"And fond of wreaking havoc on his siblings' lives, I take it."

"I know it looks that way," she countered, "but he isn't who you think he is."

"I've yet to see any evidence to convince me otherwise."

She turned belligerent. "When I was four and frightened of dogs, it was Tristan who lifted me onto his back whenever some mangy cur ran toward me. When I was seven, it was Tristan who fought three village boys for drawing a vile picture on my best cloak. When I was eight, Tristan was the one who taught me how to read and write."

"Why didn't your mother teach you?"

"She could only read French. Papa spoke French well, so . . . I suppose she saw no reason to be proficient in English. Plus, Papa was always saying he would send me away to school." Her voice hardened. "Once the war was over and they married. Which never happened."

He knew how it felt to be lied to over and over by the parents you trusted, but he couldn't imagine a parent so careless as not to make sure his own daughter could read. "Couldn't he send you to the local grammar school?"

"Tristan went, but there was no school for girls thereabouts." Her voice lowered. "Besides, Maman didn't want me going into the village when they were calling me the 'daughter of the French whore.' Tristan was better at putting up with the names the townspeople gave us."

Maximilian choked down an oath at the thought of a little girl being reviled for a simple accident of birth. "English villagers can be small-minded," he bit out.

She gave a Gallic shrug. "Especially when the whole country is at war with France." A sad look entered her eyes. "Besides, after Papa's wife died, every unattached female within twenty miles hoped to catch him for a husband. The fact that he was faithful to his 'French whore' annoyed them exceedingly."

"I imagine it did."

"We never belonged there, that's all."

"And did you belong in France?"

Pushing her wineglass away, she rose and began to tidy the table. "Not really. Here, I'm half French. There, I'm half English. I don't belong anywhere."

He certainly understood that. He'd been the second son until Peter's death, when he'd abruptly become the duke-in-waiting. Then his father had gone mad, and he'd become the heir to a terrible legacy that weighed on him more by the year. The day he'd ascended to the title had been bittersweet. But at least back then he'd known for certain that he was the Duke of Lyons.

And now?

Now, once again, he didn't know who he was. That was why this whole affair with Bonnaud angered him so.

"So you're from Devonshire, are you?" she ventured as she scraped and stacked plates.

"Not exactly. I don't live at my estate in Devonshire, though I do visit it occasionally. I live in Eastcote at Marsbury House."

She cast him an arch glance. "When you're not at your London town house or one of your many other properties, you mean. I suppose you have quite a number. You would need at least five estates to be a proper duke."

He thought about telling her that most people considered it rude and vulgar to discuss wealth so blatantly. But she probably knew that and obviously didn't care. Which rather intrigued him. "The Duke of Wellington has only one," he pointed out.

"The Duke of Devonshire has eight, not counting his London mansion." She stared coolly at him. "So how many do you have? Ten? Eleven?"

"Seven, not counting my 'London mansion,'" he said irritably.

Everyone else was awed by his riches. *She* acted as if they were a flaw in his character. Then again, what could he expect of a Frenchwoman whose poverty-stricken mother was raised during the Revolution?

"How bad was it in France after the war?" he countered, wanting to get off the subject of his filthy lucre. "Were the three of you able to manage on your own in Rouen?"

She shot him a dark look. "I never lived in Rouen."

"Paris, then," he said pointedly.

Crossing her arms over her chest, she glared at him. "You just asked me not to lie to you. So stop trying to find out where I'm from, or you'll leave me no choice."

"Ah, but then I'd get another kiss," he couldn't resist reminding her.

"Only if you *know* that I've lied," she retorted, eyes gleaming.

"Excellent point," he said with a chuckle. She was the only woman he'd ever met who gave as good as she got. Or at least the only one who also made his blood pound in his veins.

As it was doing now. Watching her busy herself with domestic tasks reminded him that she was a woman and he was a man. That they were attracted to each other. And that they were alone in this room, with no one but themselves to dictate their behavior.

As if sensing his thoughts, she colored and renewed her efforts at tidying up.

"You can leave that for the servants, you know," he said.

"Assuming that one of them ventures up here again before morning," she said testily. "The inn is packed, and their staff doesn't appear to be in any hurry to accommodate us. And I don't like having everything so messy."

He rose. "Yes, they do seem inattentive. They should have come by now to find out if we need anything else. I'll have to go remind them who's paying for all this."

She burst into laughter.

"What's so amusing?" he snapped.

"You're a land agent, remember?" she pointed out rather gleefully. "I don't think they'll be quite as receptive to *Mr. Kale's* bullying as they would be to the duke's."

Damn. He'd forgotten about their masquerade. "They will be if I give them enough gold."

"And that will draw even more attention to us than you already have by taking a suite of rooms."

He snorted. "This hardly qualifies as a *suite* of rooms."

"No? When Dom and I traveled to London six months ago, I shared an inn room—and a bed—with an elderly woman I'd never met, and he shared one with her son."

"Holy God," he muttered. "People do that?"

"All the time." A mischievous glint shone in her eyes. "Except, apparently, for the rich Mr. Kale, land agent, who can afford a suite of rooms for him and his wife, even though he claims he doesn't want to draw attention to himself."

He narrowed his gaze on her. "You're enjoying this, aren't you?"

"Immensely," she said with a grin. "Though I shouldn't tease you about it. I *like* having my own room and my own bed." Then her face fell, and she turned wary again. "That is, my own place to sleep, for of course you'll want the bed, and since we are definitely *not* sharing that—"

"Oh, for God's sake, what kind of gentleman do you take me for? I'm not going to make you share a bed with me, and I'm sure as blazes not going to make you sleep on the settee. I'll take this room; you take the bedroom."

She eyed him skeptically. "Are you sure? That settee doesn't look terribly comfortable." Her tone hardened. "And if you come crawling into bed with me in the middle of the night—"

"I wouldn't do that. Lock the bedroom door if you don't trust me." He drew himself up. "I can sleep somewhere other than a bed for one night."

"If you say so." She turned for the bedchamber, then paused. "There *is* one problem, however. I'll need help . . . um . . . unfastening my gown and my corset."

"Confound it all to blazes," he muttered under his

breath as a stark image of peeling her out of her clothing sent a jolt of hot need through him.

She faced him, her cheeks scarlet. "What?"

"I'll go fetch a servant for that." He hurried for the door.

"That would be good, thank you," she said with obvious relief. "Though they might wonder why you aren't helping your wife yourself."

"Let them wonder." With that, he fled the room.

But downstairs he found a scene of utter chaos. Apparently some rich baronet had arrived with a slew of friends to enjoy Brighton, and the inn's staff was scurrying to make them all comfortable. It rapidly became apparent that he and his "wife" were of minor importance compared to Sir Somebody. The irony of it didn't escape him.

After trying to catch someone's attention and being put off time and again, he resigned himself to the torture of attending to Lisette himself. As he climbed the stairs, he wondered how often he'd thrown an inn's staff into confusion when he'd traveled. Granted, he usually stayed with friends or at one of his own residences along his route, but occasionally he had to make do at an inn.

That was a vastly different experience. His servants were sent ahead to make everything ready, he walked into a true suite of rooms already prepared for his arrival, his meal was perfectly ordered, and he had only the inconvenience of a different bed than he was accustomed to.

Entering their room here, he looked around and

suppressed a grimace. All right, so perhaps he'd been a bit spoiled in the past. Because that bloody settee looked more uncomfortable by the moment.

There was no sign of Lisette—she must already have retired to the bedchamber, weary of awaiting his return. He knocked at the closed door. No answer. When he tried the handle and it turned, he felt a surge of satisfaction. At least she trusted him *that* much.

He opened the door and warned, "I'm coming in, Lisette." Then he walked in to find her fast asleep on the bed, fully clothed.

She lay on her side with her back to him. As he approached, he noticed that her hands were tucked up beneath her cheek like a little girl's. An unfamiliar tender emotion twisted in his chest. She looked peaceful, angelic even, with her breasts rising and falling in an even rhythm and her hair lying disordered across the pillow. She must have taken it down, for it seemed devoid of pins.

A sudden fierce urge to caress it seized him, and he choked back an oath. *None of that now.* It would only increase his disturbing attraction to her. Which was also why he shouldn't be standing here gawking at her like some besotted greenhead. He should leave.

But lying there in her clothing couldn't be comfortable for her. At the very least he ought to help her undress. Though it seemed a damned shame to wake her when she slept so peacefully.

Fine, then he just wouldn't wake her.

With that decision made, he walked to the end of the bed, where he removed her shoes. Her feet were daintier than he would have expected for such a tall, buxom woman. She had trim ankles and slender calves, what he could see of them. Her stockings had been darned a number of times, and he scowled at the sight. It wasn't right that a woman so intelligent and beautiful should have to live without something as basic as new stockings. If she were his . . .

But she wasn't, and he didn't *want* her to be. Any woman who married him would have a life of misery ahead of her, and Lisette already saw marriage as a prison. She'd also made it clear that she had no intention of being any man's mistress.

So there was no future for them. Which was why he shouldn't be standing here, drinking up the sight of her asleep, wondering what it would be like to slip into bed beside her and kiss her senseless.

Suppressing an oath, he moved to stand next to her back. He had to finish this and leave, before he did something he regretted.

But now came the tricky part. Kneeling, he smoothed her hair aside so he could unbutton her gown. Her breathing altered its rhythm for a moment, then resumed. He undid her laces, and the fabric parted to reveal a wrinkled linen chemise that made his breath catch in his throat. She would be naked beneath that chemise. It would be so easy to run his hand inside the corset along the curve of her spine. To slip it down over the full hips that were inches away . . .

With a groan, he rose and strode from the room, shutting the bedchamber door firmly behind him.

He scrubbed his hand over his face. Clearly the family tendency toward madness was seizing him early. Otherwise, why would he be contemplating caressing the woman's body while she slept?

Why would he be standing here hard and aroused, with no possibility of getting any satisfaction for it?

Cursing whatever impulse had made him loosen her gown and laces, he contemplated the settee with a scowl. He'd need a bit of fortification to be able to get any sleep on *that* ungodly piece of furniture, especially in his present state.

So he headed out the door to the taproom.

7

LISETTE LAY THERE, tense and waiting, until she heard the duke leave their rooms completely. Then she released a long breath.

She'd been sound asleep until he'd started on her buttons. At first she'd thought it was a servant, but then she'd smelled his cologne water and realized who it was. Resisting the urge to reveal she was awake, she'd waited to see just how far he would go. And she *had* asked him to help her, after all. He was just doing as she'd requested, just being polite.

Except that there was nothing polite about the brush of his hand along her spine, nothing polite about the long moment he'd spent apparently contemplating her back after he'd undone her laces.

And there was nothing polite about the way her heart was still racing. Devil take him for that.

Well, at least now she could get undressed. She briefly considered locking the door, but she doubted he would return anytime soon. Besides, if he hadn't done anything when he had the chance, he wasn't likely to do so later.

Swiftly, she changed into her nightdress, then slid back into bed, but it took her a while to return to sleep. She couldn't reconcile the haughty duke who'd assumed she was Dom's mistress and who owned seven estates with the man who'd carefully and almost tenderly unbuttoned her gown while she slept.

Who was Max? And why did she care so much, anyway? Once they found Tristan and settled this matter of the handkerchief, she and the duke would have no more dealings with each other.

Assuming that things turned out well. But if they didn't . . .

No, she wouldn't dwell on what Lofty Lyons could do to her family if it turned out that Tristan had been trying to deceive him. Tristan *hadn't*. It was impossible. So there would be no repercussions. There *mustn't* be.

That uneasy thought plagued her for a long while, until exhaustion took over and she fell into a restless sleep.

She didn't know how long she'd been sleeping when she came awake abruptly, some sound having awakened her. She lay there with her heart in her throat, the covers up to her chin. Until she heard it again. Singing. *Male* singing.

What the devil?

Sliding from the bed, she went to crack the door open just as a chair fell over in the next room.

"Shh," said a voice none too quietly, with a slight slur. "Shh, mustn't wake her."

Good Lord. It was the duke. And he was drunk. Now, *that* was something she hadn't expected. She edged into the room just as he stumbled over the chair he'd knocked over.

"Stop moving!" he growled at the chair. "I demand that you . . . that you . . ." He paused, as if trying to find his place in the sentence. "I forget. But whatever it is, stop it."

"I doubt that the chair will listen," she said dryly as she walked forward. "Chairs have a tendency to be oblivious to commands, even those given by a duke."

He whirled to face her and nearly fell over. "You're awake."

She hurried to support his swaying form. "Hard to sleep when there's so much racket."

Looping his arm about her shoulders, he said in a confiding tone, "I'm foxed."

"I know." If she hadn't already been able to tell from his behavior, she would have noticed from the brandy lacing his breath.

She led him toward the settee. "Why you would get yourself into such a condition the night before you're going to be tossed about on the Channel, I can't fathom. But then men are never logical about drinking."

As he dropped heavily onto the settee, she sat down beside him and started to untie his cravat.

He flashed her an almost boyish smile. "You took off your gown."

Blushing deeply, she kept her attention on his cravat.

"I don't generally sleep in it." And she'd rushed in here so fast, she hadn't thought to throw on her wrapper over her night rail, either.

"Good thing." His gaze scoured her, sultry and hot, making her painfully aware of just how thin her night rail was. "I like you best in your nightdress."

Fighting to hide the warmth that his words provoked, she knelt in front of him to take off his boots, something she'd done a time or two with her brothers.

Except this was different. *He* was different. When Tristan or Dom got drunk, they turned into sullen and unmanageable beasts. But Max, who until now had worn his air of stiff reserve as a knight wore medieval armor, had turned into a rumpled, seductive devil.

"You're so pretty," he murmured as she struggled with his boots. He ran his hand over her curls, tangling his fingers in them. "Your hair is like . . . it's like . . . I dunno. Something black and shiny."

She smothered a smile. Apparently when the duke was jug-bitten, he became somewhat inarticulate. "Like beetles, perhaps?" she joked. "They're black and shiny."

"Right, beetles." He blinked, then scowled. "Not *beetles*. Don't be daft." He'd filled both his hands with her hair and was smoothing it and caressing it. "Something prettier."

The ineptness of the compliment was oddly endearing, which was ludicrous. How could she take seriously a single thing he said right now?

She tossed aside the boot she'd freed, then went to work on the other one. "Well, don't expect me to provide you with a *prettier* compliment to give me. I'm too tired."

"Me too. You should go to bed. Here, let me help you." He bent forward to catch her beneath the arms as if to lift her from her kneeling position. Then he paused like that, and before she realized what was happening, he angled his palms in further to cup her breasts.

For a moment, she was too shocked to do anything but gape at him. But then he kneaded them and murmured, "These are pretty, too," which galvanized her into action.

"Stop that!" She shoved his hands away. "We had an agreement!"

He nodded solemnly. "No kisses." Then a gleam entered his eyes and he reached for her breasts again. "Didn't say anything about this, though."

Jumping to her feet, she snapped, "You can take care of your own dratted boots, Your Grace."

She started to walk away, but before she could escape he dragged her down onto his lap. Even as she tried to wriggle free, he pressed his mouth to her ear and whispered, "Want to know a secret?"

"No," she muttered as she tried to push herself off of him.

"I like you."

That halted her. She turned her head to shoot him a skeptical glance. "Do you? Or is that just the brandy fogging your brain?"

"Nope," he said, his eyes turning a molten green. "I mean it."

She frowned at him. Just when she wanted to conk

him on the head with his boot, Lofty Lyons had to come out with something like that.

Although right now he didn't look a bit lofty. He looked like any man after a long day, with his golden-brown hair mussed, a day's growth of whiskers dusting his chin, and his cravat hanging loosely about his neck. He looked appealingly ordinary for once.

There was something so intimate about being atop his lap in her night rail. It made her wonder for the first time what it might be like to sit on a husband's knee, to have him holding her and looking at her the way Max was looking at her now . . . with interest and longing and far too much heat.

Lord help her.

His gaze drifted down her body. "I like you. I do." Then he filled his hands with her breasts. "And I *really* like these."

Thrusting him away, she jumped to her feet and rounded on him to give him a piece of her mind. But he was laughing now, as if possessed by some grand joke. As she narrowed her gaze on him, he hiccupped and keeled over on the settee.

She glared at him, waiting for him to start laughing again. When he not only kept quiet, but kept inordinately still, she started to worry. She nudged his knee with her foot. To her relief, he moved, but only to drag his knees up onto the settee, turn onto his side, and . . .

Snore.

Good Lord. He was well and truly passed out.

Men!

She headed for the bedroom, thoroughly disgusted, but then halted at the door. He'd made her comfortable when she was sleeping; she ought to do the same for him, even if his sleep *was* brandy-induced.

Telling herself she was daft, she turned back to him. He lay completely inert, seemingly oblivious to his surroundings. Grumbling about fools in their cups, she marched over and finished pulling off his boots. He only mumbled and settled back into sleep. With a roll of her eyes, she found a cushion to slip under his head and managed to unbutton his waistcoat without awakening him.

That wasn't going to help him much, however. His body was too big for the settee and stuck out over the edges—an elbow here, a stocking foot there. In the morning, he was going to be stiff in every joint after being crammed into that position all night.

Feeling an unreasonable pang of guilt, she covered him with his greatcoat. It wasn't *her* fault that she'd offered him the bed and he hadn't taken it. And it certainly wasn't her fault that he'd gotten himself foxed enough to make a fool of himself, tripping over chairs and passing out and saying such ridiculous things as—

I like you.

She snorted. He probably hadn't meant a word of it—he'd just been softening her up so he could grab her breasts.

Still . . .

"I like you, too, you ill-mannered oaf." Then, annoyed with herself for even admitting as much, she added, "But if you ever grab my breasts like that again, I swear I will box your ears."

Then, turning on her heel, she marched off to bed.

✦ ✦ ✦

THE NEXT MORNING, Maximilian stood at the rail of the steam packet, staring out at the choppy waters and fighting a blinding headache. Thank God he and Lisette had arrived in time to make the journey. He'd slept past the knock that was supposed to rouse them early.

Fortunately, she'd awakened an hour later, and between her panic and his determination not to miss the boat, they'd managed to get ready with astonishing haste. They'd thrown their things into bags, paid the bill, and rushed to the docks just in time to embark with the sixty-odd other passengers headed to Dieppe.

But it had been a very near thing, and he didn't like near things. Nor did he like having to hurry onto a swaying, noisy contraption while his head still spun and his stomach still churned.

Though he supposed that was what he deserved for downing so much brandy in the space of a few hours. He wasn't sure how much, because most of the evening was a blank. He wasn't even sure how he'd gotten back to the room. Obviously he had gotten there somehow, because he'd awakened there after a night of odd dreams, but it bothered him that he didn't remember how.

Lisette came up to stand beside him at the rail. Today

she wore a bluish-colored traveling costume. The puffy sleeves, tight bodice, and broad flounced skirt accentuated her tiny waist and large bosom, although he only glimpsed them when the biting wind blew her wool cloak open. He much preferred her in her nightdress.

Wait, when had he seen her in her nightdress? He must be thinking of that morning at her brother's home. But no, she'd been wearing a wrapper then.

"The captain says that the trip should take about nine hours," she said cheerily.

Too cheerily for his aching head. "Wonderful," he grumbled. "So I've got to listen to that ungodly racket all day."

"What racket? Oh, you mean the steam engine."

He could feel her eyes on him, assessing him. Then she glanced around to see if anyone was listening, but the other passengers had all headed for the dining cabin to have breakfast as soon as they came aboard, so he and she were fairly alone at the rail.

She clutched at the rail as the boat took a sudden dip. "Have you never made the crossing to France on a steam packet?"

"No," he bit out. "I have a yacht for that."

"Of course you do."

Her sharp tone made him bristle. "I used to travel a great deal," he said irritably, "so it only made sense to have my own vessel."

"I'll have to remember to advise Dom of that the next time he finds himself with a few extra thousand pounds to spend," she said dryly. When he didn't rise to her bait, she folded her arms on the rail beside him and shot him a curious glance. "Why did you travel so much? For pleasure? Or for business?"

He debated what to tell her, then opted for the truth. "In his last years, my father was . . . ill. So we traveled in search of a cure." Which of course they never found. "Once he died, I had to see to his business concerns. My father had a great many foreign interests, so I spent a few years selling them off. I preferred to concentrate on my estates."

"Does that mean you don't travel anymore?"

"Only for pleasure, which unfortunately I have less time to do than I'd like."

"So you enjoy traveling, seeing the world."

He cast her a faint smile. "When I was young, I wanted to join the navy. I kept begging my father to buy me a commission as a midshipman."

That way he could satisfy his urge to see the world while at the same time escaping the desperate grief of his parents over their missing son, the only one who mattered.

Bitterness crept into his voice. "He wouldn't do it. And then I turned sixteen and Peter was found dead, and I became the heir. That was the end of any talk of my going into the navy." He caught the pity on her face and forced himself to lighten his tone. "So now I content myself with watching the wind fill the sails of my yacht. As I wish I were doing this very moment."

To his immense relief, she matched his light tone.

"You do realize we wouldn't get to Dieppe nearly as fast on a sailing yacht."

"But the trip would be far more pleasant. I wouldn't have that racket to add to the pounding in my head." When she opened her mouth, he cut her off with, "And before you say it, yes, I know that I brought it on myself. Believe me, I am deeply regretting those last couple glasses of brandy."

A mischievous gleam appeared in her eyes. "One would think you'd hold your liquor better, Your Grace. How much did you drink, anyway?"

God, this was embarrassing. He shifted his gaze back to the sea. "Too much. Especially for a man who rarely drinks spirits to excess."

"Oh? And why is that?" she asked, genuine curiosity in her voice.

"Getting foxed has never been my preferred entertainment. I don't like being out of control."

But last night, he'd been determined to banish his lustful obsession with the lush Lisette. Instead, he'd had wild dreams of her all night. In one of them, she'd knelt at his feet in nothing but her nightdress, her hair tumbling down about her shoulders and her breasts fitting into his hands so well that he could still feel the warm fullness of them.

If you ever grab my breasts like that again, I swear I will box your ears.

The words, so much like something she would say, brought him up short. He *had* dreamed it, hadn't he?

He must have. Lisette would never have knelt at his feet. Or been so scantily clad in front of him. And surely even drunk he wouldn't have been so foolish as to "grab" her breasts.

Would he?

The fact that she'd fallen oddly quiet gave him pause. "Lisette . . . did I . . . um . . . do anything last night that I should apologize for?"

"You mean, like grabbing my bosom?" she said as she pulled her cloak more tightly about her to protect against the spray.

A groan escaped him. "Oh, God, I didn't dream it."

"Afraid not." She sounded oddly matter-of-fact for a woman he'd practically assaulted.

He slanted a wary glance at her. "I'm sorry, I have no memory of it. Well, not much of one. I thought I'd dreamed the few bits I do remember. Please accept my apologies for . . . whatever I might have done."

She looked at him from beneath lashes that hid her eyes . . . and her thoughts. "Apology accepted."

"I'm surprised you didn't hit me over the head for it." He cast her a wry smile. "Or perhaps you did, and that's why I have this god-awful headache."

"I did not," she said firmly, "though I considered it. Unfortunately, you passed out before I got the chance."

"Ah." He began to wonder if *any* of his "dream" was a dream. "I wasn't conscious very long, then."

She avoided his gaze. "Not very."

"And the image I have of you kneeling at my feet—"

"I thought you didn't remember," she said peevishly.

"Some of it is coming back to me now," he drawled. "Nice to know that I didn't dream that particular bit."

"I was taking off your boots," she said, suddenly defensive. "I do the same for my brothers when they're in their cups."

"Wearing only your nightdress?" he murmured, keeping his gaze fixed on her face. He was enjoying her mortification. He didn't like being the only one who'd behaved foolishly last night.

The wind tossed her fringe of loose curls about her blushing cheeks as she glanced at the few people emerging from the dining cabin to walk the deck. "I simply wasn't expecting . . . I didn't realize at first that you were . . ." She glared at him. "It's not very gentlemanly of you to point that out."

He gave a low laugh. "No, but then I seem to turn into a rogue around you."

"I've noticed," she said with a sniff. "Sometimes a rogue, and sometimes an insensitive, arrogant, presumptuous—"

"Enough," he bit out. His wild French rose was showing her thorns again, which could mean only one thing. "I take it I behaved even worse last night than you've said. What else did I do? If you don't give me a thorough recitation of my sins, I can't make amends."

"There's no need for you to make amends," she said pertly. "You did nothing of any consequence."

When he would have questioned that assertion further, she drew her cloak more tightly about her and added, "Now that the crowd has thinned out, I believe

I shall go see if there's any food left for purchase in the dining cabin, since I didn't have any breakfast at the inn—thanks to a certain gentleman's neglecting to awaken when the knock came."

With her head held high, she walked off so primly that he had to laugh. His faux wife was quite a piece of work—all the pride of a duchess without an ounce of blunt to support it.

Blunt—confound it all! She was off to *purchase* food. That had gone right past him in the midst of her barbs and his cropsick state.

He strode after her. He wasn't going to let her pay for anything when he was perfectly capable of buying what she needed. Let her hold on to her pride and her surprisingly ladylike manners if she must, but she wasn't going to make him look like some negligent husband who didn't take care of his own wife.

Besides, he had to counter the impression he'd made last night, that he was some sort of ill-mannered—

I like you, too, you ill-mannered oaf.

A grin tugged at his lips. So for all her grousing and tart remarks, Lisette didn't find him nearly as "insensitive, arrogant, and presumptuous" as she claimed.

Then something else occurred to him. She'd said, "I like you, *too.*"

Too? Holy God, what exactly had he said to her while he was in his cups?

He'd better find out and put a quick end to it. The last thing he needed was for a feeling female like Miss Bonnaud to start assuming there was some hope of a respectable connection between them. There wasn't. There never could be.

He had watched his mother's heart slowly break as she witnessed Father's encroaching madness. By the end, she'd barely been capable of caring for herself, much less her son or her husband. Mother had been wholly devoted to Father—and for her trouble, she'd gained naught but pain and heartache.

No wife of his would ever endure that. When he married—*if* he married—it would be a calculated bargain with a woman who thoroughly understood what was coming. Who agreed to let others care for him in his later years. She'd have to be the sort who didn't mind giving up a love match in exchange for being a duchess. Because he had no intention of watching the light slowly die in the eyes of some woman who actually loved him.

Some woman he actually loved.

He could never put a woman he loved through that, so there could be no love match for him. And with Lisette, he knew he would want nothing less.

8

SCOWLING, LISETTE HURRIED through the crowded dining cabin. She'd been surprised this morning when Max had made no apologies for his behavior last night, but she'd attributed it to their hurry to leave and his enormous arrogance. When he'd said he'd forgotten, she'd wanted to kick herself for mentioning his grabbing her bosom—she would have preferred that he *not* remember it.

But of course he did. All it had taken was a few moments' conversation to have him casting that lazy smile over her body as if recalling every inch of her in her night rail.

Recalling and *enjoying*. She didn't want him enjoying that. She *didn't*. She didn't want his eyes scanning her body and his husky voice reminding her that last night she'd let down her defenses. That she'd liked how unreserved he'd been.

Apparently he'd figured out for himself that she'd liked it, the insolent devil. And how dare he make it sound as if she'd been doing something untoward by trying to remove his boots? *He'd* been the one to man-handle *her*! She should have left him stumbling about the room instead of trying to help him.

She reached the counter, still in a bad mood. The woman selling refreshments asked, "And what will you be having, dearie?"

Forcing a smile to her face, she asked, "Is there any breakfast left?"

"Aye. Full breakfast—boiled eggs, cold ham, toast, and tea or coffee—is two shillings. Just toast and tea is half a shilling."

She opened her reticule, observed her meager funds, and sighed. "I'll take the toast and tea, then."

"I can buy you the full breakfast if you like," said a male voice beside her.

It wasn't Max's. She kept her gaze on her reticule, well used to such unwanted attentions after all these years out in the world. "Thank you, but I'd rather the toast and tea."

The man didn't take the hint. "Now then, miss, I can see you want more." He took advantage of the crowded room to edge up next to her and lower his voice. "And a pretty girl like you shouldn't have to do without, eh?"

"And she doesn't have to, either," snapped another voice behind the man. "She has a husband who is happy to purchase whatever she wants."

The duke pushed in between them, staring down his nose at the other fellow. For once, she was rather glad of Max's lofty manner.

But the other man was surprisingly stubborn. "See here, now, guv'nor, she didn't say she was married. And she ain't wearing no ring."

"That's because we just eloped." Max placed a proprietary arm about her waist. "I'm planning on buying the ring when we reach France. You know what they say—the gold is of better quality there. Isn't that right, my dear?"

It was all she could do not to smile at the absurd idea that French gold was any different than British. "Absolutely." She smiled at the gentleman. "My husband is very clever about these things."

The other man paled as he realized that he really had mistaken the situation. "Begging your pardon, sir. Didn't know she was yours," he muttered, edging away from them.

"Well, she is," Max said with a rather convincing tone of possessiveness. "And don't beg *my* pardon. Beg *hers*."

"Max, it doesn't matter," she murmured.

"It does to me."

"Aye, sir, and you're right, too." The man had clearly taken Max's measure and realized he wouldn't win any fights with the taller, heftier man. He tugged his hat brim. "Begging your pardon, ma'am," he mumbled. Then he fled.

"Good riddance," Max growled as he followed the man's retreat with a murderous stare. "Bloody insolent scoundrel."

She laughed, oddly gratified by Max's determination

to protect her. "You're being ridiculous, you know. He didn't mean anything by it."

Max's gaze shifted to her, only slightly less angry. "Oh yes he did."

"All right, I suppose he did," she conceded. "But he was merely acting the way every man does when he sees what he assumes is an unattached female available for the taking."

His eyes narrowed on her. "You speak as if you encounter such idiots every day."

"I do," she said simply. "But I generally have no trouble rebuffing them. I can take care of myself, you know."

"The point is, you don't have to anymore."

She refrained from reminding him that his tenure as her protector was temporary. The woman serving the food was listening to their conversation with avid interest, and there were other people about. "And I'm glad of that, my dear."

She turned back to the woman. "Now, about that toast and tea—"

"She'll have the full breakfast," Max said.

As the woman nodded and set a plate with the requested items onto a tray, Lisette shot Max a long glance. "Thank you. But what about you?"

"I couldn't eat anything right now if my life depended on it."

He did look a bit green about the gills. She would have thought he was seasick if she didn't know how he'd spent the previous evening. She didn't want to feel sorry for him, but it was hard not to when he looked so utterly miserable. And yet still handsome, too, in his greatcoat and fustian breeches and boots, with his hair ruffled by the wind and his eyes looking like a storm-tossed sea.

"A little toast won't hurt you," she said gently, "and at the very least, you need to drink something." She turned to the woman. "Toast and tea for His Grace, if you please."

"His Grace?" the woman squeaked.

Good Lord, what had possessed her to say—

"It's a sort of joke between us," Max put in. "My wife finds me a bit . . . imperious."

When the woman looked confused, Lisette said, "High and mighty. He means that I find him as high and mighty as a duke."

The woman's expression cleared. "Right. Men is often that way when they first get married." She poured the tea and added the cups and a plate of toast to the tray. "Takes 'em a while to realize that we women are sturdier than they think. No woman worth her weight is a fainting flower, if you know what I mean."

"I do indeed," he said ruefully. "My wife is about as far from being a fainting flower as a woman can get." He smiled down at Lisette. "Thank God."

The unexpected compliment made her blush.

He picked up the tray, then nodded Lisette over to a table near a window, away from the rest of the crowd. After they sat down, he sipped his tea, then pushed the cup away. "Damn, that's vile."

She sipped her own and made a face. "That's all you

can expect on a packet boat. They're not going to provide you with the highest quality tea for half a shilling." She pushed his cup of tea back toward him. "But it's better than nothing. Bad as the flavor is, it will still settle your stomach and help your headache, I promise. So drink it."

"Who's the imperious one now?" he grumbled, but took another sip.

She bit back a smile. It was strange, but she rather liked looking after him. She was probably a sad substitute for his hundreds of servants, but for the moment she was enjoying playing the role of wife. And she didn't want to examine why too closely.

He was staring at her rather oddly now. She cocked her head. "What?"

"You may have been eager to act this role, but you're not always very good at it, are you?"

Good Lord, had he read her mind? And what did he mean, she wasn't good at it? "I'm *trying* to play your wife," she said testily, "but I have never been a wife, and I don't know—"

"I'm talking about your calling me 'His Grace.' That was a rather spectacular deviation from the plan."

She winced. "Oh. Right." She dug into her breakfast, all too conscious of the way he kept staring at her.

Idly he rubbed his finger around the rim of his cup. "Did you mean what you said at the Golden Cross about wanting to be one of your brother's men?"

The abrupt change of subject put her on her guard. "Yes. Why?"

"It just doesn't seem like the sort of life a woman would want."

"And what would you know about the sort of life a woman wants? You haven't ever married, probably because you haven't found a woman who would live up to your impeccable standards."

"We're not talking about me," he said, obviously too clever to be goaded into telling her what she was dying to know—why he hadn't yet married. "We're talking about you. So tell me, what *is* the sort of life a woman wants? What's the sort of life *you* want?"

The question brought her up short. She had thought about it a great deal, but no one had ever asked her to articulate it. Dropping her gaze to the cup of tea she was turning around in her hand, she considered what to tell him. "I want to be able to fend for myself, to never have to depend on a man for money." That was first and foremost. But there was more, too. "I want to see the world."

As she warmed to her subject, she lifted her gaze to his. "I want to use my brain and not have to pretend I don't have one, just so I won't trample on some man's pride. I want to help Dom make a success of his business so we can show George that we succeeded in spite of him."

He didn't laugh or make light of her words. He just kept staring at her. "And you think that the only way you can accomplish all that is by working for Manton as one of his 'men.'"

She tipped up her chin. "Yes."

"How does he feel about that?"

"He's not opposed to the idea," she said evasively. "He just wants me to learn the administrative part of the business first."

"Ah."

That one word contained a wealth of meaning. She glared at him. "You think he's not keen on it, that he's placating me. Because you think I can't do it. You think that he'd be foolish to hire me as an investigator."

"Actually, I think he would be very wise, and that you would do it very well if you put your mind to it. But I suspect you wouldn't enjoy it as much as you assume."

"Why not?"

He shrugged. "Thanks to my brother's disappearance and death, I've had vast experience with investigators, and I've noticed a few things about them. The good ones are cautious and circumspect. They listen without judgment until they have all the facts." Leaning close, he steadied his penetrating gaze on her. "Whereas you, my dear, like to speak your mind, and you don't necessarily want to wait for the facts before doing so."

"I can be circumspect when the situation warrants it," she countered.

He arched an eyebrow. "Even when a duke is beating down your door demanding action? Your brother would never have tried to throw me out, admit it. He would have been more cautious with a man who could ruin him with a word."

She bristled at that. "You insulted me and threatened my servant! Did you expect me just to . . . to stand there and take it?"

"Of course not," he said, clearly annoyed. "But there was a middle ground."

"You mean I should have toadied up to you and soothed your male temper?"

"No, I mean—" He muttered a curse under his breath. "My point is that you have strong opinions and feel passionately. And there is no room in the life of an investigator for feeling passionately."

"That's not true!" she protested, annoyed that he seemed to have figured her out so easily. When he jerked his head to indicate the other people in the room, she gritted her teeth and lowered her voice. "It's not. *Dom* feels passionately."

"And does he show it?" Max murmured. "When he questions someone, do you know what's in his mind? Do you even know what his opinions are about a case until the two of you are alone?"

She scowled at him, trying to ignore her memories of how Dom investigated a matter, which was almost exactly as Max described. It didn't mean she couldn't do the same thing. "I can hold my feelings close to my chest when I need to. I *can*."

"The question is not whether you could, but whether you would. And if you would even enjoy it. Would you really like always being circumspect, always weighing your opinions?" His eyes gleamed at her, taunting her. "Always stifling your feelings on any subject so you could get to the truth of the matter?"

God rot him. What did he know about it? She leaned across the table to hiss, "Just because you've spent two days pretending to be my husband doesn't mean you know me. You don't understand me, and you never will." She rose. "Now, I believe I shall go get some fresh air, if you don't mind. I hope that's *circumspect* enough for you."

Drawing her cloak about her, she started to walk away.

"Flouncing off in a huff merely makes my point, my dear!" he called after her.

She paused to cast him a withering stare. "Go to hell."

That only made him laugh, the conceited, arrogant lout. She stalked to the door. He thought he knew everything, him and his "vast experience with investigators." But he'd never *been* one, had he?

Neither have you, her conscience reminded her.

All right, that was true, but it was beside the point. He couldn't possibly know how she might behave until she actually served in that capacity. She was perfectly capable of curbing her emotions and listening and all those things.

His voice rang in her ears: *The question is not whether you could, but whether you would. And if you would even enjoy it.*

Drat him for that. Well, she might have to put up with Lofty Lyons's cocksure opinions when they were crammed together in a coach or some inn room, but she didn't have to do it on the packet boat.

For the next few hours she effectively avoided him, attaching herself to a group of ladies who were discussing fashions and beaus and how difficult the salt air and sun were on their complexions. It was the most inane chatter imaginable, but she nodded and smiled and pretended to be enjoying herself.

He made no attempt to invade their little group, which rather surprised her. Instead, he went off to a cabin where some of the gentlemen were playing cards. Occasionally he emerged and she could feel him nearby, watching and probably gloating at the erroneous impression she'd given him that he had won their argument, but she didn't care. She was heartily sick of the duke right now.

Hours later, when the call came that dinner was being served, she was still annoyed enough to consider dining with her new female friends. But she was also practical enough to admit that she couldn't really afford it. Besides, they abandoned her to join their husbands and brothers and other male companions anyway, which left her no choice.

So when Max came up to offer her his arm on the unsteady deck and ask, "Shall we have dinner, my dear?" she had the good sense to say, "Thank you, yes."

But she felt awkward, unsure of how to go on as they walked toward the dining cabin. When she and her brothers argued, one of them usually ended it by making a joke. Unfortunately, she didn't feel comfortable enough with Max to do that.

After a bit, he said, "You were right about the tea. Vile as it was, after the third cup, I began to feel markedly better. I swear I could eat an entire side of beef just now."

She recognized an olive branch when she saw it. "Well, I wouldn't go so far as that. Your stomach would probably rebel. But a little beef and potatoes probably wouldn't hurt."

He shot her an amused glance. "That's a very wifely thing to say."

"I'm just trying to be convincing in my role."

"I can think of several more pleasurable ways you could be convincing in your role." When she eyed him askance, he laughed. "Forgive me, but I can't get that image of you kneeling in front of me in your nightdress out of my head."

A mischievous impulse seized her. "What about the image of me on your lap?"

His amusement abruptly faded. "You were on my *lap*?"

"Oh, you have no idea the things we did last night," she said lightly. "Don't tell me you don't remember."

"I don't, damn it!" He eyed her skeptically. "Wait a minute—are you making that up?"

"Not a bit." She leaned up to whisper, "How do you think you ended up with your cravat undone and your waistcoat unbuttoned?"

He glared down at her. "You're a very wicked woman, Miss Bonnaud."

"Ah, ah, you're forgetting your role," she teased. "Mustn't do that."

"Wicked *and* annoying," he snapped.

"Not to mention hungry," she said, releasing his arm to walk over to the counter where they were handing out plates.

He followed closely behind her. "So am I. But not for food now, thanks to you."

A delicious shiver slid down her spine, despite her determination not to be affected by him. "Remember," she warned, "we have an agreement."

"Yes, and I'm beginning to regret I ever made such a foolish bargain."

She laughed. How lovely to have found a way to get back at him for his cocksure pronouncements about her character.

But as they picked their way through the dining room with their plates and mugs of ale, she found herself wondering about *his* character. Who was this duke who could be a perfect gentleman one moment and a tempting rogue the next? Had his childhood aim really been to become a midshipman? It just didn't seem like him.

The minute they sat down, she asked him about it.

"Actually," he told her as he dug eagerly into his dinner, "there's a long history of naval service among the younger sons on my father's side of the family—two uncles, a cousin, a great-uncle . . ." He paused, as if something disturbed him, then continued with a forced smile. "Some of them sent me souvenirs from their exploits sailing under Admiral Nelson. So as you might imagine, at the tender age of seven, I worshipped Nelson and hoped to sail with him myself one day."

"Did you really?" she said, trying to picture it.

"It was right after the Battle of Trafalgar, and the newspapers were full of stories about Nelson's gallant actions and glorious death. I dreamed of fighting Boney, rising rapidly through the ranks like my hero, and becoming the greatest naval captain ever to sail the seas." A rueful smile touched his lips. "Of course, I had some boyish notion that the war would go on forever."

"It did go on quite a while. Were you disappointed when it ended?"

His face clouded over. "No, because by then, any possibility of reaching my dream had vanished, anyway."

He'd turned somber again. She watched, her heart twisting as he concentrated on steadying his plate when it slid toward the edge of the table.

Trying to cheer him, she said lightly, "Forgive me, but I'm having trouble imagining you as a small boy dreaming of adventure at sea. You just seem so . . . dukely, sprung fully formed from the womb of a duchess."

"*Dukely?*" he said with an arched brow. "Is that even a word?"

"If it's not, it should be." She cast him a mischievous grin. "It means 'imperious.'"

That got a smile out of him, to her enormous pleasure. But as she watched, he sobered. "You realize that I might not actually be a duke. If Peter is alive—"

"You said it was impossible."

"It is." He drank some ale. "Well, unlikely, in any case."

Curiosity got the better of her. "They did find his body, right?"

He sighed. "They found the body of a boy the right age to be him. But by the time we learned of it and were able to travel to the Continent, he'd been buried for months."

"Then how did they know it was Peter?"

A hard look crossed his face. "He was found with his kidnapper, who also died in the fire. And his kidnapper was definitely identified by a ring he wore."

"You found out who his kidnapper was? Who *was* it?"

He flinched, then drank down some ale. "Some blackguard, that's all," he murmured and forced a smile. "So are you never going to tell me exactly what happened while I was drunk last night?"

The abrupt change of subject made her sigh. He didn't trust her even that far, did he? "No," she said, trying to match his light tone. "A woman has to have *some* secrets."

"I suppose." He pushed his plate away. "Was it your childhood dream to be an investigator?"

"Certainly not. My dream wasn't much different from yours. I wanted to be an explorer."

He laughed, and the shadows faded from his eyes.

The next few hours passed quickly. They ate their dinner, then strolled the deck talking. The sea had smoothed out into a surprising calm, which made the journey quite pleasant. As long as they skirted the subject of his brother and the kidnapping, their conversation was perfectly amiable.

The duke could be entertaining when he wanted.

He regaled her with tales about his wild friend Gabriel Sharpe, who'd settled into marriage with Miss Waverly, the cousin of one of Dom's former clients, Lord Devonmont.

But now she was all too aware of how carefully Max avoided speaking of the kidnapping, or even his life past the age when his brother had supposedly died. Other questions leapt into her mind, too, like what sort of illness his father could have contracted that made it necessary for Max's parents to take him with them searching for a cure. The more she knew of him, the more curious she became.

When the steam packet approached Dieppe, she found herself wishing that she had the courage to pry. Then again, he was adept at avoiding uncomfortable subjects. She doubted that a couple of days with her was going to unlock his reticence.

Realizing that they would be tied up for a while on the shore with customs and the like, she excused herself to visit the necessary. When she was done and had come back out to head toward where Max stood near the front of the ship, she nearly collided with a gentleman in a gray surtout who was rounding the corner toward her.

He tugged his hat down and mumbled, "Beg pardon, ma'am," then scurried into the necessary. But not before she caught the familiar vile scent of Spanish cigarillos.

Her heart stopped. Hucker.

Instantly she chided herself for being so absurd. Why would Hucker be *here* on the packet to France?

Why would he follow them all the way from London?

Still, the day before yesterday, she'd thought she'd seen him in the street opposite the house. And at the coach office she'd felt almost certain that someone was watching her.

Her blood chilled in her veins. It seemed unlikely, but . . .

She hesitated, tempted to wait until the man came out again so she could get a good look at him and make sure it wasn't Hucker. But if it were and he realized that she knew of his pursuit, escaping him might be much harder.

Then it dawned on her why he might be following her—to find Tristan. Good Lord, could Hucker actually be hunting for her brother?

She hurried down the corridor and out onto the deck, wiping her clammy hands on her cloak. Perhaps she was being hasty. Plenty of men probably smoked Spanish cigarillos. And after all these years, why would George send his man of affairs after Tristan *now*?

Once they'd left Yorkshire, George had seemed to give up the search, probably because looking for them on the Continent would have cost him a fortune since he'd had no idea where they'd gone. And from what Dom had been able to find out back then, George hadn't had a fortune. Or time to hunt down Tristan. His hands had been full dealing with the estate Papa had left behind.

As the years had passed in France, they'd begun to feel safe. It had seemed that George's thirst for blood had been sated once she and Tristan and Maman were out of his hair. It was precisely because George had no longer seemed a threat that Dom and Tristan had felt secure in having her come from France to live with—

She groaned. Good Lord, *that* would explain why Hucker might be hanging about all of a sudden. News of her living with Dom could have trickled back to George. It would have enraged him to hear that one of the half siblings he'd thought himself well rid of was living in England again, bold as brass. Knowing George, he was probably just waiting for Tristan to show up, too. The thought of them living out in the open in London with Dom would drive him mad.

But mad enough to send Hucker after her? She wasn't sure.

She had to figure it out without alerting the man that she had recognized him, or it wouldn't be nearly as easy to give him the slip. And they *had* to give him the slip, because she wasn't about to let him drag Tristan back to England to be hanged.

Ducking into the dining room, she watched furtively out of one of the windows for the man in the gray surtout. When he strolled past, he appeared to be scanning the deck for someone. Unfortunately, he kept his hat so low over his face that she couldn't make out his features.

Drat it all. She would have to ask for the duke's help. He already barely trusted her and this would ruin that. The minute she mentioned that they were being followed, he would know there was more to Tristan's situation than she'd said.

Worse yet, after how she'd hidden the truth from him, he would never agree to help her unless she agreed to tell him *everything*.

Fine, then she would do what she must. She would just have to pray that he could be trusted with her family's secrets.

9

MAXIMILIAN LEANED ON the rail as the boat approached Dieppe. He couldn't believe how much he was enjoying himself. It was a sunny day, with lazy clouds scudding above, reflected on a sea that was a sheet of green glass, unusual for a Channel crossing. His sailing yacht wouldn't have moved an inch in this calm, but the steam packet chugged along with great enthusiasm, plowing up the sea behind it.

Oddly, the noise of the engines no longer bothered him much. His belly was full, his head had stopped hurting, and he would soon be in France, one of his favorite places to visit.

Best of all, not a soul was paying him any mind. Who could have known that being a "regular person" could be so satisfying? For the first time in his life, he was truly anonymous. No one was cozying up to him because of his money and rank, no one was recording his every move to report in some gossip rag, and no one, absolutely *no one*, was watching to see if he was going mad.

Least of all his lovely companion.

He smiled. The minx never failed to surprise him. One moment, she was vowing her determination to be one of her brother's "men"; the next, she was flouncing off to talk about bonnets and fabric with a lot of chattering females.

She challenged and teased him by turns, showed an interest in his past but never pried. And she made him burn. No woman had done that since his father's madness had made him rethink his prospects for marriage. He hadn't *let* any woman do it until her.

No matter how much he told himself that his desire for her couldn't lead anywhere, he couldn't seem to stop it.

As if she'd read his mind, she came up to stand next to him at the rail, and every muscle in him went taut just at her presence. Holy God, what a fool he was.

"You were right about the steam packet," he said conversationally. "We got here much more quickly than we ever would have in my yacht."

She said nothing in answer, which surprised him. Lisette never lacked for anything to say. He glanced down to find her staring out at the sea with a serious expression.

Even that could not darken his mood. "You're not going to exult that you were right?" he teased.

"I need a favor from you," she said in a low voice,

"and I need you to do it without asking any questions. Time is of the essence."

"That sounds ominous," Maximilian said, amused by her dramatic pronouncement.

She didn't smile. "I think there's a man on board the packet who followed us from London. If it's who I think it is, we have to get rid of him."

"What did you have in mind?" Maximilian kept his tone light, though her manner was starting to unsettle him. "Stabbing? Strangulation? Or simply tossing him over the side?"

Her solemn gaze shot to him. "Don't be ridiculous. We have to keep him from following us on to . . . to where we're going."

His amusement fled. "You're serious."

"Very."

A slow chill spread over him. Why would someone be following them?

Surely she was letting her imagination run away with her. He angled his body toward her and surreptitiously scanned the deck behind them. "What does he look like?"

"He's about my height and built like a pugilist. He's wearing a gray surtout and a hat pulled low over his face."

"I do see a fellow who looks like that." What's more, the man was edging back out of his sight, as if not wanting to be noticed.

That put Maximilian on guard. She definitely wasn't

imagining it. And the fact that someone might be following them gave him pause. Because it meant there were things she hadn't told him, things other than the location of her brother.

Things he suspected he wouldn't like.

Maximilian stared hard at her. "Tell me who he is. Or who you fear he is."

"George's man of affairs, a fellow named Hucker." Her words came out in a rush. "The day before yesterday I thought I saw him outside Manton's Investigations, but I assumed I was wrong since we've had no contact with George in years. Even now, I can't be sure it's him until I see his face. I need you to help me with that."

She still refused to look at him, which turned his blood to ice in his veins. It was a sign of guilt. "I'm not helping you with a damned thing until I get some answers. Why would Rathmoor's man of affairs be following you? What or who does he seek?"

She paled. "Tristan."

Of course. Who else? "Why?"

"We don't have time for this!" she whispered, turning her face to his. It showed panic, and that made his gut twist despite his growing anger. "We need to have a plan in place before we reach Dieppe so we can throw him off the scent. I swear I will tell you everything once we're en route to . . . to . . ."

That she was still prevaricating fueled his temper. "To *where*, damn it?" he snapped.

She hesitated, but clearly she knew that he now held

all the cards. "Paris," she finally said. Her expression was full of pleading. "Now, will you help me figure out if it's Hucker? And if it is, will you help me get away from him?"

Confound her to blazes. What secret was she hiding? She had to be hiding something, if Rathmoor was sending men to follow her.

"All right." As a palpable relief flashed over her face, he added tersely, "But once we're safely away, you will tell me exactly what this is about. There will be no more evasions, no more omissions. I want all the truth. Is that understood?"

She swallowed hard, then nodded. Glancing furtively in the man's direction, she lowered her voice. "Here's what I suggest that we do, to figure out if it's Hucker."

She proceeded to describe a complicated scheme involving having Maximilian trip the fellow so that his hat fell off and she could see his face.

"I have a simpler idea," he bit out.

Turning from the rail, he headed for the wheelhouse. She followed, protesting in low, urgent whispers that he ignored. Out of the corner of his eye, he noticed that their quarry was taking great pains to avoid meeting them head-on.

He scowled. If she had said from the beginning that they might be followed, he would have been more careful. But no, she'd had to keep her cards close to her chest for her own devious purposes. He should have known not to believe her when she'd claimed she'd never lied to him. But he'd been enticed into thinking that she was unlike any woman he'd ever known.

She was, but only because she was playing a role. How had he not realized that after her convincing playacting in the coach? That should have been a clear clue that she was not to be trusted.

But he'd let himself be taken in. He'd let her distract him from his purpose regarding her brother, and now he was going to pay for it. He should have heeded his instincts. There had clearly always been far more to this situation than she'd admitted. And he would bloody well get to the bottom of it before this day was through.

After he got rid of Rathmoor's lackey.

When he entered the wheelhouse, he asked the captain to show him the passenger manifest. That required some money changing hands, but fortunately he'd brought plenty for this ridiculous escapade. As the captain returned to preparing the ship for docking, Maximilian began to scan the list.

Lisette fretted beside him. "Hucker's not going to use his *real* name."

"He has to, unless he carries a false passport about with him." He slanted a glance at her. "Is that possible?"

She colored. "I don't think so. To be honest, I'm surprised he even *has* a passport."

Maximilian returned his attention to the manifest. "Customs uses the passenger manifest to determine who's on board before matching up the names and the passports. So he had to provide his real name to book passage."

"I didn't even consider that," she said, then grabbed his arm and hissed, "Oh, Lord, what about *our* passports? They're not going to match up."

"Of course they are. My real name *is* Maximilian Cale, after all. As for you, I already told the captain that we didn't have time to get your passport changed after we married—it was a hasty affair, and we had to hurry to France to see to your family."

"You . . . you thought about the whole issue with the passports?"

"Certainly. I booked our passage." He kept scanning the list. "The captain doesn't think that your using your maiden name to go through customs will be a problem. For one thing, your name is French. For another, if they give us any trouble, I will simply offer the proper financial incentives to look the other way."

"You intend to bribe them?"

He shot her a hard glance. "Does that bother you?"

She sighed. "No. I just wish I had considered all the problems that would arise from our masquerade."

"You were in too much of a hurry to save your damned brother from me, for that," he bit out, provoking a frown from her. But he didn't care. He'd found the name he was searching for. "John Hucker? That's him?"

"Yes." She clutched at his arm again. "We have to keep him from following us once we leave Dieppe!"

"Right," he said acidly, "so he won't find Bonnaud. I grasped that. What did your brother do, steal the family treasure?"

"No! Well, not exactly." The engine noise died, and worry lit her face. "We'll be disembarking any moment. I promise that later I will tell you everything."

"You damned well will." He walked over to return the manifest to the captain, then grabbed her by the arm to urge her none too gently back onto the deck. "But for now, if you want to dodge your pursuer, you are going to do exactly as I say, without protest or complaint. Is that clear?"

She stiffened but had the good sense to nod.

"All right. Then let's go escape Mr. Hucker."

◆ ◆ ◆

LISETTE WAS IN awe of Max's efficiency. He'd thought of everything—passports, their entry into France, the possible problems with customs. She should have thought of it, but she'd only traveled to France once in her life, and she'd been with Maman, who'd taken care of everything. She was lucky she'd thought to throw her passport into her bag before she left the house.

Some world traveler *she* was.

Still, despite Max's forethought in those areas, as the day went on, she began to be skeptical of his plan, whatever it was, to dodge Hucker. The man of affairs dogged them throughout the hours they spent going through customs, though at a surreptitious distance.

Max didn't seem to notice or care. He spent his time chatting amiably with the immigration officers in very fluent French, which rather surprised her.

It shouldn't, since he was naturally well educated. And he had said that he'd traveled on the Continent a great deal. Still, she'd expected the usual English butchery of her mother's tongue, and it pleased her more than it ought to find that he was quite adept.

By the time they finally entered the Hôtel de la Ruse in Dieppe, it was late in the evening. Max seemed to know the hotel well, which made her wonder just how often he visited France. Hucker had come into the hotel with several of the other passengers, barely even trying to hide himself, probably assuming that if she hadn't recognized him up close on the packet boat, then she wasn't going to.

Meanwhile, she was starting to be annoyed that Max had made no effort whatsoever to avoid Hucker. What was the point of asking for his help?

"My wife and I would like a room for the night," Max said in English to the hotel's owner, having somehow managed to be first inside. He took a bag of coins from his bag and handed it to the fellow. "And I understand that we can also purchase the fare for the diligence to Tours here."

Tours? That was an entirely different direction from Paris. Surely he didn't mean to go gallivanting about the French countryside just to get rid of Hucker. And the diligence, the French version of a stagecoach, was a very public, lumbering vehicle. It would be easy to follow on horseback.

The hotel owner opened the bag of coins, his eyes going wide at the amount. "Oh yes, sir," the man answered in halting English. "It leaves first thing in the morning. I will make sure that you and madame have seats in the coupé."

"Thank you, that would be preferable," Max said.

The coupé in a diligence, an enclosed compartment above the driver's seat, was always the best place to sit, but right now she couldn't even find it in her heart to be pleased that he would arrange it. Did he think that taking seats on a diligence would keep Hucker from following them, for pity's sake?

"Come this way, monsieur," the owner said, walking toward the stairs. "I will see you to your room myself." He barked some orders at a footman, who picked up their bags and followed.

As the four of them headed up, Lisette murmured, "I'm not sure how this will help us."

"You promised to follow my orders without protest or complaint," he retorted. "Have you forgotten that already?"

"No, but—"

He raised an eyebrow.

"You can be insufferable at times," she said. He was beginning to give her a headache.

"It comes with being a duke," he clipped out. "I would apologize, but I'm not in the mood for apologies right now. Especially when you keep breaking your promises."

That brought her up short. What other promise had she broken?

Oh, right. The promise not to lie to him. She hadn't broken that, though he probably didn't see it that way. And he was going to be angrier still once she told him that Tristan was wanted in England for horse thieving.

The owner stopped to open a door that led into a lavishly appointed bedchamber. "This is my best room, Monsieur Kale. I hope it will suit you and your wife."

"It will, indeed," Max said, casting the room only a cursory glance before taking the bags from the footman and walking in, leaving Lisette to follow him inside.

"Shall I have dinner sent up for you, monsieur?" the owner asked.

"My wife and I ate on the steam packet," Max said. "We won't require anything else this evening, thank you."

"But monsieur, surely—"

"Did I neglect to mention that my lovely wife and I have only been married a few days?" Max slid an arm about Lisette's waist, pulling her close. "We will need nothing further this night, I assure you. In fact, I'd be most appreciative if you'd tell your staff not to disturb us until morning."

Trying not to react to that alarming pronouncement, Lisette forced a smile.

The hotel owner wore a knowing expression. "Oh, yes, of course. I understand, monsieur. There will be no disturbances."

He then handed Max the room key, sparing a wink for Lisette, who managed not to throw something at him. As soon as he'd left, she jerked free of Max and whirled to scowl at him. "If you think that I am going to—"

"Hold your tongue, for God's sake," he hissed, then hurried to crack open the door and peer out into the hall. "We don't have much time. I would wait here until everyone goes to bed, but the later we wait, the more conspicuous we'll be when we leave Dieppe."

"What are you talking about?" she whispered. "I thought we were going on the—"

"Do you want to leave Hucker behind or not?" Without waiting for an answer, he opened the door, fit the key into the lock outside, and picked up both their bags. "Quickly now, while the owner is dealing with the other passengers from the packet." Carrying their bags into the hall, he added, "Lock the door, then slide the key under it. And hurry."

She did as he said. He was already headed in the opposite direction from the stairs they'd just ascended. When he reached the end of the hall, he stopped opposite a door and indicated with a nod that she should turn the handle.

Surprised when it turned for her, she held the door open for him, then followed him into what was apparently a servants' stairwell. He nodded down the stairs, and she hurried to descend ahead of him.

"How did you know this was here?" she whispered as they crept furtively down to the ground floor.

"My family stayed in this hotel when I was sixteen. We were on our way to Paris to consult with my great-uncle's lawyer . . ." His voice turned remote. "Anyway, I sneaked down the back stairs one night."

"Oh, so you started your habit of going down to the taproom in inns at a very young age."

His only response was a foul glance, for they'd reached the ground floor. There were two doors opposite each other, and they could hear voices on the other side of one of them. "Quick, this way," he murmured and headed out the other door.

She followed, surprised to find herself in a garden. But Max didn't allow her time to pause, urging her to move behind a shed . . . and just in time, too, for someone came out the door to empty a cauldron of water onto the bushes.

As the servant lingered to smoke a cheroot, they stood there frozen, pressed against each other in the small space. Max turned his gaze to her, and her breath caught in her throat.

In the dark he looked nothing like the amiable gentleman whom she'd found so entertaining on the packet boat. Out here behind the shed, he was the forbidding duke, his eyes glittering down at her in the pale moonlight. It provoked an odd sensation in the pit of her stomach that felt remarkably like desire.

Desire? Nonsense. She did *not* desire the duke when he was ordering her about and demanding everything his way. Not in the least.

Nonetheless, as the scent of burning tobacco wafted to them on the breeze and Max continued to stare down at her, she shivered uncontrollably.

He set down the bags and drew her cloak more tightly about her. Her breath quickened. His hands lingered on her cloak, his gaze dropped to her mouth, and she half thought he might even kiss her.

Then he released her cloak as if it had burned his fingers. Edging to the corner of the shed, he glanced around it, then motioned her forward. As he went back to pick up their bags, he murmured, "There's a gate that leads to the alley. I'm right behind you."

They left the garden in stealthy silence, but the moment they reached the alley, Max quickened his pace, forcing her practically into a run to keep up with him.

"Stay close to me," he murmured as they rushed down the alley. "There's no reason to think that Hucker will be outside the hotel, but I don't know what byways we'll have to take, and at this hour men will be drinking in the taverns and weaving through the streets. I don't want them giving you any trouble."

"All right," she said through a lump in her throat. Despite his anger, he was worried for her safety. That warmed her even as he was being so overbearing.

They walked through Dieppe in silence, keeping to the shadows, taking back alleys where they could. Fortunately, the town wasn't very large. They'd walked less than a mile when they reached another hotel, the Hôtel de Londres. As they entered, he said, "If you want to visit the necessary, now is the time."

And with that enigmatic remark, he went off in search of the owner. She was dying to know what he was up to, but she figured she'd better do as he said. When she returned, Max was waiting to lead her back outside to where a coach was being hurriedly rigged up for a journey.

He handed their bags to a groom, who tied them to the back of the coach, then opened the door for her. "In you go, my dear."

As awareness dawned, she got in and took a seat in the aging but comfortable vehicle. He climbed in behind her and settled back onto the seat.

"I take it that we're headed for Paris?" she asked as the coach left.

He nodded. "The owner of the Hôtel de Londres assures me that we can be there by midafternoon tomorrow, barring any problems, especially if we go the shorter way and avoid Rouen."

"Avoiding Rouen is a good idea, anyway. It's on the road to Tours as well as to Paris."

Removing his hat, he tossed it onto the seat beside him. "We'll be long past Rouen before Hucker even sets off for Tours in the morning, but just in case . . ."

"You've made sure that if he *does* find out tonight that we've already left, he won't catch up to us in Rouen."

"That's the plan."

She gazed out at the streets dimly illuminated by gaslights. "But when he goes to board the diligence to Tours in the morning, he'll surely figure out that we slipped off in the night. Then he'll check all the hotels and find out that we left from that other hotel for Paris."

"No, he won't. I paid the owner well to keep quiet.

The trail will go cold here." His voice sharpened. "And I seriously doubt that a man as thoroughly English as Hucker would venture much beyond the coast of France if he doesn't know where to go."

He'd thought of everything, hadn't he? And thank God for it, because her head was really pounding now. She was tired of travel and she wanted nothing more than to curl up in a soft bed.

Obviously that wouldn't happen anytime soon. She took off her bonnet and placed it on the seat next to her. Then, removing her gloves, she opened her reticule and searched for her scent bottle. A sniff of the herbal perfume helped to ease her head a bit.

"You're probably right about that," she said as she restored the flacon to her bag. "George won't have paid him enough for a search of France. If I know Hucker, he'll be only too eager to return to England in the morning."

"And you do know Hucker well, I take it."

At his hard tone, she swung her gaze up to him. She could see little of his expression in the dim light, but what she saw sent a chill down her spine. He was ready for his reckoning, and he wouldn't relent until she had bared every secret her family had ever kept from the world.

She set her reticule aside. Very well, if that was the price for his help, then she would pay it. She would simply have to make him understand that despite all evidence to the contrary, Tristan wasn't the defrauder that Max was determined to make him out to be.

"Yes," she said quietly. "I know Hucker well enough. He threw me and my family from our home the day after Papa died, because George ordered it."

"Playing on my sympathies won't work, Lisette," Max said in a distant tone. "I want the truth. Now."

"I know. And you shall have it."

Even if his cold manner was cutting her to the heart. Even if his return to being Lofty Lyons was killing her.

Still, it wouldn't get any better. She might as well get this over with. Squaring her shoulders, she began to tell him the long and sordid tale of the day after Papa died.

10

MAXIMILIAN HAD SPENT the past few hours hardening his heart against her, determined not to let the devious chit mislead him. He'd prepared himself for evasions, tears, begging. He hadn't prepared himself for Lisette calmly and unemotionally relating a tale so specific in its details that it could only be the truth. Especially since it portrayed Bonnaud in a distinctly unfavorable light.

By the time she finished describing how her family had escaped England in a harrowing trip across the Channel on a smuggler's skiff, he had to grit his teeth against the feelings rocketing through him.

She'd been fourteen, for God's sake. Fourteen! Little more than a child. Her feckless father had failed to provide for his children, and as a result she'd had half her family and all her belongings ripped from her in one fell swoop.

As the thought made something twist in his chest,

he let out a low curse. He was *not* supposed to care, confound it! She'd deceived him. She was probably deceiving him even now.

"So your brother is not the saint you made him out to be when we first met," he clipped out as the coach rumbled through the night. "He's a bloody horse thief."

"He was seventeen! What would you do if your father promised you something on his deathbed and your half brother made it all disappear out of sheer spite?"

He thought back to his own father's deathbed. To his mother standing over his father's corpse, looking wild and frightened, with an empty vial of laudanum in her hand.

I didn't mean to, she whispered. *He was so unhappy and . . . he kept saying those . . . awful things and I . . . I just wanted him to sleep.*

Oh yes, Maximilian knew something about deathbed confessions and what they could do.

Determinedly, he buried the dark memories. This wasn't about deathbeds. It was about Bonnaud, who'd begun a life of crime early. Bonnaud, who was still eluding him, thanks to the man's deceitful sister.

Lisette was staring out the coach window, her expression bleak in the moonlight. "Tristan felt he had to provide for us, so he did the only thing he could think of. And he didn't consider it stealing, since Papa had left him the horse anyway."

When that tugged at Maximilian's sympathies, he

snapped, "All the same, taking and selling that horse was rash and stupid."

"That's what Dom said." Then her gaze shot to Maximilian, full of belligerence. "But without that money, we would never have made it to France. And after we reached it, we would have starved in the months it took Maman and Tristan to find work."

Her voice hardened. "Without that money to grease the palms of our 'loving' relations, we would have ended up in the street. They'd always hated that Maman had brought shame on the family by becoming an English lord's mistress. And that even after returning home to Toulon, she had the audacity to stir up gossip again by going on the stage."

"Toulon?" His temper flared again. "I thought we were going to Paris."

"We are. I told you, Tristan works for the government now."

"I said no prevarications, Lisette. Which branch of the government? Where? How can I find him?"

She blinked, then tipped up her chin. "I'm getting to that. Considering that we won't reach Paris for hours, you're awfully impatient."

"With good reason," he growled. "For all I know, you created this wild-goose chase in the first place to get me away from London so that your brother—"

"Could do what? Set up an impostor as your replacement, I suppose?" She eyed him with cool irony. "Yes, all along I've been engineering a master plan to destroy you. That's why I called you 'His Grace' when I was supposed to be hiding your identity. Why I had to rely on *you* to pay our passage . . . and our meals and the bribes for the customs officers."

Her voice grew choked. "Why I couldn't even escape Hucker without your help. Because I'm so very adept at diabolical schemes, at pretending to be someone else and trying to keep secrets and—"

"Enough," he cut in. "I see your point."

This was the Lisette he'd come to know, the one who dreamed of being an investigator and then got thorny when he pointed out that she didn't know the first thing about it. He grudgingly admitted that she was right. If she was a master manipulator, she wasn't very good at it.

For a moment, there was no sound in the carriage except that of the horse's hooves pounding the dirt and the creak of the carriage springs.

Then she dropped her gaze to her hands. "It's as I told you from the beginning—I don't know where Tristan is. The last time I saw him, when I left Paris six months ago, he was working for the Sûreté Nationale."

That threw him off guard. "The police? Your brother the horse thief was working for the *police*?"

She cast him a defiant glance. "Why do you think I didn't want you dashing over here to speak to his employer? I knew you would do your best to get Tristan dismissed."

"You're damned right I would have!" At her frown, he fought to restrain his temper. So far, he hadn't gotten anywhere with Lisette when he was angry. He forced some calm into his voice. "I assume that his employer doesn't know he's a criminal."

"No. And if he finds out . . ." She trailed off with a hitch in her voice that got him right in the gut.

Confound her to blazes. She had put him in an untenable position. Again. He didn't know which made him angrier—that her brother really had turned out to be shady or that she still persisted in championing the fool. "With such a past, how did Bonnaud even manage to get hired?"

"Well . . . it's not as if broadsides have been published across the world about his one criminal act. George had his hands full with dealing with Papa's estate, so he didn't pursue it beyond England. And he didn't know where we'd gone." She shrugged. "Besides, when Tristan went to work for the Sûreté, Vidocq was still at the head of it, and he didn't care."

"Eugène Vidocq?" Maximilian broke in.

"You know him?"

"Not personally, no, but I've heard of him from the man who investigated Peter's death. We couldn't come to France to search until after Napoleon had been routed and sent to Elba. The investigator was the one to learn that Peter had already died in that fire in Belgium."

"Was that the same trip when you came to consult with your great-uncle's lawyer?" she asked, clearly perplexed. "Did the lawyer know something about it?"

Cursing himself for saying enough that she'd connected those two in her mind, he avoided the question. "I know Vidocq is famous in some quarters, but the fellow we hired had nothing good to say about him. Claimed that he had a reputation for hiring criminals. Which does explain how your brother ended up employed by him."

With one last curious glance at him, she nodded. "Vidocq hires criminals precisely because he was one himself once. During that time he learned a great deal about how they operated. Then when a friend of his was hanged, he began to realize that criminals generally come to a bad end. So he went to work for the other side, and most effectively, too, given his inside knowledge."

He hated to admit it, but that made a sort of perverse sense. Besides, he had never been all that impressed with the man his father had hired to find Peter.

"I daresay if Vidocq had been investigating your brother's death," she went on, "you'd know far more about it than you do."

Never mind that he'd just been thinking something similar; her obvious admiration for the famous investigator gave him pause. "You seem to know the man very well."

"I do. Before he resigned last year, I worked for him, too."

Suddenly, several odd bits about her fell into place. "Vidocq is also well-known for hiring women as agents."

She shifted a bit on the swaying seat. "I wasn't an agent. I wanted to be, and he wanted to hire me as one, but Tristan wouldn't allow it."

Maximilian smiled grimly. "My respect for your brother just rose a notch."

"Now see here, I could have been very good at it!"

He lifted an eyebrow.

"All right," she grumbled, "perhaps not as good as I always imagined, but only because I had no training. If he'd had time to train me properly, I might have succeeded."

"Whether you would have or not is immaterial," Maximilian ground out. "It's one thing to help Manton question people. But being an agent for Vidocq would be treacherous work. Your brother would have been a fool to let you put yourself in such danger."

She looked out the window. "You're just like him, you know."

"Vidocq?" he said incredulously.

"Tristan. Both of you think you know everything. You're both proud and overbearing, and you both—"

"Care about you," he finished for her. When her gaze shot to him, he cursed his quick tongue. "Enough not to want to see you hurt."

A long silence spun out between them, catching them both in a tangle of frustrated desire. He fought to ignore the fact that they were alone in the dark, that she sat inches away from him, looking pretty and vulnerable and lonely. As lonely as he felt right now.

No, he wouldn't let himself be ensnared by her charms, confound it! "So if you didn't work for Vidocq as an agent, what *did* you do for him?"

"The same thing I do for Dom, mostly. Vidocq used

to keep track of every criminal he'd ever dealt with. He had their features, their aliases, their criminal habits, their known haunts—everything—written down on cards. By the time I went to work for him, he had sixty thousand, and they all had to be organized. It took four of us working full time just to keep track of them all."

"Now, *that*, I imagine, you were good at."

A soft smile lit her face. "I was, actually. You may have noticed that I like to keep things tidy." She gave a rueful laugh. "And Vidocq has no idea what tidy is, I swear. If not for me, that office would have been a nightmare of discarded disguises and boxes of cards and Lord knows what all. The man is brilliant as an investigator, but he's not very good at taking care of himself."

The obvious affection she felt for her former employer stung him. As he recalled, Vidocq was also known for being something of a rogue around women. "So you didn't just take care of his office," he said hollowly. "You took care of him, too."

"You might say that. Especially after his wife died and everything went to hell in a handbasket."

"He was unmarried when you were working for him?"

"The last few years, yes. Why?"

"So you valiantly stepped in to look after the poor man." Though he could hear the jealous edge in his voice, he couldn't seem to stop talking. "And what did that entail, exactly? Making him tea? Darning his stockings? Warming his bed?"

To his annoyance, she burst into laughter. "Are you mad? Vidocq is old enough to be my father, for pity's sake."

"But he's *not* your father, is he?" Maximilian said, jealousy still riding him despite her levity on the subject. "And he has quite the reputation with women, I'm told."

As the depth of his obsession seemed to sink in with her, she cocked her head to regard him intently. "Indeed he does." Her eyes glittered in the darkness. "He *is* rather handsome for his age. And he can be quite charming when he wants."

"Oh, I'm sure he can," he grumbled, not sure whether she was deliberately tormenting him or simply being honest. "That's all that matters to you, I suppose. Never mind that the man used to be a criminal, that he knows half of the underworld. He's handsome and charming, and that's good enough for you."

"It's better than being baleful and irritating like a certain troublesome duke," she shot back. "At least Vidocq knows how to treat a woman."

"What's *that* supposed to mean?"

"He doesn't assume at every turn that she's some untrustworthy creature engaged in plans to ruin him."

He gritted his teeth at that apt description of how he'd reacted. "Can you blame me for being suspicious? Your brother is a thief and you didn't bother to tell me."

"If I had, would we even be here? Or would you have had me arrested and forced to reveal his whereabouts?

Would you have destroyed Dom's business just to find Peter?" She crossed her arms over her chest. "I was protecting my family. You of all people should understand that."

He did, damn her. He understood and sympathized. That was the trouble with wild roses—they grew under a man's defenses when he wasn't watching. Despite all of his determination not to be taken in, he'd been taken in.

Or perhaps he'd just recognized what he'd sensed all along—that at her core she was forthright and loyal. The kind of woman his mother had been, sticking by her husband's side to the very end, standing up for him throughout the worst of Father's madness. The kind of woman he would want for a wife.

He thrust the thought from his mind before it could tantalize him.

She was right about one thing—if he'd known of Bonnaud's past, he wouldn't have been so eager to take this trip. He wanted to think he wouldn't have had her and Manton arrested, but he'd been quite angry that morning. There's no telling what he might have done.

But now that he knew her better, it was hard not to see things from her perspective. "So what happens now? We speak with the new head of the Sûreté to find out where your brother has gone?"

"Actually . . . um . . . I was thinking we should talk to Vidocq first."

The nervousness in her voice put him on edge. "Why? If Tristan works for the Sûreté, then they're more likely to know where he went on his last case."

"Well, yes, but the new head of the Sûreté doesn't exactly *like* Tristan."

Maximilian scowled at her. "Why does that not come as a surprise?"

The moon through the window cast a soft glow on her tense features. "My point is, the minute a duke of your consequence starts asking questions—"

"You're afraid I'll get your brother dismissed."

"Well, you *did* just say that you would."

"I was angry. And I was speaking of what I would have done before."

"But not now?" When he didn't answer, she added, "Vidocq is more likely to know where Tristan is, anyway. They are great friends and Tristan wouldn't take on any big case without talking to Vidocq. The Frenchman has such excellent instincts, and he is so knowledgeable about—"

"You just want to see Vidocq again," he snapped. "Admit it."

A frown furrowed her brow. "I don't know what you mean."

"Oh yes you do. Vidocq is more *charming* than I am, more *knowledgeable*, more *brilliant*." Driven once more by a jealousy he was at a loss to comprehend, he shifted to the seat beside her so he could glare down at her. "Clearly you can't wait to see him again."

She gaped at him. "You're utterly mad."

"Yes, I am. You make me so, every time you open your mouth and start praising that bloody Frenchman."

"Oh, so now you're going to blame *me* for your surly—"

He cut her off with a kiss. A hard one, born of jealousy and bad temper and a need to blot Vidocq out of her mind.

But it only took a moment for it to turn into something more. A real kiss, born of obsession, need, and bone-deep desire. God, it was sweet to kiss her again. So bloody sweet.

Hooking his hand behind her neck, he held her still while he molded her mouth with his, exulting when she moaned and parted her lips. At once, he deepened the kiss, driving his tongue deep, claiming her in the only way she would let him, the only way he should let himself.

For a long moment, there was no sound in the carriage but that of his roaring pulse in his ears as he drank from her mouth over and over, reveling in the heady taste of her, the scent of French perfume in her hair, the feel of her hands clutching his coat, drawing him closer.

Suddenly she thrust him away. She stared at him, her eyes wide and wary, her breath coming in urgent gasps. "We said no more kisses. You promised."

"*You* promised never to lie to me," he countered. "You broke your promise."

"No," she whispered. "I never once lied to you, I swear. Not once."

He wanted to argue the point, but as he thought back over their conversations, he couldn't remember her ever speaking any actual lies. Still, that didn't change anything. "You may not have lied, but you deceived me about your brother, which is practically the same thing."

"No, it's not. Strictly speaking, I followed our agreement to the letter."

"Then *strictly speaking,* I will follow our agreement to the letter, too."

Hauling her onto his lap so that she faced away from him, he clamped one arm about her waist to hold her still.

"What do you think you're doing?" she protested as she tried to wriggle free.

He pressed his lips to her ear. "We agreed to no kissing, but we said nothing about touching. And if you can call it fair to deceive me, then I can call it fair to touch *you.*"

Then he swept his hand up to cup her breast inside her cloak. She froze. He didn't wait for her protest; he just fondled her shamelessly, teasing her nipple to a taut little point through her gown. Ever since last night, he'd been haunted by half memories of what he'd done, how she'd felt in his arms. So this time, by God, he was going to do it while he could remember it.

He half expected her to argue or at least make some attempt to break free. But she just sat there breathing hard. The more he caressed her, the more she arched back against him, her hands digging into his thighs.

"Max," she said hoarsely, "you shouldn't . . . you oughtn't . . ."

"Yet I am," he murmured against her ear. "And you like it, too—admit it."

Sliding his hand over to caress the other breast, he tugged at her ear with his teeth. The little whimper she gave in response fired his blood almost as much as the feel of her lovely breast filling his hand.

"You probably don't remember," she choked out, "but last night I swore . . . I'd box your ears if you ever . . . grabbed my bosom again."

"I remember. I just don't care. Besides, you can't reach my ears," he murmured, feeling cocky now that he had her melting in his arms. "And you don't want to box them anyway, do you?"

She twisted her head to look up at him, her breath a rapid staccato. "I want . . . I want . . ."

"Tell me what you want, dearling, and I'll give it to you." He released a long, shuddering breath. "You feel like heaven in my hands. Pure heaven. I've wanted to do this practically from the moment I saw you . . ."

Her eyes were lost and luminous in the moonlight. "Liar," she whispered. "You wanted to throttle me."

"Only so I could get my hands on you. I wanted to touch you so badly I could hardly think straight." He slipped his hand down her leg so he could inch her skirts up. There was more he wanted to touch. "Last night was sheer torture . . . unbuttoning your gown . . . unlacing your corset . . . You may not realize it, but I was the one who did that while you slept. Not some servant."

"I know," she said, surprising him.

"But you have no idea what I suffered doing it. Why do you think I went to the taproom and drank myself silly? So I wouldn't climb into bed with you and put my hands all over you, the way I wanted to when I was unlacing you."

"I kept expecting you to. I waited for you to . . ." she whispered.

"You were awake?" he said incredulously.

"Part of the time. I held my breath and waited to see what you would do . . . I was so afraid . . ."

He froze just as his hand brushed her stocking-clad knee . . . "Surely you know I would never harm you, dearling."

Her eyes met his. "That's not what I was afraid of. I was afraid that if you climbed into bed with me and put your hands all over me, I might just . . . let you."

His heart thundered in his ears. She desired him. What's more, she was *admitting* she desired him.

That was all it took to have him kissing her again. She was in his arms now, and he desperately wanted, *needed*, a taste of her. So to hell with their stupid bargain. He had her now, and he wasn't letting her go until he got his taste.

11

CLEARLY LISETTE'S EARLIER headache had turned her good sense into Swiss cheese. That was the only explanation for why she was letting Max caress and kiss her.

He called you dearling. *Twice.*

The absurdity of that thought made a laugh bubble up in her throat, but his kisses were so fierce and ravenous that it died there. She shouldn't care about such a silly thing as an endearment.

But she did. Max wasn't angry. He wasn't holding her prisoner or retaliating. He was kissing her as if she held the key to the meaning of life, as if he meant to gain it by making her desire him madly.

His hand slid between her legs and inside the slit in her drawers, startling her. "Max!"

"Let me give you pleasure, dearling," he said hoarsely, melting her objections again with that one sweet word. "Let me show you what desire feels like."

Then he cupped her tender parts, and every inch of her leapt into high alert. "Oh, Lord . . . *Max* . . ."

He began to rub her there, stroking her so devilishly that she groaned. Did he know how it made her yearn for more?

"You like that, do you, minx?" he said in a self-satisfied tone.

Oh yes, he knew. "It's . . . very . . . interesting . . ."

"Interesting, hmm." He teased her mercilessly. "I can do this all night. Admit it. You like it."

"You're a devil." She dug her fingers into his arm. "All right, yes . . . I like it. Please . . . Max . . . please . . ." She didn't know what she was begging for. All she knew was there was more. She could sense it, feel it, just beyond her.

"I'll do whatever you wish, dearling. Just tell me one thing." He raked kisses down her jaw to her throat. "Did I really have you on my lap last night?"

His hot caresses made it hard for her to think. She fought to clear her mind. "Yes . . . On your lap . . . yes . . ."

"Like this?"

"No!"

"Thank God. I'd want to remember *that*, for damned sure."

She choked out a laugh. Then his finger slipped inside her where she felt aching and slick and hungry, and her amusement turned to pure hot desire. He slid his finger in and out, playing with the little button there, making her squirm and press against his hand like a shameless wanton, wanting more.

"Well, minx?" he said hoarsely. "How do you enjoy that?"

"You're making me . . . insane . . ."

"Good," he whispered against her ear. "You've been making me insane since the day I met you."

The swaying of the coach made her rock atop his lap, and now she felt something hard pushing up against her bottom. His arousal? It must be. She knew *that* much about a man's body. Oh, Lord, was that what his . . . his *braquemard* felt like? So thick and sturdy?

She wriggled her bottom over it again, and he groaned. "Holy God, Lisette . . . don't . . . do that."

"It's my turn," she said coyly, repeating the motion. "How do *you* like being teased?"

"I like it . . . too damned much," he growled.

Taking her by surprise, he suddenly shifted her to sit sideways across his knees. Then he fumbled with his breeches, and next thing she knew he was pressing her hand down onto something heated and long and hard.

Ohh, it was his *braquemard*. How fascinating. She'd never thought it would be that firm. Yet supple, too.

"Please," he said in a guttural voice. "Stroke me, dearling."

"How?"

"Like this." He closed her hand around his flesh, then showed her how to pull on him. "Not too hard . . . yes . . . Oh, God, yes, exactly like that."

His moan made her exult. He was as much a prisoner to desire as she. How thrilling to have him so seemingly helpless in her hands, as thrilling as when she'd realized he was actually jealous of Vidocq. Max had even admitted to caring for her. The haughty and powerful duke laid low by *her*? It seemed impossible.

Yet he was breathing even harder than she, his *braquemard* was rigid as stone and growing longer and harder with each stroke, and he was calling her *dearling* and *minx* with what sounded like real affection.

Then he released her hand so he could return to fondling her between her legs, and she gasped. It felt *wonderful*, more wonderful than she'd ever expected.

And the best part was that it was Max doing it, Max kissing her neck and shoulder, Max who was thrumming that sweet little button between her legs with such an expert touch that she could feel something rising deep in her belly, a twisting tension fighting to break free.

"Max . . . Oh, Lord, *Max* . . ."

"Yes, dearling," he rasped. "Take what you want . . . take it . . ."

Her blood was like a fever in her veins and her heart was racing and any minute now she was going to come apart like a piece of glass . . . vibrating so furiously that it shook . . . shook . . . *shattered*!

"Lord save me!" she cried, rocked by a piercing pleasure.

Then he came apart, too, in her hand. As he released a cry of his own, something wet spilled over her fingers and onto her bared thigh, startling her.

For a moment they both just sat there, their bodies shaking and their breathing heavy.

Then he brushed a kiss to her ear. "Lisette, my wild French rose . . . you're a wonder," he murmured, his mouth trailing languid kisses over her hair and down her neck.

A powerful embarrassment overtook her, and she ducked her head against his shoulder to hide her flaming cheeks, which was ludicrous because it was dark. What had she done? She had sworn not to let him this close, and now . . .

He drew a handkerchief from his pocket and began to wipe her hand. After he had also wiped his own, she took the handkerchief from him to wipe her thigh.

Mortification swamped her. What was wrong with her? How could she have encouraged this, reveled in it? Was it because of pleasures like these that Maman had become so enthralled by Papa?

Men were devils. Amazing, sweet devils who made a woman forget who she was.

"Lisette . . ." he began in a low voice.

Gaslight suddenly flooded the carriage. She jerked her gaze to the window to see houses flashing past them. They were in a town, and now the coach was slowing down.

"Oh no," she whispered, "we're stopping to change horses!" Had that much time passed already?

Muttering a string of French curses that would have done Maman proud, she vaulted off his lap and onto the other seat, then began dragging her skirts down.

He was cursing, too, as he hurriedly rebuttoned his breeches.

"We should have drawn the curtains," he grumbled.

"No. We shouldn't have . . . have . . . done what we did at all." Good Lord, she didn't even know what to call what they'd just done.

He stared at her, his jaw going taut. "Right," he clipped out. "You're right."

Her heart sank. He didn't have to agree with her so readily. And how could he regret it already? Not that she could blame him. *She* regretted it already.

Didn't she?

The carriage halted in an innyard, and the grooms hurried to change the horses. To her shock, Max opened the door and leaped out. "Dinner was hours ago," he said as he held the door open for her. "I'll get a supper packed up for us. And you probably want to visit the necessary."

Though both suggestions were considerate, they took her aback, coming on the heels of what they'd just done. But she nodded her agreement, incapable of speech as she snatched up her reticule and let him help her down. In a few blessed moments they were inside the inn where she could flee him, at least temporarily.

The coaching inn had a rather nicely appointed retiring room for ladies, which was abandoned at the moment. Thank God. A glance in the mirror told her she looked a fright even by candlelight, her bonnet missing and her hair mussed and her lips a bright red from Max's many kisses. Anyone who looked at her would know her instantly for the shameless wanton she was.

Then again, she was supposedly married.

A mad laugh escaped her. Well, at least there was that. And Max was even behaving like a husband, going right from touching and caressing her to talking about fetching supper. How like a man! He'd had his pleasure, and now he was ready to have his belly filled.

You had your pleasure, too.

She swallowed. Yes. She'd behaved like some trollop, letting him touch her all over, caress her all over, kiss her until she ached and yearned and—

Stop that! she chided as her body began to melt all over again, just remembering the things he'd done. She wasn't supposed to let some arrogant Englishman make her feel like this, all because he'd given her pleasure and she'd done the same to him.

Glaring at her offending hand, she bit out a curse, then filled the washbasin from the pitcher nearby and began scrubbing her hand with the soap, as furiously as Lady Macbeth could ever have done. When she'd rubbed it raw, she lifted her skirts and washed her thigh.

Odd how her body looked exactly the same as before, but it felt so utterly different. *She* felt utterly different.

That's when the tears began to flow. Truth was, she would do it again if she had the chance. Not merely because she'd enjoyed it, but because Max had been the one giving her the enjoyment. Somewhere along the way, what he thought of her had begun to matter. She'd begun wanting him to . . . to desire her. No, to *care* for her.

How utterly foolish. She knew better! A duke of his consequence could never feel anything but desire for a woman like her. And that wasn't what she wanted. Or it wasn't *all* she wanted, anyway.

She dried her hands and blew her nose, then set about making herself look more presentable. Time was ticking away and they had to put as many miles between them and Hucker as possible, but she felt an urgent need to return everything to the way it was.

For a moment, she stared at herself. Her eyes were red, but she looked halfway decent. Unfortunately, she still smelled of . . . of what they'd done, the way Maman's bedroom had always smelled after Papa's visits.

With a groan, she jerked out her scent bottle and dabbed some perfume on her wrists, then added some to her neck for good measure. She'd probably overdone it, but she didn't care. It was better than smelling of something that would remind him of what they'd been doing. Because she absolutely could *not* let herself fall into the same trap with him as Maman had done with Papa.

When she returned to the coach, Max was waiting to help her in. If he noticed her heavy perfume, he didn't say anything. And once they were in the carriage together, a different scent took over—a heavenly one of baked goods and roasted meat from the box he'd set on the floor.

"I prevailed upon the innkeeper's wife to sell us some leftovers from dinner," Max said in a low rumble. "She even included a bottle of wine."

Lisette hadn't realized until she smelled the food

how truly hungry she was. That might even explain her headache earlier.

As the coach set off, Max pulled out a crusty loaf of bread, some pont l'évêque cheese, and a couple of roasted pigeons wrapped in paper. She fell on the meal like a ravenous dog, partly because she was hungry and partly to avoid talking to him.

After a few moments, she became aware that he wasn't eating quite so avidly. Instead, his gaze was fixed unnervingly on her. Normally she would relish the French cheese and bread that she'd dearly missed in London, not to mention pigeons cooked with some flavor to them and not in the boring fashion of the English. But having him watch her so intently dampened her enjoyment.

"About what happened earlier, Lisette—"

"No, we don't need to talk about it. I understand." She couldn't bear to hear him speak the usual lies; she'd just as soon pretend it hadn't happened.

She bent forward to remove an apple from the box, but he caught her by the arm to stay her. "We *do* need to talk about it, and you *don't* understand. I didn't mean for it to happen. I need you to know that I—"

"I *know*!" Snatching her arm free, she hunched back into the seat and drew her cloak about her like a shield. "I already know what you'll say. That it was a mistake. That we shouldn't have gotten carried away. And I agree." She forced a lightness into her tone that she didn't feel. "We enjoyed ourselves, but it didn't mean anything."

"It damned well meant something to me," he ground out.

"Did it? What, exactly?" When he let out a curse and glanced away, she added, "You don't have to say it. You enjoyed . . . what we did together, but you're a duke and cannot marry someone like me."

His gaze shot back to her. "That's not what I would say." He dragged in a heavy breath. "All right, I can't marry you, but not because of who you are, because of your parentage or station or any of that rot. Not even because I'm a duke. I just . . . can't."

That was why she hadn't wanted to talk about it, curse him! She was already growing to care for him deeply, and she couldn't stand the humiliation—the pain—of hearing exactly how little he cared.

"As I said," she bit out, "I understand. So there's no reason to speak of it any further. You can't marry me and I don't *want* to marry you, so—"

"You truly have no desire to marry me." His hands flexed on his knees as if he fought the urge to reach for her. Or throttle her. "Not even a little?"

What did he want? For her to beg him to marry her so he could trample all over her pride while he continued on with his *I can't marry you*? She would not do it! "No, Your Grace, not even a little. I like you, but I'm not seeking a husband. So let's just forget what happened earlier, shall we?"

"You can do that?" he said, his voice suddenly ragged. "Because I don't think I can."

"You will have to. I refuse to engage in an affair, and you have no interest in anything else. So once again, we find ourselves at an impasse. Except that I don't think this particular impasse can be resolved."

He dragged one hand through his hair, then offered a tight nod. "Perhaps you're right. Perhaps it *would* be better if we try to forget what happened."

"Yes, I think that would be best," she choked out, then steadied her shoulders. "Now, didn't you say there was wine?"

His eyes glittered at her in the dim light of the carriage, and for one long, tempting moment, she thought for sure he would throw caution to the winds and drag her into his arms and kiss her again. And if he did, she knew she would not have the strength to resist.

But he didn't. With a shuddering breath, he turned to hunt in the box.

As she watched his bent head glistening golden in the moonlight and remembered how sweetly he'd kissed her, her throat ached with unshed tears and her heart felt ripped from her chest. Yes, it *would* be best if she forgot how he'd stroked her and caressed her and called her pretty names. It really would.

So it was a wretched shame that there was no chance in hell of that ever happening.

12

MAXIMILIAN SAT THERE numb, long after Lisette had fallen into a fitful sleep. He'd handled the whole thing badly. First he'd accused her of all manner of perfidy and behaved like a jealous, besotted fool, then he'd nearly taken her innocence, and finally he'd made that idiotic speech about not being able to marry her.

No wonder she'd withdrawn from him to cloak herself in her pride.

If that was what she'd been doing. Perhaps she'd really meant it when she said she had no desire to marry him. Given what she'd endured watching her father muck up her mother's life, it would be understandable.

But he'd gone to the retiring room to fetch her, and heard her crying through the door. The sound of those tears still echoed in his brain. No, she hadn't meant it.

It was one more measure of how different she was from other women. Any other woman would have pressed her advantage, tried to extract some promise of a future from him after he'd put his hands all over her so insolently.

Not his Lisette. She was too proud for that. Instead she went off and cried her heart out alone. And even knowing that, he had still hurt her.

He *was* an insensitive, arrogant arse.

At the very least, he should have revealed why he couldn't marry her. He should have told her that both his great-uncle and his father had died raving mad, that odds were good he would as well, and that she would *not* enjoy watching it.

But after hour upon hour of having the woman treat him like a regular person, he hadn't wanted to give that up. Because if she knew the truth, she would look at him the same way every other woman did—as the duke who was sure to degenerate into madness any moment.

At least other women weighed the advantages of being married to a rich duke against the possibility of madness and sometimes chose to ignore the latter. But she didn't care about the former, so she would only see the latter. That would kill him. Better to have her think him an arse.

Not only an arse but a heartless rogue.

What had she said? *I refuse to engage in an affair, and you have no interest in anything else.*

Little did she know. The idea of marrying Lisette had begun to have an intoxicating appeal. He knew it would only end in tragedy, yet he couldn't stop imagining what it would be like.

She would turn the *ton* on its ear. Ladies would gossip endlessly about her, and when they realized she didn't care a whit, they would lionize her. Because the *ton* always worshipped whoever had no use for them, especially when that person was the wife of a wealthy duke.

In those long, lonely nights at Marsbury House, he would have her to hold, her to joke with, her to tease. He would no longer have to lie in his bed waiting for the madness to start. She would distract him from it.

But only until the day when his mind started to go. And since Lisette would undoubtedly care deeply about him by then, the thought of what it would do to her was more than he could stand.

She shifted restlessly on the seat, pulling her legs up beneath her cloak as if trying to get them warm. It *was* rather cold in the coach. It might be spring, but the nights were still cold.

Telling himself he just wanted to make her more comfortable, he slid onto the seat beside her, pulled her against him, and covered them both with his greatcoat. With a sigh, she burrowed into him, and his heart constricted in his chest.

He closed his eyes and laid his head back, pretending that they *were* married, that she was his wife and they were traveling to Paris for pleasure. He sat like that a long time, thinking he would never be able to fall asleep himself, with her so fragrant and warm in his arms.

But to his shock, the next time he opened his eyes,

it was broad daylight. Sometime in the night, he must have stretched out on the seat with his back to the squabs, for she lay stretched atop him. Her raven curls had come loose from their pins, and he couldn't resist the urge to stroke them.

Rousing, she opened her eyes to stare up at him in clear confusion.

"Good morning . . . Lisette," he murmured, choking off the word *dearling* just in time.

"Max." A soft smile touched her lips that made his heart soar. Then, to his chagrin, she came fully awake and cried, "Max!" and threw herself off him and onto the other seat.

She wouldn't look at him as she straightened her skirts. "I'm so sorry. I don't know how I ended up using you for a bed."

"It's all right. I didn't mind."

If that was the closest he could get to having her in his arms, even temporarily, he would take it.

"I suppose I look a fright," she murmured, running her fingers through her wild curls.

"You couldn't look a fright if you tried."

She shot him a wary glance, then gazed out the window. "We made good time, didn't we? We can't be more than an hour from Paris. I think we should go to Tristan's lodgings and see what we can find out there. That will also give us a chance to make ourselves presentable before we talk to Vidocq."

Clamping down on a burst of jealousy, he said, "We don't have time to dillydally, Lisette. Let's only spend as much time at your brother's as we need, assuming that he doesn't turn out to be there."

"All right."

"And we can consult with Vidocq, but if he doesn't know anything—"

"We will have to speak to the head of the Sûreté. I understand."

"Good." Because no matter how tempting he found her, he wouldn't relent in getting to the bottom of this matter with his brother and Bonnaud.

To Maximilian's surprise, Bonnaud's lodgings turned out to be in the Faubourg Saint-Germain, an aristocratic area of the city. Either the man had done well for himself in Paris, or he had a friend in high places who'd rented to him.

But as it turned out, his street, the rue de l'Hirondelle, was mean and narrow and his rooms, situated in a slice of the block of buildings, looked deserted. When they entered using Lisette's key, it was clear no one had lived there in some weeks. Dust lay thick upon the furniture and the carpetless floors.

"What next?" he asked. "Does your brother have a desk or safe where he might have kept notes or letters regarding his business affairs? We might trace him that way."

"The room he used as a study is through there." She pointed to a closed door. "I suppose we might find something in his records."

A voice speaking French came from the doorway. "It's about time you returned for a visit, my angel."

Maximilian turned to see an imposingly tall man in his fifties enter the room. Despite his bushy eyebrows, the fellow was what some might consider attractive, with a sanguine complexion, eyes of bright blue, and fair, curly hair.

"Vidocq!" Lisette cried and ran over to press a kiss to the man's cheek.

Tensing, Maximilian watched the blasted investigator, but Vidocq's expression was more like that of an indulgent father than of an impassioned lover.

"I suppose you are looking for your brother," Vidocq continued in French, casting Maximilian a shuttered glance.

"We are indeed," Lisette replied. "This is Maximilian Cale. He is in something of a hurry to find Tristan."

Maximilian was pleased that she hadn't introduced him as the Duke of Lyons. If they could learn of Tristan's whereabouts without having to reveal his full identity, so much the better for her reputation, especially if Vidocq could be counted on to be discreet.

"I've heard much of you, sir," Maximilian said in French, holding his hand out to the man.

"How odd," the man said in English, refusing to take Maximilian's hand. "Because I have heard nothing of *you*. At least not from my little angel."

With an anxious glance at Maximilian, Lisette switched to English as well. "Forgive me, Vidocq, but we don't have much time. We have urgent need of Tristan. So if you know where he is—"

"I know where he was headed when he left here." Vidocq stared hard at Maximilian. "But I will only tell you after you explain why you're traveling alone with the Duke of Lyons."

As Maximilian groaned, Lisette said, "You *know* who Max is?"

"Of course. The Cale family had dealings with the police when they came here in search of the young heir years ago. The name of their surviving son was mentioned often. It's a hard name to forget."

"Especially for a man rumored to have an excellent memory," Maximilian said dully. He couldn't believe he hadn't considered the possibility that Vidocq might know of his family. Father's investigator had probably consulted with the Paris police a number of times in the course of his search.

"Come," Vidocq said, offering Lisette his arm, "let us go to my house where we can be more comfortable. You will join me for *le déjeuner* and tell me what this is all about. Then I will tell you where Tristan was headed last." He cast Maximilian a veiled glance. "I suspect that you will both find it most interesting."

Maximilian forced a smile. "We would appreciate any help you can give, sir," he said, "and we'd be honored to join you for breakfast." Even if he did feel as if he'd just stumbled onto a stage without a script.

Vidocq's house turned out to be through a courtyard into the next building. When Maximilian shot Lisette a questioning look as they headed into the more spacious rooms, she murmured, "Tristan rents from Vidocq."

As soon as they were seated in a small but expensively decorated dining room with servants scurrying off to arrange their breakfast, Vidocq turned to Lisette with a bright smile. "I have found a publisher for my memoirs. I don't suppose you would consider moving back here to help me edit them, my angel?"

"Your 'angel' already has a position helping Mr. Manton with his business in London," Maximilian said tightly, inexplicably annoyed at the possibility of Lisette returning to Paris to live. "I understand it's a very good position."

"And now you speak for her, too, Your Grace?" Vidocq said smoothly. "In addition to dragging her about the country without a chaperone and ruining her reputation so she will never be able to find a respectable husband?"

"Enough, you two," Lisette cut in with a dark glance at Maximilian. She turned to Vidocq. "I came of my own accord. We're traveling as a married couple: plain Mr. Kale, the land agent, and his wife."

At that moment, one of the servants reentered the room, and Lisette said in French, "If you would please give us a few moments . . ."

The servant nodded and left.

Lisette scowled at Vidocq. "If you really do care about me, then you must maintain the fiction in front of the servants. My neighbors already think I got married. And His Grace pointed out that it will be easy for me to tell people that my husband died conveniently while we were abroad."

At Vidocq's snort, she added, "You are likely the only

person in the world who would recognize the duke's actual name. Not a single person has questioned our disguise."

"Disguise!" Vidocq said. "It's hardly a disguise when you use real names." He cast Maximilian's clothing a contemptuous glance. "And His Grace looks as much like a land agent as I do a duke. His fingernails are too clean, he wears fine linen beneath that fustian suit, and he speaks with an Etonian clip."

"Oh, for God's sake—" Maximilian began.

"You see?" Vidocq said. "Like that."

"Stop it!" Lisette chided. "Tell me where Tristan is, before His Grace challenges you to a duel or something else absurd. He's very volatile."

"I am not," Maximilian grumbled.

She merely raised an eyebrow at him, then scowled at Vidocq. "Tristan, if you please?"

"Very well," Vidocq said. "He left two months ago, pursuing an escaped forger up north to Belgium."

"Belgium!" Maximilian exclaimed.

"Isn't Belgium where your brother was found dead?" Lisette asked.

Maximilian leaned forward, his eyes boring into Vidocq. "*Where* in Belgium was Bonnaud headed?"

"Antwerp," Vidocq said. "Which makes it very curious that you are here looking for him, Your Grace, because Antwerp is close to—"

"I know what it's close to," Maximilian bit out.

Vidocq's eyes narrowed. He glanced at Lisette, then

back at Maximilian. "Tell me, does my little angel know about your family?"

Maximilian released a low oath.

That brought Vidocq's thick eyebrows up a notch. "I thought not. And you don't want her to know, do you?"

"But you're going to tell her anyway, I suppose," Maximilian countered, feeling his stomach twist into a knot.

Vidocq shrugged. "She will find out sooner or later." His voice hardened. "Better that it be sooner if you are trying to take her into your bed."

"Vidocq!" Lisette cried, a blush staining her cheeks. "He is not . . . we are not . . ."

"I'm not blind, my angel." Vidocq's gaze never left Maximilian's face. "I see how he looks at you. I see how you look at him. And since he is a duke and marriage is not all that likely, that leaves only—"

"Tread lightly, old man," Maximilian bit out, "or I might challenge you to that duel to uphold her honor." He steadied a dark gaze on the man.

Vidocq sat back to stare at him consideringly, though without apparent fear.

Lisette glanced from Maximilian to Vidocq. "What is it that Max isn't telling me about his family? What is Antwerp close to?"

With this new information, there was no way to avoid telling her the truth.

"Antwerp is close to a town called Gheel," Maximilian said, his throat suddenly tight and raw. "Gheel is sometimes referred to as the Colony of Maniacs, because it's where many of the mad go in a last attempt to get cured."

He gave a shaky breath. "It's also where my insane great-uncle took my brother in the final years after kidnapping him. And where they both died in a fire."

13

AT THAT MOMENT, the servants entered with a typical Parisian breakfast—roast beef and chicken, pastries, grapes and pears, a ragout, and some good bread and cheese, not to mention tea, coffee, and *vin ordinaire*.

It was an excellent distraction for Lisette, since she could hardly take in what Max had just revealed. It wasn't only his words that stunned her, either—it was his haunted tone. He looked suddenly weary, and she wanted nothing more than to comfort him.

But not in front of Vidocq. Her old friend had already guessed too much about her and Max. And why had Max not told her this, anyway?

Because he was a duke. Dukes didn't talk about weakness or illness. They didn't reveal dark secrets about their families.

Still, it hurt that he hadn't felt he could trust her with the knowledge. She remembered what he'd said when she'd asked who the kidnapper was: *some blackguard*. That left out an awful lot.

"So, Max," she said flatly after Vidocq dismissed the servants, "it was your great-uncle who kidnapped your brother. Why?"

"I wish I knew. I didn't even know he was the one to do it until the fire." His tone hardened. "I was almost four when Peter disappeared; Father just told me he'd been stolen by a blackguard. For years, I feared that there were blackguards everywhere waiting in the bushes to steal me from my parents."

"Oh, Max, that's awful," she said in a sympathetic tone that had Vidocq raising an eyebrow at her. She ignored him.

Max seemed to grow even tenser. "When I got old enough to question what I'd been told, my parents said they had investigators searching England and America for Peter. They told me they had no idea who'd taken him. That was a lie. Yet they held to that until after the fire, when they couldn't keep it from me anymore."

She remembered what he'd said about being lied to by his family. *This* was what he'd meant. "Perhaps they didn't know that the kidnapper was your great-uncle."

"They had to know." Max served himself some food. "It took me years to piece together the whole tale, but apparently my great-uncle Nigel, a dashing naval captain, was rather wild. He and Father were only ten years apart, so they used to go drinking together whenever Uncle Nigel was on leave, before Father married. Or so I was able to make out from things Father said and stories I heard from other family members. It rather surprised me. Father never seemed the wild type."

Max picked at a hot roll. "And apparently Father's wild days didn't last long. A couple of years after marrying Mother, Father quarreled bitterly with Uncle Nigel one night. I can only assume that Father refused to be his companion in sin anymore. Whatever provoked it, my great-uncle went back to his ship and wouldn't have anything more to do with the family."

He stared blankly forward as if looking into the past. "They heard nothing from him for five years. Then the Peace of Amiens came, and the war between France and England ceased. Uncle Nigel, who was in his early forties by then, requested and was granted retirement. He came to Marsbury House wanting to make amends, but I gather it didn't go well. A few days later, he disappeared . . . and so did Peter."

Lisette frowned as she poured tea for her and Max. "Then it was obvious who took him. If your parents knew that, why couldn't they find your brother?"

"He left no word with the navy or anyone else of where he was going. My parents assumed he was in England somewhere. They sent investigators across the country, but my great-uncle and brother had vanished. Father would have sent men to the Continent, too, but by then the war had resumed, and no one could travel from England to France."

"Why didn't the authorities attempt to find him?" Vidocq asked.

"They, too, tried, but their hands were somewhat

tied. My parents inexplicably refused to let them speak about my great-uncle to the press." A faint hint of disgust entered his voice. "I think Father was mortified at the idea of a member of his family doing such a thing. And I suspect he always hoped that my great-uncle would just bring Peter home one day, when Uncle Nigel got tired of caring for a child."

"So your great-uncle raised Peter in Gheel?" Lisette asked as she served herself some ragout.

"We don't think so, but I never heard where he was before that." Max ate a moment in silence. "You have to understand—when the fire happened, no one knew of their connection to us. Uncle Nigel told everyone Peter was his son and never mentioned his relations, of course. He and Peter even went by their real names. But it was Belgium during the war—who would associate Peter Cale with the missing heir to the English Duke of Lyons, especially thirteen years after the kidnapping?"

He dragged in a heavy breath. "Fortunately, after the fire, someone had the foresight to save the ring my uncle was wearing, or later they wouldn't even have been able to identify for certain who he'd been."

Lisette shuddered to think that Max might have gone his whole life never knowing what happened. "How did your family even learn about the fire?"

"The deaths were eventually reported in the Paris papers, which was noticed by the investigator Father had hired shortly after Napoleon's exile to Elba. The man wrote to my father. While we were en route to

Paris, the investigator went to Gheel to see what he could learn. Of course, by the time he got there, the bodies had long been buried. He questioned the residents and brought the ring back for my father."

Max gave a long sigh. "He did learn that my great-uncle had a lawyer in Paris, and apparently my father spoke to the man, but the attorney had been entirely unaware of my uncle's perfidy. Or so I was told."

"Did your investigator discover anything in Gheel about why your great-uncle kidnapped your brother?" Vidocq asked.

"No. No one knew anything about that."

"The rift between your father and your great-uncle must have provoked it," Lisette put in. "Clearly your great-uncle did it to get back at your father."

"That's one explanation," Max said tightly. "Although kidnapping Father's heir seems rather extreme. And he couldn't have done it for money either, since at the time he was far down the line in terms of heirs. I was second in line, so why not kidnap me, too? It's never made any sense to me."

Vidocq cut his roast beef into precise squares. "Your uncle might initially have acted impulsively. The way you've described him points to a man who rarely thinks ahead. But once the deed was done and his temper cooled, he found himself in a quandary. If he returned your brother, he would face a possible trial as a kidnapper, perhaps even execution. Perhaps he just decided to raise the boy himself to avoid the consequences of returning him."

"I suppose," Max said. "Then there's always my mother's explanation—that he was simply insane. The investigator did determine that Uncle Nigel was in Gheel for that reason. And having read some about the place, I know that they allow their madmen to live peaceably with a family who is hired to look after them. I suppose since Peter was believed to be his son, he lived with them, too."

"Madness *will* cause people to do strange things." Vidocq steadied his gaze on Max. "As you well know, Your Grace."

Before Lisette could wonder at that, Max scowled at Vidocq. "I don't see how any of this helps us find Bonnaud."

"You still haven't said why you're looking for him." Vidocq drank some wine. "What has Tristan got to do with your family troubles?"

"Tristan sent the duke a note implying that Peter might be alive," Lisette explained. "He said a friend of his had Peter's handkerchief. And given that Tristan was recently in that part of Belgium, it might even be true."

Max eyed her askance. "Or *because* he was in that part of Belgium, he heard the full tale of my brother's death and decided to capitalize on it. When we determined that Peter was dead, we said no more to the press than that he died in a fire on the Continent. That was the official story, and that's the story your brother knew years ago when I met him."

Broadening his gaze to include Vidocq, he added, "You said he went to Belgium in pursuit of a forger.

Well, perhaps he struck a deal with the man and convinced him to produce the copy of the handkerchief in exchange for Bonnaud's agreeing to let him go."

Before Lisette could protest that outrageous supposition, Vidocq said, "Tristan would never do that. He is a man of character."

"For a horse thief," Max snapped. When Vidocq shot her a surprised glance, Max added, "Yes, I know all about his criminal past. Rathmoor sent someone to follow us, which is why Lisette had to tell me about it—so we could take measures to evade the man."

"Then you know why Tristan stole that horse," Vidocq countered. "To save his family. I do not blame him for that."

"Obviously, since you hired him," Max muttered.

"I hired him because he was clever and willing to learn. I saw potential. And I was right about him, too. He's very good at what he does."

"What he does is act as an agent for the secret police, which requires some degree of deception. Perhaps he thought it was time he used his talents for his own good. And with a forger in his power—"

"You claimed that the handkerchief couldn't be copied," Lisette said hotly.

"Bonnaud doesn't know that," Max pointed out. "He might have thought it possible. We never saw the end result, did we?"

"If Tristan was so convinced he could deceive you with an elaborate fraud," she answered, "then why didn't he show up in London?"

Vidocq snorted. "Because Tristan would never go to London."

"That's what *I* said!" Lisette glared at Max. "But he won't listen to me. I keep telling him it makes no sense. Tristan simply wouldn't risk getting caught."

Max shot her a dark glance. "But a man would hazard much for a chance at a ducal fortune. If he and the forger were in it together—"

"For all you know," she shot back, "the forger kidnapped him and forged the note."

"Then how did the forger know of my previous connection to your brother? If the forger is involved, they have to be in it together." Max sat back to cross his arms over his chest. "*Your* theory is the one that doesn't make sense."

Vidocq muttered a curse under his breath. "You might as well be married, given how you two quarrel. Would one of you explain all your nonsense about Tristan being in London?"

Max took out the note and the rubbing of the handkerchief that Tristan had sent, then tossed them across the table to Vidocq. "I got this from Bonnaud a few days ago. That's what sent us traveling here in search of him. He summoned me to meet with him and then didn't show up."

His curiosity obviously roused, Vidocq took out a pair of spectacles to examine the note more closely. Without a word, he left the room, only to return moments later with another sheet of paper. Shoving aside his plate, he laid Tristan's note beside the other sheet, which Lisette could see held Tristan's signature, too.

As Lisette ate a pastry and Max began to pick apart a chicken leg, Vidocq glanced back and forth between the sheets repeatedly. Finally he announced, "I can say for certain that the note isn't forged. Tristan did write it."

"Yes, but where was it sent from?" Max growled. "Was he actually in London? And where did he disappear to after he wrote it?"

"It's very strange," Vidocq remarked. "This bit about not trusting his messenger—he's being evasive."

"I could figure that out myself," Max grumbled.

Vidocq smelled the note and rubbed the paper between his fingers.

"I don't think the paper will up and announce where it's been," Max said dryly.

Lisette kicked him under the table. When his gaze snapped to her, she said, "Let Vidocq work. This is his forte. He made his fortune developing tamperproof paper for banks."

"And paper *can* tell you where it's been," Vidocq added with a sharp glance at Lisette. "I would say from the uneven texture that this paper has been someplace where it absorbed moisture over time."

"At sea, perhaps?" Lisette said.

"Perhaps." Next Vidocq examined the rubbing of the handkerchief. "And this is an actual rubbing, not some artist's rendition. The paper is raised in the right places."

Max blinked. "It didn't occur to me that an artist could create a rubbing."

"A forger would certainly be able to fool the eye. But fooling the hand would be virtually impossible." Vidocq removed his spectacles. "If the two of you can remain in Paris today, I will go to the Sûreté and see what they can tell me about Tristan's mission. At least I can learn if Tristan reported having found the forger. Then we can rule out the possibility that he is working with the man. His superior might even know exactly where Tristan was headed next."

"I wanted to speak to the chief of the Sûreté first myself, but she wouldn't let me," Max said with a nod at Lisette.

"Because you wanted to get Tristan dismissed!" Lisette countered. "You admitted it!"

"The chief wouldn't have told you anything, anyway," Vidocq said smoothly. "You're an English duke. He would have flattered you and promised to look into the matter, and then, as Lisette says, he would have dismissed Tristan without a hearing. The man is an arse."

"A *stupid* arse," Lisette muttered. "He's taking his best agent for granted."

"The man doesn't recognize brilliance, or even mere competence," Vidocq said. "He cares only whether the rules are followed. And Tristan always cared more about results than the methods required to get them."

"So if this chief doesn't appreciate 'brilliance,'" Max

said with the faintest sneer, "how will you get him to tell you the information you need?"

"Certainly not by consulting him. Better to keep him out of it entirely." Vidocq gave his sly smile. "I have connections, others I can talk to. Don't worry—I'll know everything the Sûreté knows about Tristan by nightfall."

"That will give us time to have a more thorough look at Tristan's house," Lisette said. "We might find something there to tell us who this friend of his is. The one he thinks is Peter."

Max nodded. "It's worth a try."

"And it will give His Grace a chance to tell you all the parts of the story he's left out about his family," Vidocq said, his gaze on Max.

The color drained from Max's face. "Thank you for reminding me, Vidocq." Max stared grimly into his cup of tea. "Aren't you supposed to be going somewhere?"

Vidocq rose. "If you have not told her by the time I return, I will tell her myself."

"I understand." Max drew himself up. "It doesn't matter if she knows anyway," he added in a tone that told Lisette that it mattered very much to him. "She was bound to learn of it eventually."

"Very well. Then I'm off to the Sûreté. The two of you should finish your *déjeuner*. You are welcome to stay as long as you like, either here or at Tristan's rooms. Ask my servants for whatever you need, 'Mr. Kale.' They will be happy to attend you. They know Lisette well."

He walked over to brush a kiss to Lisette's forehead, then murmured in French, "Careful, my angel. You're playing a dangerous game with this duke."

She leaned up to whisper in his ear, "He's not as bad as you seem to think."

Vidocq looked skeptical but didn't answer. He merely tipped his head to Max and left.

She returned to her breakfast, all too aware of Max's gaze on her as she bit into a pear. He wasn't eating. Instead, he sat there drinking tea and tearing the remainder of his roll into crumbs.

It broke her heart. He looked so lost. "Max, I don't know why Vidocq is suddenly so eager to pry into a stranger's affairs, but—"

"He only wants to protect you." He gave a choked laugh. "I certainly understand that."

His surprising defense of Vidocq caught her off guard. "Do you?"

Max looked bleak. "You seem very . . . comfortable together."

"We are," she said simply. "He's like a father to me."

"I could tell."

At least he didn't say it with the jealous edge he'd had last night. She relaxed a fraction. "He hired Tristan at a time when Maman and I desperately needed the funds. Then, after Maman died, Vidocq gave me a position as well. So I am very grateful to him." After wiping her mouth with the napkin, she rose from the table. "But that does not mean that I do whatever he says."

She'd seen enough to know that Max's pride and

dignity had been bludgeoned rather thoroughly today. If she truly cared about him, she needed to give him his privacy. No matter what Vidocq said.

In that moment, she made a decision. "Just ignore Vidocq's demands that you tell me the 'truth.' You may keep your secrets, Max. They are of no concern to me."

14

Lisette was tired of trying to figure Max out, tired of how it obsessed her. If he wanted to close himself off from anyone who might care about him, then she would let him.

With that resolve, she left the table and headed out the dining room door. One of the servants called to her in French from the other end of the hall, "Is everything all right, miss? Is there anything we can get for you?"

"No, nothing," she responded. "We won't require your services any further this afternoon. We have some work to do at my brother's lodgings."

"Very good, miss," the servant said.

As Lisette hurried down the hall, she heard Max's chair scrape in the dining room. Then he was striding after her as she passed through Vidocq's house and the courtyard to the other house.

"My secrets are of more concern to you than you realize," Max clipped out as they entered Tristan's rooms.

When she would have kept going through Tristan's small public area to the study, Max hurried ahead of her to block her path. "My secrets are the reason I cannot marry you. That I *will* not marry you."

He wore that shuttered look that always made her feel as if she should tread softly. Only this time, she could see the pain behind it.

Suddenly her heart was pounding. It was foolish of her, but no matter what she'd told herself until now, no matter what she'd told *him*, she wanted very much to be his wife. And the way he kept bringing it up told her that it was something he'd considered.

Either that, or he was just like Father—playing with her emotions.

She forced her voice to be light. "Don't tell me you have a secret wife stashed away somewhere, like the English king with his Mrs. Fitzherbert."

His dry laugh relieved her. "No, the only secret relation I have may be a brother. Or not. I no longer know."

She pounced on that to avoid revisiting his refusal to marry her. She didn't think she could bear to hear his reason for it. It must be serious indeed if Vidocq knew of it. "So do you now think that Tristan might actually have found your brother?"

"It's possible, I suppose," he said. "The tale of the fire has always left me with too many questions. If my uncle was mad, how was he sane enough to go to Gheel to seek a cure? Or was he put there? And if the authorities jailed him there, as they sometimes do violent madmen, why aren't there records of it? The trouble is,

I will never be able to get answers to my questions. The investigator is long dead, and the reports he gave to my father are gone."

She blinked. "Why?"

"My father burned them not long before he died."

That shocked her. "But that . . . that makes no sense! Why would he do such a mad thing?" She instantly regretted her poor choice of words.

But Max just said flatly, "Probably because he *was* mad."

A sudden unnamable fear seized her heart. "What do you mean?"

"That's what Vidocq wanted you to know." He gave a shuddering breath. "I not only had a great-uncle who went insane in his later years, but a father who did so as well. And given such a history, it is likely that I, too, will go mad before I die."

Mad? He thought he was going to go *mad*? Her blood ran cold. Her poor dear Max! *This* was the secret he'd been keeping from her?

Without waiting for her response, Max turned on his heel and stalked off to Tristan's study.

Her mind raced as she used the new information to reexamine everything he'd said and done in the past few days. But one thing stood out above the rest. "No," she said as she hurried after him.

That made him halt, then whirl to face her. "What do you mean, *no*?"

"Just because your father and great-uncle went insane is no reason to believe that you will, too."

"God help me, Lisette, you have to listen to—"

"No! I won't!" Perhaps it was only desperation driving her, but she knew in her heart that he was making a leap he should not. "Was your grandfather mad? And your great-grandfather?"

He stared bleakly at her. "No, but that doesn't mean anything."

"Of course it does! You're not like your father, I'm sure of it. You're the sanest man I know."

"For *now* I am. Who knows what I will be in ten or twenty years? It didn't strike them until they were older."

She stared at him, comprehension dawning. "Is this why you don't let anyone near? Because you have this awful fear hanging over your head that you will end up insane?"

"Do not patronize me!" he ground out. She flinched, and he softened his tone. "I didn't let you close because I didn't want you to know." His eyes, so deeply haunted, searched her face. "For the first time in my life, a woman regarded me without prejudice, without measuring me by my wealth *or* by the gossip about my family."

The yearning in his face made her heart ache for him.

"You were the only woman who didn't look at me and wonder, every time I said anything out of the ordinary, 'Is it starting? Will he pick up a fork any moment and jab me with it?'"

His voice turned cold. "That's how society found out about Father. One day at a dinner with the Duke of Wellington, he imagined he saw some assailant, and he stuck a fork in the arm of one of Wellington's fine guests. After that, there was no hiding the fact that he was losing his mind." He steadied a hard gaze on her. "And there was also no hiding the fact that I was likely to be the same."

"If that is what people in your fine circles have been telling you, then they are mad, too," she said.

"Perhaps," he gritted out. "But they still watch me, wait for me to show signs of it. And *I* know, if no one else does, that with two such relations in my family, I am very likely to inherit it."

She could see that he really believed it. Fighting back tears, she laid her hand on his arm, but he shook it off. "Don't pity me either, damn it!" he growled, anger flaring in his face.

But this time she wouldn't let him push her away. "Do not mistake concern for pity." She choked down her tears, struggling against the urge to weep for all he'd suffered. "I am sorry for what you've endured, but you won't convince me that it means you're destined for the same fate. I can't believe it. I *won't* believe it."

"That's the other reason I didn't tell you about Father. Because I knew you would ignore the obvious." He gave a harsh laugh. "The same woman who believes in her brother's goodness, even when everything points in the other direction, is certainly not going to believe that a man who seems perfectly sane right now might not remain so." He lowered his voice to an aching murmur. "Especially when it's a man she cares about."

Her heart leaped into her throat. "I do care about you. Too much to let you go on fearing that you might have such an awful future. Sometimes you just have to ignore your fears."

"The way you ignore yours?" he clipped out.

She froze. "What are you talking about?"

"You're so afraid you'll end up like your mother, left alone with a couple of children and no means to take care of them. So afraid that men will disappoint you. I don't see you ignoring *your* fears, Lisette."

He was right. She'd been so busy protecting herself against having her heart trampled by the duke that she hadn't noticed the tortured man inside the golden castle.

Well, she was certainly noticing now. This was the secret that kept him rigid and remote and afraid of his own desires, fearing that one little slip would reveal some lurking madness. It was the secret that made him ache for all he'd lost when his brother had died, leaving him to inherit the dukedom.

It was also the secret that made him behave kindly at times. Because he knew what it was like to be covertly mocked. Who would have guessed that she and a duke would have such an essential thing in common?

"Yes, it's true," she managed as she fought back the sympathy she was certain must show on her face. "I've let my fears govern my life far too long. But I begin to think I cut myself off from a great deal in the process. Perhaps it's time I stop living in my mother's past."

Clearly that wasn't the response he'd expected, for he began shaking his head. "You're wise to worry about men, and most assuredly about me. I will definitely disappoint you."

"At least you never lie to me," she said. "You aren't like Father, who used the hope of a marriage to get Mother into his bed. You never once claimed that we could have anything beyond your . . . your . . ."

"Wild passion for you that possesses me despite all my attempts to stomp it out?" His gaze burned into hers. "No. But that doesn't make this any easier."

She didn't *want* to make it easier for him to throw his life away out of some fear that might never come to pass. "So you mean never to marry?" she asked bluntly. "Or is it just me you are determined you 'can't marry'?"

He squared his shoulders. "Whether I marry depends largely on whether Peter is alive. If he's not, I have to provide an heir for the dukedom. There's no one to inherit, and I refuse to break up all my property and sell it. I have tenants who depend on me, thousands of servants at my estates—I cannot let them down by not marrying."

That confused her. "So you do mean to marry."

"If Peter isn't alive, yes. But it will have to be a particular kind of match."

"And what kind is that?" she managed.

"I watched my mother die slowly inside as my father went mad. She was so destroyed by it that I swore I'd never put a woman I cared about through that. Nor one who cared about me." When she frowned, he added, "But there are women who would gladly forego a love match for the privilege of being a duchess. Women who care more about their rank and station than about affection, whose hearts won't break when they see their husbands go mad, as long as they know that their place in society is assured for all time."

"And you actually think you *want* that sort of woman taking care of you if you should go mad?" she cried. "Some . . . some grasping harpy who will stand over your bed waiting for you to *die?*"

He paled at her blunt description. "Better that than a weeping half widow, half wife, living in hell for as long as the madness lasts. For my father, it lasted four years. *Four years,* Lisette. Imagine watching someone you care about forget everything he ever was. To go from being a man of great position to a joke whispered about in the halls of fine houses."

"That doesn't mean that the answer is to find someone who *doesn't* care about you."

"It will take someone like that to agree to my conditions." Obstinacy made his jaw go taut. "Any woman I marry must agree to give me over to caretakers once the madness begins. My mother wasted away trying to care for my father in his final days, which is why she died only a year later."

"Perhaps she just missed him," Lisette said gently. "Married couples often follow each other into death, especially if they were particularly close."

"That's not why," he bit out. "She died wracked by a foolish guilt. She blamed herself for his death, because he died after she administered some laudanum to help him sleep. That was after she spent the years of his madness carrying him about the Continent seeking a cure, during which I accompanied her."

Ah, so that was why he'd traveled so much, why he had a private yacht. "I would have done the same thing."

"Exactly!" he ground out. "You would never agree to leave my welfare to others. You would never wash your hands of me. You're not that kind of woman."

"Certainly not, thank God!" Outraged over his idea of the only marriage allowed him, she asked, "Has it ever occurred to you that married couples endure watching their spouses grow old and feeble and senile all the time? That it's part of marriage? A hard part, to be sure, but not so hard that one just gives up on the institution altogether."

"That's not the same thing." He glared down at her. "They've had a lifetime together, plenty of time to be with each other, to relish the good parts of marriage, so they can be sustained through the bad parts."

"Did my father have a lifetime with his wife, who died bearing Dom? No, he did not. And that happens more often than you think. People die young sometimes. That's life."

She cupped his dear, tormented face in her hands. "That's why you must savor it while you can. Because you never know when it will be snatched away. Papa kept putting off what he knew he must do, sure that he would have time later. And later never came."

"I'm not putting it off," he said softly, covering her hands with his. "I'm just not doing it at all." His gaze grew fierce. "And that's why if Peter *is* alive, I won't marry anyone. Let him be the one to pass on the legacy of madness if he wants. It will be out of my hands then, thank God."

He stepped away and began to pace. "Father's will made no provisions for my inheritance or position in the family if Peter is alive, so I'll have to depend on my brother's largesse. Which means I might not . . . be able to afford the doctors and attendants needed to deal with someone gone mad. So I won't inflict that burden on a wife, too."

She marched up to catch him by the arm and halt him. "Instead, you mean to cut yourself off from anyone who might care about you? To live some sterile existence in a cold and loveless marriage or without any marriage at all? That's your plan for your future?"

Stiffening, he met her gaze with an angry one. "You can't possibly understand. It is far easier for me not to let myself . . . care about a woman than it is to care about her with the knowledge of what a future with me will bring her."

"First of all, you don't know for certain what your future might bring. None of us do." When he started to answer, she pressed a finger to his lips. "And secondly, it's too late to keep yourself from caring." She caressed his stubbled cheek. "You already care. About me. You said so last night. Unless that was a lie."

"You know that it was not," he rasped.

Because he never lied. And the full reason for that hit her. He never lied, because his parents had lied to him from his childhood on. Because madness itself was one giant lie, playing tricks on one's mind.

That was why he so abhorred deception. And why she could be nothing but honest with him.

It was time to be honest with herself, too. Aside from her brothers, she'd never met a man as honorable and fine as him. So tossing him aside because he didn't meet the stringent conditions she'd created to protect herself from heartache seemed ludicrous.

She might only have one chance with him, and this was it. Once they found Tristan, anything could happen. But for these few hours, she wanted to be his, to know what it was like to lie in the arms of a man she loved.

Loved? No, she wasn't *that* foolish. Because he would almost certainly break her heart.

But it didn't matter. If he was to put aside his fears, then she would have to put hers aside first. "If you care about me, then show me." She looped her arms about his neck. "Because Lord knows I care about you."

His expression turned stark, raw. "Lisette, don't do this."

"Care about you? Want you? That won't go away just because you have decided it must." She could feel the tension in him, the way he held himself apart still, as if to deny his own desires by sheer will.

He was fighting very hard not to react. "What happened to your not wanting to be a duke's mistress?" he choked out.

"I have no desire to be *any* man's mistress." Giving in to the impulse to throw caution to the wind, she pressed herself against his rigid body. "But that doesn't mean I want to spend my life as a nun, either."

That got a very firm reaction, both in the flex of his jaw above, and in the flex of . . . something else entirely below.

He was obviously aware of it, too, for he grabbed her arms as if to pull them from around his neck. "I am not going to ruin you for any other man."

She held on to his neck, determined to win what she wanted—him in her bed. "Too late. Do you really think I could even look at another man after you?"

When heat sparked in his eyes and he clutched her arms more like a man drowning than one fighting, she pressed her advantage.

"If I am to spend the rest of my life without you because of your conditions and your rules and your fears for the future, then at the very least give me something to remember and let me have one afternoon in your bed."

The word *bed* had the desired effect. He stared at her a long moment, his internal struggle evident in every chiseled line of his bold features.

Then he muttered, "I was right—you really are a wicked, wicked woman."

And his mouth crashed down on hers.

15

MAXIMILIAN KNEW HE shouldn't be doing this, but she hadn't balked when she'd heard about the family curse. She hadn't looked at him any differently. Throughout it all, she'd remained Lisette. *His* Lisette.

Fisting his hands in the puffy sleeves of her gown, he kissed her wildly, exuberantly. He ravished her mouth, then her jaw, then her throat, and when he felt her pulse leap beneath his lips and heard her soft, sweet moans, he started at the beginning again.

He told himself he would just kiss her long enough to savor this one sweet moment. He told himself he would put her away from him after he'd drunk his fill. But he knew he lied. The minute she'd started fighting for him, he'd started losing the battle to resist her.

And how could he ever end this when her fevered responses showed her to be willing and just as eager as he?

"We should stop," he growled against her throat. "Someone will come in."

"No, they won't." She shoved his coat off his shoulders. "Vidocq won't be back for hours, and I already told the servants we didn't need them."

Even as that fired his imagination—and his desire— it spiked his alarm. Especially when she began to undo his waistcoat buttons.

Grabbing her hands, he tried to set her firmly from him. "What are you doing, dearling?"

She stared up at him with a minxish tilt to her lips. "Tempting you," she murmured, exactly as he'd done in Brighton. Then, with eyes gleaming, she rubbed her lower body against his rapidly hardening cock and added, "And it seems to be working rather well."

God help him. When had she turned into such a talented seductress? "You mustn't do this," he choked out.

"It's your fault." She lifted the hand that still gripped hers and pressed it against her breast until he could feel her taut nipple even through her gown. "You started it. You introduced me to desire, taught me to feel it, to want it. So the least you can do is satisfy the urges that you aroused."

When she swept his hand over her breast again, he groaned and released her, but only so he could fondle her himself as he ached to do. Flashing him a temptress's smile, she stretched up to kiss him.

He caught her about the waist with one hand so he could knead her breast with the other while he ravaged her mouth over and over. She tasted like butter and honey, so damned delicious he could scarcely keep from eating her up.

Confound it to blazes, he was losing this battle. He'd wanted her too long, needed her too long. His blood sang, *More. Now. More of Lisette*, and his body heeded the cry with great enthusiasm.

After all, he didn't have to take her innocence. They could just do what they'd done in the carriage—give each other pleasure. He could satisfy her enough to sate her curiosity—and take the edge off his hunger—without ruining her.

With that decided, he swept her up in his arms and growled, "Where?"

She blinked but caught him around the neck like a wild rose sending out runners, then cast him a sultry look that made his blood run hot. "My bedchamber." She nodded to a half-open door next to her brother's study. "There."

"You have a bedchamber here?" he asked even as he strode toward it.

"I lived with Tristan for three years after Maman died."

"Ah, right." At the moment it was all he could do to remember his own name, with her lying soft and fragrant and yielding in his arms.

He carried her inside the high-ceilinged room, then stopped short. Papered in a lavender-and-white pattern with tiny violets trailing along the stripes, the bedchamber was quite a feminine sanctum. Ribbon embroidery adorned every chair and covering, and the draperies were lacy and frilly.

Then Lisette was peeling off his waistcoat and unbuttoning his shirt, and every lucid thought fled. All he saw was her trying to seduce him with a mixture of naïveté and anticipation that only a virgin could exhibit. It made his breath race and his blood turn to fire, even as he reminded himself that he was *not* going to take that innocence.

Giving him a quick, nervous smile, she turned her back to him. "You'll have to undo my gown. I can't manage it."

He hesitated. Holding to his plan to only pleasure her would be decidedly more difficult if they were both entirely naked. But he couldn't bear to give up his one chance at seeing what lay beneath the nightdress that had tantalized his thoughts over the past few days.

With an urgency born of a fervent need to touch her and hold her and see her as Nature had intended her, he stripped her down to her shift, then turned her back to face him.

"Take it off," he growled, wanting to watch her do it.

She gazed at him from beneath lowered lashes. "Only after you take off your clothes, too."

He didn't hesitate. He wanted her hands on him, wanted her running those long, delicate fingers down his chest and belly and straight to the cock that was so hard for her, it was already fighting to get free of his trousers.

Once he'd undressed down to his drawers, he said hoarsely, "I want to see you naked, dearling. Let me see you."

Suddenly shy, she dropped her gaze and concentrated on untying her shift. Then she pulled it over her head and let it drift to the floor, and he thought he'd died and gone to heaven.

Or perhaps hell, because the sight of her, so perfect, so beautiful, made him want more than he could ever allow himself to have.

Her skin was like fine porcelain that begged to be stroked and caressed, and her breasts . . . Oh, God, her breasts were full and heavy, her pink nipples so enticing that it was all he could do not to throw her on the bed and bury his face in her bosom.

But there was more he wanted to see, so he trailed his gaze down over her faintly curved belly with its beckoning navel to the soft dark curls that hid the mysteries of her female flesh.

The flesh he couldn't wait to taste and suck and plunder.

"You're a goddess incarnate," he rasped as he caught her in his arms. And for now, she was *his* goddess incarnate.

He kissed her a long moment, indulging his urge to fill his hands with her sweet bare breasts. Only when he had her gasping and leaning into him did he ease her down onto the bed and lay beside her so he could suck at the taut nipples that were teasing him sorely.

She fisted her hands in his hair, holding him close as she panted and moaned beneath the lashes of his tongue over her lush breasts. "Oh . . . *mon coeur* . . . that feels so . . . very . . . *good*."

She'd called him *my heart*? Reveling in the endearment, he kissed his way down her belly to the dewy center of her he wanted to devour. When he covered her flesh with his mouth, she nearly shot up off the bed.

"Max! What are you doing?"

"Satisfying your desire," he murmured against her silky skin.

Then he got right to it. And God, was it heady to taste her, to have his tongue inside her the way he ached to put his cock inside her. Since he couldn't do the latter, he used all the knowledge he'd gained in his youthful flings with opera dancers and actresses to rouse her and tease her, until she was writhing and begging beneath his mouth.

When she gripped his head and began to pant, he knew she was nearly there, and it took every bit of his control not to rise up and thrust into her.

Instead he redoubled his efforts, satisfaction roaring through him when she pressed up hard against his mouth and found her release so forcefully that he felt the spasms against his tongue as she cried out.

Long after she came, he stayed there between her lovely thighs, kissing her, stroking her as he fought for control over his eager cock. Did he dare ask her to do again for him what she'd done in the carriage? Could he keep a grip on his control if she did?

Because having her just pleasure him with her hand was no longer enough. It could never be enough. As soon as he finished, he'd want her again and again, until he made her his. Which was why he should leave the bed right now.

Yet the temptation to have her hands on him was

too great to resist. Lying alongside her, he shoved off his drawers, then closed her fingers around his cock.

To his surprise, she resisted. "No," she whispered. "I want you inside me."

"I won't do it," he choked out. "If you don't want to pleasure me, that's fine, but I'm not going to take your innocence."

Stubbornness flared in her face. "You think not, do you?" She scooted close enough to cradle his cock against her belly. Then she undulated against him.

"Damn it, Lisette," he gritted out as his cock went from hard to stone, "you're playing with fire."

"I'm not playing. I'm fighting. I *want* you to take my innocence. Only you."

When he tried to pull away, she grabbed his hips and added desperately, "I swear, Max, that this is the only thing I will ask of you. I don't need a promise of marriage—I know that you can't offer that. I only want this one time with you. And you want it, too. I know you do."

"You deserve better," he said hoarsely, thrusting helplessly against the satin skin of her belly. "You deserve everything."

"But are you sure I'll get it? Even if I find another man to be with me, how can you be sure he'll treat me well? I might lose my innocence to a man who proves heartless or cruel."

He closed his eyes against the words, but that only made it worse, because now he could imagine it in stark detail. He could see her with some arse who at best would take her for granted and at worst might hurt her. Who would almost certainly never appreciate her as he did.

"Then again," she added in a wounded whisper, "perhaps that doesn't matter to you."

His eyes shot open. "You bloody well know that it does." And leave it to her to fight with logic, not tears. She knew how susceptible he was to a reasonable argument. "You don't play fair."

"I play as fair as you, who taught me to desire you and now expect me to forget that I ache for you, that I *need*—"

He kissed her hard in an attempt to blot out her words, but it didn't work. Because he needed her, too. And she knew it, his tempting minx.

Rolling atop her, he growled, "Damn you, Lisette." He kissed her roughly as he parted her thighs with his knees. "Damn you," he rasped against her lips as he found the entrance to her silken passage. "You won't rest until . . . you have me utterly in thrall to you . . ."

"Yes . . . *mon coeur* . . ."

With those sweet words ringing in his ears, he slid inside her.

Lisette's heart soared. Hardly able to believe she'd won, she gasped her relief against his mouth. She'd won and he hadn't left her, which meant he cared. It meant that no matter what he said about what they should or shouldn't do, no matter what his conditions and his rules, he had deep feelings for her.

She had him at last.

But she seemed to have a tiger by the tail, for he was

thick and hard inside her, much larger and more intrusive than she'd expected.

"Oh, God, Lisette," he murmured, "you feel bloody wonderful."

"So . . . do you," she managed to choke out, telling herself it was only a little untrue. It did feel wonderful to have his body surround her, his strong arms bracket her, his hair brush her cheeks whenever he kissed her brow or her lips or her throat.

He stopped inching inside her and drew back to stare at her, an unholy amusement in his eyes. "You haven't lied to me yet, minx. Don't start now. I know that it can't be comfortable for you." He bent to whisper, "So, imagine us alone together on my private yacht on a beautiful summer day in the Mediterranean."

She relaxed a fraction, and he slipped deeper inside her.

"That's it," he whispered. "Imagine the sun warming our skin. Imagine us lazing away the day, feeding each other oranges and drinking wine."

Closing her eyes, she pictured it, and she relaxed a little more. He settled his *braquemard* farther in, but it felt less . . . uncomfortable somehow.

"Better now?" he rasped.

This time she told the truth. "A bit."

He nodded. "Hold on to me, dearling. It'll be rough sailing at first, but once you get your sea legs, it'll be better than you expect."

"I certainly hope so," she said archly, making him laugh.

Then he plunged hard. Her eyes shot open and she gripped his arms. But the pain was really only a pinch and it didn't last long. It wasn't even as bad as Maman had described.

He stayed motionless, kissing and caressing her until she stopped gripping his arms. "All right?"

She swallowed, then nodded.

That's when the real lovemaking began. As his mouth dragged hot, sweet caresses down her neck, he slid in and out of her in long, slow strokes that seemed at first awkward, then interesting, then rather warming.

It was the most deliciously intimate experience.

His smoldering gaze on her made it even more so, although looking away didn't change that, for she could still hear his sharp breaths, still smell the faint scent of eau de cologne beneath the musk of pure male beast . . . still feel the hard thrusts of him inside her that quickened and grew more enjoyable by the moment.

He was panting now, and so was she. Some instinct made her arch up against him, and a promise of pleasure shuddered through her that made her do it again and again.

"Ah . . . dearling . . . yes . . . like that," he rasped against her throat.

She'd thought nothing could equal having his mouth arouse her, but having him inside and around her, making her ache and yearn, was even more enchanting. His flesh teased a storm up from below that rapidly grew into a tempest and then into a whirlwind that tossed away every barrier between them.

And as his thundering thrusts quickened and she dragged her fingers down his back, as his labored breaths twined with hers and their bodies moved in tandem, they became one being, dancing in the whirlwind until they vaulted into a glorious sky.

They hung there together for one splendid moment as she felt him spill himself inside her. Then they tumbled to earth and he collapsed on top of her.

Tangled with him, spent and warm and content, she felt like she could lie forever in his arms.

As she held him close, pleasure still quaking through her body, he whispered, "Ah, my dangerous temptress . . . You slay me."

If anyone had done any slaying, it was him. He'd slain her resistance to him, to her desire to be independent, alone. Yet he'd also slain her bad memories, her insecurities . . . her fears. For that, she'd always be grateful.

Now it was her turn to slay *his* fears and bad memories. She wanted him for her own, and the only way to have him was to banish the past and teach him to embrace the future. But she wasn't sure how to go about it. Max wasn't like any man she'd ever met.

With a ragged sigh, he rolled off her, pulled her close so that they lay together spoon fashion, then nuzzled her neck. Her languid contentment returned. At least he cared. She knew that much for certain.

"You always smell so good," he murmured.

She laid her arm over the one he'd draped casually around her waist. "So do you."

"Not at present, I fear. I do hope your brother has a tub somewhere."

She turned her face up to him and grinned. "Missing your dukely comforts, are you?"

"A few of them," he admitted, smiling down at her and brushing a kiss to her lips. Then he cast the room a quick glance. "This is quite comfortable, though. Not nearly what I would have expected of a bachelor's lodgings."

"We are indebted to Vidocq for that," she murmured.

"Is Vidocq responsible for the décor as well?" he asked in a teasing tone.

The duke was actually teasing her? She was making progress already, and without even trying. "You can blame that on me. Lavender is my favorite color."

He propped his head up on one elbow as he gazed about him more slowly. "I would never have guessed," he said dryly. "But I wasn't actually commenting on the wallpaper or the embroidery everywhere. It's the African carvings nestled among the flounces on your dressing table, the ivory tusk propped against your ormolu clock, and the ebony dagger atop your flower-embellished chest of drawers that provide a somewhat exotic note."

She laughed. "Oh, those came from Papa. He always brought something back from his trips for me. And of course I have to display them all." She regarded her treasures wistfully. "They're a reminder that one day I hope to gather some foreign treasures of my own."

His gaze grew thoughtful. "To me, they're a reminder that you're a study in contradictions."

Turning to face him fully, she ran her hand over the heavily stubbled cheek that represented his own contradiction—the rigid, proper duke with two days' growth of beard. "Tristan says my room looks like a princess's castle that a pirate has invaded."

"Does that make me the pirate?"

"Certainly not. It makes you the prince who has come to slay him."

Though he was certainly built like a pirate—muscular and masterfully put together. The very idea of his going mad seemed ludicrous, when he lay there supremely healthy and hearty, looking like some dashing, notorious corsair with a lust for princesses.

"Of course, you'll look more like a prince after you've had a bath and a shave and a change of clothes."

"You don't need anything to look like a princess." He ran his fingers through her hair. When she smiled, he added, "Or a duchess."

Her breath caught in her throat. "Max—"

"You know that we have to marry. Today, if possible, but certainly as soon as we return to England."

For a moment she exulted in his offer, which was more than Papa had ever given Maman. Oh, and how she wanted to accept! To be his wife—she couldn't imagine anything more wonderful.

If it was a real marriage. But she could tell from the way he'd said it that it wouldn't be a real marriage. "No," she answered. "We don't."

He searched her face. "Don't you want to marry me?"

More than life. "Only if you forget about your conditions. The ones that say I must not care too deeply for you. That I must leave you to suffer alone in your final days. That I must abandon you when the situation grows too hard."

A muscle ticked in his jaw. Then, muttering an oath under his breath, he fumbled for his drawers, which lay tangled in the coverlet, and left the bed. "I'm sorry, but those conditions aren't negotiable."

Despair gripped her as he dragged his drawers on over his exceedingly firm behind. "Then I won't marry you," she said softly. "I will not be a wife by halves. Not to anyone, but especially not to you."

He stood a moment with his back to her, saying nothing. Then he turned to her with a determined look. "You don't understand."

"I do. You want to control your future." She sat up and pulled the coverlet over her breasts, tucking it under her arms. "But you also want to control mine. And I won't be controlled."

He stared at her, then jerked his head to indicate where her blood stained the sheet beneath her. "You have no choice. I've ruined you."

"At my bidding. I'm certainly not going to punish you for it by making you adhere to some rule of conduct that even my own mother flouted."

"It would not be a punishment, damn you!" he said, and the fire in his face briefly gave her hope. Then he turned his back on her again to hunt for his clothes.

"And it's the only choice we have. Unlike your father, I believe in behaving honorably. I mean to take care of you now that I—"

"Only if you let me take care of you in return," she said softly. "I hold you blameless in this, Max. I know that a wife like me was not in your plans."

"Plans change," he bit out.

A lump stuck in her throat. "You have enough things changing in your life right now. This is no time for hasty decisions."

"You mean, you don't want to marry me if I turn out not to be the duke after all," he said peevishly.

The sheer ludicrousness of that made her laugh. "You know perfectly well I don't care if you're the duke. But there is nothing we can do about it at the moment, anyway. It's not as if we can marry today—we're not even French citizens."

"Trust me," he snapped, "I could get it arranged."

He probably could, too. "Ah, but then the press would find out and be gossiping about you marrying some nobody, and they'd start digging for information, and everything you were worried about in the first place when you refused to travel with me would come to pass."

When he swore under his breath, she added, "We're better off remaining incognito at the moment. I don't think we should act on anything until we find out what's going on with your brother and mine." A thought suddenly occurred to her, and her stomach clenched. "Besides, you might not want to marry me after we learn the truth about that."

His expression softened. "Whatever your brother is up to has nothing to do with our future together. Not for me, anyway. That much you can be sure of."

That gratified her enormously. Perhaps they might still have a chance together. One day. "All the same, we should wait to make a decision until your life and future are settled." Until she could be sure that his feelings ran deeper than mere passion. That he was willing to be together in sickness and in health, till death they did part. She wouldn't accept anything less from him.

And love? What about love?

Her throat tightened as she skittered away from that thought. Love was too much to ask for. If she pined for that from him, if she let herself fall in love with him, there really was a good chance he would break her heart.

Unfortunately, her heart didn't seem inclined to listen to her cautions. It was already half in love with him.

It was prompting her to hold her hand out to him. "I'm weary of talking," she whispered, wanting to forget, if only briefly, the complications of their present situation. "Come back to bed. Vidocq won't return until evening, so we have a few hours together. We should make the best of it."

She wanted to lose herself in him once more.

Heat flared in his face, and his eyes trailed a path of fire down her body. Then he steadied his shoulders and snapped his gaze back to hers. "Until you agree to marry me, we aren't doing this again."

Shock rapidly gave way to irritation. "Are you trying

to blackmail me into doing as you wish, Your Grace?" she said tightly. "Because I assure you that while I enjoyed what we did together, I'm not so desperate for male attention that I will agree to any demand of yours in order to get it."

"It's not blackmail." He crossed his arms over his chest. His still bare, still magnificent chest. "But every time we make love, we risk conceiving a child, and I won't let you bring a bastard into this world to be mocked and ridiculed."

She gaped at him, her heart dropping into her stomach. "Of all the insulting . . ." Her anger flaring high, she leaped from the bed, dragging the coverlet with her. "How could you think I'd ever let my child suffer the cruelties of being a bastard?"

He gazed steadily at her. "You refuse to marry me. What else am I to think?"

She strode up to poke her finger in his chest. "If I do find myself with child, I assure you that I will marry you. I'm not so foolish as that!"

When a sudden satisfaction glinted in his eyes, awareness dawned. Devil take her temper! She'd just told him exactly what he wanted to know—that he had a way to *make* her marry him.

"In that case," he drawled, catching her hand and trying to pull her to him, "let's go back to bed."

She snatched her hand free. "Oh, no you don't. You are not going to swive me silly in an attempt to get me with child." Turning on her heel, she marched over to the closet and found a wrapper she'd left behind for whenever she visited. "I believe you're right, Max. We *shouldn't* do this again." At least not until he realized that the only marriage worth having was a real one.

Changing the coverlet out for the wrapper, she shot him an airy look. "Now I think I'll go call for a bath. Might as well put to good use the time we must spend waiting for Vidocq."

She started for the door, but hesitated as she thought of something. Returning to the bed, she jerked off the bloodstained sheet and tossed it into the fireplace. Max watched in silence as she started a fire on top of it.

But as she fanned the flames, he said, "Getting rid of the evidence, are you?"

Sparing a glare for him, she gathered up her clothes. "The servants believe we're married, remember?"

That infuriating eyebrow of his quirked up. "That's not what worries you. You're worried they might tell Vidocq what happened, and he might tell your brothers about it, which would send them straight to me." His voice turned cocky. "And you know damned well that if they confront me, I won't hesitate to tell them I'm not the one balking at marriage."

Ooh, he was so sure of himself! And so abominably right.

Refusing even to dignify his remarks with a hot retort, she hurried toward the door. She had to get away from him before she did something reckless, like . . . like shove the arrogant, annoying arse off a balcony!

Or accept his offer of marriage, infernal conditions and all.

Tears stung her eyes. Curse him—Max was the only man she knew who could turn what should have been the most romantic moment in the world into a calculated business proposition.

But as she started to leave, he added in a low voice behind her, "I warn you, dearling. I don't play fair either when it comes to getting what I want."

A thrill shot through her. All right, so perhaps his proposition hadn't been *entirely* cold-blooded. But that didn't make it any better. Or any more acceptable.

Fighting for calm, she faced him. Despite his rumpled hair and unshaven chin and lack of decent attire, he still looked every inch a duke. He still wore the air of supreme self-confidence that both tantalized and maddened her.

And his eyes gleamed with resolve. "I'm not giving up easily, Lisette."

She stared him down. "Neither am I."

Then she fled.

16

WITH HIS HEART in his throat, Maximilian watched Lisette leave. Holy God, he'd handled that badly. What the hell was wrong with him? Even a duke couldn't *command* a woman to marry him. Women didn't appreciate that sort of disregard for their feelings.

He scrubbed a hand over his face. Unfortunately, something about the dark and sultry Lisette shattered his self-control every time and made him behave like an oblivious fool.

She'd probably expected sweet words and promises of love and a long life of connubial bliss. Not logic and reason and a blunt statement like *You know that we have to marry.*

But damn it, logic and reason were all he could offer her. A long life of connubial bliss was highly unlikely. Though love, perhaps . . .

Gritting his teeth, he began to dress. He was not in love with Lisette, damn it! He couldn't be that foolish. Being in love made men do things like give up control entirely to the women they loved. He wasn't going to do that, no matter how much he'd enjoyed having Lisette in his bed.

He paused with his shirt in his hand. He really *had* enjoyed it. And not just the part where they'd made love, either—the way she'd tempted and provoked him into bedding her, then given herself to him with such unbearable sweetness.

That had been memorable, but it was the part afterward that he would never forget. Lying there so companionably with her, having her gaze up at him with a melting tenderness in her face . . . even having her refuse his offer of marriage.

Despite everything she'd said about marriage being a prison for women, he'd half expected her to play on his sense of honor and demand that he wed her. Any other virginal female would have done so, especially when the person who'd taken her innocence was as eligible a bachelor as he.

But not Lisette, oh no.

You know perfectly well I don't care if you're the duke.

And she'd laughed! She wanted him for himself, not for his title or wealth. She wanted him in spite of the truth about his family's curse.

A lump caught in his throat. Only Lisette would look past the gossip to the man. Not the Duke of Lyons, but Maximilian Cale. Or Max, as she so jocularly called him.

That, too, was something he wasn't used to. She dared to tease him. No woman had ever done that, not even his friends' sisters and wives. They were all too intimidated by the cold and aloof duke.

But Lisette treated him like an equal. It was bloody intoxicating. It made him want her as his duchess so badly, he would slay dragons to have her.

He groaned. That in itself should serve as a warning that he must proceed with caution. He had to marry her, of course—he wasn't about to let her suffer the consequences of her ruination—but he would have to make sure that she did so under his terms. She would have to understand and accept the peculiarities of his situation.

The problem was she felt too deeply, wanted too much. She had to learn not to do that if they were to have an acceptable marriage.

And yet.

Mon coeur. She'd called him "my heart."

His pulse quickened. Just the memory of the words, spoken with such affection, stirred the feelings he'd struggled for so many years to imprison within his heart's fortress. Like the wild rose she was, she was growing over the walls, into the cracks, breaking the stone—

No, damn it! He was *not* letting her destroy his walls. That way lay pain and suffering. Hadn't he had enough of that in his life?

He would make her his wife. He would do his duty by her, and he would enjoy it, but that was all he would allow himself. Love . . . No, love was not part of it. Couldn't be part of it, not if he wanted to protect her in the end.

Glancing around at the room that was so visibly hers, he swore and headed out the door. For now he had to put the enchanting Lisette from his mind long enough to shore up his defenses. Perhaps some time spent searching Bonnaud's study would do that.

Unfortunately, after an hour, he realized there was nothing in the damned place that told him anything of use. There were boxes filled with papers . . . but none of them had anything to do with his family.

And Bonnaud's notes were written in some cryptic code that showed the man to be even more paranoid than Father at his most insane. Though that was probably to be expected of an agent of the French secret police.

He'd just closed the last box when the sound of a cleared throat arrested him. He turned to find Vidocq's butler standing in the doorway.

"Yes?" Maximilian said in French. "What is it?"

"Madame says that you may wish to have a bath."

With a little clutch in his heart at Lisette's thoughtfulness, Maximilian said, "I would indeed. Thank you."

The servant let out a typical Frenchman's huff of annoyance. Maximilian was used to the impudence of French servants, but this went beyond the pale. "Is that a problem?" he snapped.

"I merely thought you should know that you may have to wait a while for it. Madame insists that you have fresh water, and it will take time to heat it. If fresh water is what you prefer."

Now Maximilian was bewildered. "Of course I prefer fresh water. What else is there?"

The butler rolled his eyes, as if frustrated at dealing with someone so oblivious as Maximilian. "Wives and husbands often share bathwater in France, Mr. Kale. I forgot that you English can be . . . fastidious."

Several things hit Maximilian at once. One, he'd forgotten he was supposed to be married. Two, he'd forgotten that the servants didn't know he was a duke. And three, people actually *shared* bathwater?

Before he could even comprehend such an outrageous thing, Lisette showed up. She informed the butler that he had better draw her husband a fresh hot bath and quickly, or Vidocq would have his head. The butler responded with a few choice words about the English and their nonsense, and she countered with a few of her own.

Meanwhile, Maximilian had stopped paying attention to the conversation the minute he realized how well Lisette's wrapper skimmed her appealing curves. Her hair was wrapped up in a towel, but a few tendrils fringed her neck, making her look even more delectable than usual. And God, she smelled like flowers.

She always smelled like flowers. It made him want her all over again.

As she apparently won the argument and the butler slunk away to do her bidding, she glanced at Maximilian. "Did you find anything in Tristan's papers?"

"No." That was all he could choke out past his image of a naked Lisette.

Fortunately, she didn't seem to be aware of how much he was enjoying the sight of her scantily clad body. "I was afraid of that. Let's hope that Vidocq finds out something at the Sûreté."

"Yes, let's hope."

"Well, then, I'm going to take a nap. Enjoy your bath."

"Lisette!" he called to her as she walked away.

She halted to face him. "What?"

"Do married couples really share bathwater in France?"

A smug smile crossed her face. "In France, in England, and probably in half the countries in Europe, Your Grace. It saves the trouble of heating and hauling buckets of water. And it's not just married couples, either. Sometimes whole families bathe in the same water."

"Holy God," he muttered. "That's . . . that's . . ."

"Disgusting? Yes, it is. Be glad that Vidocq's servants will make allowances for your being one of those 'fastidious English.'" She laughed merrily. "When it comes to baths, I'm one of those 'fastidious English' myself."

"A pity," he said quickly before she could leave again. When she cast him a quizzical glance, he raked her body with a heated look. "I might enjoy sharing a bath with *you*."

She blinked. Then color rose in her cheeks. "What a shame, then, that you're unlikely to ever get that chance." She marched off, her back rigid, but he'd accomplished his aim.

If he couldn't win her by using logic and reason, he'd win her by seduction. She was a sensual female who desired him. Surely that would be enough to get her to marry him in the end.

That did him no good at the moment, however. As she disappeared into her bedchamber, he was left once more fruitlessly aroused. Suppressing a sigh, he walked back through the courtyard to Vidocq's house for his bath, attended by a pair of more accommodating man-servants than the one who'd complained about heating bathwater.

By the time he was done, he was ravenous. Fortunately, Vidocq's cook was apparently kindly disposed toward Englishmen and piled a tray full of bread and cheese and fruit for him to take over to Bonnaud's lodgings to share with Lisette.

Maximilian found her sound asleep, and he sucked in a ragged breath. She looked so fetching when she slept, with her delicate hands tucked up beneath her cheek, her hair tumbled across the pillow, and the ala-baster skin of her shoulder displayed where her wrap-per had slipped down.

He ached to caress her the way the setting sun's rays did, dancing across her body. He wanted to climb right into the bed and awaken her with long, lazy kisses.

But she needed the sleep. There was no telling when they would next get a chance of it, depending on what Vidocq found out.

So he went off to the small dining area where he'd put the tray of food, sat down at the tiny table, and began to eat. He hadn't been there long when Vidocq arrived.

The Frenchman joined him at the table. "Where's Lisette?"

"Sleeping. She was tired."

"You told her the truth?" Vidocq asked.

Maximilian stiffened. "I did."

"How did she take it?"

"Better than I expected," Maximilian said coolly.

Vidocq sat back to survey him with unnerving thoroughness. "Did you bed her?"

A fierce surge of anger welled up in him. "That is none of your damned affair."

"Which means that you did."

Maximilian rose, his fists clenching at his sides. "Now, see here, Vidocq, if you ever say one word to anyone about your scandalous suppositions—"

"I would never harm her or her reputation." He cast Maximilian a hard stare. "But I'm not sure I can say the same for you."

Maximilian flushed, which never happened to him. But then, he'd never before been faced with the substitute father of a woman he'd just bedded.

"I offered her marriage."

"Did you, indeed?" Vidocq said, oddly enough not sounding surprised.

"She turned me down."

Vidocq turned thoughtful. "Now, *that* is unexpected."

"With her, the unexpected *is* the expected," Maximilian snapped. "I've never met a more unpredictable woman in my life."

"She does tend to go her own way." Vidocq gestured to the chair, and Maximilian grudgingly resumed his seat. "But you can always count on her having a soft spot for lost causes. And you are certainly that, Your Grace."

Maximilian rubbed the bridge of his nose. "Then why did she turn me down?"

"Perhaps she thinks *that* is the way to save you."

I can't be saved.

But that wasn't something he dared admit to the far too perceptive Vidocq. The man already knew too much about him and his affairs. "Whatever the case, that has nothing to do with why we're here." He crossed his arms over his chest. "What did you find out about Bonnaud?"

Vidocq stiffened, then gave a quick nod in the direction of Lisette's bedchamber. Maximilian turned to see her in the doorway, looking rumpled and sleepy and thoroughly enchanting.

Except for the glint in her eyes. "I do hope you weren't planning to have this discussion without *me*," she said, walking languidly toward them.

Vidocq smiled. "I wouldn't dream of it, *mon ange*."

As Maximilian rose to give her his chair, he wondered if she'd heard the other part of the conversation. He hoped not. She wouldn't appreciate their talking about her behind her back.

She took a seat, and Maximilian leaned against the scarred buffet that seemed to serve as the "kitchen" part of the room. He only wished she were wearing more than that damned wrapper. It made it hard for him to concentrate on anything but her.

"I wasn't able to learn much," Vidocq said, "but I did discover two things of importance. While he was still in Antwerp two months ago, Tristan wrote and asked for a month of leave, which was granted to him. And they don't know why he still hasn't returned." Vidocq's voice tightened. "Apparently they all believed he had simply left the Sûreté to work for me without bothering to resign."

"Instead he went off to follow his own plan," Maximilian said cynically. "It's just as I've said all along—he's found a better way to ensure his future than working his way up to prominence in the Sûreté."

When Lisette glared at him, Vidocq said, "Actually, I don't think that's it, either. Tristan captured the forger and placed him in a cell in Antwerp, then wrote to his superiors to send someone to fetch the prisoner because of personal matters Tristan had to attend to."

"Where?" Lisette asked.

"London, obviously," Maximilian put in.

"I hope not," Vidocq said. "Ostend is where Tristan would have gone to take the packet boat to London, and there's been a recent outbreak of cholera there."

"Oh no," Lisette said anxiously.

Vidocq patted her hand. "He's young and healthy. I'm sure that even if he went to Ostend, he didn't catch cholera."

"Well, he was obviously still in good health last week when he wrote me that note," Maximilian pointed out. "Unless he was delirious with fever at the time."

"That couldn't be," Lisette said dismissively. "If he'd had cholera, they wouldn't even have let him into—" She halted, her eyes going wide. "Quarantine!"

Maximilian instantly followed her thoughts. "Yes. That would explain a great deal. There needn't even be sickness on board a ship for the quarantine laws to go into effect. The captain is required to raise a yellow flag whenever his vessel comes from a city where an infectious disease is rampant. So the minute the ship reached London, it would have been quarantined, even without disease on board. The Privy Council has a tendency to be—" He stopped, noticing the odd way Vidocq was staring at him. "What is it?"

"You know an awful lot about quarantine, Your Grace."

"I've traveled a great deal," he said defensively. "And several members of my family served in the navy." When Vidocq just lifted his eyebrow, Maximilian drew himself up stiffly. "And I have a friend on the Privy Council."

Lisette eyed him askance. "Of course you do."

"My point is, the Privy Council decides whether to quarantine a ship, and it tends to be overly cautious. Once the decision has been made, quarantine can last for weeks."

"That would explain why Tristan couldn't just go to your house with your . . . with his friend," Lisette pointed out. "No one would have let them off the ship, even if they weren't sick. The rules are very strict."

Holy God, it began to look more and more as if Bonnaud might actually have found Peter.

His heart began to pound. For the first time, he let himself hope that his brother might be alive. He might no longer be alone with the family curse.

"It's an interesting theory," Maximilian said, pushing away from the buffet to pace the floor, "but it doesn't explain everything. Let's assume that Bonnaud paid off a quarantine officer to smuggle out that note he sent to me. It's highly illegal, and anyone who agreed to it would be risking the permanent loss of his position as well as a hefty fine—but it could be done."

He paused to face them. "Getting a *person* off a quarantined ship is dicier, however. Boats patrol those ships nightly to make sure no one tries to swim off. So how could Bonnaud have thought to meet me? It sounded as if he was sending that note right from the meeting place, as if he were already there waiting."

"Anything is possible with enough money," Vidocq said, "especially when it comes to bribing poorly paid government officials."

"But would Bonnaud have enough funds for that?"

Vidocq shrugged. "Whatever quarantine officer was helping him would have to know he was trying to reach a duke. Tristan might have promised that you would offer enough of a reward."

"On the other hand," Lisette said, "Tristan might have had enough money to get one person smuggled off the ship but not two. That's why he couldn't bring his companion. Although I don't understand why he didn't just wait on board until the quarantine was up."

Maximilian pointed out, "The other question is, if he went to so much trouble to get off the ship in the first place, why didn't he stay around to meet me?"

"You said you were late," Lisette replied. "Perhaps the quarantine officer got him as far as the London docks but grew impatient when you didn't show up right away. The man might have started worrying that they'd be caught. As you say, the consequences of that are great."

Vidocq nodded. "He might even have decided that Tristan had mistaken the situation, or didn't have a connection to the Duke of Lyons after all. Who knows? When you're dealing with English customs officials, any number of things can happen."

"God knows that's true," Maximilian said.

"And another thing," Lisette said. "It's always bothered me that Tristan didn't try to contact me or Dom. But he couldn't have if he was in quarantine and it was so difficult."

"Actually," Maximilian said, "it would have made more sense for him to contact you two and get you to meet with me to bring me to him."

Vidocq shook his head. "Tristan would never risk involving Dom or Lisette. If George found out, he might charge Lisette, perhaps even Dom, with harboring a fugitive."

"Unfortunately, that's true," Lisette said with a sigh.

"And Tristan would definitely keep us out of it if he thought it was safer."

"All of this is still supposition," Vidocq said. "We don't even know for certain that Tristan was ever *in* Ostend."

"Could we speak to the forger?" Maximilian asked. "Perhaps Tristan told him something of his plans."

"If he did, then the man took them to his grave," Vidocq said. "He was executed last week."

Maximilian blinked. "So quickly?"

Vidocq shrugged. "The fellow had been convicted and sentenced to the guillotine before he escaped. So there was nothing left to do but carry out his sentence once the officers brought him back here."

"And I don't suppose *they* spoke to Bonnaud."

Vidocq shook his head no. "He was already gone by the time they got there. You could speak to the gaoler. Perhaps he could tell you more."

"We can't travel to Belgium, Max," Lisette said with an anxious look. "Dom returns to London soon, and if I'm not back, he's likely to come after you with daggers drawn. I can't trust Skrimshaw not to tell him who I'm off with."

"I can handle Manton," Maximilian assured her. He would just tell the man he meant to marry her, and that would be that. "But I agree—a trip to Belgium, trying to retrace Bonnaud's steps up there, is out of the question. It would take too long, and if he *is* in quarantine in London and it might end any moment, every minute counts."

Besides, the longer he traveled with Lisette, the more she risked having her reputation irreparably damaged. While that might be to his advantage in forcing her into marriage, he didn't want that for her.

"So I think," he went on, "that our best choice is to return to London and explore which ships are in quarantine. It will be easy enough to find out if Bonnaud is on any of them. All we need do is ask to see the ships' manifests."

"Tristan won't have used his real name," Lisette pointed out.

"Perhaps not, but my brother would have." Maximilian sighed. "*If* Bonnaud really has found Peter, that is."

"It sounds as if he at least *thinks* he has." Vidocq rose from the table. "I can give you a list of Tristan's usual aliases. I'm sure he'd use one of those to travel. And actually, there's only two for which he has official documents."

"Knowing the aliases will help, thank you." Maximilian stared down at Lisette. "Have you had enough of a chance to rest? Do you think we could leave at once?"

She nodded. "There's a diligence that departs from the Messageries Royales de la rue Notre-Dame-des-Victoires for Calais."

"Why Calais?" Maximilian asked. "I thought Dieppe was the nearer way."

"We can't go back through Dieppe. We can't risk Hucker still being there."

"Ah. Excellent point."

"You are not traveling by diligence," Vidocq broke in. "It is far too uncomfortable. You will take my traveling coach. My coachman will deliver you to Calais and then bring my carriage back. If you leave now and post through the night, you can be there by tomorrow evening and on the steam packet to London the next morning."

"There's a packet that goes directly to London these days?" Maximilian asked.

"Yes," Vidocq said. "It takes about twelve hours and sets you down at the Tower. But you spend more time in choppy water, which is why most people go by Dover or Dieppe. Is seasickness a problem for you, Your Grace?"

"Only if he doesn't spend too much time in the taproom," Lisette said archly.

Maximilian ignored her. "It's not a problem."

"But honestly, Vidocq, there's no reason we should use your carriage," she said. "It won't save us that much time, and we don't mind traveling by diligence. Do we, Max?"

He started to agree with her; then it dawned on him why she wanted to ride in a lumbering omnibus with ten other people. She didn't want to be alone with him. Which meant she was probably more susceptible to him than she cared to admit.

He would take full advantage of that. "On the contrary," he said, "we need every extra hour we can get." He used the one tack sure to sway her. "There's a chance that your brother could be found out and arrested the longer he stays trapped aboard a ship. And that's a risk we shouldn't take."

She paled, then turned to Vidocq. "Thank you, then we will use your coach."

Vidocq was eyeing him suspiciously, but Maximilian didn't care. To gain Lisette as his wife, he would need plenty of time alone with her so he could court her.

And he'd just bought himself that time.

17

THE NIGHT PORTION of their coach trip went
better than Lisette expected, mostly because she was
too tired from all their traveling to do anything but
sleep. Max also fell into a doze as soon as they'd left
Paris, and thankfully he stayed on his side of the carriage all night.

But everything changed once the sun came up. First,
she awakened to find the carriage halted and Max gone.
In a panic, she leapt out just in time to see him and the
coachman in rolled-up shirtsleeves preparing to push
the equipage up a steep hill that the horses were having
trouble with. She could only stand there gaping as they
put their backs into it.

Last week she would never have imagined that
Lofty Lyons could—or would—shove a carriage up a
hill. But Max did his part so admirably that long after
the coach had reached the top and they'd continued on
their journey, she was unable to blot out the image of

him with forearms flexing and windblown hair shining golden in the morning sun.

It got no better as the day went on. He was up to something; she knew it. He made no mention of the conflict between them, but he kept *touching* her. At first, she'd thought it was accidental—his booted calf bumping hers in a turn, his elbow brushing her thigh when he leaned forward to get something out of his bag, which was stowed beneath her seat.

But the coach was not *that* small; there was no call for him to touch her. And when they disembarked to dine at an inn midday and his hand lingered on hers while he helped her out of the carriage, she realized what he was up to. He was subtly trying to seduce her, the sly devil. He was still bent on trying to get her with child, so she would have to marry him on *his* terms.

Very well. He would fight the battle his way. She would fight it hers.

So as soon as they climbed back into the coach, she drew out the ribbon embroidery she'd brought with her but hadn't had the chance to work, and began to ornament a pillowcase. The next time he "accidentally" rubbed his knee up against hers, she "accidentally" jabbed his knee with her needle.

"Ow!" he cried and scowled at her, rubbing his knee. "What the blazes was that for?"

She cast him an innocent glance and continued to work. "I don't know what you mean. It's such close quarters in here that you have to expect a bit of bumping up against each other."

He eyed her suspiciously. After watching her for a few sullen moments, he asked, "Do you do that often?"

"What? Stab randy dukes in the knee with my needle?" she quipped.

"Embroider. I noticed a great deal of it in your room and at Manton's and on your gown. Did you do it all yourself?"

She was surprised to find him so observant. "As a matter of fact, yes."

He crossed his arms over his chest. "It seems a rather domestic activity for a woman who wants to be an investigator."

"I had a great deal of time on my hands when I was a girl, and I was the restless sort," she explained. "So whenever I got too rambunctious, Maman would sit me down with a needle and cloth and ribbons and teach me how to do ribbon embroidery."

"That worked?"

"For me it did. It calmed the frenzy in my mind." She paused to gaze out the window, remembering. "I used to love those times with Maman. She'd learned the skill from *her* mother, whom I didn't know, so I got to hear stories about my French family. Eventually, I chose to do the embroidery for my own pleasure. I still do; it calms me when I'm agitated."

And she was certainly agitated around him.

Forcing that thought from her mind, she held up

what she was working on. "Of course, my subjects aren't exactly . . . typical."

When he caught sight of her silver ribbon rendering of a dagger Papa had brought back from one of his trips, he burst into laughter. "Leave it to you to figure out how to combine domesticity with a yearning for adventure."

With a smile she went back to her work.

After a moment, he said, "My mother used to embroider."

Something he'd mentioned a few days ago tugged at her memory. "Did she embroider that handkerchief that you said was so distinctive?"

"She did, actually."

Not wanting to pry, she bent her head over her work.

He watched her a moment, then said, "What makes the handkerchief distinctive is what lies between the embroidery and the linen." He pulled open his coat to reveal a hidden pocket behind the lapel. Then he drew out a handkerchief of ivory-colored linen that she hadn't seen before.

He stared at it, softness spreading over his features. Then he handed it to her.

She slid closer to the window to examine it in full sunlight. At first it just looked like a very fancy handkerchief, with the ducal crest embroidered in a variety of colored threads, including gold and silver ones. But given what he'd said, she noticed that the bits of the cloth that showed through the embroidery weren't creamy linen. They were white, possibly cotton or muslin.

When she looked at him in bewilderment, he said, "My mother took a piece of our christening gowns and sewed it to a handkerchief for each of us, then embroidered over and around it. It's not the kind of thing anyone would notice without knowing to look for it. It's certainly nothing that Bonnaud would have noticed upon seeing my handkerchief for a few moments years ago."

"Why did you show it to him back then?"

Max took the handkerchief from her and gazed down at it. "When I was a boy, I was more casual with it, carrying it about in the same pocket with my regular handkerchief. But I was always reaching for a handkerchief and pulling out the wrong one, which is what I did with your brother that day. Then I felt compelled to explain why I had two, one of which was ornate. Of course, I didn't tell him about the christening gown fabric." He lifted his gaze to lock with hers. "I've never told anyone but you."

The fact that he trusted her touched her deeply. "I won't tell a soul."

He nodded, then tucked the handkerchief reverently into its secret pocket.

"The work on it is very fine. Your mother must have been talented with a needle."

"She certainly spent enough time at it. Before Father . . . grew ill. After that, she was too busy to do much but take care of him."

"How old were you then?" she asked.

"Twenty-one. I had just come of age."

"Tell me about it," she said softly.

When he tensed, she thought for certain he would retreat into his self-imposed prison. But then he began to talk. And her heart broke a little more for him with each word.

By the time they neared Calais, she began to understand why he was so afraid of letting anyone too close. Perhaps she would be, too, if she'd watched her father forget her name, make wild accusations about her mother, and run amok from mad delusions that people were trying to murder him. Worst of all were Max's tales of holding his father down to keep him from hurting his mother or himself. Those made her want to cry.

Clearly he was telling her all this to convince her that his idea of a marriage was the best. But it made her even more determined never to abandon him to the indifferent care of servants and doctors.

They reached Calais after nightfall. The inns were teeming with passengers headed for England the next day, and they had to go to three hotels before they found lodgings.

As soon as they entered their small room, she groaned. It contained only a bed, a dresser, and a spindly chair.

Max came to take her cloak. "We'll share the bed. We both need a good night's rest. There's no telling what we'll find once we reach London."

"But—"

"I promise to be a gentleman," he cut in. "Trust me, I'm too tired to be anything else."

Though she cast him a skeptical glance, she knew he was right about them needing their sleep. "All right." She forced a lightness into her tone. "Just stay out of the taproom tonight, will you?"

"Oh, for God's sake," he said irritably, "I've gotten drunk in a taproom only once in my entire life, and you happened to be around for it. I suppose I'll never live that down."

"I beg your pardon, but what about when you were sixteen and sneaked down to the taproom at that inn in Dieppe?" she teased. "Didn't you get drunk then?"

He flushed. "That's not why I sneaked down those stairs. I was going out to the garden to meet with a maid who'd flirted with me at dinner. I was feeling my oats, that's all."

Her heart tightened as she imagined a young Max, full of youth and vigor, trying to steal a kiss in a back garden. Before his life was ripped away from him by responsibilities and duties and tragedy.

"After all, isn't that the second son's job?" he joked halfheartedly. "To be a rapscallion?"

"Well, you're not a second son anymore, so you'd better keep your hands to yourself tonight."

"If I don't, you can always stab me with your embroidery needle," he said dryly. "You seem to have mastered that technique."

She managed a smile. "I doubt that will be necessary."

An uncomfortable silence descended upon them. Muttering something about seeing to their supper, he disappeared.

The rest of the evening was as difficult as she'd expected. Sharing a room with him felt distinctly different now that she'd shared his bed. Conversation at supper was stilted, and preparing for bed was awkward since she had to have his help in taking off her corset.

His hands undoing her gown felt intimate, his fingers unlacing her corset felt intimate . . . just feeling his breath on her neck felt intimate. He didn't do a single thing that was improper, yet it didn't matter. Everything he did made her want him.

He climbed into bed wearing only his shirt and drawers and faced away from her. She sat on the bed and took her time brushing her hair, waiting to hear the even rhythm of his breathing. Thankfully, it came soon.

Only then did she slip off her loosened gown and corset and petticoats, leaving her in her shift and drawers. She wasn't about to change into her nightdress; that would be tempting Fate.

She carefully slid under the covers to avoid waking him, but he didn't even rouse.

That ought to have made her relax, yet she lay there for a long time thinking about what he'd told her, wondering if she was making a mistake to be so insistent about how they should go on together. He had offered her marriage, for pity's sake. Was she being foolish to turn him down?

When at last she fell asleep it was to dream of Max, strong and hearty, shoving Vidocq's carriage up a hill. Except that in her dream Max wore nothing but a hat. Though she told him he should be careful—since he was naked and all—he merely tipped his hat to her and went right back to shoving the carriage.

Suddenly, the carriage began slipping backward and Max started sliding down the hill, unable to control it, and she tried to scream, but she couldn't, and she ran toward him down the hill and ran and ran—

She came awake with a start. She was gripping something warm beneath her. Still half asleep and disoriented, she stared about her and realized she was using Max as a bed. Again.

Then she felt something hard pressing into her belly, which seemed to grow harder by the moment. As she caught Max's gaze glinting up at her in the gray light of dawn, he drawled, "If you want me to keep my promise to be a gentleman, dearling, I suggest that you retreat to your side of the bed."

For a long moment, she just stared down at him—at his tousled hair and his whiskered chin and his tight jaw. At the face that became dearer to her by the day. Then she kissed him.

He tensed as if in shock, then swiftly rolled her beneath him. His hands bracketed her shoulders, and he lowered his mouth to within a few inches of hers. "Tell me you want this," he growled.

The rampant heat in his eyes made her swallow, but she'd already decided what to do.

Perhaps it was the lingering memory of her dream. Or the feel of his body so warm and real against hers, or the way he'd lain perfectly still the whole time she'd been sprawled across him. Perhaps it was the fact that she knew they might not have another chance to be alone like this.

Whatever the reason, she had to feel his mouth on hers once more, had to touch him and be with him. Really *be* with him.

She slid her hands up beneath his shirt. "I want this. I want—"

He smothered the word *you* with a hard kiss.

After that, there was no turning back. As he plundered her mouth, she put her hands all over him, pressed her body against him, filled her senses with him. She couldn't get enough of him.

Apparently he felt the same. The sun rose as he sucked her nipples hard through her shift while fondling her below with long, firm strokes of his clever fingers, making her even more impatient for him.

"Max," she whispered, "Max, please . . . please . . . I need you *now*."

"Good," he said hoarsely as he settled himself between her legs. "Because I can't wait any longer to have you."

Next thing she knew, he'd entered her right through the opening in her drawers. She nearly came out of her skin as he buried himself to the hilt.

"Lisette," he choked out. "Oh, God, Lisette . . ."

Then he began to move. It was so different from

before—no pain, no awkwardness. Just Max joined to her, claiming her, making her his own.

The reckless glitter in his eyes as he drove into her with hard, eager thrusts told her that when they were like this, he was not the duke. He was her wild lover.

"This is how . . . it should always be," he rasped as he quickened his strokes. "You . . . in my bed . . . in my arms . . . Always."

For the moment, she gave herself up to that dream. He was thunder and lightning and rain, and she was the earth and flowers that drank up the storm. He was the only man she wanted, the only man she would ever want, and she was his only mate.

She felt her release approaching, rising to seize her in its grip and drive her up . . . up . . . up . . . until Max gave one final thrust inside her and let out a ragged cry that triggered her own glorious explosion.

In that moment, as he clutched her to him and filled her with his seed, she knew she'd lost the battle to protect her heart. She loved him. Oh, Lord, how she loved him.

After a while, his breathing slowed. He bent his head to kiss her cheek and nuzzle her neck. Then he slid off to lie next to her on his back, staring up at the ceiling.

Though she knew she had just done the most foolish thing of her life, she snuggled up against him. "You make an excellent bed."

He laughed. "Feel free to use me as one whenever you like." He curled his arm about her and held her, stroking her hair. "We could wake up like this every morning, you know."

She rubbed her cheek over his chest. "At least until you started imagining that you saw signs of madness in yourself. Until you sent me away to protect me, whether or not I wanted or needed protection."

When he uttered a long sigh, she swallowed her disappointment. The man was so stubborn! And so determined to have everything his way.

She slid off the bed. "We have to go. The packet boat will be leaving shortly."

He sat up. "Lisette, I want you to know that no matter what happens once we find Bonnaud, my offer of marriage stands. I don't care what your brother has done or who your mother was, or whether I prove to be the duke or not. You're the only woman I would ever choose to marry."

Trying not to cry at those sweet words, she smiled sadly. "And my answer still stands. It's *because* you're the only man I want to marry that I must have a real marriage. That isn't going to change."

He muttered a curse under his breath. But at least he didn't argue with her.

An hour later, they were aboard the steam packet headed for London. This time, the crossing proved every bit as miserable as her mood. A squall arose, tossing the boat on the churning sea as easily as a matchstick. So they spent their time huddled in the main cabin with the other passengers, trying to stay warm and dry.

"Do you still miss your yacht?" she asked him. "I

daresay it would have been torn to bits during this storm."

He shook his head. "I have an able captain and a very seaworthy vessel. It has made the crossing more times than you have, I'll wager." His eyes gleamed at her. "And it will make the crossing many times more. After all, I intend very soon to take a wife who has family connections in France."

She sighed and averted her gaze. He wouldn't give up, would he? She didn't know whether to be thrilled over his determination, or to despair that he continued to insist it be on his terms.

But one thing was certain: If she didn't get away from him soon, he would win. Because with every passing moment, she lost more of her will to resist him.

18

MAXIMILIAN STOOD ON the dark London dock with Lisette and their bags, having spent the hours since their arrival in arranging this meeting. His heart pounded as he watched a lamplit boat being rowed toward them through the night. He couldn't see the cargo ship beyond it, but he knew it was there. The *Grecian* had been quarantined right here, under their noses, ever since it had arrived in London flying a yellow flag six weeks ago.

He'd found two names on the passenger manifest— Jack Drake, a common alias of Bonnaud's, and Victor Cale. Maximilian wasn't sure why Peter had chosen to go by another Christian name after the fire, but it couldn't be coincidence that the surname was Cale. He and Lisette had found the needle in the haystack at last.

Amazing what a man could discover once he knew where to look . . . and once he was able to use his title. Maximilian had spent the past few hours bullying Privy

Council members and shipping officials alike to gain information and arrange to be taken aboard the *Grecian*.

A cynical smile crossed his lips. Apparently getting *onto* a quarantined ship was a damned sight easier than getting off of one. Especially when the authorities couldn't agree if there was even anyone with cholera aboard.

In this case, the madness in his family was a help to him. No one was terribly surprised that the Duke of Lyons would do something as insane as to go aboard a quarantined ship. He'd been careful not to reveal why. He hadn't even mentioned the names of the men he wanted to see. No point in giving the press more fodder before he knew the situation. Besides, there was the matter of Bonnaud traveling under an assumed name and being a wanted man.

It had been harder to get the authorities to agree to let Lisette on board, especially since he'd refused to tell them who she was. But a few covert bribes had convinced them.

He glanced at Lisette. "Are you sure you want to do this?" he asked, fighting not to grab her hand in front of the quarantine officer accompanying them. "Once we're aboard, they may not let us leave until quarantine is lifted. What is your half brother going to think if he arrives from Scotland to find that you're still not home?"

"I sent a messenger with a note for Skrimshaw to give to Dom, in case he returns soon." She cast the quarantine officer a furtive glance. "I didn't tell him where I was—just that I was safe. I didn't want to alarm Dom over the quarantine. But I did warn him about Hucker."

"Good idea. The man is bound to have returned to England by now, and he may very well return to watching Manton's Investigations."

"I know. That's why I have to go aboard with you—I have to talk to my . . . friend about what he's risking by coming here."

"I understand." That was why Maximilian hadn't pushed her into going home. After all they'd been through, she deserved to have her concerns about Bonnaud laid to rest.

Besides, a tiny, selfish part of him wanted her there for this encounter with the man who might very well be his brother. He was too agitated to think straight at present, and he knew that she would.

"So is there anyone on board the ship with fever or not?" Lisette asked. "If the ship has been here for six weeks and everyone has a clean bill of health, it should be out of quarantine by now. Since you made me stay in the carriage for most of your visits to the government officials, I never got the full story."

"To be honest, neither did I. At most there is one ill passenger on board. They couldn't tell me if it was cholera or not, however. My friend on the Privy Council would only say they'd been consulting with doctors." He shot her a quick glance. "That's my only worry about taking you out there. The thought of you catching cholera sends a chill down my spine."

A soft smile lit her face. "I feel the same about you. But I doubt it's cholera, and if only one passenger has it, we may not even encounter the ill individual."

He bloody well hoped not.

The boat reached the dock. They made the short trip out to the ship in a silence punctuated only by the slap of the waves against the boards and the swish of the oars through the water.

Once they boarded, they were met by the ship's captain. The quarantine officer introduced them as the Duke of Lyons and his "lady companion," which made Maximilian wince but didn't seem to overly concern Lisette. Then the official beat a hasty retreat to the boat.

"Well, Your Grace?" the captain asked when they were alone. "I do hope you've come to get the quarantine lifted."

That caught Maximilian off guard. "Actually, we need to see two of your passengers—Jack Drake and Victor Cale."

The captain's eyes narrowed. "Are they friends of yours?"

"You might say that," Maximilian retorted. "Why?"

"Because Victor Cale is the reason the *Grecian* is still sitting here. After we were forced into quarantine, Cale got ill. My ship's physician, whom I would trust with my life, is convinced he has pneumonia, so there's no reason for continuing the quarantine just for him. But the damned quarantine officers won't lift it without permission from the Privy Council, and the Privy Council is too afraid to stick its neck out. So my men and my cargo are trapped here until he recovers. Or dies."

Maximilian tensed. "Is there a chance of him dying?"

"He's been very sick for over two weeks. Dr. Worth is beginning to despair. And Cale's friend Drake spends every waking hour helping to tend him."

Maximilian grabbed for Lisette's hand. She squeezed it comfortingly, and that settled him a little. "Then I should like to speak with Drake and the doctor."

The captain nodded and inclined his head toward a hatchway. "They're both below deck in the infirmary."

"Thank you," Maximilian said.

Once they descended the hatchway, they didn't have to go far before finding the infirmary. It was the only cabin with a light burning from beneath the door. Before they could even enter, however, a man stepped out into the dim passageway, the lantern light from inside briefly illuminating his face.

"Tristan!" Lisette cried, apparently forgetting all about her brother's alias as she squeezed past Maximilian to launch herself at the man.

"Lisette?" he said in clear bewilderment as she hugged him. He pulled back to look at her. "Good God, it *is* you! What the devil are you doing here?"

"I should ask you the same thing!" She lowered her voice. "Have you lost your mind, coming to England? George has had a man snooping about Dom's, and if he should learn that you're so close . . ."

Bonnaud flashed her the cocky grin that Maximilian remembered from their chat at the races years ago.

"Surely you and Dom were too careful for that." Then he peered past her. "How did you know I was here? Is that Dom with you?"

Maximilian moved into the light. "No, it's the Duke of Lyons."

Bonnaud gaped at him. "You found me!"

"It took some doing," Maximilian said, "but yes."

Bonnaud glanced back into the room behind him. They could hear violent coughing coming from inside. "This way," he said, pointing down the passageway. "We can talk."

"I want to see him first," Maximilian snapped.

Not needing to ask who he meant, Bonnaud said, "He's very ill."

"The captain told us as much," Maximilian said.

As Maximilian entered with Lisette at his side, he stared at the emaciated figure in the bed. Next to the bed sat a young man who was trying futilely to get the patient to drink a chemical-smelling draught.

"Your Grace, this is Dr. Worth," Bonnaud said. "He's been looking after Victor." He glanced at the doctor. "Dr. Worth, this is the Duke of Lyons, a . . . possible relation of Victor's. And the lady with him is my sister, Miss Bonnaud."

When Maximilian shot him a sharp glance, surprised that he'd given the man her actual name, Bonnaud shrugged. "The doctor and I have spent days together. We no longer have any secrets. He's the one who arranged for me to be smuggled off the ship last week."

"We couldn't wait for quarantine to be lifted," Dr. Worth explained. "The possibility that Mr. Cale might die became more pronounced with each day, and Mr. Bonnaud thought you might wish to see him before . . . he got too ill."

Bonnaud scowled. "That cursed quarantine officer wouldn't let me go beyond the docks or reveal to you that we were from a quarantine ship, for fear that you would show up here and get him sacked. He got sacked anyway, smuggling contraband off a couple of days later."

He shot Maximilian an apologetic glance. "I really thought I'd have a chance to speak to you, or I wouldn't have been so secretive in the letter. But the damned officer got spooked when he saw soldiers and insisted that I return with him at once, since we'd already waited a while for you."

"I know, I'm sorry." Maximilian's eyes were fixed on the man in the bed. "I was out when your message came. But I remembered your connection to Manton and went to his lodgings. Manton wasn't there, but Miss Bonnaud was, and she eventually figured it out."

No point in revealing how—or the fact that they'd spent the last several days alone together.

Victor began another fit of coughing, and Maximilian tensed. Lisette tucked her hand in the crook of his arm. "Are you all right?"

"No." Raw fear tightened his throat. "He looks very ill indeed." He squeezed her hand, then stepped nearer the bed. "How long has he been like this?" he asked Dr. Worth.

"He's been sick for two weeks, Your Grace," the physician said. "It wasn't too bad at first, but then he took a turn for the worse a week ago, and he's been feverish and insensible ever since. The next few days are crucial. He'll either survive it or die. I've seen men of his youth and vigor survive pneumonia with no ill effects after treatment. And I've seen men stronger than him die under the same treatment. At this point, it's hard to know which he will do."

"Is that you, Father?" said "Victor," fretfully pushing away the doctor's cup. "Don't want any more gruel. Hate gruel."

Maximilian caught his breath. Gruel had been Mother's favorite cure for illness. Had it been Uncle Nigel's, too, for the boy he'd treated as his son? Or was Victor possibly even remembering further back, to his childhood illnesses at home?

The man looked as if he *could* be Peter. He seemed the right age, and he faintly resembled Father. Peter had been blond as a child, whereas Victor's hair was a medium brown, but Maximilian's was only a shade lighter than brown, and he'd been blond as a boy, too.

"What color are his eyes?" Maximilian asked.

When the physician blinked, Maximilian realized that must seem a very odd question. "They're hazel," the doctor said. "Why?"

Peter's eyes had been hazel.

He gripped Lisette's hand. Could it be? Or was he

grasping at straws, desperate to have his brother back? "Is there nothing you can do for him?"

"I'm making sure he drinks saline and sulfur draughts. Some doctors insist on cupping and bleeding the patient as well, but I've never been fond of such a treatment." The physician sponged the man's brow with a damp cloth. "It would help, however, if he could leave the ship. The air here is too wet for his lungs, and the noise of the sailors disturbs him. He needs to be in a calm, dry, *quiet* place."

"You're sure he doesn't have cholera?" Maximilian asked.

Dr. Worth snorted. "He's not vomiting, he's not voiding his bowels every hour . . . of course he doesn't have cholera. I have explained that to the quarantine officers repeatedly, but they will not act."

"They will *now*," Maximilian said grimly, "if I have to bring every damned member of the Privy Council down to the docks to ensure it."

The doctor flashed him a tired smile. "Thank you. Lifting the quarantine would do him a vast deal of good, I think." As Victor went into another fit of coughing, Dr. Worth mopped his brow. "I swear I'll do all in my power to save him, Your Grace."

"If you succeed," Maximilian clipped out, "I'll gain you any medical appointment you desire."

The physician said gently, "Whatever happens will be his own choice, I fear, not mine or even yours. He'll have to fight it if he wants to live."

Maximilian nodded, but felt the same helpless despair come over him that he'd felt during Father's madness and Mother's last days before death. What good was it to be the bloody Duke of Lyons if he couldn't save the ones he loved?

Assuming that this man *was* one of the ones he loved.

He turned to Bonnaud. "It's time we had that talk."

With a nod, Bonnaud led them from the room and down the passageway to a small cabin. Apparently it was the one Bonnaud had shared with Victor, for it contained two bunks fitted one above the other.

Bonnaud dropped wearily onto the lowest bunk and Lisette hurried to sit next to him. Maximilian understood why, but it made something lurch in his chest to see the two Bonnaud siblings ranged against him.

It did, however, reinforce how uncanny was the resemblance between brother and sister. Both had eyes of crystal blue, both had pointed jaws, and both had dark curls, though Bonnaud's were cut to just under his chin.

One thing was certain—Bonnaud looked wrung out. He did *not* look like a man engaged in some sort of fraud.

"I suppose you want to see the handkerchief first," Bonnaud said, reaching under the bunk for a small trunk.

"No." Maximilian crossed his arms over his chest. "I want to know why you risked your very life to return to this country with a man you believed to be Peter Cale. You and I met only briefly years ago—why go to so much trouble for me? Because I don't believe it's out of the goodness of your heart."

Though Lisette shot him an injured glance, Bonnaud met his gaze evenly. "It's not. I don't know how much Lisette has told you, but I'm wanted in England for stealing a horse when I was seventeen. I was hoping that if I could reunite you with your brother, you would use your influence to get the charge against me dropped."

Maximilian blinked. He hadn't expected *that*. And he had to admire the man for not only admitting his crime, but not trying to excuse it.

"Don't misunderstand me," Bonnaud went on, "I enjoy my work in France for the Sûreté. But I miss England." He took Lisette's hand in his and squeezed it. When he went on, his voice was choked. "And I miss my brother and sister. With Lisette and Dom both here, I have no one. My landlord, Eugène Vidocq, is very good to me, but—"

"He's not family. I understand that." Especially as someone who'd been left alone for the past few years, with no one to share his pain and grief.

Until Lisette had come along. "I assure you, Bonnaud, if Victor Cale proves to be my brother, I'll do everything in my power to restore you to England and your family. It's the least I can do."

"Thank you, Your Grace," Bonnaud said as Lisette cast Maximilian a melting smile that warmed his heart.

"So how did it begin—your finding Victor?" Maximilian asked.

"I've known him off and on for a few years. I never connected him with your family because I didn't remember that your surname was Cale. When I met you, everyone referred to you as Lord Maximilian."

That had been before the fire, when Maximilian was still only a second son.

"Besides," Bonnaud went on, "neither Victor nor I talked much about our pasts. To be honest, I thought he was an orphan. He'd spent some years after the war serving in Prussia's standing army, having fought with them against the French at Waterloo."

"Peter would only have been eighteen then."

"I think Victor was seventeen when he joined, yes."

Maximilian mused a moment. "That would probably have been right after my great-uncle died. The timing fits." He stared at Bonnaud. "But how did he escape the fire? Who was the boy killed in the fire if it wasn't Peter? And if Victor is Peter, why did he change his name?"

"I don't know. I didn't know enough details about the fire even to be able to ask him the right questions, and he won't talk about it anyway. He says he'll only tell *his family* about it."

That roused Maximilian's suspicions. He needed to be careful here and not let his desire for this stranger to be Peter take over his good sense. "Tell me how you met him."

"A few years ago, I was on a case in Antwerp. I needed an interpreter and I was referred to Victor, since he speaks several languages and he'd left the army to work on his own. After he helped me with that case, I used him whenever I needed an interpreter. Most recently he aided me in tracking down a forger."

Bonnaud took a long breath. "One night during that investigation, Victor and I went drinking. He pulled out a handkerchief, and I recognized it as being just like yours—down to the fancy embroidery. That's when I remembered that your family name was Cale."

"Show me the handkerchief," Maximilian said.

Dragging out his small trunk, Bonnaud removed a folded piece of linen. With shaky hands, Maximilian took it and held it up to the lantern's light. It was worn and frayed and dingy, but the embroidery was still intact, and it was exactly like that on Maximilian's handkerchief. He didn't really need to see the swath of white showing through it. He'd already felt the thickness of the extra fabric in the middle.

His heart began to pound.

"Well?" Lisette asked softly.

He handed it to her. "It's Peter's. At the very least Victor knew him, or knew someone who knew him." He stared Bonnaud down. "So when you saw the handkerchief, you told him what? That it belonged to the heir to a duke?"

"God, no! I'm no fool. Victor's a decent enough fellow, but he has led a rather rough existence. Ever since he left the army, he's been a soldier for pay for whoever hires him. I thought it wise to be circumspect."

Relief surged through Maximilian. Now he knew why Vidocq had spoken highly of Bonnaud.

Then something occurred to him. "But you told the doctor who I was."

Bonnaud rubbed his bleary eyes. "Once Victor worsened and grew delirious, there seemed no point in keeping this affair secret from Dr. Worth. I didn't tell him that Victor might be your brother; I just said he might be related to the Duke of Lyons. Victor doesn't even know his own name right now, much less what we are saying. Most of what he babbles is nonsense. And I had to confide in someone, if only to gain help in getting off the damned ship."

That made sense, especially under the circumstances. "Go on then, continue your story. You were drinking in a tavern, you saw the handkerchief . . ."

"I asked him how he came by it. That put him on his guard. He wanted to know why I asked, and I told him I'd seen one like it in England. That got him excited. He said he'd had an English father, who'd died in a fire at Gheel a few months before Waterloo."

Excitement coursed through Maximilian. It didn't get much plainer than that. But how could that bloody investigator have missed that Peter was still alive? *Damn* him! Maximilian had never liked the man, and now he liked him even less.

Bonnaud went on. "He said he'd been told he had no other family, but he'd always wondered if that was the truth."

"Told by whom?" Maximilian demanded.

"I don't know. The minute I started asking questions, he closed up. He asked if I knew who his family was, and then *I* closed up. I didn't think you would want me to reveal too much."

"You were right," Maximilian said. "Thank you."

"So we came to a sort of agreement. I said I'd take him to meet his family, if he would let me set up the meeting. But I'm sure he already suspects that his family is of some consequence. He commented on the fact that the embroidery seemed to be a family crest."

"Why didn't you just *write* to the duke with all this information?" Lisette put in.

Bonnaud eyed her askance. "I didn't even know if Lyons remembered our conversation all those years ago, and I wasn't going to take the chance that he might never see the letter. Besides, Victor was adamant about wanting to meet him, and I—"

"You were hoping for my help with the horse thieving charge," Maximilian said dryly.

"Exactly. We both thought that coming in person was the best idea."

Lisette snorted. "Yes, because taking a ship from a city infested with fever is always a good plan."

"It wasn't that bad when we got there," Bonnaud grumbled. "And anyway, how was I to know he would get sick? For God's sake, he was wounded at Waterloo and survived." He shook his head. "I can't believe he got through that only to be laid low by some damned pneumonia."

Maximilian sat there a moment, taking in everything Bonnaud had said. "So all you know for certain is that Victor's English father died in a fire in Gheel?"

"And that his surname is Cale, and has been all the time that I've known him. He absolutely refuses to say any more about his family as long as I refuse to tell him any more."

Maximilian scrubbed his hand over his face. He'd thought to get answers. Instead, he only had more questions.

The door to the cabin opened, and Dr. Worth thrust his head in. "I need to mix up more of my draught. Can one of you sit with him?"

Lisette stood. "I will."

"No, you won't," Maximilian put in. "You're exhausted. I'll sit with him. It's too late to do anything about the quarantine tonight. I'll deal with it in the morning."

The physician smiled at Lisette. "If you'd like, Miss, you can rest in my quarters. I've been sleeping in the infirmary anyway—I won't leave Mr. Cale until the worst is past."

"Very well," she said, "but I'm not going to sleep long. Tristan is obviously too worn out to do anything more tonight, and Max needs sleep, too, if he's to be of any good to us tomorrow."

"Max?" Bonnaud interjected. "You're calling the Duke of Lyons *Max*?"

When she blushed, Maximilian said, "Your sister and I have become friends through the midst of this. That's all." At least until he could convince her to marry him.

Bonnaud's eyes narrowed, but he merely said, "Then it's settled. His Grace will get the quarantine lifted, and Lisette and I will take turns sitting with Victor until he's better."

Assuming that he gets better. Maximilian squelched the thought. The man *had* to live, damn it. He refused to accept any other outcome.

◆ ◆ ◆

THE NEXT NIGHT, Lisette walked into the doctor's cramped quarters and tossed her ribbon embroidery onto the tiny table bolted to the wall. She felt like a sack of potatoes that had been dragged across a rocky hill and tossed down a ravine.

Tristan entered behind her, having come to play lady's maid for her before she retired.

"Any word on whether the quarantine has been lifted?" she asked him.

"I just saw the duke, and he said they were coming in the morning to make it official that we can all leave the ship."

She let out a breath. "Thank God."

"How is the patient?" Tristan asked.

"The worst I've seen him," she said, choking down her despair. "His fever is still awful and his delirium gets worse by the moment."

Thank God Max had been too busy today dealing

with the Privy Council and quarantine officers to spend time in the infirmary with Victor. Yesterday she'd seen the haunted look in his eyes when Victor coughed so violently. "If Victor dies, I don't know how Max will endure it. Yet I don't see how Victor can survive, no matter how many of those draughts Dr. Worth slips down his throat."

"Victor's stronger than he looks. Don't count him out yet." Stepping behind her, Tristan undid Lisette's buttons. "Dr. Worth is a nice man."

She sighed. "Not that again."

"I'm merely pointing it out. He's young, he's handsome . . . he speaks well of you."

"I'm not interested in marrying Dr. Worth," she said sharply, "so stop it."

He was quiet a long moment. "I hope you're not so foolish as to have set your sights on 'Max.'"

"Why not? He's young, he's handsome . . . he speaks well of me."

"Very funny," Tristan growled as he worked loose her laces. "But I'm not joking, Lisette. He's a duke. That means something here in England."

"You think I don't know that?"

Watching Max use his rank to deal with all those officials last night and today reminded her rather forcefully that he was oceans above her in station. Impending madness or no, he could have any woman he wanted. And any other woman would gladly meet his conditions.

But having seen his anguish, she knew she could

never do so. She loved him too much to leave him in the hands of strangers in his final hours. And considering how dedicated he'd been to seeing to the welfare of a man he wasn't even sure was his brother, he ought to understand.

"Of course, if Victor does turn out to be Lyons's brother," Tristan said as he finished loosening her laces, "then Maximilian Cale is not the duke anymore, is he? So I'd better hurry off to the infirmary, or he might have figured that out and decided to finish Victor off."

She whirled to scowl at him. "Don't you *dare* say such a vile thing! Don't even think it!"

"I was joking, Lisette." Tristan stared hard at her. "And I take it that you *have* set your sights on the duke."

Tipping up her chin, she glared at him. "Don't be ridiculous. Just because I defend his character—"

Her brother snorted. "You don't just defend his character. You cater to him as I've never seen you cater to anyone, not even me and Dom. When you weren't looking after Victor today, it was 'Max needs this' and 'I should make sure Max eats.'"

Good Lord, she hadn't meant to be so transparent. She let out her breath in a long sigh, and the urge to confide in someone, *anyone*, was too overwhelming to resist. "You don't understand. I'm in love with him."

A look of pity crossed his face. "Oh, dear heart—"

"Don't say it. I know it's hopeless." Though not for the reasons he thought. "And I'm fine, really."

"You don't seem fine. The two of you practically set fires off each other when you're in a room together."

His eyes narrowed. "It makes me wonder what went on between you while you were trying to find me. Especially since you persist in not telling me how you managed it."

"It was nothing," she lied. "And nothing went on. Max—the duke—was a perfect gentleman."

"Hmm."

"Don't keep the doctor waiting," she said lightly.

Tristan cast her another concerned glance, then left. As soon as he was gone, she changed into her night rail and dropped onto the narrow bunk. She should let the rocking of the ship lull her to sleep.

But Tristan had her agitated now, obsessed with wondering the same thing she'd been wondering since yesterday. If Victor proved to be Peter, how would Max react? And if Peter—Victor—died—

Oh, Lord, that didn't bear thinking upon.

A knock came at the door. She got up and opened it, only to find Max standing there. It startled her. He hadn't once tried to see her alone since they'd come aboard the ship.

He stared at her, his face ashen and his eyes bleak in the lantern light. Seemingly oblivious to her scanty attire, he came into the tiny cabin and sat on the bunk, saying in a shattered voice, "I finally find my brother, and he's going to be ripped from me before I even get to know him. He's dying."

19

MAXIMILIAN FELT AS if Fate had been toying with him for its own amusement. What good was it to have found Peter, only to lose him in the end?

"You saw Victor?" Lisette asked in a shaky voice.

"Just now. I . . . I went in to tell the doctor that the quarantine had been lifted, and . . ." His throat closed up. "Victor was so ill that the doctor had resorted to bleeding him. He was thrashing, and I had to help . . . hold him down. Oh, God, my brother is dying. And there isn't a damned thing I can do to stop it!"

After shutting the door, she came to sit beside him on the bunk. "First of all, we're still not even certain that he *is* your brother." She patted his hand reassuringly. "And secondly, we're definitely not certain that he's going to die."

Maximilian ignored the part about Victor not being his brother. The resemblance to Father was too strong to ignore. Victor had to be Peter.

Lisette threaded her fingers through his. "Tristan says he's stronger than he looks."

"Not tonight, he isn't." Maximilian stared at her, his throat raw with fear. "He's so bloody hot with fever. And he's raving like . . . like—"

"I know," she whispered. "And I imagine it's even harder for you to watch than for me."

"Seeing Victor's ravaged body buck the doctor's hold is like watching Father all over again," he admitted.

"It's not the same thing, though," she said kindly. "Victor's delirium comes from fever. It will pass."

"Assuming that he lives." Squeezing her hand, he choked out, "And I don't think . . . I don't think . . . he will."

"Shh, *mon coeur*, shh," she crooned. She hugged him to her. "It will be all right."

"It will never be all right!" he cried, jerking back from her as fear scored his heart. "All these years, I've tried to approach my future logically, to plan for my end to be dignified. For it not to hurt anyone but me. I thought I could hold fast to that plan. But I realize now, watching him . . ."

Gripping her hand in both of his, he struggled for breath. "I'm not that strong. I can't bear to end up like Victor, raving mad. At least he has us. But I'll have no one. Only some coldly efficient doctor, some attendant struggling to subdue me."

Pity spread over her face, and it was a mark of how terrified he was that he didn't even care.

"Oh, God, Lisette, I can't stand the thought of it,"

he bit out. "I meant to stay in that damned room with him tonight, but watching him d-die is just too hard. I can't . . . I can't . . ."

She pressed a kiss to his mouth as if to calm him. But it only made him more desperate for touch, affection . . . life beyond the grave.

Grabbing her face in his hands, he kissed her fiercely, passionately. He needed her to blot out the fear, to make him feel in control again.

"Promise me you'll marry me, Lisette," he whispered against her lips. "Promise me you won't let me die alone."

"Max, I—"

"No, you can't refuse me this time. You mustn't." His breathing grew ragged, harsh. "I won't let you."

Pulling her onto his lap, he began to devour her mouth. He needed to feel whole, alive. He needed to know there was one person on this earth who cared about him. Because if Victor died he would be alone again, and he simply couldn't bear it. The thought of going on in his empty existence without anyone . . .

He dragged openmouthed kisses up her cheek to her ear. "I thought I was resigned to my solitary future with a woman I didn't care about. I thought that I could manage . . . to accept my lot." His voice grew choked. "Then you came along, and I learned what real hell is. It's meeting the one woman you want and realizing you can't have her."

"You *can* have me, Max," she whispered as she pulled back from him. "If not for your conditions—"

"To blazes with my conditions," he growled. She'd breached his walls, and he knew he could never build them back. He no longer wanted to. "I'll take you however I can have you, dearling. It's utterly selfish, but I can no longer bear the thought of going mad without you beside me to ease the way. Especially if it means I'm to be deprived of you for the part of my life that's worth living."

Her eyes were full of a melting softness that soothed his ragged pain. "You don't have to be deprived of me, *mon coeur*," she murmured, brushing kisses over his cheeks and jaw and lips. "I will never leave you now. Never."

He searched her face. "You promise? You swear it?"

She smiled. "I swear it."

"You'll marry me."

"Yes. Oh yes, Max. As soon as you want."

"Thank God," he rasped, relief swamping him. Even if Victor did die, he wouldn't have to be alone anymore.

He kissed her again, achingly, thoroughly. "I want you, dearling." He worked loose the buttons of her nightdress. "I need to be inside you. I need to be reminded that there is life somewhere outside this cursed ship. You're the only one who's ever given me hope, and I never knew how desperately I needed it until you came along. Even if it's a futile hope, I need to believe that my future isn't all bleak."

"It's not," she gasped as he shifted her so he could drag her night rail off over her head. "I know it's not. We'll have a lifetime together, I swear."

"Don't make promises you can't keep, Lisette," he whispered. "Whatever time we have is enough. We'll make it be enough."

Hastily, he undid his trousers, then his drawers, desperate now to have her. He settled her astride him. "Make love to me, dearling." He rubbed his rampant cock against her.

Her eyes went wide. "A woman can . . ."

"Yes," he said hoarsely. "Kneel up and take me inside you."

Just saying the words had aroused him even more—the image of her riding him possessed him. So when she murmured, "Very well," he thought for sure he'd come off right there.

Especially since she looked so very lovely perched astride him, with her skin luminous in the lantern light and her eyes gleaming. And when she drew herself up and came down on him like some intoxicating goddess, he gave himself up to her. She enveloped him, his wild French rose, growing into every crack in his walls, surrounding him with the scent of perfume and the sweetness of her petals.

And he knew he could never root her out now. That was what made her so very dangerous—he no longer wanted to.

He cupped her breasts, kneading them, glorying in them as she began to undulate on top of him. His cock was like iron inside her. He scattered kisses over every inch of skin he could reach, branding her as his for all time.

"Take everything," he choked out. "It's yours."

"I only want you."

She kissed him then, entwining her tongue with his, then teasing it back into her mouth. As she engulfed his cock below, he drove into her mouth above, setting a rhythm that she echoed in her motions.

His blood sang as she rode him. She was a natural wanton, sure of her feminine power and using it to hold him in thrall. He'd always feared just this thing—being possessed by desire. But she'd taught him not to fear it. And next to the fear of being alone, it was nothing.

"Do you like that, my pirate?" she teased, leaning over to thread her fingers through his hair, her breasts pressing against his face. He sucked them hard, feeling his release coming.

"Faster, dearling," he rasped against her sweet bosom. "More. Ride me harder."

"Yes, *mon coeur*." She quickened her motions. "Whatever you want."

"I want *you*."

"You have me already." Her breathing grew broken, rough. "You have it all, if you will only take it . . . my body . . . my heart . . . my love . . . I love you, Max."

The words sent him over the edge. He thrust up hard into her, then lost himself inside her. As she cried out and milked him dry, her sweet words thundered in his head.

I love you, Max.

And in that moment, the fortress surrounding his heart cracked from top to bottom.

✦ ✦ ✦

LISETTE LAY IN Max's arms, her body curled into his on the narrow bunk. He was still fully dressed and she was naked, which ought to embarrass her. But she'd passed the point of embarrassment with Max. Which she supposed was a good thing, since she'd accepted his proposal of marriage.

She only wished she hadn't proclaimed her love for him. He wasn't ready. If she wasn't careful, too much closeness would have him pushing her out.

Yet he held her so sweetly, so tenderly, kissing her hair, stroking her hip. "Did you mean it?" he murmured behind her.

She tensed. There was no mistaking what he was talking about, but she had expected him to pretend she hadn't said it. "I promised never to lie to you, remember? Of course I meant it."

Turning in his arms, she stared up at his shadowed face and tried to read what he was thinking.

His expression was pensive. "No woman—other than my mother, of course—has ever said those words to me."

She cupped his cheek. "Then you've been spending your time with a lot of foolish women."

A ghost of a smile crossed his face. "Perhaps."

"Or you've locked them out so thoroughly that they didn't dare."

He sobered. "That is probably closer to the truth. Though to be fair, no woman has ever fought quite so hard to get past my locks as you have."

She smoothed back his hair. "Does it bother you?"

"Sometimes. I'm not used to . . . letting people close."

"I noticed," she said, hiding a smile.

A frown furrowed his brow. "Lisette, I . . . well, it's just that . . ."

She pressed her fingers to his lips. "You don't have to say anything." Although she yearned to hear *I love you, too*, she wouldn't rush him.

"It's just . . . My world has been at sixes and sevens since the day your brother sent me that note. But there's one thing I'm sure of: I want you as my wife."

She caught her breath. "For richer or poorer, till death do us part?"

He nodded. "No conditions."

With a hitch in her throat, she snuggled into him. "That's good enough for me." For now.

They lay there companionably another moment. Then he propped himself up on one elbow. "I should go. I should be with Victor."

His tortured words earlier came into her mind. *I meant to stay in that damned room with him tonight, but watching him d-die is just too hard. I can't . . . I can't . . .*

"No," she said firmly. "Tristan and the doctor are with him. You need rest. You spent all day fighting for him, and you're exhausted. If it looks as if Victor really is at the end, Dr. Worth will come fetch us."

"Another reason I should leave. It's probably not a good idea for anyone to find us here like this."

"Because they might force you to marry me?" she quipped.

He smiled. "Good point."

"Come now," she said, stroking his face. "Sleep."

"You're bossy, do you know that?" he said, but he lay back down.

"That's what my brothers tell me. But I'm really not. It's just that men think no one should ever tell them what to do, unless it's some general brandishing a sword on the battlefield."

He chuckled. "A pity for Napoleon that he never had you in his army," he murmured, his eyes drifting shut. "He would have won the war. Or maybe just . . . just . . ."

When he fell silent and his breathing slowed, she smiled and curled back into him. After a while, she too slept.

She didn't know how long she'd lain there when a knock came at the door. It must have been some time, though, because she could see sunlight through the porthole. When the knock came again, a fraction louder, she sat up.

"Yes?" she called out.

"It's Dr. Worth," the physician's voice said beyond the door.

Her heart froze in her chest. She felt Max tense beside her and knew that he too was awake, but that didn't stop her from hurrying to the door.

She opened it just enough to see the doctor standing there. "What is it?" she asked, her blood pounding. "What's happened?"

He smiled broadly. "Mr. Cale has come around. His fever broke a few hours ago, and he slept a real sleep for the first time last night. He's still very weak, but he's awake and he's lucid and it looks as if he will fully recover."

"Thank the good Lord," she said hoarsely. "That's wonderful news!"

"I went to tell the duke but he wasn't in Bonnaud's quarters."

She forced a smile. "I'll find him and tell him."

"Thank you. I need to return to my patient."

Shutting the door, she leaned back against it, then smiled at Max, who was sitting there looking stunned.

"I can't believe it," he said hoarsely. "I was so afraid . . ." A smile split his face. "I may actually have a brother."

"But that means you might not be the duke anymore," she couldn't refrain from pointing out.

"It doesn't matter," he said, his gaze warm. "I have you. Unless you're planning to throw me over if I prove *not* to be the duke," he teased.

She pretended to consider that for a moment. "Well . . . I *do* hope you get to keep your yacht."

When he blinked, then laughed, she relaxed. They both knew their lives would never be the same after this moment. But if he didn't care, she didn't care.

As long as she had him, as long as she had the hope that one day he could learn to love her, she was content.

20

A SHORT WHILE later, as Maximilian followed Lisette down the narrow passageway to the infirmary, he wondered why he'd balked at telling her he loved her.

Because he *did* love her. He loved how sweet she could be, and how tart. He loved both the rose and the thorns. He loved that one minute she could coddle him and the next remind him that he'd been damned lucky to be born a duke to two parents who'd loved him, madness or no.

So why hadn't he said the words to her?

He sighed. Because after laying bare his fears last night, after showing her how desperately he needed her, he'd felt compelled to keep one part of himself still invulnerable. One part of himself still under his control.

Coward.

Perhaps so. But baring one's heart was a risk, even with his dear Lisette. He simply wasn't ready to take that risk.

Though when she gave him a soft smile just as he

opened the door to the infirmary, he nearly changed his mind about that.

Then he caught sight of the man he'd wanted to meet all his life, and the moment passed. Because a gaunt and pale Victor Cale, sitting upright and looking decidedly more lucid than before, with his brown hair tousled and his beard quite advanced, was the spitting image of Father in his final days.

Choking down the lump in his throat, Maximilian walked into the room with Lisette at his side. "Mr. Cale," he managed to say formally, "it's good to see you looking well."

Victor turned his gaze from the doctor to Maximilian, curiosity in his hazel eyes. "Who the devil are you?"

This was no time to mince words. "I believe I may be your brother."

Victor's face changed, grew even paler, if that were possible. He glanced at Bonnaud. "He's the 'family' we've come to see?"

Bonnaud nodded. "And that's my sister Lisette there with him. I've told you about her."

"Yes," Victor said, casting Lisette a cursory glance before turning to study Maximilian with an oddly hostile glint. "I always knew that my bastard of a father had another family somewhere. He was always so cagey with Mother about his trip to England that one time."

"Mother?" Maximilian said hoarsely. "What mother?"

"*My* mother," Victor said.

"You never said you had a mother," Bonnaud put in, startled.

"You never asked. In any case, she died long before I met you." Crossing his arms over his chest, Victor scanned Maximilian coldly. "And yes, *brother*, I'm sure you would consider her far beneath our family's dignity. I can tell just by your clothes that you have quite a bit of it. She was only a tavern maid, and my bloody father never let her forget it. But she loved the bastard until the day he died, and that ought to count for something."

Maximilian fought to comprehend the strange turn of this conversation. "Are you saying that Nigel Cale not only pretended to be your father, but foisted a pretend mother on you as well?"

It was Victor's turn to be startled. "There wasn't anything pretend about my mother, I assure you. And unless she was lying to me, Nigel Cale *was* my father."

Maximilian was all out to sea. "No, your real father was Sidney Cale, and your real mother was Tibby Cale. Nigel kidnapped you when you were nearly five."

"Kidnapped me!" Victor said. "The hell he did. I remember when I was five, and Father had already left the navy to—" He froze. "Peter," he whispered. "This is about *Peter*."

Lisette moved up beside Maximilian. "You're not Peter?"

"No," Victor said. "He was my half brother. My father told us that . . . Peter was a by-blow of his whose mother died." His expression grew bleak. "I should have known that was a lie."

Grief struck Maximilian so hard he could hardly breathe. Victor wasn't his brother. Victor wasn't Peter! Maximilian had been so sure— "But you have Peter's handkerchief," he said hoarsely. "I assumed that . . . that . . ."

"You assumed wrong," Victor said, turning belligerent again. "Peter left it in his bureau when he headed off in a temper to see Father at Gheel."

"You didn't live in Gheel?" Lisette asked.

"No," Victor said tersely. "The three of us—Mother and Peter and I—lived in a cottage in the next village, where Mother made a little money doing laundry to pay for Father's 'cure,' which never came." He paused to cough a bit. "Peter and I were carpenters' apprentices . . . but we talked about joining the army and fighting Boney together."

Maximilian heard all of that as if through a fog. Peter, a duke's heir, had been forced to work as a carpenter's apprentice? Holy God, what had Uncle Nigel been thinking, to carry him away from his family for *that*?

"The day Peter went to Gheel," Victor continued, "something he'd seen or read had set him off. He said he was going to get the truth out of Father about who his mother was." Victor wheezed a bit, grief shining in his eyes. "He never came back. Somebody at Gheel later told me that he and Father argued. The general opinion was . . . that one of them knocked over a candle that set fire to the cottage."

Somewhere in the midst of Victor's recitation, Lisette had taken Maximilian's hand, and he realized he was squeezing it hard enough to imprint his nails on her palm.

She didn't seem to notice. Her eyes were filled with tears. For him. Because of him and his loss. "I'm sorry, Max. I'm so sorry."

Victor began struggling for breath, and Dr. Worth looked at Maximilian. "Could we continue this later?"

"No," Victor choked out. "I just need . . . a moment. I came all this way . . . to find my family. Now I want to know the truth."

With concern in his face, Dr. Worth pressed a glass of wine into his hand. Victor swallowed some and his breathing calmed. He then stared up at Maximilian. "So you're *Peter's* brother," he said in a hollow voice. "Not mine."

"Yes," Maximilian managed.

Clear disappointment crossed Victor's face. "I thought perhaps Father had . . . another legitimate family in England. That I might even have another half brother." His expression looked as empty as Maximilian felt. "But I have no one."

"Actually," Maximilian said, sympathetic to the man's grief, "since Nigel Cale was my great-uncle, if you're his legitimate son, then you're my first cousin, once removed."

"Am I?" Victor said, a sudden hope in his voice. But then he scowled. "That hardly counts, does it?"

"What do you mean?"

"This has all been about Peter. Finding Peter." He coughed a few minutes. Then his voice lowered. "No one ever gave a damn about finding *me*."

Irritation scraped Maximilian's nerves raw. "I didn't even know you existed until now. No one did."

Victor shook his head. "That investigator must have made a report to your father. Which he ignored. And *you* ignored."

"What investigator?" Maximilian asked sharply.

Suspicion lined Victor's face. "Don't pretend you don't know about him. He showed up in our village a month or so after the fire." Victor breathed heavily a moment, then pressed on. "He came to question Mother and me about Father. When Mother asked . . . if we had any relations, the man said he didn't think so, but he'd let us know."

Victor's voice hardened. "About six months passed, and the man showed up while I was out working. He talked to Mother. Told her that she was due some money . . . Father's inheritance." He wheezed a moment. "That she'd get it all as long as she agreed to sign some paper. She couldn't read English, so she didn't know what the paper said, but she signed it. Anything to get us money."

A muscle ticked in Victor's jaw. "That was the last time we saw the fellow. And I never found out what that damned paper said, either."

It took him a moment, but when the truth dawned on Maximilian, anger roared up in him. "Damn him. Damn him to hell."

At the virulence in Maximilian's voice, Lisette and Bonnaud exchanged glances. But Victor merely narrowed his gaze. "Who?"

"My bloody father. He knew. He had to have known. That investigator—Father paid the man to find out what had happened to Peter. If that investigator talked to your mother, then he knew Uncle had a family. And he had to have told Father. Father just didn't want *me* to know."

"Why the devil not?" Bonnaud asked.

Maximilian's gaze locked with Lisette's. "Because Victor would be next in line for the dukedom."

Victor gaped at him. "Wait a minute. My father was related to a *duke*?"

"Your father was the youngest son of the sixth Duke of Lyons," Maximilian said dully. "And thus brother to the seventh duke and uncle to the eighth." He paused to stare at Victor. "He was also great-uncle to the ninth duke. Me."

"Bloody hell," Victor muttered. He eyed Maximilian warily. "I'm your heir?"

"Not directly. That's not how it works. But you and I are presently the only male descendants of my—*our*—great-grandfather, the sixth Duke of Lyons. If I die without a male heir, you inherit the dukedom." Maximilian curled his hands into fists. "And clearly Father despised the idea of his uncle's progeny ever having a chance at inheriting the dukedom. Not after what Uncle Nigel did."

"That's why your father burned the records," Lisette said softly.

A cold chill swept down Maximilian's spine. "He did it deliberately, because he didn't want anyone to ever know of Victor's existence. I thought it was done in a fit of madness, but now I'm not so sure."

"Madness?" Victor said. "*Your* father went mad, too?"

Swallowing hard, Maximilian said, "Afraid so. It's the family curse."

Victor's expression hardened. "Do you happen to know if your father ever had syphilis?"

Maximilian froze. "As a matter of fact, he did. What has that got to do with anything?"

"My father had it, too. One of the physicians at Gheel believed that syphilis can cause madness later in life, even if you banish the disease early."

"I've noticed that as well," Dr. Worth put in. "I've seen a number of cases of insanity where the sufferer had contracted syphilis at some point in his life."

"So the madness might be a result of the disease?" Lisette asked in an excited voice. "It might have nothing to do with anything but that?"

Maximilian held his breath, a sudden ray of hope opening in his dark future.

"Possibly," Dr. Worth said. "Look at how 'mad' the pneumonia made Victor. It is my firm belief that disease works on the mind as well as the body. And syphilis is a virulent disease."

His blood pounding fiercely through his veins, Maximilian seized Lisette's hand. She beamed at him as she clearly grasped the direction of his thoughts.

If the madness had been a result of the syphilis . . .
Holy God, he might actually have a hope of a *life*!

Bonnaud was frowning. "It's rather an odd coincidence that both the duke's father and great-uncle
should contract syphilis, don't you think?"

"Not necessarily," Maximilian said. "They used to go
drinking together."

"Drinking is a far cry from whoring," Bonnaud said.
"And you'd expect the duke at least to be more careful
about such things."

Maximilian nodded. "I know—I always thought
it was odd myself that Father would have gone to a
whore. He never seemed the type."

"Perhaps he didn't get the syphilis from a whore,"
Victor said coldly.

"He didn't have a mistress, either," Maximilian put
in, not sure why it mattered how Father had gotten
syphilis. "He was wild for my mother. Of course, that
all happened before he married her."

"You know that for a fact?" Victor coughed some,
then went on relentlessly. "You know for certain he got
sick *before* he met your mother?"

Something in Victor's hard tone was beginning to
irritate Maximilian. "No, the doctor told me of it after
he went mad. But I'm sure—"

"Because there's another possibility." Victor's gaze
bore into Maximilian's. "Perhaps my father got it and
gave it to a woman that he and your father were both
intimate with."

"But who would that—" Maximilian tensed as his

father's final words came to mind. *So I only have the one son, then?*

Holy God. Oh bloody, bloody hell. *That* was what Victor was getting at?

"No. The very idea is revolting," Maximilian said sharply. "It's impossible."

Victor scowled at him. "My father always claimed that Peter was his son, even during his mad ravings, even when he was out of his mind. Peter was *his son*. He never deviated from that, never spoke of a kidnapping, never mentioned a nephew."

"I don't give a damn what he spoke of!" Maximilian cried. "He was lying, the damned bastard! He kidnapped my brother!"

"Why would he do that?" Victor asked. "What reason could he possibly have had to do such a thing if Peter *wasn't* his son?"

The question had haunted Maximilian and his parents for years. But this . . . this was not the answer.

"He was mad," Maximilian gritted out. "You said so yourself."

"Don't get me wrong—Father was an arse, but he didn't go mad until I was nearly fourteen, long after he brought Peter home." Victor struggled for breath. "By the time he lost his mind, he'd been in the army as an enlisted man for years . . . fighting for his country and moving us all over the Continent. He was lucid enough to keep hold of his position as a soldier . . . until the day he . . . tried to strangle Mother. Which is when we brought him to Gheel."

Victor glanced away, his face darkening, and Maximilian felt a moment's sympathy for the man who'd shared his own hell. But his sympathy vanished when he remembered what the man was trying to claim about Mother.

"You're wrong," Maximilian hissed. "My mother was a saint, I tell you. She would never have had an affair with her husband's uncle. Even the thought of it is appalling!"

Lisette put a hand on his arm. "You said she was wracked with guilt. Is it possible that you mistook the source of her guilt? If she knew that she had given your father syphilis after being with his uncle—"

"No!" He snatched his arm free of her. "No! It *isn't possible*! You won't convince me otherwise!" He stared at her, swamped by betrayal. "And how could you for one moment believe what my cousin is saying? The cousin I never even met until today! I told you what my mother suffered, what she endured. How dare you take *his* side?"

"I'm not taking anyone's side, Max," she said softly. "I'm just saying that it's one solution that makes sense."

"You think so, do you?" He gazed about at them, at the pitying looks on their faces, and every inch of him recoiled. "Just because your mothers were whores doesn't mean that mine was, too, damn it!"

The room fell eerily silent.

When Lisette's face turned to ash, Maximilian could have ripped out his tongue. He reached for her but she brushed his hand away.

"I'm sorry, Lisette. I didn't mean—"

"Yes, you did." She went to stand by her brother with a look of such pain that it cut him to the heart. "We will always be beneath you, won't we?"

Bonnaud put his arm about her protectively as he shot Maximilian a steely glance. "I told you, dear heart. He's a duke. He's not like us."

Hearing that her damned brother had obviously been warning her against him spiked Maximilian's temper higher. "You're right, Bonnaud." He stared the man down. "I'm *not* like you. I don't speak ill of a man behind his back while at the same time currying his favor." He shifted his gaze to Victor. "And I don't make vile accusations about people I don't know. I don't—"

He choked off anything else he might have said, aware that he was out of control. Very, very out of control. Turning on his heel, he clipped out, "To hell with this. I must see to the quarantine officers. They'll be coming aboard any minute."

And before he could shatter completely, he strode for the door.

But he hadn't yet reached it when a small voice asked, "What about me, Your Grace? What cruel thing have *I* done to you?"

His heart twisted in his chest to hear the hurt in Lisette's voice.

You made me fall in love with you.

He choked back the words. He wasn't that much of a fool. He'd given up enough to her already. He'd deviated from his plans, offered marriage . . . and for what? So she could look at him as some . . . pathetic, misguided fool who couldn't see that his family was a decadent cesspool of humanity?

"You did nothing, Lisette," he managed to say. "You have always behaved above reproach. Now I must go."

And with that, he escaped the infirmary.

21

As soon as Maximilian walked out, Lisette pulled away from Tristan, headed for the door.

"You are *not* going after that arse, I hope," Tristan said as he grabbed her by the arm.

She halted to glare at him. "He's not an arse."

The doctor said, "I should go help His Grace with the quarantine officers. They'll need to speak to me." And he hurried out the door.

As soon as he was gone, Tristan snapped, "He called our mother a *whore*."

"And my mother, too," Victor cut in. "I don't know about your mother, but mine was legitimately married to my father. She might have been a tavern maid, but that didn't make her a whore."

"Stop saying that word!" Lisette cried, wrapping her arms about her waist in a futile attempt to contain her pain. She'd finally shared herself with Max, body and soul, and even told him she loved him, and he'd knifed her in the heart.

How could he? He had always seemed to sympathize, always seemed to understand about Maman.

Unbidden, she saw again the betrayal on Max's face when she'd agreed with Victor's opinion of the kidnapping.

My God. That is why he said it. Max had only done what anyone would do when cornered—he'd struck back hard. And they had cornered him in the worst way. No doubt he'd felt abandoned all over again . . . by his mother, by his father and uncle, and this time, by her. It wasn't fair of him and it wasn't right, but she could understand it.

Leveling a bleak glance on both her brother and Victor, she said, "Do you realize what you've both done? And for no reason, either, except to hurt him. None of what you pointed out really matters—it's all in the past. Yet you both felt compelled to tell Max that his mother, whom he has worshipped all his life, might have had an affair with his great-uncle. That the man might have sired a child on her. That his sainted mother might even have caused his father's madness."

She swallowed hard as everything hit her at once. "And now he realizes that his entire life has been a lie. That everything he thought about his past was a lie, that every story ever told him by his parents about his brother's kidnapping was a lie. That his father even lied about his having a cousin. And Max abhors being lied to more than anything."

She tipped up her chin. "So how did you expect him to react? To thank you for unveiling the blackness beneath his family's lies? Did you expect him *not* to draw back in horror and strike at us all? Wouldn't you?"

Tristan's frown softened a fraction. "Well, when you put it like that . . ."

"And he was right about you, too, Tristan. You returned to England wanting something from him. Then, the minute he didn't handle all your speculations with great aplomb, you turned on him by insinuating that you and I had been talking about him behind his back. Which has been done to him over and over all his life. He hates it."

She turned to Victor. "As for you, sir, why did you even come here? Was it really to find your family? Or was it just so you could punish them for abandoning you?"

Victor glared at her. "Considering how they cut us out of their lives completely, I think I had the right to punish them."

"Well, you certainly found a good way to do it," she said smoothly. "And now the man who had nothing whatsoever to do with your abandonment is up on deck using all his influence to have the quarantine lifted so *you* can convalesce somewhere more comfortable than the bowels of a ship. He really is a terrible man, isn't he?"

She whirled for the door. She wasn't sure what to say to Max, but she couldn't leave things the way they'd left them.

"Tell me one thing, Lisette," Tristan called out from behind her. "Where was this paragon of virtue last night? He wasn't in our cabin. And he damned well wasn't in here."

Her heart dropped into her stomach. She might be as much to blame for her "ruin" as Max, but Tristan would never see it that way. "Where was he?" she said stiffly. "He was mourning the brother he thought he was about to lose yet again."

Then she walked out and headed for the hatchway. Let the two of them stew a bit. Victor had been relentless in his speculations, and Tristan had been the one to bring them up in the first place. No wonder Max had recoiled. They both could have done it more gently.

She hadn't helped, either. She'd just been so excited at the idea that the madness might not be hereditary after all, that Max might finally have some answers. She hadn't stopped to consider how he would regard what they said. That it would destroy his faith in his mother.

Just because your mothers were whores doesn't mean that mine was, too, damn it!

Despite understanding why he'd said it, the fact that he would include her in such a cruel sally made her reel. Because if deep down, he really saw her only as the bastard child of a whore . . .

She'd actually begun to believe that he didn't care about her illegitimacy. But clearly he did. What if he could never let that out of his mind? What if he were ashamed of her?

Steadying herself for the prospect of seeing him, she

took a breath, then climbed out of the hatchway. But she was surprised to find the deck nearly empty. There was no phalanx of officials, just the captain writing something in a notebook and Max standing with the doctor in deep conversation.

She approached the captain, because that was easier than approaching Max. "What happened to the quarantine officers?"

"They're gone. It was all over in a matter of minutes." The captain nodded over to the mast, where a seaman was lowering the fever flag. "They came, they informed us we were out of quarantine, and they left."

Max and the doctor approached them, and she tensed. Especially when Max refrained from looking at her.

"Captain," he said, "can you spare a couple of men to help Mr. Cale up onto the deck? Dr. Worth and I agree that he's much too weak to climb the ladder on his own. And my carriage is already on the dock, waiting for him."

"Certainly, Your Grace," the captain said. "I'll see to it right now."

Lisette stared at Max. "Where are you taking him?"

"To my town house, where he can be looked after properly. Dr. Worth has agreed to oversee his convalescence."

"You would do that for Victor . . . after what he said? It's very good of you."

"Hardly." Max's cool gaze met hers. "He's still the only other heir to the dukedom. And he's still my only close family—even if he does seem to resent the fact at present."

And Max was nothing if not loyal to his family.

Just then a seaman emerged from the hatchway behind them and reached down to catch Victor under the arms as another seaman handed him up. The doctor hurried over to supervise Victor's being put onto a litter. She could hear a boat rowing up to the ship. Another sailor hurried to secure it to the side.

Then she heard the sailor say, "Are you His Grace's servant, come to help us with the sick fellow?"

"No," said a familiar voice, "I am definitely not His Grace's servant."

As Max turned toward the sound of the voice, Lisette groaned. "Dom has arrived."

Her half brother had a look of fire in his eyes as he climbed onto the deck from the ship's ladder. When Max stiffened, as if bracing himself for another contentious encounter with a member of her family, she hurried toward her brother to head him off.

"What are you doing here?" she asked. "How did you know where to find me?"

"It wasn't exactly hard, dear girl," he growled, shooting Max a murderous glance. "Skrimshaw told me when I arrived yesterday evening that you'd run off with Lyons—alone and unchaperoned—on some wild-goose chase to find Tristan. So I went to the duke's town house, and his servants told me where he was. Then I came here. To throttle the bastard."

"You're not going to throttle him."

"Oh yes, I am," Dom said, pushing past her.

But Max was already striding forward to meet him. "You needn't worry about your sister's reputation, Manton. I've already offered her marriage."

That took the wind out of Dom's sails. "You have?" He glanced to Lisette. "Is that true?"

She just stood there gaping at Max. She hadn't expected him to mention that, not after what had just happened in the infirmary.

Still, it didn't matter. He'd made it very clear that he *didn't* really want to marry the daughter of a French "whore." He couldn't even say he loved her! He was merely trying to save her honor—and he needn't bother.

"It's true," she told Dom. "He did offer marriage, but I refused."

Max looked even more surprised than Dom. She could see him withdrawing into himself, shuttering his expression.

Her heart sank. He was going to seize the chance she was giving him to escape marrying her. And she couldn't blame him. They weren't nearly as well suited as she'd thought.

"That's not how I remember it, Lisette," Max said.

The husky words caught her off guard. He wasn't seizing the chance after all?

For half a moment, her heart leaped. He *did* want her. She nearly threw herself in his arms to say that it wasn't how she remembered it, either.

Just because your mothers were whores doesn't mean that mine was, too, damn it!

That halted her. No matter what he claimed right now, he would never be able to forget who she was. And she would never be able to fit into his world. What had she been thinking?

Besides, he no longer had to worry about dying mad and alone. He had his cousin, and given what Victor and Dr. Worth had said, there was a good chance madness would not be in his future. So she refused to hold him to an offer he'd made under vastly different circumstances.

He would appreciate it later, and congratulate himself on having made a narrow escape. As would she.

Or so she tried to tell herself. "Perhaps it's not . . . exactly what I said," she remarked softly. "But I think you'll agree that it's for the best that we don't marry."

"The hell it is," Dom put in. "According to Skrimshaw, the two of you set off to travel halfway across England and France—"

"Under aliases," Lisette said. "My reputation is intact." She'd deal with Mrs. Greasley later. No point in telling Dom right now that his sister would soon have to pretend to be the grieving widow of a land agent.

"Reputation is one thing," Dom snapped. "But if Lyons laid one hand on you, Lisette, I swear—"

"His Grace was a perfect gentleman," she said, swallowing down the tears clogging her throat. She clasped her hands behind her back to hide their shaking from Dom. "I have nothing to reproach him for."

Something flared in Max's eyes—though she couldn't tell if it was anger or desire. Or both.

But before he could speak, the captain came up to

him. "Mr. Cale is on shore now, Your Grace. They're waiting for you."

"Thank you. Tell them I'll be there shortly." Max faced Lisette. "I must go get Victor and Dr. Worth settled in, and I have several important matters to attend to. But I will call on you in a few days, I promise. This is *not* over."

Then he strode off.

She wished she could believe him, but she knew better. Once he realized that he had no more reason to fear marrying someone of his own rank, he would forget her.

A pity that she would never forget him.

Tears welled in her eyes that she fought mightily to contain.

"What the hell just happened?" Dom asked. "And who is Victor Cale? Skrimshaw told me the two of you went off to find the duke's brother, but I thought he said his name was Peter." His eyes narrowed on her. "And why are you crying?"

She brushed the tears ruthlessly away. "I'm not. It's just this sea air. It makes my eyes water."

"Lisette—"

"I don't want to talk about it, Dom." Heading for the hatchway to see what was keeping Tristan, she changed the subject. "I assume you avoided having Hucker follow you here."

Dom froze. "Hucker? George's man of affairs?"

Her blood chilled. She turned back to him. "You received my note, right?"

"No, I didn't receive a damned thing. What are you talking about?"

"You had to have gotten my note!" How could he have not? Oh, Lord, what if Hucker had followed him? "We have to get Tristan off this ship. Now, before Hucker and George get here!"

Tristan's voice came from the opened hatchway. "Why are Hucker and George coming here?"

The minute he caught sight of his half brother, Dom paled. "Are you out of your mind, you damned fool? What are you doing in England?"

"It's a long story," Lisette said. "We need to leave. We probably don't have much time."

"Where's the duke?" Tristan asked.

"Gone. And I'm sure he'll honor his promise to you if he can, but I don't know if there is much he can do if you actually get yourself arrested. So we have to get you off this ship!"

"Let me fetch my trunk," Tristan said and hurried down the hatchway.

She climbed down after him. "There's no time, drat you!"

But he was already in his cabin, packing up. When she rushed in and tried to get him to leave, he said, "Relax, Lisette, even if Hucker did follow Dom to the dock, he's got no reason to think Dom is coming to see *me*. Why would he think that?"

Oh, Lord, she'd forgotten that Tristan didn't know she'd been in France with Max. "Because the duke and I went to France after you, and he knows it."

"*What?*" Tristan said. "You traveled alone with Lyons?"

"We don't have time for this!"

"She's right about that," Dom said from the doorway. "If George had Hucker follow her to France, he must really be eager to arrest you."

"Exactly!" she cried. "So come on!"

The two of them got Tristan onto the deck. Then he halted. "What about your bag, Lisette?"

"It doesn't matter!" she said, frustrated. "We have to get you off the ship!"

"Too late for that," said a new voice.

Lisette's heart dropped as she slowly turned to find George climbing on deck with Hucker following behind. And after them, half a score of officers swarmed aboard. "Lord save us," she whispered.

"Damn you, George," Dom growled.

Their brother ignored them both. "Good morning, Tristan," George said with a look of pure satisfaction. "I hate to tell you, but the only way you're leaving this ship is in chains."

He nodded to Tristan, and one of the officers hurried over to seize her brother. "Tristan Bonnaud, I arrest you in the name of the king for . . ."

She couldn't hear the rest of it over the blood pounding in her ears. Despite all her attempts to prevent it, George had finally gotten Tristan exactly where he wanted him. And there wasn't a thing she could do about it.

22

As the carriage fought its way through morning traffic in London, Maximilian could only stare out the window. Dr. Worth had taken a hackney coach to his own abode, saying that he would gather some medications and then meet them at the town house. Victor, who lay on the seat opposite, was sleeping after his exhausting transfer from the ship to Maximilian's coach.

Maximilian was numb. Lisette had refused him. Thanks to his cruel words, he'd lost her.

He shouldn't have called her mother a whore. He deeply regretted that. But damn it, he'd had a right to be angry. She thought him a pampered aristocrat, an arrogant arse who wouldn't even admit to the vices of his family—vices that *she* and the others had drummed up out of some assertions from his lying madman of an uncle.

"You're a bloody fool, you know," came Victor's voice across from him.

He stiffened. That was the last thing he needed right

now—more idiocy from his cousin. "Thank you for your opinion, but at the moment I don't want to hear anything from you. I believe I've heard enough today already."

A long silence fell between them, punctuated only by Victor's coughing. Then the man struggled to sit up, and Maximilian scowled at him. "Stop that. The doctor says you need to rest."

"I don't like being a damned invalid," Victor grumbled, though he drew the blanket over his lap. "And you're going to hear my opinion whether you like it or not, cousin."

Maximilian scowled at him. "I've had just about enough of your disgusting insinuations about—"

"I wasn't referring to that." For the first time since they'd met, Victor looked distinctly uncomfortable. "I . . . er . . . shouldn't have speculated on the relationship between your mother and my father. As you said, I didn't know your family—I had no right to assume anything. Miss Bonnaud made that very clear."

Maximilian froze. "Did she?"

"She gave us quite the lecture after you left the infirmary." He coughed a bit, then got it under control. "She told us we ought to be ashamed of ourselves for saying things that served no purpose except to wound you. And she called us both ungrateful."

"Both?" Maximilian said, surprised.

"Yes. Bonnaud got the worst of it. She thought he behaved badly, in light of what you *said* you'd do concerning the warrant against him."

"I meant what I said," Maximilian retorted. "As soon as I get you settled, I will see to having the charges against him dropped. I have to find out more about it and learn who's the magistrate who swore out the warrant, but we should have time for that. Since he traveled under an alias, no alarms will be rung at customs. And I'm sure Lisette and Manton will find a place to keep him hidden in the meantime."

Though he probably should have spoken with Manton about all that. He'd just been so . . . angry over the situation. He hadn't been thinking about Bonnaud's troubles.

"Tristan couldn't really blame you if you chose *not* to help him," Victor clipped out. "He didn't actually find your brother, did he?"

Maximilian leveled him with a steady glance. "No, but he found a member of my family, and that is just as valuable to me. I haven't had much of anyone until now."

"Neither have I. That's why I traveled here." He raked back his disheveled hair. "Although Miss Bonnaud accused me of coming to England not to find my family, but to punish them."

"Is that true?" Maximilian asked.

"Partly, I suppose." His gaze turned resentful. "My mother died a few months after Father. She never recovered from the loss of both him and Peter. Even though she'd been told that he was just the result of some previous liaison of Father's, she loved your brother like a son."

"I'm sure she did," Maximilian choked out. "But Peter had a mother who missed him desperately. Who died asking for him. What your father did was . . . unconscionable."

"Yes, but what your father did in response was cruel, too. How could he have hidden the fact that Mother and I had family? His investigator gave her a pittance, which barely covered our debts in Gheel regarding my father's care. And once Mother died, I had to use what little was left to bury her." His voice hardened. "My fine relations could have shown some Christian charity and at least made sure she was taken care of, even if they didn't want to acknowledge me."

Maximilian stiffened. "I'm sorry. I agree that Father was wrong to do what he did. Though you can hardly blame him, considering that his son had been kidnapped by your father."

"I had nothing to do with that!" Victor said hotly. He reined himself in and added, "Mother had nothing to do with that. We didn't even know about it."

"And I had nothing to do with Father cutting you off. I swear it."

"Yes, I gathered as much." With a sullen look, Victor crossed his arms over his chest. "But Mother *was* my father's legitimate wife, no matter what you said about her."

Maximilian winced, remembering his heated words. "Do you have any proof of that?"

"As a matter of fact, I do. I knew that would be asked of me, so I brought it with me." Reaching into the satchel they'd placed in the coach with him, he pulled out an old piece of parchment and handed it over.

Maximilian examined it. Marriage lines, between Elizabeta Franke and Nigel Cale. He supposed the document could have been forged, but to do that Victor would have needed to know beforehand how significant it would prove to be, and he hadn't, according to what Bonnaud had said.

"Father met Mother while the British Navy was in port in Ostend," Victor explained. "She was a Belgian tavern wench, and he got her with child. So he married her."

Taking the document from Maximilian, he restored it to his satchel. He breathed hard for a moment before continuing. "Now that I know he was a duke's son, I realize that's nothing short of miraculous, but Mother did always say he loved her. That was the reason he gave her for retiring from the navy—so he could be done with that life."

"That may have been the truth. The war was halted at that point. Perhaps that was why he visited England—to set up a place for you and your mother. As a retired naval captain, he could have had a comfortable life here, assuming . . ." Maximilian mused a moment. "To reinstate himself in English society with a lowborn foreign wife, he would have needed Father and Mother to accept her into the family. Perhaps he mentioned to Father what sort of woman he'd married and Father refused to help him. So Uncle Nigel kidnapped Peter out of spite."

Or perhaps Father refused to help him because he knew of Uncle Nigel's affair with Mother.

The errant thought made him stiffen. That was *not* what had happened, damn it!

"Perhaps," Victor said, obviously now wary of saying anything on the subject.

Maximilian should drop it, since it gave them both so much pain. But he couldn't let it go. Not understanding why Peter had been taken had always gnawed at him, and he had to get to the bottom of it. "So after your father brought Peter back to Belgium, he enlisted in the British army. Right?"

Victor nodded. "He said he had to do his part for his country once the war was back on. Mother asked why he didn't return to the navy, but he gave her some reason he couldn't."

"Well, he couldn't go back to the navy because my family would have found him. And he couldn't very well have been an officer anymore—he might have run into someone who knew him. He had to stay low. If he intended to remain in the military, he had no choice but to enlist."

"He always said that fighting was all he knew how to do. So I suppose being in the army was the next best thing to being in the navy. And since he took all three of us with him to his postings, it was better than when he was at sea."

"Did Peter . . ." Maximilian swallowed. "Could he remember his family from before? Or what happened when he was taken?"

"If he did, he never told me. You have to realize, I wasn't yet four when he was brought home. I don't even remember it. To me, he was always just . . . my big brother." His voice grew choked. "Why do you think I kept his handkerchief all these years? Because it was his."

"I had just turned four myself when he was taken, so I don't remember him at all." Maximilian felt the unfairness of it like a punch to the gut. He had all sorts of Peter's things at Marsbury House, but they meant nothing to him. "Tell me about my brother. What was he like?"

On the long journey from the dock to Mayfair, Victor regaled him with stories about Peter. It was bittersweet for Maximilian, hearing about his brother secondhand, but at least it kept his mind off of Victor's speculations earlier.

Not to mention keeping his mind off Lisette.

They had already entered Mayfair and Victor had fallen silent, staring out the window at the grandeur they were passing, when he suddenly said, in a halting voice, "So your father went mad, too."

Maximilian tensed. "Rather spectacularly, yes."

"That's a good way to put it. It nearly killed my mother to watch it."

A lump caught in Maximilian's throat. "Mine too."

It dawned on him that not only had he found family now, but he'd found family who understood what he'd suffered. That meant a great deal. It meant that perhaps he'd also found a friend.

Depending on what his new cousin thought of him, that is. "You said earlier that I was a damned fool. You never said why."

Victor turned a direct gaze on him. "I don't know Miss Bonnaud very well, only what Tristan has told me about her, but I can tell she cares deeply for you. She defended you vigorously, even after what you'd said. And she seems like a woman who would stick with a man through thick and thin. Yet you left her there."

His heart lurched in his chest. So she did still care. She *didn't* think the worst of him.

And yet . . . "I offered her marriage. She refused."

"Then you didn't offer it right."

Maximilian released a shuddering breath. "Actually, last night I had gotten her to agree to marry me, but this morning she reneged."

"After what you said in the infirmary."

He nodded. He couldn't think of it now without loathing. "She told me that we both knew it was for the best if we parted ways. Which means *she* thinks it for the best that we part ways."

And perhaps it was. Being married to Lisette would mean opening his heart to the knife, tearing down his walls, giving up his precisely ordered existence to a woman who always spoke her mind. If they dined with the king, she would probably inform His Majesty that he could use more exercise.

When that thought made Maximilian smile, he shook his head. Might as well admit it—he would give his right arm to see her speak her mind to King George.

He would stand there with a glass of champagne in his hand, cheering her on and enjoying every minute. Then he would take her home and make love to her until the sun came up.

Images filled his mind—Lisette lying in bed in her frilly bedchamber, Lisette slipping off that nightdress . . . Lisette comforting him last night as he fell apart.

His pulse quickened in spite of everything. Being married to Lisette would also mean passion and light and love. It would mean the end of his solitary nights and lonely days. It would mean children.

For the first time since he'd met her, he thought about having children with her. Children who would banish the curse on his family line by growing up healthy and strong and beautiful . . . like their mother. Children who would populate the long-dead nursery, who would pick flowers in the massive gardens at Marsbury House and float miniature ships in the pond and—

"Damn it, she was wrong," Maximilian bit out. "It is *not* for the best that we part. Not for either of us."

Victor cast him a hard stare. "Did you tell *her* that?"

Maximilian thought back to the conversation, how he'd stood there protecting his heart and his dignity. How he'd walked away just as she'd finished telling her brother she had nothing to reproach him for.

Coward.

"No," he said, regret hitting him like a blow to the chest.

"Ah." Victor lifted an eyebrow. "Do you love her?"

"Yes." Funny how he didn't even have to think about it. He knew it bone-deep, just as he knew that marriage to Lisette would be wonderful.

"Did you tell her *that*?"

He groaned. He really had botched their parting, hadn't he? "No."

Victor snorted. "Well, there's where you went wrong, cousin. I don't know much about women, but I do know that telling a woman you love her—assuming that she loves you too—is the only way to gain her. Because if she believes you love her, she'll follow you to the ends of the earth." He shook his head. "Women are irrational like that."

"Not Lisette. She's perfectly rational."

Then again, when he first met her she'd had some fool idea about wanting to become one of Dom's agents. And it had been her idea for him to masquerade as a "regular person." She'd been the one to throw herself into his bed full-bore because she couldn't bear that he intended to spend his life in a "cold and loveless marriage."

Come to think of it, the woman wasn't rational at all. Or at least not when it came to him. So perhaps he did still have a chance with her.

If not for one thing.

"I called her mother a whore." He choked down bile. "I really hurt her. And she didn't deserve that."

"If she loves you, she'll find a way to forgive you. As long as you make it clear that you're truly sorry." Victor turned pensive. "No, that's not enough. My father used to throw my mother's low birth up at her whenever they argued, and then apologize after. It used to infuriate me." He gave Max a long look. "You have to apologize *and* never do it again."

"Trust me, I have no intention of repeating my mistake."

They were pulling up in front of his palatial London town house now, but Victor merely cast it a quick glance before returning his gaze to Maximilian. "And speaking of calling people's mothers 'whores,' I'm sorry about what I said, too. I didn't mean to sully your mother's memory."

"Apology accepted," Maximilian said tersely.

"I wasn't just being cruel, though. I really did think that an affair between your mother and my father explained a great deal." When Maximilian glared at him, he said quickly, "But obviously I was wrong."

"Obviously," Maximilian said as the carriage halted.

Nonetheless, long after he'd introduced Victor to the staff as his cousin and had got him situated and had greeted the doctor, Victor's words lingered in his mind.

Maximilian hated to admit it, but it *did* explain a great deal. It explained those strange words of Father's near the end. And the fact that Father had contracted syphilis despite never having been the whoring type.

It even explained Mother's guilt, which he had never understood. Not that an affair would have given her reason to blame herself for the madness—she wouldn't have thought there was any connection between syphilis and madness.

But it might have been as Lisette had hinted—Mother's guilt over the affair and the resultant abduction had made her fiercely determined to make up for those things by nursing Father devotedly in his final days.

After Maximilian changed into clothes more befitting a duke, he stood staring out at the garden, his throat tight and his hands clenched. There was one person who might shed light on the subject—the Cale family physician. Assuming he was still alive, he would surely know if Mother had ever had syphilis . . . and more important, *when* she and Father had contracted it.

So before Maximilian went courting, it might be good to have all the facts straight in his mind.

It took him only a few hours to hunt the man down. The doctor was nearly ninety and his memory faulty, but he had kept copious notes on his patients, and he was perfectly happy to show them to the man whose family had practically made him rich.

And there, buried in the notes, was a reference to Mother's bout of the "pox"—almost exactly nine months before Peter's birth. Then Max went through the rest and found the notation of the first signs that Father had the "pox." It had apparently been more virulent than Mother's. And it had come *after* Mother's.

He left the doctor's home in a turmoil of emotion. All these years, he'd had everything wrong. He had planned every detail of his future, basing it on a monumental lie. Perhaps it was time he stopped trying to predict the future. Perhaps it was time he embraced the present.

Or rather, perhaps it was time he embraced the one woman who made the present livable. The one woman who'd never wavered in her faith in him.

The only woman he could ever love.

Victor was right—he was a damned fool if he didn't at least attempt to convince her to marry him, no matter what she thought was "best" for both of them.

With that decision made, he headed off for Manton's Investigations. When he arrived there, the place looked eerily quiet. Odd—it was only eight o'clock.

He knocked at the door. When no one answered, he kept knocking louder until the door opened. Manton's odd butler stood there glaring at him while tying on a voluminous cloak.

"Would you inform your mistress that I wish to speak with her?" Maximilian said.

"You certainly took your sweet time getting here, didn't you, Your Grace?"

Maximilian blinked. "What are you talking about?"

"Miss Bonnaud sent a desperate message to you hours ago."

His heart leaped. She'd changed her mind? She'd actually asked him to come to her? "I haven't been home for hours. So if you'd just announce me—"

"She's not here," Mr. Shaw said with a sniff, obviously not yet ready to forgive him for his negligence, "and I am late for rehearsal."

As the butler hurried down the front steps, Maximilian kept pace with him. "Where is she?"

"Not that it's any of *your* concern, Your Grace, but

after she and Mr. Manton tried unsuccessfully to get Mr. Bonnaud out of gaol—"

"What the devil? How did he end up *there*?"

Shaw eyed him askance. "Rathmoor had him seized before they could even leave the ship. Apparently Mr. Manton unknowingly led him there, since that scoundrel Mr. Hucker intercepted a note from Miss Bonnaud that was supposed to warn Mr. Manton off. It seems Mr. Hucker has been watching the place."

"Holy God," Maximilian said as the full reality of that crashed down on him. "After Hucker lost us in France, he must have come back here to resume his spying until he could find us."

Shaw trotted along the road. "Mr. Manton spent the afternoon attempting to convince Sir Jackson Pinter, his friend in the magistrate's office, to release Mr. Bonnaud, but that didn't work."

Maximilian's heart pounded. "No, Pinter isn't the sort to bend the law for someone who broke it, even Manton's half brother. Besides, Bonnaud did steal a horse and sell it. The facts are irrefutable, from what I understand."

"Then 'the law shall bruise him,' I'm afraid." When Maximilian eyed him oddly, he added, "It's Shakespeare."

"It's not helping. So if they weren't successful at Bow Street, where are they now?"

"Gone to Rathmoor's to beg his lenience." Shaw frowned and picked up his pace. "There is no point in that. 'For pity is the virtue of the law, / And none but tyrants use it cruelly.' Rathmoor is most assuredly a tyrant."

"Then tell me where I can find him," Maximilian snapped. "I am not going to let Tristan Bonnaud hang."

Shaw halted. "Do you have a plan to prevent it?"

Maximilian thought for a moment, and a smile spread over his face. "I believe I do. But I'll need help in pulling it off."

Shaw sighed heavily. "I suppose they can do without me at rehearsal for one night." With a flourish of his long cloak, he walked back toward where Maximilian's carriage sat waiting in front of Manton's Investigations. "I do hope your plan is sufficient to free Mr. Bonnaud."

"I believe it will be. Here is what I need you to do . . ."

23

LISETTE PACED THE substantial parlor in George's town house. She turned to Dom and asked, "Do you think George has really gone out? Or is he just pretending to be gone to make us stew?"

Dom crossed his arms over his chest. "Knowing George, it's the latter."

"Then we should search the house for him and hold him down until he agrees to withdraw his claim of thievery against Tristan," she bit out.

"So he can have us charged with attempted murder or some such nonsense? We're lucky he failed at having us charged with harboring a fugitive this morning. If he'd had Tristan seized at Manton's Investigations, or if the captain hadn't been good enough to claim we had just boarded the ship, we'd be sitting in gaol with Tristan right now."

Lisette sighed. Dom had a point. "But what's to stop him from claiming that we stole something from him after we leave here?"

"The fact that we have nothing in our pockets?" Dom quipped.

She glared at him.

"I know, it's no time to joke. Pinter is doing his best to see what legal recourse we have, but the truth is, right now George holds all the cards. So if our sitting here awaiting his leisure gives him some petty satisfaction, then sit here we will."

"You know George will never relent. Why should he?" she said despairingly. "I'm trying to hold on to the hope that Max will respond to my note, but that hope gets smaller by the moment."

"He may yet. Don't count him out."

Dropping into a chair beside Dom, she shook her head. "I dare say the minute he was back in his fine town house, he thought better of ever offering for me."

"You can't blame him if he did. You turned him down. Most men don't take that well, but a duke? Might as well shoot him in the arse."

"I always knew he would break my heart in the end," she said softly.

Dom cast her a searching glance. "It has been my experience, dear girl, that if one goes into a thing certain of the outcome, one does everything in one's power to ensure that outcome."

She tipped up her chin. "What are you saying? That I brought this on myself?"

"No. I'm saying that you need to stop thinking of yourself as Claudine's illegitimate daughter, doomed to follow in her footsteps. You can do whatever you set your mind to. Especially if you can learn to see yourself the way we do—as a vibrant, beautiful woman with a great deal to offer any man."

Was Dom right? Had she done her best to scuttle any chance she had with Max? Had she wrapped her heart in so much protective wool that it no longer had air to breathe?

"Excuse me," came a feminine voice from the doorway, "but are you here to call on someone? I heard talking and . . ."

The voice trailed off as Dom rose. "Jane?" he said hoarsely. Then he stiffened. "Forgive me, Miss Vernon. I forgot that you might be here."

Lisette leaped up from her chair, too. Jane Vernon was cousin to George's wife. She had also once been Dom's fiancée. Until Dom had ended up penniless.

The pretty young woman paled. "Good evening, Mr. Manton. I had no idea . . . I was unaware . . ." She looked at Lisette, and that seemed to help her master herself. "I didn't realize that you two were waiting. We're at dinner upstairs. I don't know why the butler didn't send you up."

Dom eyed her askance. "Come now, Miss Vernon, you're no fool," he clipped out. "You know perfectly well why the butler didn't send us up."

Jane steadied her shoulders, then stared at him. "I see that you haven't changed at all, Mr. Manton. No polite niceties for a clever fellow like you." She cast Lisette a half smile. "I will fetch George. I assume that he's the one you've come to call upon?"

Lisette nodded. "Thank you."

As soon as Jane had left, Lisette whirled on Dom. "You didn't have to be nasty to her."

"I wasn't being nasty. I was being truthful."

Seeing Jane had obviously upset the generally even-tempered Dom. Lisette's eyes narrowed. Wasn't that interesting?

A knock came at the front door, startling them both. The butler hurried to open it, and a tall figure brushed past him into the hallway. "Thank you, my good man," said an arrogant voice she recognized only too well. "Please inform the Viscount Rathmoor that the Duke of Lyons is here to speak with him."

Lisette froze, caught entirely off guard, as the butler practically knocked Max over with his bowing and scraping.

Max had come! He'd done it for Tristan, of course, because that was the sort of man he was—a man of honor and character. But perhaps a little of it was done for *her*?

Her blood began to pound, and she tried not to hope too much. But it was difficult when Max was standing there in the flesh, proving that he hadn't forgotten her—or her family—at all.

The butler got a sudden panicked look on his face as he apparently realized that the entrance parlor was filled, and that perhaps he shouldn't put the duke in with such low creatures as the estranged brother of the viscount and their illegitimate sister.

But while he was still floundering, Max looked over

into the parlor and caught sight of them. "Ah, I see my friends made it here before me. I'll just join them, thank you."

The butler stammered, "V-very good, Your Grace," and practically vaulted up the stairs.

"Well, that should bring George down in a flash," Dom muttered to her.

Max strode up to them with an urgent look on his face. "I take it you have not spoken to your brother yet?"

She shook her head, unable to do more than stare at him.

"Good. Then the two of you must allow me to handle this. Do you think Hucker is around?"

"Probably," Dom said. "He's never far. Why?"

"Because if he recognizes me as Mr. Kale, it will only help the plan Shaw and I have cooked up."

"Shaw?" Lisette said. "*Our* Shaw?"

"Yes. Good man, that. Though a little odd."

She didn't know whether to agree or laugh hysterically. "Do you really think you can get Tristan freed, Your Grace?"

He arched an eyebrow. "Not if you keep calling me that, dearling. What happened to 'Max'?"

He'd called her *dearling*. Tears stung her eyes. "I wasn't sure if Max was still around," she said, fighting a smile. "You were being so dukely just now."

"Well, being dukely is apparently what I do best, according to a certain tart-tongued female."

George appeared in the entrance to the parlor.

"Don't worry, my love. Everything will be all right," he murmured.

My love? Oh, dear, he was making it difficult for her to hold fast to her resolve not to marry him.

With her blood pounding in her ears, she watched as Max turned to greet her half brother. "Good evening, Rathmoor."

George eyed him warily. "Have we met, Your Grace?"

"No, I don't believe we have." Max's tone chilled. "Though I've heard a great deal about you from my friends here."

The blood drained from George's face. "Friends?" he squeaked.

"Yes. They tell me that you've arrested a man who is in my employ."

As Lisette stifled a gasp, George scowled. "Tristan Bonnaud is in Your Grace's employ."

"Indeed he is. I hired him and Miss Bonnaud and Mr. Manton to find my lost cousin and return him to the arms of his loving family. They succeeded admirably. Victor Cale, the man who was the reason for their being on that ship you boarded, is now ensconced in my town house."

Lisette could scarcely contain her excitement. What a brilliant scheme! And it helped that he could use his title like a bludgeon when necessary.

He was quite dukely as he stared George down. "I only regret I was not there when you arrived to carry off Mr. Bonnaud. My cousin is recovering from a nasty bout of pneumonia, so I had to get him into a doctor's care immediately. If I had known that you were going to show up and arrest my best investigator, the man who is primarily responsible—"

"You're saying you *hired* Tristan, a known fugitive, to find your cousin," George put in, a vein throbbing in his temple.

"I didn't know he was a fugitive. I am rather shocked to hear it. He worked for the Sûreté Nationale in France for some years."

That seemed to give George even more of a shock. "The French secret police? All this time?"

"According to Eugène Vidocq, he's a very competent agent. What is Mr. Bonnaud accused of?"

"Stealing a horse," George said tersely.

"That *is* rather difficult to get around. When did this happen?"

George tugged nervously at his cravat. "Twelve years ago."

"I see. I suppose he stole it from a prominent citizen, too."

"He stole it from *me*."

Max feigned shock. "But aren't you his relation?" He let that sink in, then added, "Ah, I see. A young boy taking a horse for a ride. So this is more a matter of a family spat than of actual thieving."

George bristled at that. "It is *not* a 'family spat,' Your Grace. He stole a very expensive Thoroughbred and then sold it for his own gain."

"You have witnesses? Evidence?"

"I have a witness," George said uneasily. "And the evidence is the missing horse, which was never recovered."

Max lifted an eyebrow. "Sounds like a flimsy case to me. Especially given that it happened twelve years ago. I'm not sure you'll be successful in having it prosecuted. And it seems a damned shame to ruin a man's life and future over a misunderstanding."

"It is not a misunderstanding!" George growled. "And forgive me for my impertinence, Your Grace, but it is also none of your affair."

"Ah, but it is." Max shot George a thin smile. "He is in my employ now. And I would hate to think that after all he's done for the dukedom, he would end up hanged. I would take that as a personal affront."

At that moment, Hucker walked in. When he caught sight of Max, he hurried over to George to murmur something in his ear.

George glanced over at Lisette, then narrowed his gaze on the duke. "Hucker tells me that this entire tale of yours is made up out of whole cloth. You didn't hire them at all. He says you've been traveling alone with my half sister under an assumed name."

"Was Mr. Hucker *following* us?" Max said in pretend outrage.

That made George a bit uncomfortable. "Only so it would lead him to the fugitive."

"Your *half brother*, you mean," Max said in a hard tone. "We did travel together, Miss Bonnaud and I, to the Continent to find Mr. Bonnaud after we heard no word from him on his mission. We didn't know that he'd been detained in quarantine here with my cousin. I couldn't use my title on our trip—I didn't want to alert the press to the fact that my possible heir had been found, not until I was sure of the facts." He picked lint off his coat. "Of course, Mr. Manton was with us. I assume Mr. Hucker neglected to tell you that."

"That's a damned lie!" Hucker cried. "Mr. Manton weren't with you at all. He went to Scotland."

"Did he really? You saw him there?"

Hucker blanched. "Well, no, but . . . I heard . . ."

"You *heard*. I see."

Lisette fought to keep a straight face. For a man who hated deception, Max could be very good at it when he needed to be. Although most of what he said was the truth—just creatively realigned into something else.

"He weren't with you on that trip," Hucker persisted.

"Not on the coach ride to Brighton, but he was waiting for us there inside the inn. Surely you saw him."

"Well . . . no . . . I . . . I didn't go into the inn."

"Did you not?" Max arched one eyebrow. "How odd for an investigator. In any case, Manton left London early so he could travel to Brighton to secure us inn rooms and tickets for the packet boat. Surely you saw him on the packet boat."

"No, I did not," Hucker said stiffly. "He weren't there."

"There were sixty people aboard. You looked at them all?"

"I . . . I . . ."

"What you mean is, you didn't see him." He cast his eyes heavenward. "Surely you saw us on the road to Paris."

Hucker blinked.

"And followed us to Monsieur Vidocq's house? No?" Max acquired his best arrogant tone. "What a competent investigator you have there, Rathmoor. If he had been doing his job, speaking to the people we spoke to, et cetera, he would have learned that we consulted with Vidocq and the Sûreté. Thank God Mr. Manton and Vidocq were able to piece together the fact that my cousin was being held incommunicado on a quarantined boat."

A lump filled her throat. Max was lying with a vengeance. For her.

George glowered at Hucker. "You said you followed them. You said Manton wasn't with them."

"I didn't see him! I-I mean, he *wasn't* with them."

"Begone, you fool," George growled. "I should never have left you in charge of something so important."

"But what about the note!" Hucker cried. Fumbling in his pocket, he took out a folded message and waved it wildly in the air. "You see? Miss Bonnaud sent a note to Mr. Manton! She wouldn't have sent a note if he'd been traveling with them!"

She suppressed a gasp. Max didn't know her note had been purloined by Hucker—but he showed no sign of surprise. He took the note, looked at it, then tossed it back to George with a huff of impatience.

"It's not addressed to Manton, but to his servant. And all it says is, 'I am safe and well and tell Dom to beware Hucker.' There's no mention of Mr. Bonnaud, nothing that implicates anyone for anything."

A muscle ticked in George's jaw. "Leave us, Hucker."

"But my lord!"

"Leave us! I don't need you making things worse." As soon as Hucker left, George glanced beyond Max to where Lisette and Dom were keeping very quiet. "Don't think you've fooled me for one moment, Your Grace. I see what you're doing. You've trumped up this entire tale about Tristan's being in your employ in a vain attempt to save him."

He cast Lisette a withering glance. "I suppose you want to impress my half sister, to get her into your bed. If she hasn't been there already. She'd be a fool not to fall into the bed of a man as rich as you."

Dom stiffened beside Lisette, but she put a steadying hand on his arm.

Max had gone dangerously still. "Actually, she has turned down two of my marriage proposals. But don't worry—I mean to make sure that she accepts the third, if only so she can look down her nose at you at every social occasion."

"*Marry* her!" George said with a sneer. "Don't you know she's the bastard daughter of my father's French whore?"

This time Dom had to put a steadying hand on *her* arm.

"Whore?" Max said in a deceptively soft voice. "I was under the impression that her mother was a retired actress." He glanced at Lisette, his heart in his eyes. "Isn't that right, my love?"

My love. He'd said it again. And he was defending Maman. He was trying to make amends for what he'd said earlier. "Yes, that's right," she managed, though she could hardly speak for the thickness in her throat.

Max turned a malevolent look on George. "In my world, we don't consider a woman who is faithful to her lover for her entire life a whore—we consider her a rather fine mistress." He smiled grimly. "Of course, I can always hire investigators to learn the truth of all that, too. I would want to make sure that the facts are straight for the newspaper."

George paled. "Newspaper! What are you talking about?"

Max lifted his head. "I believe that's the press I hear approaching now."

As if on cue, a clamor was heard in the streets in front of the town house. George flew to the window and looked out. "The press! What the hell? What are they doing here?"

"Mr. Shaw invited them here on my behalf," Max said coolly. "I thought they might find my 'trumped-up tale' interesting, especially when I announce that Mr. Manton and his brilliant team have found my long-lost cousin. Of course, the reporters will also be very interested to hear that one of those investigators now languishes in gaol because his own half brother is holding a twelve-year-old crime over his head. They'll find that very newsworthy, I expect."

George was staring out the window, his face ashen. "You bloody, damned—"

"I would take great care just now if I were you, Lord Rathmoor." Max's voice was pure ice. "A choice is before you. You and I can go out there and announce with great pride the part your family has played in saving a possible heir to the dukedom. We can have Bonnaud out of gaol before they even get wind that he's there, simply by your telling the authorities that you were mistaken about the horse. Your miserable part in his arrest can all be swept under the rug in a heartbeat. Or . . ."

When he paused for effect, George faced him, his features drawn. "Or?"

"I can go out there and make you sound like the devil incarnate." Max's eyes glittered at him. "You might still succeed in getting Bonnaud hanged, though I wouldn't count on it—given my connections and the competent barrister I will hire for his defense. But it will be a hollow victory when those jackals out there get done vilifying you in the newspaper."

George was seething, but he had obviously begun to realize that this wouldn't end the way he'd planned.

Max glanced at Lisette, his eyes softening. "Either way, I mean to marry Miss Bonnaud." He shifted his gaze to George. "So you can either be a friend to me and my future relations, who also happen to be *your* relations. Or you can be an enemy. Simple as that." He walked to the window and glanced out as the noise rose in the streets. "But I'd make your decision soon. The crowd grows restless."

For half a moment, it looked as if George might resist. Then he bit out, "You give me no choice, Your Grace."

"None," Max said. "How clever of you to realize it."

George glared at her. "You really got your hooks into him, didn't you, Lisette? You must have learned from your whore of a mother exactly how to—"

"One more thing," Max ground out as he turned from the window. "If you ever again speak of my wife or her mother in anything but the most respectful tones, I will eviscerate you." Striding toward George, Max went in for the kill with a ruthlessness that made her proud. "You will be blackballed from every club, you will be unable to get loans, you will find that my influence stretches into places you didn't even dream existed." He halted to loom over George like an avenging angel. "Is that perfectly understood, sir?"

George blinked, clearly taken aback by the force of the duke's rage. He had the good sense to bob his head in assent.

A smile of triumph crossed Max's lips. "Excellent." He gestured to the door. "Now, if you don't mind stepping into the hall with Mr. Manton, I'd like a word alone with my fiancée before we announce to the press the 'great friendship' between our two families."

Resentment flared in George's face, but clearly he'd finally realized the depth of trouble he'd landed himself in.

George stalked out and Dom slid past her with a quick wink, closing the parlor door as he left.

She was alone with Max at last, but she felt suddenly awkward after what had passed between them this morning. Her heart was so full, and she didn't want to get it wrong this time. Especially when he was so very much the Duke of Lyons just now, dressed in great splendor, with the full power of his title behind him after routing George.

Might as well begin with that. "Thank you, Max, for saving Tristan. For bringing him back to us." Tears filled her eyes. "You don't know how much it means to me. I know you did it to hold to your promise to him, but—"

"I did it for you," he said hoarsely. "All of it was for you."

The way he was looking at her, with his heart in his eyes, made her knees go weak and her blood quicken.

He stepped closer. "I'm just glad that the plan actually worked."

She smiled through the tears she was trying to hold back. "Your plans always work. It's mine that don't, remember?"

"I beg to differ. You found my cousin. I could never have found him without you." He came even nearer. "I'm sorry it took me so long to get here. I wasn't at home. I was out speaking to the family physician about Victor's speculations. It appears he might have been right about my mother and my great-uncle, after all."

"Oh, Max, I'm so sorry."

"I'm not. It's gratifying to have answers. To know that the family curse might not be a family curse after all." He seized her hands, holding them against his heart. "To know that I can have a future now."

"Yes, but that also means you don't have to settle for marrying an illegitimate daughter of—"

He kissed her hard, then drew back to stare intently into her eyes. "Don't ever call yourself that again. I don't think of you that way. I never have." He dropped his gaze to their linked hands. "I realize that this morning I . . . made you feel as if I might, and I have no excuse for that. I can only promise it will never happen again, and I beg you to forgive me for being an arrogant arse—"

This time she kissed *him* hard. "Don't ever call yourself that again," she echoed, then shot him a teasing smile. "I'm the only one allowed to call you that. Besides, sometimes I love that you're an arrogant arse. Especially when you're threatening dire harm to my horrible half brother who—"

This kiss was mutual, a fierce coming together full of heat and need and passion. When at last they parted, the great Duke of Lyons had entirely vanished and her own dear Max was gazing into her eyes.

"Does this mean you'll marry me, dearling? Because

I don't think I can go on if you don't. I love you, and the thought of spending my life without you is worse than the fear of going mad ever was."

"You *love* me?" she said, hardly able to believe that he'd actually said the words.

"Of course I love you. I'm not mad, you know." He smiled at his little joke, and the fact that he could joke about it at all warmed her heart. "How could I not love the woman who refused to marry me because I wouldn't let her take care of me until the very end? The woman who nursed my cousin, whose face lights up whenever she gets to travel . . . who never, ever lies to me."

She teared up.

He cupped her cheek. "Of course I love you. Do you think I bully viscounts every day?"

She blinked, then eyed him askance.

"All right, so perhaps I can be a bit overbearing at times." He pulled her into his arms. "But that's precisely why you should marry me. Who else but you will be able to keep me humble?"

She beamed at him. "I do believe you're right. You need a wife who will remind you not to be so dukely all the time." She reached up to deliberately set his cravat slightly askew. "In light of that, I accept your offer, *mon coeur*."

"Thank God," he said, breaking into a broad smile. He caught her mouth in a profoundly wonderful kiss that had her tingling to her toes and reminded her that he wasn't always dukely.

When he was done, he offered her his arm. "Now we'd best get out there and announce it to the rest of the world."

"What will you tell them about Victor?"

"That I've found a long-lost cousin, the son of my great-uncle. No one ever knew Uncle Nigel had a part in the kidnapping, so that shouldn't be too scandalous."

"No. Not too scandalous," she agreed. As they walked toward the door, she added, "I suppose this means the end of any future for me as one of Dom's 'men.' A duchess doing that sort of work would probably be *very* scandalous."

"True. Still, think of it not so much as ending that future," he said blithely, "but as changing employers. You'd be surprised how much organizing and investigation is part of running a dukedom. I could really use the help. So I will be very happy to have you be one of *my* men." He cast her a side glance. "Except in the bedchamber, of course."

And as she burst into laughter, they stepped through the doors and out into their future.

EPILOGUE

FOUR MONTHS AFTER his wedding, Maximilian was comfortably ensconced in his study, with Lisette doing her usual flitting about being useful, when Victor walked in, dressed in what was clearly traveling attire.

"Well, I'm off to Edinburgh," he said.

"Scotland? Whatever for?" Maximilian said.

"Didn't your wife tell you?" Victor said with a quick glance at Lisette.

She colored. "I . . . um . . . was waiting for the right moment. I thought you weren't leaving until tomorrow."

"I thought so, too," Victor said. "But Manton got a letter that made the matter more urgent, so—"

"What has Manton got to do with this?" Maximilian asked. When his wife and his cousin exchanged glances, he felt a sinking in the pit of his stomach. "Somebody had better tell me what's going on right now."

"Victor is joining the Duke's Men," Lisette said baldly.

Maximilian narrowed his gaze on his cousin. Manton's Investigations had been dubbed "the Duke's Men" after the newspapers had run the story about the successful search for "the duke's long-lost cousin." "Why? Don't I offer you a sufficient allowance?"

Victor tensed. "It is more than sufficient. This has nothing to do with money. I don't mean to be ungrateful, cousin, but—"

"Victor is accustomed to a more active sort of life," Lisette put in. "He spent years in the army and then aiding various officials with sticky situations. He's not used to sitting around doing nothing."

"Then I'll find him something to do." Maximilian stared at the cousin he felt he was just starting to know. "I'm sure there's something that needs doing around here."

"You and Lisette and your massive staff have all of that well in hand." Victor tugged at his cravat. "Besides, I'm not . . . well suited to all the balls and dinners and pretending I give a damn about who appeared at the theater wearing the wrong color of waistcoat. I can still barely believe I'm cousin to a duke, much less that anyone cares what sort of boots I wear."

"It is a lot to take in all at once, I know." Lisette shot Maximilian a veiled glance. "And we've hardly given you a chance to get used to it, throwing you into English society with little preparation."

Maximilian had to bite his tongue. *She'd* managed to handle it quite well. Why couldn't he? "But Scotland is so far."

"Manton has a new case up there that promises to be lucrative," Victor said. "But since he's in the middle of a big case of his own, and Tristan has his hands full with several others, he suggested that I might like to take this one on. And I have . . . reasons of my own for wanting to have a go at it."

"Like what?" Maximilian prodded.

Victor closed up. "Nothing to concern you." Then, before Maximilian could react to that bald statement, Victor forced a smile. "Besides, it will give me a chance to think about . . . what I want to do with my future."

When Maximilian let out a long sigh, Lisette said, "Max . . ."

"I know. You're both right." Maximilian rose from behind the desk to stare at his cousin. "You should be able to live as you please. And I realize that while I was raised in this life, you weren't." He forced a light tone into his voice that he didn't feel. "Who's wearing the wrong color of waistcoat actually interests me."

"It does not," Lisette said softly.

As usual, she always knew what he was feeling. At first, it had been a little disconcerting to have someone about who understood him so well, but that had long since passed, and now he found it rather exhilarating.

"All right, so that part of my life can be tedious," he admitted. "But I find managing the estates for my future heirs very rewarding. I had hoped that in time you would regard it that way yourself, cousin, so that I could teach you to take over in case—"

"You'll have plenty of heirs to take over for you, Max," Victor said dryly. "Judging from how often the two of you 'retire' early, I'll end up being fifteenth in line for the dukedom."

"God forbid," Lisette muttered. "I like children, but fourteen?"

"The point is," Victor went on, "you'll have at least one son, perhaps several, to pass the dukedom on to. You don't need me. And I need something more than this." He swept his hand to indicate his surroundings. "Or at least something different from this."

"I understand," Maximilian said, though he didn't entirely. He was so utterly content with his life that he couldn't imagine anyone else not being so. "And you won't be up there forever, I suppose."

"I hope not," Victor retorted. "I understand it's rather bleak."

"Depends on the part of Scotland you're in." Maximilian smiled. "If you're going to be staying in Edinburgh for any length of time, you can use my house there. I'll send a letter off right now to have it opened up for you."

"Thank you. That may prove useful." Victor glanced at the clock. "Well, then, I'm off. My coach leaves in an hour or so."

"Good luck," Maximilian said.

"Be careful," Lisette said, and pressed a kiss to Victor's cheek.

"I'm always careful," Victor drawled.

It was only after he was out the door that their interchange really registered with Maximilian. "*Be careful?* Is this a dangerous assignment?"

She gave him a bright smile. "Not too dangerous."

"Lisette . . ." he said in a warning tone.

"I'm teasing you. As far as I know, there's no danger involved. And even if there were, Victor is quite capable of taking care of himself."

"Holy God," Maximilian muttered as he dropped into his chair. "Remind me to throttle your brother the next time I see him."

She laughed as she came over to stand beside the desk. "I swear, you and Dom are always threatening to throttle each other, yet I've never once seen either of you attempt it."

"That's only because we know you would blister our ears lecturing us afterward. But, to be fair, your brother has more cause to be angry with me than I with him."

"He does, indeed. He will never forgive you for turning Manton's Investigations into 'the Duke's Men.'"

"It's not my fault that the newspapers came up with that," Maximilian grumbled. "I merely said that I hired the three of you to find my cousin."

"I know," she murmured soothingly. "And when he isn't being annoyed by it, he grudgingly acknowledges that business increased tenfold after that. So you did him a favor. Even if he hates to admit it."

He glanced up at her. "You don't mind it, do you?"

"I *adore* it. It keeps my brothers from being too full of themselves. Not to mention that it serves as a constant reminder of how much you love me." She flashed him the soft smile that never failed to stir him. "How much you did for me—and them—that day."

That sobered him. "I suspect we haven't seen the last of Rathmoor. He truly hates the two of you, especially Bonnaud. And I'm not sure why."

"Me neither, but he always has." She took a deep breath, then said lightly, "Let's not think about him, shall we? Besides, I have to go tell Cook that it will be just the two of us for dinner." She grinned down at him. "You see? There are certain advantages to having Victor gone. For example, now that I need not consider *his* wishes for dinner, you can have whatever your heart desires. So tell me, my lord duke, what might that be?"

He dragged her onto his lap, taking her off guard. "I'll tell you exactly what the duke desires, my wild rose. And it's not dinner."

"You want us to take another jaunt to France on your yacht?" she teased. "Or even Spain this time?"

"Much as I enjoyed the last trip we made, I had in mind something a bit closer to hand." His eyes gleamed as he reached beneath her gown. "All Victor's talk about my heirs has made me think we should get right to work on producing them."

With a sensual smile, Lisette looped her arms about

his neck. "I thought we'd already been working rather hard at it."

"You know me." He gazed into the face of the woman who had changed his life, who had given him hope and passion and a future, and his heart flipped over in his chest. He lowered his mouth to hers. "A duke's work is never done. Thank God."

Author's Note

Eugène Vidocq was a real person—and is widely considered to be the first private detective and the father of modern criminology, not to mention the founder of the Sûreté Nationale. When Scotland Yard was first established, Sir Robert Peel twice sent men to consult with Vidocq and observe his methods. Several details in my story come straight from accounts of his life. Vidocq really did start out as a criminal, and decided to switch sides after watching a cohort hanged. He really did have a staff of four clerks to keep up with his sixty thousand cards detailing all the characteristics of criminals he'd dealt with. He really did make a fortune by inventing tamperproof paper for banks. And he really did hire female agents!

There actually is a town named Gheel (now Geel) in Belgium that became famous in the early 1800s as a "colony for maniacs." It had one of the most forward-thinking programs for dealing with the mentally ill of its time—the people of the town took care of them at a price, and in exchange, the mentally ill were housed with their caregivers and given useful work to do. Those patients who were harmless were allowed to roam the streets at will; those who grew violent were restrained or kept in irons until they could be rational again. A committee oversaw the program. Geel still places some patients with town inhabitants. How revolutionary!

Syphilis doesn't always cause madness, but it can, and it can show up years after the illness seems to have "gone away." It was often called "the great imitator" because of the varied paths the disease can take, which confused diagnosis in the days before we knew about bacterial infections. Although the link between syphilis and madness was only confirmed much later than the period depicted in my book, I figured that some doctors would have to have noticed the connection, even if they couldn't yet prove it scientifically.

The quarantine situation is taken right out of the quarantine laws of the time. No one was very sure about what or who needed to be quarantined, so they erred on the side of caution. Then the merchants complained about it so much that the laws were changed . . . and changed and changed. Eventually, the Privy Council really was given the power to decide, which allowed for judgment calls to be made. I would imagine there was more than one man of consequence who tried to persuade the Privy Council to act in his favor!

Want even more sizzling romance
from *New York Times* bestselling
author Sabrina Jeffries?
Don't miss the first book in her
sexy new Sinful Suitors series,

The Art of Sinning

Coming in Summer 2015 from Pocket Books!

LADY YVETTE BARLOW stood at the edge of the duke's ballroom, watching the dance with a hollow ache of envy in her stomach. She loved to dance. And the chances of her being asked were slim to none. She towered over half the men in the ballroom. Not to mention that the whole world had recently learned of her brother Samuel's perfidy. Even her eldest brother, Edwin, the Earl of Blakeborough, couldn't avoid being tarred by that brush.

As if she'd conjured him up, Edwin's voice sounded behind her. "Yvette, there's someone I'd like you to meet."

Good Lord. He'd been trying to cheer her up ever since they'd arrived, and he was very bad at it. Heaven only knew whom he thought might serve the purpose.

Pasting a smile to her lips, she faced him and his companion. Then her heart dropped into her stomach.

Standing beside Edwin was the most attractive man she'd ever seen—a golden-haired Adonis with eyes as deep a blue as the estate's prize delphiniums. Indeed, the man stared at her with an intensity that quite sucked the air from her lungs.

He was tall, too. Heavenly day. A decided improvement over the gentlemen Edwin usually foisted on her.

"May I introduce my new friend, Mr. Jeremy Keane?" Edwin said.

The man bowed. "I'm delighted to make your acquaintance, Lady Yvette."

His deep voice resonated through her like a piece of particularly delicious music. Even his accent was compelling. American perhaps? Oh, she did like Americans. They were so refreshingly forthright. And they used such interesting slang, too. Perhaps she could expand her collection of street cant to include American terms.

She dipped her head. "The pleasure is mine, Mr. Keane." But even as she said it, she put together the accent and the name. Oh dear, he was *that* Mr. Keane.

As if to confirm her realization, the man raked her in a blatantly admiring glance. A *rogue's* glance.

She groaned. Not again. Could she never meet a gentleman who was *not* a scoundrel?

Edwin went on. "Keane is an artist from—"

"I know all about Mr. Keane." When Edwin scowled, she caught herself. "From the exhibit of his works, of course."

Mr. Keane's warm gaze poured over her like honey. "I don't recall ever seeing *you* at my exhibit. And trust me, I would have remembered."

A shiver danced down her spine before she could

steel herself against reacting. Very nicely done. She'd have to be on her toes with this one. "We attended it in the morning. I daresay you were still lying foxed in some gaming hell or nunnery."

"Good God, here we go," Edwin muttered under his breath, recognizing the cant for brothel.

"I am rarely foxed and never in a nunnery," Mr. Keane retorted, "for fear it might tempt the 'nuns' to bite me."

"I should love to know what you consider 'rarely,'" Yvette said. "That you even know that 'bite' means 'cheat' in street cant shows how you must spend your days."

"And how you must spend yours," he said with a gleam in his eye. "After all, you know the cant, too."

She stifled a laugh. Mustn't encourage the fellow. Still, she was impressed. Rogues always fancied themselves wits but seldom did she meet one who really was.

"Mr. Keane has kindly agreed to paint your portrait, Yvette," Edwin cut in. "Assuming that your tart words haven't changed his mind."

The scoundrel had the audacity to wink at her. "Actually, I like a little tart with my sweet."

"More than a little, I would say, having seen your paintings," she shot back.

Suddenly he was all seriousness. "And what did you think?"

The question caught her off guard. "Are you fishing for compliments, sir?"

"No. Just truthful opinions."

"That's what everyone always says, though they never mean it."

"Are you calling me a liar, Lady Yvette?" he said in that deadly tone men use when their honor is questioned.

"Of course not," she said hastily. A man's honor was nothing to be trifled with. "I was just speaking generally." When he continued to look at her expectantly, she struggled to put her uncertain feelings into words. "As for your work, I would say that your idea of 'tart' borders on the 'acidic.'"

"It does indeed," he drawled. "I prefer to call it 'real life.'"

"Then it's no surprise you've taken up with Edwin. He considers real life to be acidic, too."

"Oh, no, don't drag *me* into this," Edwin put in.

Mr. Keane's gaze searched her face. "And you, Lady Yvette? Do *you* consider real life acidic?"

My, my. Quite the persistent fellow, wasn't he? "It can be, I suppose. If one wants to dwell on that part. I'd rather dwell on the happier aspects."

A sudden disappointment swept his handsome features. "So you would prefer a painting of bucolic cows in a field."

"I suppose. Or market scenes. Or children."

The mention of children sparked something bleak in the depths of his eyes. "Art should challenge the viewers, not soothe them."

"I'll try to remember that when confronted at my breakfast table by a picture of vultures devouring a dead deer. That *is* one of yours, isn't it?"

Mr. Keane blinked, then burst into laughter. "Blake-borough, you forgot to tell me that your sister is a wit."

"Trust me," Edwin said wearily, "if I'd thought it would get you to agree to our transaction sooner, I would have mentioned it."

"Transaction?" She stared at her brother. "What transaction?"

Edwin turned wary. "I told you. Mr. Keane is going to paint your portrait. I thought that a well-done piece of art showing what a lovely woman you are . . . might . . . well . . ."

"Oh, Lord." So *that* was his reasoning. A pox on Edwin. And a pox on Mr. Keane, too, for agreeing to her brother's idiocy. Clearly, the artist had been coerced into doing so. Mr. Keane was well-known for *not* doing formal portraits. Ever.

She fought to maintain her composure, to act nonchalant, though inside she was bleeding. Did Edwin really think her so unsightly that she needed a famous artist to make her look appealing?

"Forgive my brother, sir," she told Mr. Keane with a bland smile. "He's set on gaining me a husband, no matter what the cost. But I happen to have read the interview where you said you'd rather cut off your hands than paint another portrait, and I'd hate to be the cause of such a loss to the world."

Mr. Keane gazed steadily at her. "I sometimes exaggerate when speaking with the press, madam. But this particular portrait is one I am more than willing to paint, I assure you."

"Eager for the challenge, are you?" Such raw anger boiled up in her that it fairly choked her. "Eager to try your hand at painting me attractive enough to convince some hapless fellow in search of a wife to ignore the evidence of his eyes?"

Belatedly, her brother seemed to realize how she'd taken his words. "Yvette, that's not what I was saying."

She ignored him. "Or perhaps it's the money that entices you. How much did my brother offer in order to gain your compliance in such an onerous task? It must have been a great deal."

"I didn't offer him money, Yvette," Edwin protested. "You misunderstand what I—"

"I *want* to paint you," Mr. Keane snapped even as he glared Edwin into silence.

With betrayal stinging her, she gathered the remnants of her dignity about her. "Thank you, but I am not yet so . . . so desperate as to require your services."

She turned to leave, but Mr. Keane caught her by the arm. When she scowled at him, he released her . . . only to offer her his hand. "May I have this dance, Lady Yvette?"

That took her by surprise. Only then did she notice the strains of a waltz being struck. She had half a mind to stalk off in a huff. But that would be childish.

Besides, other people had begun to notice their exchange, and she could *not* endure the idea of people gossiping about her making a scene at the wedding breakfast of her friend . . . who happened to have jilted her brother.

"Lady Yvette?" Mr. Keane prompted in a steely voice.

She cast him the coolest smile she could muster. "Yes, of course, Mr. Keane. I would be delighted."

Then she took his hand and let him sweep her into a waltz.

As soon as they were moving, he said, "You have every right to be angry with your brother."

"My feelings toward my brother right now are none of your concern."

"I was telling the truth about wanting to paint you."

She snorted. "I don't know how much money Edwin promised—"

"But not for a portrait." He bent close enough to whisper in her ear, "Though he doesn't know that."

That caught her so off guard that when Mr. Keane pulled back to fix her with a serious gaze, she couldn't at first summon a single answer.

"I see I finally have your attention," he said.

"Oh, you always had my attention," she said testily. "Just not the sort of fawning attention you probably prefer."

A faint smile crossed his lips. "Tell me, Lady Yvette, do you have something against artists in general? Or is it just I who rub you the wrong way?"

"I don't trust charming rogues, sir. My other elder brother was one of your kind, so I know all your tricks."

He arched one eyebrow. "I seriously doubt that."

When he then twirled her in a turn, she realized with a start that they'd been waltzing effortlessly all this time. That almost never happened with her. Few men knew how to deal with an ungainly Amazon like her on the dance floor. But clearly he was one of them.

That softened her toward him a little. A very little. "So what exactly *do* you want to paint me for, anyway?"

"An entirely different work," he said. "And agreeing to your brother's request seemed the only way to get close enough to you so I could arrange that."

She eyed him skeptically.

"Ask Blakeborough if you don't believe me. Before I knew who he was, who *you* were, I wanted you to sit for me. I decided it the moment I saw you enter the room. I asked your brother who you were, he asked why I wanted to know, and I told him."

His gaze locked with hers, as sincere a one as she'd ever seen. But then, Samuel had always looked very sincere, too, when he spun some tale. "Why on earth would you want to paint *me*?"

"No clue. I never know why particular models intrigue me; just that they do. And I always follow my instincts."

Yvette blinked. He *could* have claimed it had something to do with her looks. The fact that he hadn't lent more credence to his assertion. "That's the most ridiculous thing I've ever heard." Yet a tiny part of her found it enormously flattering.

"It *is* ridiculous, isn't it? But true, I swear. No matter what gossip you've heard about me, I'm always honest, no matter the cost."

"Fine. Then tell me this: Exactly what are the terms of your 'transaction' with my brother?"

He flinched. "Your brother is an ass."

"Not really. Just rather oblivious to other people's feelings sometimes." She cast him a hard stare. "Answer the question."

With a long-suffering sigh, he tightened his grip on her hand. "I am to paint your portrait. In exchange, he is to drum up some gentlemen who might be interested in courting my sister."

She gaped at him. "What a pair of nodcocks you are! Has it occurred to either of you that your sisters are perfectly capable of finding husbands on their own if they so choose? That perhaps we— Wait a minute, I thought your sister lived in America."

"She's on her way here. She means to drag me home to help her with the family mills." He cracked a smile. "I mean to fob some other fellow off on her who can go in my stead."

His look of boyish mischief seduced her. Briefly. Until she put herself in his sister's shoes. "First you abandon her to go flitting about Europe. And now that she has tired of waiting for your return, you think to get rid of her by marrying her off." She shook her head. "Your poor sister."

"Trust me, there is nothing 'poor' about my sister. Amanda can take care of herself." His smile smoldered. "As, it appears, can you. Which is probably what made me want you for my painting in the first place."

She fought not to be intrigued. "What is this painting about, anyway?"

"It's allegorical, about the sacrifice of Art to Commerce."

That took her by surprise. "Something like Delacroix's paintings?"

"You're familiar with Delacroix?"

His voice held such astonishment that it scraped her nerves. "I do read books, you know. And attend exhibits and operas with my brother . . . when I can drag him to town."

"Operas, eh? Better you than me," he teased. "I can't imagine anything more tedious than an evening of such screeching."

"My point is that I'm not some ninnyhammer society chit who only keeps abreast of fashions."

"I didn't think you were." He bent close enough to say in a husky tone, "Unlike your brother, I am fully aware of your attractions."

The words melted over her skin like butter. And when he then tugged her slightly closer in the turn, she let him.

Not because of his devastating attractiveness, no. Or his deft ability to dance. Or the glint of awareness in his startling blue eyes. None of that had any effect on her. Certainly not.

Fighting to keep her mind off the breathlessness that suddenly assailed her, she said, "So, which character would I play in this allegorical painting of yours?"

One corner of his mouth tipped up. "Does that mean you agree to sit for it?"

"Perhaps. It depends on your answers to certain questions."

The music was ending. Oh dear, and just when the

conversation was getting interesting. Unfortunately, it would be highly improper of him to ask her for another.

But apparently he'd thought of that, for he waltzed her toward a pair of doors that opened to reveal a set of steps descending into the sunlit garden. And almost as soon as the notes died, he offered her his arm.

Cursing the curiosity that prompted her to take it, she let him lead her outside, but she was relieved to see that they weren't the only people strolling about. At least she needn't worry about rousing further gossip.

Besides, she was ready to be out of the stuffy ball-room. Here in the chilly autumn air, she could breathe at last.

"Now, then, madam," he said. "Ask me whatever you wish."

"Who am I to play in your painting? What am I to wear? Will sitting for your picture ruin me for life? Is that why Edwin would only agree to a respectable portrait?"

"That's quite a lot of questions," he said dryly. "Let's start with the last. Your brother and I didn't get as far as my describing the concept of my work. The minute I said I wished for you to model for me, he flat-out refused to let you be part of any painting that wasn't dull as dirt, even though I told him you wouldn't be recognized."

"Won't I?" She felt a stab of disappointment at the thought that he didn't really want to paint *her* as she was. And why did she care, anyway? "So I'm to be wearing a mask or a cloak or something?"

"No, indeed. But you will be in some kind of Greek costume quite different from your normal attire. I can even change your hair color if you wish. And you'll only be in profile, anyway. I doubt anyone will realize it is you."

She gave a harsh laugh. "Right. Because no one will notice that the woman in your painting happens to have my ungainly proportions."

"Ungainly!" He shook his head. "More like queenly. Majestic, even."

The compliment came so unexpectedly that it startled her. She was used to being teased for her height, not praised. She had to turn her head so he wouldn't see how very much the words pleased her.

"But your proportions are unlikely to signify, anyway," he went on. "You'll be lying down."

That arrested her. How had she managed to forget he was a rogue? "Why would I be lying down?"

He gazed at her as if she were witless. "'Art' sacrificed to 'Commerce'? Were you even listening? Damn, woman, I can hardly depict a sacrifice without laying you across an altar."

Stunned by his matter-of-fact tone, as if it were perfectly obvious to anyone with sense, she mumbled, "Oh, right, of course. I don't know what I was thinking."

Actually, she did know. She thought him quite mad. When he spoke of his art, there was no trace of the rakehell in him. Was it by design? Was he *trying* to rattle her?

Because he was certainly succeeding at that.

"Will you do it?" he asked. "Assuming we can find a way to manage it?"

"Managing it isn't a problem," she said, thinking aloud. "Artists doing portraits generally reside with the family during the process. So if you come to our estate for the portrait, we can arrange some way to meet for the painting you wish to do for yourself." She slanted a glance at him. "If you're willing to leave London for a bit, that is."

"Oh, I don't know." He stopped beside a marble fountain to smile teasingly at her. "It would take me away from all those gaming hells and nunneries. However will I survive?"

"I'm sure you can find a sympathetic tavern maid or two in nearby Cheshunt to tide you over," she said dryly.

"So, no nunneries in your neck of the woods?"

"Trust me, if there had been, my other brother would have uncovered them long ago."

When he looked at her oddly, a blush rose in her cheeks. She didn't know why she'd said that. She couldn't seem to forget the request Samuel had made of her just before he'd been sent off to serve his sentence of transportation.

"I'll be fine, I promise," he said silkily. "Though you still haven't given me your permission to paint you. For *either* work."

And suddenly it hit her—the solution to her problem with Samuel. "I haven't, have I?" She stared him down. "Tell me something, Mr. Keane. Are you as willing to make a bargain with me for your painting as you were to make a bargain with Edwin for my portrait?"

His eyes turned wary. "It depends. What sort of bargain are we talking about?"

Avoiding his gaze, she twirled the water in the fountain with one finger. "I will sit for you—clothed, of course—as much as you like. You may draw as many pictures of me as you please."

"And in exchange?" he prodded.

"You will find some way to get me inside a nunnery in Covent Garden."

Don't miss the first book in the sexy new "Sinful Suitors" Regency historical romance series by *New York Times* bestselling author Sabrina Jeffries!

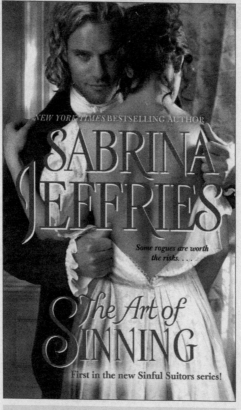

NEW YORK TIMES BESTSELLING AUTHOR

SABRINA JEFFRIES

Some rogues are worth the risks. . . .

The Art of SINNING

First in the new Sinful Suitors series!

On sale summer 2015!

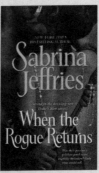
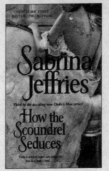